DEATH
BY STATION
WAGON

DEATH
BY STATION
WAGON

A Suburban Detective Mystery

Jon Katz

A PERFECT CRIME BOOK
DOUBLEDAY
NEW YORK   LONDON   TORONTO   SYDNEY   AUCKLAND

A Perfect Crime Book

Published by Doubleday
a division of Bantam Doubleday Dell Publishing Group, Inc.
666 Fifth Avenue, New York, New York 10103

Doubleday is a trademark of Doubleday, a division of
Bantam Doubleday Dell Publishing Group, Inc.

Book design by Tasha Hall

Library of Congress Cataloging-in-Publication

Katz, Jon.
Death by station wagon : a suburban detective mystery / by Jon Katz.
p.   cm.
"A Perfect crime book."
I. Title.
PS3561.A7558D4 1993
813'.54—dc20
92-29809
CIP

ISBN 0-385-42112-5

To Jane and the Open Door

DEATH
BY STATION
WAGON

1

The old man reached over and turned off the alarm, knowing without looking that the small digital clock would read 3:55 A.M., feeling the biting cold in every one of his seventy-five-year-old bones. On mornings like this—the cold wave was breaking records as well as testing elderly joints—he regretted that things hadn't worked out as he had planned, so that he could be sitting on his butt in Florida this time of year with Gloria, God rest her soul.

But then, he supposed, he was lucky to have a rent-free place in a nice suburb like Rochambeau. His boys fussed at him constantly to quit and head south, but he wasn't one to give up his independence and hang around with old folks like fruit spoiling in the sun. Most days, he was proud of his job. Without it, he couldn't afford to live here at all anymore, not with tiny rowhouses right next to the train tracks fetching close to two hundred thousand.

Getting up in the middle of the night to patrol the grounds in his dented old Chevy wagon wasn't that great a price to pay. If he didn't make his rounds, the goddamn kids would come spray-paint every brick and bust every window in the big old house now that Old Man Brown was dead; they'd probably cart off or wreck the old furniture that remained inside while the lawyers squabbled on about who would get this tract on the hill.

He knew, had read about it often enough in the *Rocham-beau Times*, that the Brown estate had become a battleground. It was one of the biggest remaining undeveloped parcels of private land within commuting distance of New York City. Some of the townspeople had organized to try to keep it from the developers, and the developers had countered by hiring big city firms, until the whole damn mess had become another way for lawyers to get fat. After a while, the old man had little doubt, the developers would prevail. He'd lived in this town his whole life and he'd seen lots of fights over development, but only one outcome.

When he went to the hardware store or the Rochambeau Coffee Shop, people would ask what was going to happen to the old place. He would tell them it was the oldest story in the suburbs, wasn't it? The Brown estate was going to wind up either a giant mall or a couple hundred condos, a shame either way.

Sitting up, the old man listened as the automatic coffee maker hissed on. On nights as cold as this, he slept in his flannel shirt and corduroy pants. He had just a wool shirt and heavy boots to pull on over them, and his quilted parka over that. He'd need two cups of coffee—black, spiked with two fingers of rum—to get cranked up this morning.

He checked what he called his millionaire's view. From the second-floor window of the caretaker's cottage, even at this hour, Manhattan glowed and sparkled from twelve miles away, especially in the clear, arctic air that had gripped the area for days. If ever there were a day he yearned to crawl back into bed, this was it. At his age, once the cold seeped into your feet, it was summer before it got out.

But he threw off the blankets. With Gloria gone six years, he had to be his own scold. Eustace Brown had remembered him in his will, stipulated that he be kept on as caretaker, provided he made his rounds.

The executors would be happy to strike him off the estate's expense sheet if he started sleeping in. They had already jumped all over him when somebody pried off the expensive tiles that lined the walkway into the garden last winter. One of the snooty young gents had actually suggested that somebody younger might make a more effective watchman. Hell, he'd retorted, the whole Rochambeau PD couldn't keep every kid off of two hundred wooded and untended acres. Besides, these were suburban kids, playing at being bad more than actually doing much harm. Let's see the bastards pay for a private security service to come out and drive around at 4 A.M., he'd fumed to himself.

At least he could complete his circuit quickly this morning, ten minutes at the most. He wasn't getting out of the Chevy, that was for sure, not unless he saw someone walking out with the drapes. Crossing the twenty feet from his little cottage to the garage would be enough to chill him for the rest of the day.

Minutes later, cursing the wind, his wagon thawing but far from comfortable, his ears stinging even under the Russian-style fur cap his grandchildren had given him, the coffee in its plastic holder already growing cold, he switched on the hand-controlled spotlight mounted on the side of his car and began rolling down the long driveway that circled the house.

He loved the oversized chrome-plated police car light he'd ordered through a local mechanic. The same garage that serviced the town's cruisers had painted "Security" in white letters on the doors of his Chevy. Kids often thought he was a cop and ran off when he drove up, especially at night when the light froze them in their tracks and they couldn't see how beat-up the wagon was.

The big light sliced through the blackness as he swept its beam across the garden. In spring, people took to stealing the irises from Mr. Brown's once lovingly tended garden, but there was nothing much to steal now. He rolled past the giant stone house and flashed the light over the windows. Taking one shortcut tonight, he didn't get out of the car to test the front door. He could see it was tightly shut.

He looked over the drained pool, and passed the vegetable garden; all that was left was to eyeball the old hollow once occupied by tenant farmers. In the winter you could still see the foundations of the old farmhouse, razed by Mr. Brown's great-grandfather just after the Civil War. There was almost no natural light there—the old oaks and pines formed a canopy over the road—and he'd have to pay careful attention to stick to the asphalt.

Even randy teenagers didn't neck down in the hollow. It was overgrown and the site of too many legends and rumors to keep track of. Some crazed young farmhand had been hung down there in the 1800s, it was said, after the boy had gone on a bloody rampage all over the town. The old man always drove by quickly.

Perhaps it was because his mind was already on the thick comforter waiting back in his bedroom that he didn't see the Volvo wagon until he was almost upon it. Or maybe it was because the car was midnight blue.

Fortunately his reflexes were quicker than his thoughts these days, he later recalled to the police. His headlights bounced off the wagon's rear window and somehow that registered, because he managed to swerve around the Volvo, braking abruptly alongside the car.

He was puzzled at first, as he sat clutching a hand to his chest and fighting to catch his breath, by the sound of another engine running. His had stalled out; the warning light on his dashboard glowed red. It was the Volvo's engine that was running; in his rearview mirror, he saw wisps rising from the other car's exhaust.

The Volvo's right front window was only a foot or so from where he was sitting. He turned his spotlight on it like a weapon, which in a sense it was. He was, of course, unprepared for everything he saw: for the Volvo's windows to be open, for the young face to be staring at him, eyes open, tongue protruding, rope knotted around her neck, a crooked trickle of blood running from her nose to her lip. "Oh, Jesus," he whispered, afraid that if he spoke louder he'd scare himself to death.

Beside her, in the driver's seat, he could see a Rochambeau High School soccer jacket, the blue and white colors the young boys wore so proudly. The boy had his back to him and appeared to be hanging partway out of the window, away from the girl. He didn't answer the old man's confused cries. The spotlight picked up a heavy rope that seemed to run from the driver's side away to a big old stump a couple of dozen feet away.

The old man couldn't take the girl staring at him that way, he admitted later. But it was when he glanced in his rearview mirror that he panicked and frantically restarted his engine. He'd had the sensation—it had once saved his life at Inchon—of somebody standing among the trees, watching. It was pitch dark, and the shape that loomed indistinctly in the mirror was a blur, but he was positive he'd seen someone in some kind of cloak or cape and one of those tall hats, the kind you always saw in pictures of Lincoln. You live long enough, go through enough, and sometimes you just trust your instincts, he told the detectives, who smiled at each other and nodded. There was somebody else there, he would swear to it, and that was why he hadn't stopped to make absolutely certain of what seemed clear, that the boy and girl were both dead.

Don't worry about it, the detectives said soothingly. The two kids were long beyond help. Any sane man would have done what he'd done, which was to floor the Chevy in reverse, turn the car around, and race like hell up the road to the guardhouse. Bloodhounds would search the area thoroughly, the detectives said, and if there were any trace of anyone having been there, they'd find it. But he knew that the detectives didn't really believe him, thought he was trying to explain away his fear. They didn't figure he was sharp enough to take in the notes the younger cop was writing, but the old man saw him jot it down: *liquor on guard's breath.* Most folks treated the elderly and the young the same way, as cute but unreliable. The suburbs were especially cruel to the old, making them feel invisible amidst all the bustling family life.

But he told the rest of the story anyway. He'd made it back to the caretaker's house in under a minute, gotten out his hunting rifle and pointed it at the entrance, prepared to blast through the door at the slightest sound, and called the Rochambeau PD. Looking out his window toward the town, he could see the first flashing red lights in seconds, heading up the hill's winding drive; in a few more seconds he heard the first sirens. Soon it was Coney Island up there on the old estate: the chief himself arrived, then three Rochambeau cruisers, three state troopers, two county crime lab vans, the medical examiner's wagon, a county helicopter circling overhead, police dogs barking down in the hollow. A tow truck for the Volvo appeared shortly afterwards, followed by two or three reporters and newspaper photographers, two ambulances, and a few stray cops from nearby towns who'd been listening to their scanners and couldn't resist stopping by. They didn't get to see murder scenes very often. The top of his quiet mountain must have looked like an airport runway, all that flashing and blinking.

He had to say, the old man told his kids the next afternoon, he was happy to see them all charging up the hill the way they did; Inchon was like a trip to the Jersey shore compared to what he'd felt in that hollow.

The old man was in Florida for good a week later, telling his new cronies that the shock had broken him, ruined him for security work forever. He'd take his Social Security and pensions and spend his time being warm, like he should've done years ago.

Sitting on the bench in front of the condo he'd rented for the coming year—his kids had found it for him—he knew he had the best story anybody in the whole complex could tell and, aided by his thick stack of already fraying newspaper clippings, he told it and told it.

2

Rochambeau had been a town with musty old family-run businesses and sprawling clapboard houses long before it became an upper-middle-class suburb where three out of four backyards are equipped with organic wooden climbing gyms. Maybe that's why I like it so much.

It's old enough to have a history that predates New York sprawl and yuppie acquisitiveness, to have Victorian porches and parks with statues and giant aging trees. Its homes sort of peek out from overarching swathes of green, as if the buildings and the trees have grown together. I had become a late but enthusiastic convert to the cause of defending it from the rapacious mall-making that was under way in the rest of the suburbs. I thought it a noble effort, though my wife claimed I wanted to preserve Rochambeau because we could no longer afford to move anywhere else.

It was my friend Benchley Carrolton who had politicized me on the subject of preservation, which had never figured much in coffee-break chat on Wall Street. Mostly as a favor to Benchley, I had agreed to attend the Historical Society dinner at the Rochambeau Inn last night.

People who care about town history and environmental issues are pretty much one and the same in Rochambeau. The dinner was supposed to raise money to restore the old Daltrey house, but the conversation over cocktails was of little but the fight over what would happen to the Brown estate now that it was on the market. Every developer between here and Dallas lusted for it. The land alone was worth at least sixty million dollars. Developed, Benchley figured, close to a half-billion, conservatively.

The Historical Society was wandering away from its charter a bit, gearing for a fight to have the town acquire the Brown estate by eminent domain or maybe persuade the state or county to turn it into a park. That did not seem a likely prospect, cake sales and petitions versus billionaires and their law firms. Nevertheless, the dinner had attracted nearly a hundred local do-gooders—garden ladies, recycling zealots, high school history teachers, Civil War buffs—willing to plunk down fifty dollars for bad food to preserve good land from split-levels and shopping plazas. I was happy to be there, although, unlike Benchley, I would always feel self-conscious about do-gooding. It was just a few years ago that I was refueling every morning with coffee and doughnuts, psyching myself like the Ninja trading warrior I was for the daily test of nerve, stamina, and greed that was my capitalist career. Conservation gatherings came as naturally to me then as picnics on the arctic tundra.

Benchley Carrolton had selected the Rochambeau Inn for economic, certainly not culinary, reasons. It was one of those ornate suburban catering palaces that could turn over two thousand people as efficiently as I made toast. Such places were truly ecumenical, chicken-and-whipped-potato melting pots that stood as unintended but eloquent testaments to commercial brotherhood. On the list of events you could find anything from a bar mitzvah to a Bahai wedding to Harry and Martha's fiftieth. The inn had charged twenty-two dollars a head for last night's roast beef, limp beans, anemic salad, and dollop of tasteless chocolate pudding. The Historical Society got to keep the rest.

The bitter January winds soon penetrated even the ersatz brick walls of the inn and everyone was rushing through the dinner. This kind of cold was rare for northern New Jersey. Everybody had gotten got quite excited about it—the radio dispensing frostbite avoidance tips, the few kids remaining on the street swaddled like newborns, Benchley worrying about his greenhouses. I was remembering that I had never gotten around to putting up the storm windows, despite Jane's increasingly testy predictions that our oil bill would probably soon top my legal debts.

After the dinner I dropped Benchley off, wishing as usual that I looked as lively at forty-two as he did at eighty. Benchley has aged as graciously as he does everything. But he had recently forgone night driving, arguing that he wanted to quit before he hurt somebody, not after.

His home is behind his Rochambeau Garden Center, just down the hill from the Brown estate, on land that Carroltons have owned practically since the time General Lee was heading for Gettysburg. Benchley's wife had died a few years earlier, but it was not in his nature to brood or whine. He simply took on another dozen or so causes, a physical rehabilitation center downtown, the local literacy program, Meals on Wheels. If everyone were like Benchley, there would be no poverty or cruelty in the world.

I'd known him for several years. After the steamy afternoon five years ago when I'd reached an agreement with the U.S. Attorney exiling me from the financial world for life, I'd had, for the first time I could recall, lots of time to fill. I filled it in various ways, coaching my son's soccer team, walking my black Lab, Percentage, studying for my private investigator's license—and gardening. Boy, did I garden. I pulled up every weed, pruned every tree and bush, seeded every bare inch of lawn, and planted three maples, two dogwoods, a row of tomatoes, six rose bushes and too many pachysandra to count. All these items were purchased at the Rochambeau Garden Center, along with appropriate shears, trowels, rakes, and sacks of mulch and topsoil. Jane says we don't have to worry about the rain forest anymore; it's being replaced in our backyard.

Rochambeau is too small a town and Benchley too sharp a merchant for the greening of Christopher Deleeuw to pass unnoticed. I hadn't realized until he pointed it out to me that I wasn't the only middle-aged man browsing thoughtfully through the Garden Center. Benchley says Wall Street types head for the gardens like a shot when they're out of work. His theory is that after years of making money through shell games, crap shoots, and paper shuffles, the urge to grow something real and useful is too powerful to resist.

He had startled me one afternoon by inviting me behind the back greenhouse—he had a couple of lawn chairs set out under the burlap-bound shade trees—for a drink. I startled myself by accepting. Benchley, angular, white-haired, eternally dignified, liked to sip from a (recyclable) bottle of mineral water with one hand and, with the other, train his hose on the burlap bags. We shot the breeze for hours. This, too, was quite new for me. On Wall Street, the closest I got to real friendship were those murderous hours on the racquetball court.

Last night, though, even Benchley's hospitable instincts lost out to the cold; he thanked me for the ride and scuttled inside.

Jane woke me up with the news. I was slow to rise,

burrowing deeper under the quilts. Percentage didn't rouse either. The dog, not usually blessed with an abundance of intellect, has figured out a clever way to sleep on the bed while technically obeying the regulations against doing so. He crawls up onto the bed, burrowing between the covers while leaving his hind legs on the floor. I let him get away with it on especially cold nights.

After rousing the kids, Jane had gone down to fire up the wood stove and bring in the paper, a chore which in some households, I am told, is the province of the dog. Very quickly she was back, standing beside the bed in her bathrobe, her arms folded against the cold. She wore a President-has-been-shot or we're-at-war look.

"Kit," she said, "I just heard it on the radio downstairs. Two kids from the high school were found dead on the Brown estate this morning. There aren't many details, but the police are saying it looks like a murder-suicide."

We looked at one another and reacted as hundreds of other Rochambeau parents must have done at that moment: We pictured ourselves getting that call from the police and wondered, since it was impossible to actually comprehend it ourselves, how we could ever come to grips with so stunning a loss. It took me another moment or two to think of Benchley, whose Garden Center practically adjoined the death scene.

I sat up, pushing Percentage to one side, and reached for the phone. The voice that answered sounded uncharacteristically fatigued.

"Benchley, it's Kit. I only have a second. Got to get the kids off. You're okay?"

He wasn't, of course. Benchley is a Quaker, and he has never gotten used to the reports of violence that pour out of the media daily. Each incident seems to hit him personally.

But to have two people killed right up the hill—I knew he'd be devastated. "I heard the sirens around four," he told me. "I waited for them to stop but they kept coming for hours. I brought coffee up to the officers on the estate and told them they could use my house. It was so awfully cold, Kit. Two seniors from the high school. It seems that the boy choked the girl, then hung himself somehow. I'm not clear on the details. I saw the bodies. . . .

"They said it must have happened while we were at the dinner," he resumed after a moment. "I know it's silly, but I feel guilty. The thought of those two kids up there dying while we were passing canapés." He was closing the Garden Center for the day, Benchley said. He thought it inappropriate to do business at the bottom of a hill when two children with most of their lives ahead of them had just perished at the top.

I hung up and saw Jane staring out the window when she should have been pulling on her pantyhose. Although she sees plenty of misery and suffering at the clinic where she works, that seemed as far removed from our quiet street as the ghoulish reports every night on the evening news from New York—mothers stabbed in front of their kids, sons mowed down on playgrounds, toddlers shot as they napped in their strollers by warring drug dealers. This was harder to look away from.

But reality intrudes in an especially relentless way on Monday mornings. Jane glanced at the alarm clock and realized that, tragedy or no, a school bus would pull up in twenty-five minutes and Ben and Emily had to be ready to get on it. Jane would be late for work if we didn't hustle, and I would be late for the cases I had been insisting I had to finish up.

I scrambled downstairs to make the lunches, reverting to

boxed chocolate milk, emergency peanut butter sandwiches, bananas, plastic containers of pudding, and bags of corn chips. The two-minute lunch—it wasn't pretty, but it got the job done. It was enough to keep them from getting hungry and me from feeling guilty.

I can't quite break myself of the habit of constantly taking the temperature of my relationship with my kids, a practice that seems most futile and pathetic in the morning. My standard is, if you can love your offspring before 9 A.M., you can love them for the rest of their lives.

Children don't seem biologically programmed to rise early for school, at least not mine. Ben especially has to be growled into getting out of his bed (and then making it), offering something resembling human speech over breakfast, clearing his dishes, collecting his book bag, jacket, and gear, and getting to the school bus on time. Between the time he silently drags himself downstairs and the time he trudges out to the curb, he is at his sullen, resentful, uncommunicative best. Emily hasn't quite gotten the hang of being sullen yet.

"How's school these days, Ben?" I repeated the question across the table three times. "C'mon, there, Ben. You can do it. You can speak. Go for it." I persisted. I always persist, foolishly. When will I ever learn that you can't win contests like that? "School-ish," was his reply most days. Em, otherwise the chirpiest and most cheerful of kids, whined her way through breakfast. They should have been left alone; we really had nothing much to talk about in the morning. Jane and I weren't exactly cooing lovebirds at breakfast either.

"Did Em have her vitamin? Ben, you know you have a dentist appointment this afternoon? Kit, have you got fruit for their lunches?" Jane called as she rushed into the bathroom to fuss with her hair.

"Don't I always? Do I need lessons on making lunch?" I called after her, indignant as always when Jane insisted on reminding me about my parental duties. She meant it as simple backstopping, of course, but I was touchy. Jane is a wonderful mother, but I think I handle some of the details better than she did, back when I used the house to sleep in and spent my waking life on the Street and she, along with a nanny and a housekeeper, ruled the home front.

My wife—her name is Jane Leon—is one of those feminists who keeps her name and thinks a woman's place is in the House of Representatives, but who fights to the death to keep from relinquishing a single domestic chore, especially one involving kids. For all that she adores the kids, Jane doesn't really have a domestic gene in her body. Once I started working closer to home, it made sense for me to take over most child-care duties, and I'm pretty good at them now, after some admittedly false starts. But try getting her to back off and leave you alone while you do your daughter's hair or decide what jacket your son should wear in the rain.

We were really play-acting at fighting. Since my previous life had suddenly disintegrated, our marriage had taken on surprising and delightful new dimensions. Jane had quickly announced she'd taken a full-time job at a mental health clinic in Paterson that, while hardly high-salaried, would buy me some time to build up my new business while our savings dwindled to nothing, which is where they continue to hover. She loves her work and I love mine, the variety, the freedom, the fact that I'm my own boss. Without money to pay for help, I took over kiddie care. I love that too, although it had never occurred to me how difficult and draining it is to do it right.

I see it as a sort of low-intensity civil conflict. There are sweet moments of affection, sure, but mostly my children conduct an indefatigable guerrilla resistance against healthful food, reasonable bedtimes, minimal neatness, courteous conversation, and me.

But it's funny—until my troubles, our marriage wasn't really a partnership. I made most of the money, Jane's career sputtered and languished. When I stumbled, she rose to the occasion. Before, we lived separate and somewhat distant lives within the same household. Now, we make one another possible. Besides, she has a weekly paycheck and a health plan, the private investigator's best friend.

I ran through my daily checklist.

"Kids! Lunches? Backpacks? Homework? Ben, you're walking over to the dentist after school, right?"

"Jesus, Dad, Mom already reminded me. How many times do you have to ask me?"

My son was at that painful and obnoxious stage of adolescence where every component of his life seemed in turmoil and he was uncomfortable talking about any of it. His body changed almost daily. I could smell sweat for the first time, and I guessed that the testosterone was at full boil. One morning he was chunky, the next lean and an inch taller; one day he loathed girls, the next he was hiding copies of *Playboy* in the attic.

Of all the family, I think Ben was the most affected by my troubles. I could only imagine the ribbing he'd taken from other kids, though he'd never mentioned it. And I would have to imagine it, since he would never discuss it. I suspect he wondered what most of the people around me had wondered at one time or another: Was I a thief? The government didn't hassle innocent people, did it? I had tried a hundred times to sit down and explain it all to Ben, but I'd gotten nowhere.

Emily would never for a second consider the notion that I was capable of disabling a fly. One of my daughter's girl-friends once told her I was a crook, and Emily had delivered a roundhouse shot that almost took out two teeth, according to the teacher's stunned and horrified report. The child's father called to tell me Em was out of control and that he wasn't going to sit by and allow his Katie to be subjected to violence.

That was not typical; Emily was a TV sitcom kid, freckled, skinny, funny, bubbly, trusting, adoring, and adored. Unlike Ben, she wanted to know every detail of every case, and pestered me day and night to come to my office and hang around. My office isn't the kind of place most nine-year-old girls in town would frequent—it's sort of a dump, actually—but I loved having Emily around, and so did the salespeople in the shoe store and everyone else. She was the unofficial mascot of the American Way Mall.

Outside, the numbing wind sneaked around the window-panes of our big old house. The iron wood stove in the kitchen, which we originally bought because it was atmospheric but now used to save money, wasn't quite equal to this mid-January morning. It was so cold the kids weren't even fighting about the mittens, scarves, and parkas I was hauling out of the hall closet, common sense triumphing over fashion for once.

"You'll probably hear about this in school," I said to them, trying to strike a line between matter-of-factness and gravity. "Two high school kids died last night." I wanted to prepare them for the inevitable rumors, but I didn't want to scare them out of their wits.

"Oh, my God," said Emily. Ben dropped his standard bored expression and looked genuinely shocked.

Why shouldn't he be? We'd never encountered anything like this in the ten years Jane and I had been living in Rochambeau. Unlike cities, suburbs don't like to dwell on violence. There are no tabloids to keep crime alive with lurid headlines. In fact, few suburban newspapers acknowledge crime of any kind for longer than they have to. Murder tends to take the gloss off property values; city dwellers reason that if they're going to get killed, they might as well stay where they are. But there would be some coverage in the local paper, which came out that afternoon, and the kids would probably be hearing stuff all day.

Both kids were paying unusually rapt attention. But there wasn't time.

"Look, guys," Jane put in from the bathroom doorway. "I want to talk with both of you about this, but we should sit down tonight after dinner when we can really discuss it, and when we know more. But you'll probably be hearing some wild things, meantime, and a lot of them probably won't be true. We'll clear it up tonight. Daddy will give you enough details so you'll know what everybody's talking about, but the rest will have to wait, okay?" I caught the warning in the last word and glance. Psychology was, after all, her turf. She would undoubtedly know the best way to air a tragedy like this one without leaving permanent scars.

"God, we're gonna be late," Ben announced, returning to consciousness, and he and Em struggled to slide their backpacks over the layers of winter clothing and headed towards the door.

"Dad, please, please, please don't forget the fiberboard for my atom," Emily reminded me.

"Okay, sweetie, I wrote it on a Post-it and I'll put it

on the Volvo dashboard. I won't possibly be able to miss it."

She looked skeptical but had no time for further pleading. I peeled the Post-it off the pad and stuck it on my forehead, the only fail-safe way I'd devised for remembering domestic chores. I would see it when I looked in the rearview mirror before backing the car out of the driveway. The neighbors sometimes looked at me strangely, but what the hell.

Jane gathered up her overstuffed briefcase and worn canvas shoulder bag and headed toward the back door, chuckling. The sight of a yellow square affixed just below my receding hairline had temporarily driven away thoughts of dead children and grieving families. Percentage, dozing in the hallway, acknowledged her passing with a thump of his tail.

"Kit, don't forget your meeting with Mr. Kelley. We have to get her English teacher changed." In Rochambeau, things like class assignments were not distant bureaucratic problems: They were life and death dramas. Parents watched their mailboxes carefully, waiting for the envelope with the school system logo—a well-proportioned tree in full foliage.

They were on the phone to one another in a flash, comparing assignments, pretending to be indifferent or resigned, then fighting for the best teachers as if they were battling over crumbs for their starving kids. Parents handicapped teachers the way track junkies mastered every horse. The rule of thumb, from what I could see, was this: If your kid had a problem, attack. Mr. Kelley, the principal, stopped answering phone calls at this time of year, as a new semester was beginning. The man aged dramatically from year to year. He had developed a nervous tic in his right eye, his hair was graying visibly, and he had acquired a hurried, furtive style that could get him from the school's front door into his car in seconds.

I had done all right with him the last couple of years, though I didn't really know if that was unusual or not. In the suburbs, people freely trade information about housing prices and tax bills, but they guard closely whatever tricks they've learned for dealing with the school system. We all talked about how important it was to let our kids solve their own problems, but they rarely got the chance.

Em's English teacher was, in fact, an idiot, a pompous authoritarian martinet who had given her detention for forgetting to have a parent sign her perfect spelling test. He'd once made her rewrite a book report because she'd put the date on the top right corner instead of the top left. I try to stay out of these things, I swear I do, but at such moments I want to storm the school and run blockheads like that out of the building and into the Department of Motor Vehicles where they belong. Of course a few years earlier, it was rare for me even to know what any of my kids' teachers looked like. I was never home for parent-teacher conferences or "Back To School" night.

"I know about the meeting, Jane, I've got it on my calendar." It was a comparatively full calendar that morning. I was working on three runaway cases and one missing wife, investigating a couple of liability claims for Foundation Mutual, and trying to track down a husband who was ducking his child support. I enjoyed nabbing and confronting those bastards, sometimes scouring through records for the places they hid their money. I also had a couple of background checks to make, routine screenings of employees for a local electronics company. Compared to the car repos and divorce snoopings I sometimes had to do, this was high-class stuff. And there was a fair amount of it, in contrast to my early months when I would dial the weather number just to make sure my office phone was working. I was just beginning to realize how much I loved running my own life, especially now that holding on to our house was at least a possibility as opposed to an absurd fantasy. Someday we might even be able to paint it again.

3

I fiddled with the radio trying to learn more about the deaths as I waited for the old Volvo to warm, an increasingly uncertain and time-consuming prospect in weather as bitter as this. The car never actually failed to start, but sometimes it took a fair amount of cranking, grinding, and whirring. The only news reports I could find were from the New York all-news stations, which were already loving the story—death in suburbia, what a delightful twist. I wasn't hearing much more than Jane had—two Rochambeau High School kids, a boy and a girl, found by the night watchman at the Brown estate in what police were tentatively calling a murder-suicide.

Names were being withheld until relatives could be notified. Town stunned, etc. I wondered how the reporters could know. Most of the town hadn't even heard about it until half an hour ago.

Backing out of the driveway, glancing in my rearview mirror, I was startled to see a Post-it with a message that was backwards but readable enough: FIBERBOARD. On the way from the house to the car I had naturally forgotten all about it. I decided to stop at the hobby store—excuse me, at Creative Expressions—before trying to track down my third fiscally irresponsible ex-husband of the week.

Could the dead kids have lived nearby, on these peaceful streets that comprised our neighborhood? Could it have been Willie Doehler, in the red brick on Fairfield? He was a

24

brooder. Or Marli O'Bryan in the Tudor on Windsor? I'd
never seen her smile in the six years she'd lived there. She
took every social ill personally, gloomily but admirably ringing our bell every other week for gun control or animal rights
or no-nuclear-anything. We always gave, always signed.
Could it be one of the kids I saw pedaling their bikes around?
Kids that could be mine in a few years? The really chilling
thing was that some parents in town already knew. The ones
whose kids were dead.

I couldn't decide whether I was hoping for murder-suicide or whether any other possibility just seemed too incon-
gruous for the quiet, prosperous suburban houses I was cruising past. News had a way of suddenly landing close to home.
I had learned that as I had approached forty, when phone
calls could suddenly mean Mom or Dad or Aunt Sally had
died or that an overweight, overworked buddy from the firm
had crumpled on the trading floor with a coronary.

The parking lot behind the huge Victorian house that
now housed Creative Expressions was blessedly empty on a
weekday morning, a stark contrast to the madhouse the store
became on weekends. Sid was sipping coffee from a paper
cup. We exchanged head-shakes and clucks over the dreadful
headlines and both hoped they were nobody we knew.

"I heard it was kids from the next town," Sid said reassuringly. "From Caldwell. They were found here, but they
weren't from here. That's what they told me in the coffee
shop, anyway." Reports from the Watchung Coffee Shop. Reliable stuff.

I handed Sid the list for Emmy's science project—fiberboard, three kinds of colored thumbtacks, a yellow Hi-liter
and some adhesive tape, soon to be on exhibit at Lucretia
Mott Elementary School.

"Oh, Mrs. Shipper's atom." Sid chuckled appreciatively.

"It's a good project, every winter. You might as well get the pins and paper for the maps of North America—that'll be her next project. You need thumbtacks for that too, for the cities. But can I be honest? Between us, Mrs. Shipper's a sucker for multicolored states. Get this colored posterboard. It's a little more expensive, but it will stand out. This white will look blah compared to what the other kids are using." Sid winked. Inside intelligence on Mrs. Shipper's map assignment. Maybe that would provide the edge that would turn a Brown University admission counselor's head in ten years.

As I fumble and fuss over my new life, I often think appreciatively of Sid Green, unheralded genius of suburban transitions. I worry every morning—*every* morning, as regularly as shaving (it clearly has something to do with this most male of rituals, which underscores my responsibilities to my family)—about how to pay the mortgage, how to send Ben and Em to college, whether I will ever be able to retire and, if so, how. I am plodding and witless next to Sid Green, who has read Rochambeau more skillfully than any gypsy ever read a tarot card.

At fifty-one, he was downsized without warning out of his $120,000 job as vice president of Americal Insurance after twenty-eight years of devoted service, and it was the proverbial first day of the rest of his life. I used to ride the train into the city with Sid, a cigar-smoking horse freak who tucked the *Racing Form* inside his *Wall Street Journal* every morning.

At the time he was laid off he had two kids in college, one more headed there, a wife whose main job was hosting the Rochambeau Concert Series fund-raising dinners, a $3,000 monthly mortgage, two Volvos, weekly piano lessons and soccer uniforms and ballet shoes to pay for, a house on Cape Cod, $6,000 a year just in country club dues, and a new

$150,000 kitchen in midrenovation. He and Ginger immediately scaled back their expenses, sold their summer place, and used the proceeds to buy the old Rochambeau Hobby Shop, which sold mostly model sets, balsa wood airplanes, paint, glue, and popsicle stick kits. The Hobby Shop was unselfconsciously frayed around the edges, a place you wandered into now and then when your kid wanted to learn how to twist balloons into dachshunds or build a plastic F-16.

Sid had instantly renamed the store Creative Expressions and held a lavish breakfast reception for every public and private art, science, and social studies teacher in town at which he stuffed them with croissants and pastries, solicited their philosophies, programs, and likely classroom assignments, and offered them and their students fifteen-percent discounts for all eternity. He boarded up his ripped-up kitchen and used the balance of the home improvement loan to redesign and renovate the old store. He threw out the bellicose models and divided the store into age groups, according to the classifications followed by the town schools: Toddler, Preschool, Elementary, Middle, and High School. Each group had its own displays: science, reading, social studies, geography, math, creative play, noncompetitive games.

Creative Expressions sponsored science fairs all over town (the winners got displays in his windows), opened a dinosaur habitat center (with take-home dinosaur models), and sold home environmental kits.

Perhaps Sid's most brilliant stroke was converting the shop's entire second floor, previously a dusty storeroom, into the Gifted and Talented Department, "For Children With Special Gifts in Need of Special Means of Expressing Them." In Rochambeau, a line like that should have been illegal; someone might as well have given him a machine to print

money. Along with soccer games and the video store on Saturday (sleepover) night, Creative Expressions had become
one of those weekly must-stops for Rochambeau families. Sid
watched kids in town grow up, there at every step of their
creative development to lend a hand or a paint kit. Parents
felt virtuous about avoiding Toys "R" Us. Junior high school
kids used it as a pick-up place. Em made play dates there for
Saturday afternoon. Sid made money.

"Sid," I would hear a parent say, "Evan is going through
an active period"—what four-year-old boy wasn't?—"and I'd
like to encourage him to be more creative." Sid might mutter
something under his breath about slipping the kid a Valium,
but he and Evan would go off hand in hand (parents were
encouraged to hang back so that Sid and the kid could form a
relationship; most parents foolishly complied) to the preschool "active" section and return with armfuls of beanbags,
oversized marbles and chutes, foam bats and balls, and eighty
bucks' worth of plastic building blocks.

Emmy had once told Jane and me at breakfast one Saturday that she was "really, really, really" interested in painting.
Before noon, she had an easel, a smock, three brushes, three
canvases, and a paletteful of washable nontoxic oil paints. The
easel is in my office at the American Way, where it holds my
chart of current cases. Would Em ever know how elaborately
the world around her was constructed?

Sid grinned at me as I left with my supplies. "Don't you
just love science?" he called, nodding as a young couple eyed
the Gifted and Talented sign and headed upstairs. He grabbed
my arm as I headed towards the door. "Kit," he whispered.
"My brother called from the city. Jersey Girl in the sixth at
the Meadowlands. It's a gift." He waved good-bye. I shook my
head. I thought it would be rude to tell him I never gambled
—I couldn't afford to.

I hoped he was right about the dead kids; I hoped they were from another town. I didn't particularly relish explaining murder or suicide to my kids that night; I wanted a way to make death sound remote. This wasn't really what we had moved to suburbia for.

With my Creative Expressions bag in the rear of the Volvo, I checked Dave Savastano's home address: Glenside Road, Jersey City. The Jersey waterfront towns—Hoboken, Jersey City, Weehawken—were increasingly popular first stops for Rochambeau's newly divorced men, and increasingly frequent destinations for private detectives in search of those delinquent in their alimony and child support payments.

In modern America, any private detective worth a hamburger can find these errant daddies between breakfast and lunch. They can put up protective screens around their calls and visitors in the city, but if they rent anything, buy anything, lease anything—and divorced daddies do all these things—I can find them. Finding their hidden assets is harder. Peeping on extramarital affairs is stomach-churning and distasteful. Tracking down irresponsible leeches who stick it to their wives and kids while they furnish trendy new apartments with smoked-glass coffee tables is a joy. A few of them are broke, but most of those I track down are just unbelievably selfish and irresponsible.

Two miles down from the American Way Mall, where my office is tucked away on the seldom-seen-or-visited second floor, is one of the state's biggest credit agencies. For three hundred dollars, one of the computer clerks will plug in any name I need. I show up in the parking lot the next day, even the same day if necessary, and wait next to the Salvation Army clothes drop. The clerk comes out at lunch time, drives by, and drops the disc out the window of his car next to the clothes drop. I wait a few minutes, pick it up, go back to the office, and look up my delinquent dad's current financial history. In some respects, this is the most useful work I have ever done. It is illegal, of course, but how else to track down alimony deadbeats: the yellow pages?

Savastano had been a partner in a substantial real estate development firm. He took off with his secretary two years ago, leaving his wife behind in a big house in Rochambeau with a dog, two cars, and two small children. During the settlement, he had been all remorse and responsibility. His wife Julia—a physical therapist who had gone back to work and who I liked a lot (why do they always work over the nicest ones?)—had moved to a smaller house and was trying to hold things together. Then six months ago, Savastano suddenly sold his shares in the firm, and vanished. People in town saw him around from time to time, but no one knew where he lived. He stopped contacting his family and his child support payments lapsed.

"He's probably in Sante Fe," Julia had told me through a puff of cigarette smoke. She'd taken up nicotine again, she told me wearily, but wouldn't go near liquor because "I'd be an alcoholic in a flash." Savastano, she said, had always fantasized about moving to New Mexico. "But I can't afford to send you there looking for him, Kit."

I had tried to reassure her. "Look, I don't know if this is good news or not, but I'll wager Dave's within a stone's throw of here. They usually are. He's in the city, in the Village or SoHo, or he's in some apartment near Hoboken. He'll give me some song and dance about hard times, and then he'll pay for a few more months. Then he'll probably stop again. But at least your lawyer will know where to nail him," I said.

The fact is the system stinks. While clogged courts and

high-priced lawyers wrangle for months about payment schedules and agreement violations, families like the Savastanos get pretty desperate. Julia was not looking to hook the bastard; she just wanted him to do what he had agreed to do so that their kids could have some sort of normal life. The last thing she wanted was for him to come back. She wasn't much of a complainer, but I got the sense, from the boxes of canned soup and generic cereal, the peeling paint and threadbare sofas, that she and the kids were right on the edge.

"If you find him, just tell him to do what he promised. And would you ask him to call the kids, please? They want to talk to their father once in a while, and much as I'd like him to get out of our lives for good, he *is* their father." I had heard those words before.

Maybe, I told her, he was just feeling guilty about the divorce.

"Yeah, maybe I'll get invited on *Jeopardy* and win fifty grand."

Savastano popped up right away in the credit agency file. He had applied for a new Gold Card so that he could secretly furnish his new bachelor's pad in Jersey City; that month alone, he'd racked up four thousand dollars in furniture from Macy's. I knew just what it looked like, too: The first thing these guys got was black leather furniture, then a big stereo, then a waterbed or other king-size monstrosity they hoped to spend a lot of time in. He probably had started a new business in the city or in some other part of North Jersey too. Stalking him would not be unpleasant; it was social work.

The street in Jersey City was two blocks from the PATH train station in a neighborhood of renovator townhouse specials and dingy old apartment houses. None of the bells by the door were labeled Savastano, naturally, so I parked across the street and broke out a novel. I would turn the Volvo engine off whenever the car warmed up, then back on when I couldn't stand the cold. I didn't dare leave for a cup of coffee, because if I missed the chump I could easily spend the whole night sitting there wondering if he'd shown up. I cursed myself for not remembering to bring a thermos of coffee. No real detective, private or official, would ever be caught on an extended stakeout without coffee. An embarrassing lapse. I jotted COFFEE on a Post-it and pressed it on the dashboard. Post-its are the neatest invention since blue jeans.

Every half-hour, I tried to remember to turn on the news to see if there was anything fresh on the dead kids, though often I forgot what time it was. Toward afternoon the victims acquired names—the cops must have released them—but I didn't recognize them and there weren't many new details. The New York stations were diverted by a subway derailment on the Lower East Side and were broadcasting death and injury counts instead of new developments in Rochambeau's drama.

I may have forgotten the thermos, but I did use my plastic urine bottle for those unexpected little emergencies. Twice in the past, my squirming with the bottle had brought calls to the cops from some old busybody at her window. Now I brought a blanket along to throw over my lap, which made the whole procedure even more awkward but was markedly preferable to an indecent exposure bust. I also carried a supply of granola bars, nearly frozen, and a stack of cold war spy novels, which I skimmed but dared not immerse myself in.

I always tried to park facing away from the subject's house so that I could watch from the extended rearview mirror, but in this case the street was one-way, and I was stuck in the only available parking space twenty feet from the door. I had a five-hour wait. From Julia's description, and the family photo album, there was absolutely no question it was Savastano—beefy, balding, dyed jet-black hair swept over his blank spot, the obligatory leather jacket open to show off some sort of gold chain. Men. They are not complicated animals, most of them.

I was out of the car in a flash, ID high, breath steaming in the air, moving nearly at a trot. I took a lot of abuse in Rochambeau, from real cops and other people, but delinquent husbands wet their pants when they saw me, all deference and pleas.

"Oh, shit," he said. "How'd you find me? Look, I'm sorry, I'm sorry, I'm not a bad guy, but I had to get settled here." He tried the usual—bribe, threats, whining—but I left with a check for three thousand dollars, and a promise that I'd be back that very night if it bounced. I had ways of checking, I falsely assured him. Julia was glad to get the money, but I thought she also seemed a little sad that he hadn't gone all the way to New Mexico.

"Even when you work at it," she told me, with a tired smile, "it's hard to like men." I nodded. In my work, you get to see a lot of the ways men end up hurting people, physically and emotionally. Not that women are incapable of causing pain. It just doesn't seem so ingrained a trait.

The *Rochambeau Times* was sitting out on the kitchen table when I got home that evening just after 6 P.M. The dead kids were, in fact, from Rochambeau, though I did not know them or their parents. Ken Dale and Carol Lombardi, among the senior class's best-liked students, said the paper. Papers are very charitable in death. Have you ever read a story describing a murdered kid as unpopular?

The details remained sketchy. The paper quoted Rochambeau Police Chief Frank Leeming as saying it appeared to be "a just about open-and-shut" case of murder-suicide. I had been a private investigator long enough to dwell on the "just about." The car was found at 4 A.M. by an elderly watchman on the grounds, engine still running. The boy had apparently strangled the girl, then hung himself by attaching one end of the rope to his neck, the other to a tree stump, handcuffing his hands to the steering wheel, then taking his foot off the brake, allowing the car to coast down the hill and choke him to death. The exact time of death would be difficult to pin down, the chief conceded, because the car windows were all left open, the heater was off, and it was awfully bitter up on that hillside.

The probable motive, the chief said, was what Ken Dale's friends described as his "despair" because Lombardi was seeing someone else. I thought about the kids' parents, about so much being taken from them for good. People bounce back from almost anything, but could I ever bounce back from something like this? This was not a story you could put down while you passed the meat loaf and chirped about what had happened in social studies that day.

Em had heard all about it at school. "There's a murderer loose in town and he's trying to kill all the kids who go out in the park," she informed me calmly. "Georgia said her dad told her she wasn't coming to school until he's arrested." Em seemed unimpressed by the rumors, willing to accept my reassurances that whatever happened on the mountain didn't involve her or her friends, that she would be well protected and taken care of. We would all talk about it as we learned more, I promised her. I made a note on a Post-it to keep the hall light on at bedtime and read her a story. Then she and I spent an hour working on her model atom. She had unfortunately chosen silver, which had forty-seven damned protons.

Jane called to say she'd be late—two of her clients had been beaten bloody that day, one by a father, the other by a mother—so could I start supper? She reminded me that Ben had a piano—excuse me—keyboard lesson after his dentist's appointment. We had joined car pools for the innumerable lessons our kids were rushed to and from and, fortunately, this wasn't my night. When he got home, Ben had an hour's homework and was too wiped out to talk about death. He'd heard even wilder rumors than Em, but being an adolescent male, had no interest in sharing them.

Benchley often talked of his wonder at how people could listen to the grisly stories they heard on the news every day, then go about their lives as if nothing abnormal was going on. There wasn't much mystery to it, I thought. How could any of us survive otherwise? I had no sense that the deaths on the mountain were about to intersect with my own fledgling new life. I would surely have slept differently if I'd had even a clue.

4

In a few years, they'll try to buy the American Way Mall off
Route 6 and move it down to the Smithsonian, into one of
those cavernous halls where they display old steam engines
and other Americana. It's ready whenever they are. The
American Way was built in the flush of the suburban expan-
sion in the early sixties, when twenty-five thousand dollars a
year would buy two cars and a gleaming new split-level on a
cul-de-sac named Willowdale or Elmwood.

Now the Amway, with its chipped stucco walls, could fit
easily into the fast-food court of the newer malls they're
building. My office is on the second floor.

Benchley Carrolton was a good advisor when I first set
up shop. You'll be busy, he said. There's lots of grief in suburbia, it's just more diffuse. Suburban life revolves almost completely around children, homes, and cars, he told me, and if
you pay attention and have connections with all three, you'll
prosper. While I haven't exactly prospered, I have survived, a
minor miracle in itself.

At nine-fifteen, when I usually arrive, it's still peaceful at
the mall. The video game room beneath my office hasn't been
fired up yet and isn't beeping, ringing, chirping, and blasting
as it will from 10 A.M. to midnight. The lights aren't on in the
Cicchelli Furniture window display. I always expect the com-
pleat suburban family—George, Cindy, two kids, friendly

beagle—to be sitting in it, comfortable on the beige-uphol-
stered chairs and sofa, chatting warmly about work and
school.

Murray Grobstein, the monarch who rules Shoe World,
usually waves to me from his window, where he's unpacking
and displaying his sneakers *du jour.* As near as I can tell, the
life span of a contemporary sneaker is about forty-eight hours.
In my next life I'm coming back as an archaeologist studying
the footwear rituals of late twentieth-century American suburban youth, and Shoe World will be my first excavation site.

Murray drives into Brooklyn every Saturday afternoon to
see what the black kids are wearing, then calls his wholesalers
Monday morning to order thousands of pairs of whatever he
sees on their feet. Murray drives a Jaguar XKE. He is not
without a certain sense of irony. "My father ran a grocery
store, worked sixteen hours a day six days a week, if he made
nine thousand dollars at the end, I'll eat a Nike Air," he said. If
you've ever seen one of those, you know that's no small promise. "Me, I can't sell sneakers fast enough, sometimes two,
three pairs a month to the same kid. I'm gonna build a shrine
to basketball stars. I got sneakers in there for a hundred bucks
you have to pump up with air. I tell Bess I never know if these
kids are going to jump high or explode."

I like to ogle Murray's Jag; there's a tiny though dwindling part of me that covets it. Maybe it reminds me of the
days when I could have driven one. I never wish I was back on
Wall Street, but how can you not miss the junkets to Europe,
the secretary who types your letters and makes all your reservations, and all that money?

My new life is well symbolized by my yellow Volvo
wagon, its odometer heading towards 100,000 miles. I may
need to drive it another 100,000 before I can replace it. Some

people are self-conscious about owning Volvo wagons, thinking the car brands them too clearly as upper-middle-class suburbanites. Not me; I ride mine as enthusiastically as Roy rode
Trigger. I can't remember a time when we haven't been able to
stuff whatever we needed into it: mountains of athletic equipment; firewood, mulch, and topsoil; used clothes ferried to
school tag sales; numbing numbers of bags of groceries.

In the morning, I can park it anywhere I want, since
there isn't a teenager, or many shoppers, who are up at that
hour.

This early in the day, the smells from the Lightning
Burger downstairs ("Food In A Flash") haven't turned greasy
yet. I have a terrible weakness for those home fries they keep
in a freezer and plop into boiling oil. The oil they're cooked
in doesn't turn brown until noon, so Luis Hebron, who runs
the place, makes them in the morning for me, extra crispy,
the kind of nuclear cholesterol hit that sends Jane up the wall.

Luis and I became friends before either of us quite noticed it, I think, passing from polite chitchat to occasional but
longer exchanges, and finally to long talks about my cases.
Luis never talks much about himself, and I finally realized I
wasn't being gracious by constantly asking him about his life.
His new country and his new work were the hands he'd been
dealt, not subjects he wanted to discuss.

He was one of Havana's foremost criminal attorneys before fleeing to Jersey City. He tried to get through law school
at Seton Hall, but couldn't quite pull it off and keep his family
together. So he's tossing burgers on a grill all day in the
Amway Mall, riding herd on the surly teenagers who work
and eat there. His dignity and bearing remain intact, however. I have never heard him complain about the twists and
turns his life has taken.

If he's not too crazy from interviewing monosyllabic teenagers or filling in for them when they don't show up for work or preparing for a health inspection, he'll bring me a cup of coffee from a fresh pot and we'll brief each other on the day's events. His are often more eventful than mine—fries overcooked, drunks threatening his staff, teenagers vandalizing his booths.

More than once, Luis and I have closed up the place with coffee and doughnuts and Luis's brilliant mind picking apart a case I'm working on—pathetic stuff, I'm sure, when compared to what he used to work on.

The guys from mall security were just trickling in, charging up their walkie-talkies. City crime gets all the media attention, but even in a small, peeling-around-the-edges mall like this, constant vigilance is required against pickpockets, shoplifters, car thieves, check-kiters, the creepies who goose the salesgirls, plus the occasional fistfight or drug deal, though it's almost unheard of for blood to be spilled.

"Kit," said Tim Leland, the mall's security chief, who was walking the perimeter. "Bunch of kids were waiting. Said they had to see you." He shrugged. "They looked clean-cut enough, so I told them to wait upstairs outside your office. That okay?"

I nodded, although I couldn't imagine who they might be or what they would want; most of my work comes through referrals and over the phone. But when I climbed upstairs there was, in fact, a gaggle of boys milling in the hallway outside my door.

Suburban teenagers vary in style and class, from the jocks in their letter jackets to the muleheads in their rat tails and fifty-pound sneakers, but one curious trait most of them share is the desire to sound and dress as much like city street kids as they can. To my knowledge, black city kids never seem to try to act like white suburban kids, and how could they? They'd be parodying themselves.

The group that stood awkwardly in the hall that January morning were of the moneyed, athletic variety. They reeked of entitlement—rangy, attractive, unable despite their faded letter jackets and worn jeans to hide their health and good grooming. I'd heard them high-fiving each other as I walked down the hallway, trying to jive and sound streetwise. But when I came up and introduced myself, they fell silent.

I could tell they were a bit disappointed, as people often are when they meet me. They always expect Philip Marlowe, trench-coated and taciturn, cigarette dangling from his lips, half-empty bottle of cheap hootch on the desk, waiting for Violets McGee to call from Homicide.

Instead they get me, middle-aged and ordinary looking, an inch over six feet, trim if not lean, slightly bookish in tortoise-shell glasses, flannel shirt, navy wool V-neck from Land's End, corduroys, and loafers, looking for all the world like a casual, off-duty version of the hotshot Wall Streeter I had been just a few years earlier.

At first I thought the boys had made a mistake, that they were looking for the mall employment office down the hall or per-haps had come on a dare. What could these kids want with a private investigator? If they were in *real* trouble, they'd go to Mom or Dad or Uncle Chip. But I motioned them inside.

My office is small, two rooms set off by thin wallboard from the insurance agency I pay rent to. The rent is minimal, three hundred a month. In exchange, I get access to their janitor, fax, Xerox machines, and the occasional jug of min-eral water. My outer office is set up as a reception area, though I can't afford a secretary. It has a ratty sofa, Formica table, and lamp. In my inner sanctum are a water cooler and the desk I dragged from my study at home. Modern technology allows me to plug into the world, but also gives the office the look of a low-budget Third World espionage operation: I have an answering machine I leave on twenty-four hours a day, and an Apple II originally purchased for Ben.

On the wall is the only souvenir of my Wall Street days, a poster of Winston Churchill I'd bought on one of my monthly trips to London. Below the familiar, bulldog face is the stern caption "DESERVE VICTORY." In the corner, poorly camouflaged by a hardy but ugly plant, is the three-hundred-pound safe that holds my contracts and current files and my Smith and Wesson .38, which I'm terrified either to bring home (because of the kids) or to carry (because I might use it).

The six boys and I piled into the outer office, where there was barely room to stand, let alone sit and talk.

"Mr. Duh-low," began the tallest kid, the leader, tentatively.

"It's pronounced Dee-loo," I said. "Christopher Deleeuw. Dutch, actually. And you are?"

"Sam. Sam Mellman," he said, stepping forward. There was a lot of muscle in the room. I felt exceedingly flabby and middle-aged. Athletes, unquestionably.

They looked as if they'd jump out of their Nikes if I coughed. They stared everywhere but at me, shuffling their heavy sneakers, pulling at their jackets. Sam, in his Greenpeace sweatshirt, looked to me a more sensitive version of the genre, his green eyes piercing in his thin face, his brown hair all over his forehead. He seemed to be struggling to launch an explanation of their presence. I noticed that he and his buddies were too cool to bundle up in what the radio said was a two-degree wind chill.

"Look, this is uncomfortable," I said. "If you're speaking for the group, why don't you step into my office, and the others can wait out here? I feel like we're clowns stuck in a closet."

The group seemed relieved. Sam nodded and followed me into my office, pulling out of his jacket pocket an inch-thick wad of bills. He still seemed to be trying to figure out how to tell me what he was doing here.

"Ummm . . . Mr. Deleeuw . . . this is money we all collected from jobs we've had and from allowances and whatever." He sat abruptly in the chair across from my desk, cleared his throat, and stopped, as if that made it all clear.

"What's this for?"

"It's a retainer. A down payment. We want to hire you. Otherwise, nobody's going to listen to a bunch of high school kids."

"How old are you, Sam?"

"Seventeen. I'm a senior," he added quickly, as if to dispel any suspicion that he might be young. "I'm going to Oberlin next fall."

"Do your parents know you're here, you and your friends? You're a minor, you know. Of course, you know." What a dumb remark; no wonder kids couldn't abide talking to adults.

Sam took a deep breath. He didn't give the impression of being someone in trouble as much as someone in pain. "My dad knows I'm here. He said it was okay."

I plugged in my Mister Coffee.

"Sam, I don't know what this is about, but you can't hire me to do anything without your parents' consent," I commented as I puttered. "So even though I trust you, I'd have to call your father or mother before I could agree to go to work for you; I just want that clear up front. I ask all my clients to sign contracts, and one of your parents would have to cosign it, so don't tell me anything you wouldn't want your parents to know."

He nodded, apparently untroubled. Rochambeau parents generally were not the type who inspired fear in their kids.

"Sam?" I coaxed. I had to go to Trenton that afternoon, and before that I had to face a real drama: my confrontation with Mr. Kelley at Lucretia Mott School. This was a case where being a private detective helped, because people had these silly notions from reading mysteries and assumed that you had to be tough. I sure wasn't going to slug an elementary school principal, but I sometimes got the feeling, when I walked into his office, that Kelley was looking to see where the shoulder holster was. It didn't hurt; Em usually was assigned the best teachers in school. I suppose it could have been because she was smart.

I needed Sam Mellman to start talking, or my day would be a mess. He was reminding me of Ben.

He shifted in his chair, holding the wad of bills against his Greenpeace sweatshirt. "My dad has agreed," he said finally. "He's supportive. Ken Dale's dad is his oldest friend. The guys out there are all on the soccer team with me. Ken Dale was our captain. We want to hire you to clear him."

"Clear him?"

"I couldn't believe it when they said his name on the radio yesterday. I just couldn't believe what I was hearing. In the papers this morning they're saying that he killed Carol and then himself. Ken and I were best friends since sixth grade. I can tell you, man, he didn't kill Carol. He couldn't kill anybody, and he would never, never kill himself. He was real down about Carol seeing some other guy—I mean, you can't blame him for that. They were going together for three years, man, I don't think he ever loved anybody else—"

"She broke up with him?" Once Sam got started, it was clearly going to be hard to get him to stop. I looked up at the clock. I couldn't imagine this conversation would result in any work for me, but I confess I wanted to hear anything the kid had to say about the deaths on the mountain.

"Well, it was weird. I think the hardest part for him wasn't just that she broke it off, but that he never knew who this other guy was or what was going on. She seemed so upset about it all, would start crying in class right in front of everybody. That wasn't like Carol. She was really together usually. All she would say was that she wished she could tell Ken about it, and that she'd always love him. What kind of stuff is that? It had him crazy. But he thought they would get back together, that she was signaling him that they would. And like, she was the last person he could have killed—that just wasn't in him."

"So you were a friend of the girl—Carol?"

"Sure." I thought I saw Sam's eyes redden. Kids, especially this age, rarely let outsiders see what they're feeling. I don't think they often know themselves. Sam Mellman's loyalty and grief were powerful, a strong testament to his friend Ken, I thought. I had not been drawn to the jocks I'd met in my life, young or old, but this one seemed atypical of the species.

"She was great. She was probably the most decent person I knew. No way this figures. I was shocked, we all were, when Carol stopped seeing Ken. It was almost like she was dying or something, you know, like she had some disease and she wanted to spare him, that was the feeling I had. But what she told him was, there was somebody else."

I shifted in my chair and glanced out at the parking lot, already beginning to fill with compact Japanese and American cars and vans. Whereas Mountain Lakes, the elegant mall that had superseded this one a decade ago, sometimes resembled a giant Mercedes/BMW dealership.

"Did she have a best friend?" I started taking notes, just out of courtesy.

"Yeah. Judy Cole. Judy's at home—they say she's on some kind of medication, she's in shock. Mr. Handley's staying home today, too. But he called all of us at home last night, all of Ken and Carol's friends, which was a nice thing to do. He didn't have to do that. He's real broken up, but he was worrying about us."

"Richard Handley?"

Coincidentally, although not remarkably in a town the size of Rochambeau, Richard Handley had been at my table at the Historical Society dinner the night before last. He was a history teacher who had written a couple of books about early Rochambeau that sold steadily in the town's two bookstores. I'd read one of them and it was pretty good. Few suburbs have any history to speak of, but Handley was quite adept at tracing the early life of the town to its present state. I'd only talked to him for a few moments, but Benchley, who was a friend of his, often praised him as a wonderful teacher. I was hoping Ben would have him next year.

"Was Handley Carol's teacher?"

"And Ken's too. They were both in the honors program and took Mr. Handley's history class. Ken was working on a paper, something about some crazy man who used to live in town just after the Civil War. He was into it."

I stood and pulled up the blinds. Cicchelli's Furniture was having its winter sale, and people were already dragging chairs and lamps out to their vans. It had to be opening time. I could hear the video emporium beeping to life downstairs. The jingly-jangly tune of *Ms. Pac Man* used to stand out above all the others (I used to hum it, to the ridicule of my children and the horror of my wife). That was before *Afterburner* and the sounds of jet fighters roaring across enemy territory. Who played video games at ten in the morning?

"So you don't buy the police notion of murder-suicide, not because you have evidence to the contrary really, but mostly because you're loyal to your buddy. Right?" I sounded a little sharper than I'd meant to, but I wanted Sam to understand that this wasn't kid stuff. While I had no intention of taking these boys' money, I had no doubt that they could find someone who would.

I pushed the pile of folded bills back across the desktop. "Sam, I admire your loyalty. I mean it. But you know as well as I that even close friends can fool you sometimes. Ken was found in his car with a rope around his neck. You need something concrete, something more than an instinct to call that into question. Anyway, I can't take your money. First, you're a minor; second, there's really nothing for me to go on."

"My dad will sign any agreement, I told you that. He's great. He never even hesitated. He said to call him if you need to. And my dad said to make sure I told you that Stan Keiser sent me to you. He said we could trust you."

If you were going to utter one phrase likely to stop me in my tracks, that was the one.

Stan Keiser represented my baptism by fire as a private investigator, the case that initially terrified me but wound up letting me know I just might make it. His father Lou was a bank vice president, I think head of the loan department at Rochambeau National, so desperate and distraught when he came to me that he didn't notice he wasn't exactly signing up the Pinkertons. Lou Keiser knew me because he'd approved our mortgage application—I doubt he would now—and I guess he'd heard about my new line of work.

His son, sixteen at the time, had dropped out of school. He rarely came home, would never explain where he was or what he was doing. Shrinks, school counselors, and family therapists hadn't gotten anywhere with him. Stan was the suburban nightmare come to life, the lovingly cared-for, wonderfully educated, promising kid who goes bad overnight. When Lou found the white powder secreted in the tool shed, he understood.

I followed the kid for weeks, remembering my army training, finally trailing him to a shabby frame house in West Passaic where lots of upper-middle-class kids like Stan seemed inexplicably to be coming and going. I also noticed the police cruisers that seemed to drift back and forth without ever stopping or getting suspicious about what the kids were doing there.

I hired another investigator from Jersey City, and the two of us grabbed Stan one night as he was getting into his car in West Passaic. He was in no shape to put up much of a fight—fortunately, for neither was I.

We locked him in the basement of my house and called the state police drug squad. They were busy handing down indictments for close to six months after that. Lou was grateful that I kept his son completely out of it. After eight weeks in a drug treatment center, Stan was back in high school.

The case was a turning point for me. Not only did I start doing work for the bank, but the word got around, as it always does in small towns, that I could help kids in trouble and do it discreetly. There's more mischief to get into in the suburbs than most people who live there want to admit or care to know about.

Stan and I stayed in touch. We still had him to dinner when he came home from college; sometimes he joined me and Ben for a Yankees game. I liked him, and if he'd sent Sam to me, that meant he agreed there was something wrong about the way this story had come down.

Sam seemed to notice right away that my attitude had shifted and drove his advantage home. "It sucks, Mr. Deleeuw. It's crap. We've all been on the phone for twenty-four straight hours, man. We've even been using our parents' faxes to round up support. These people, they give their kids lots of things, money and cars and all, but they don't know what we're like. There's a couple of kids outside that door"—he gestured towards the anteroom—"that if they'd been pinned with this, I'd say, 'That's bad news, man,' but I might believe it. But not Ken.

"Look," he said, reaching into his pocket and pulling out a folded-up wad of computer paper. "Ken and I both want— wanted—to be writers. You don't talk about that in school, not if you're a guy. We wrote these stories together; we were going to try to get them published. Read them. See for yourself."

"Wait," I said, as he began to collect his lanky frame from my small wooden chair. "I don't know if I'm going to take this case or not. But if I do, I'll have to ask you this, so I might as well ask now. If Ken Dale didn't kill Carol Lombardi and then himself, then that means somebody else killed them. That means somebody hated them enough to murder them. That's what you're talking about, isn't it, Sam? Have you thought that through? Do you know anybody in the world who would put a rope around your friend's neck and kill him up on some mountain in subzero weather in the middle of the night?"

That seemed to shock him. Premeditated murder was an almost unimaginable notion for Rochambeau.

Sam dropped back into the chair. He put his right hand over his mouth, initially stymied, but working it through. When he was ready, he looked me in the eye. "I guess I hadn't put it quite in those terms. But yeah, that's what it would mean, I see that. That is incredibly heavy. Murder." He made a whooshing sound, almost like a *whew*. "I don't think I know anybody who'd kill another person. That's why I came here, 'cause I couldn't imagine Ken doing it. Everybody loved Ken. He was one of the most popular guys in the school. The only guy he had any serious trouble with was Jamie Harte, and I'm not saying Jamie could've killed him—"

"Tell me about Jamie Harte," I said, jotting the name down.

Sam shrugged, as if there were hardly words to capture Jamie Harte. "He's just this real crazy, angry, macho guy. He's in our class. His father's supposed to be a drunk who took off when he was little, and Jamie is real trouble—bad news. He works out every day in a gym, practices karate; he always wants to punch somebody out. He can hurt people, too—he's been suspended for fighting. He's real bad news about girls, always making cracks about their bodies and things he wants to do to them."

"And how did he get tangled up with Ken?"

"Well, he came on to Carol last year. I think Ken and Carol had some sort of argument, and were cooling it. There were rumors around that Carol and Jamie actually went out a couple of times—somebody said they saw them driving somewhere, but it could have been a rumor. Jamie kept brushing up against her in the hallway and claiming it was an accident, and she started getting upset. He would make kissing noises in her ear. One day she stayed late after school and was getting books out of her locker and when she turned around Jamie was there. He pressed his, you know, his crotch up against her, something like that, and she yelled for him to stop. Ken had been hanging around, waiting to walk Carol home, and he heard her yell."

"They fought?"

"It wasn't much of a fight, really. Ken just slammed Jamie in the nuts with his book bag, hard, before Jamie could do his karate shit. Jamie went down and threw up all over the floor. Loss of face, if you know what I mean. The school suspended him, made him get counseling. He never came near Carol again, far as I know, but he really had it in for Ken. Whenever he saw him, the guy's whole face lit up with hate. I have to say, honestly, this guy Jamie is the baddest person I know, though that's not saying *that* much in Rochambeau High. If he'd ever caught Ken in a parking lot or something, that would have been ugly. But I truthfully don't see him killing anybody. I mean, jeez."

Sam forgot to shake hands as he got up and left. I promised only to think things over, maybe make a few calls. I reminded him that I'd have to get his parents' permission to take on this case.

The other boys hadn't waited around to say good-bye. I suspected they were on the umpteenth level of Super Mario downstairs.

When I want to think, I pull the blinds up in my office and stare out at the parking lot. Today I didn't have much time. I had to meet Mr. Kelley. Then I had to head for Trenton to plow through some auto insurance records for a fraud case I was working on. It had led me to a bend of the Passaic River with what I suspect were about four dozen cars dropped in it, all falsely reported stolen, I was sure. I would be out of my office all afternoon. My next appointment, tomorrow morning, was with a man who claimed that more than a year ago a brick had fallen from the top of a four-story office building in downtown Rochambeau and struck his shoulder. He was asking for $1.5 million, claiming he couldn't work as a plumbing inspector anymore or even walk upright. He shoulder had been banged up all right, but the owner of the building couldn't find any broken brick, and the suspicious insurance company asked me to investigate. The first five times I checked him out, he had his sling carefully in place and walked with an exaggerated stiffness. But amateurs are never vigilant for too long, and I had a crystal-clear color time-coded snapshot to show him of the wonderful form he exhibited (it was a spare) at the Happy Lanes Bowling Alley last week. The cluck could have settled for $100,000 a year ago, no questions asked. I was sure he knew what was coming. They were usually relieved, in a way.

But Sam and his friends were asking me to cross a threshold I hadn't before, to deliver in a way I hadn't yet had to. Sneaking after insurance cheats or running computer checks on runaway parents was one thing. Taking on a case like this, especially when there wasn't the hint of a lead beyond a teenage boy's loyalty, was something else.

I concede that I didn't take the matter all that seriously at that point, thinking Sam's father would do what I would have done if Ben had pulled the same stunt, and tell me to disappear. Even if Sam was correct and his father didn't, the odds

were that I would call the boy within a day or two to report
that the police version of the deaths seemed solid and that I
had nothing much to add.

Plunging into a sensational murder-suicide would, on
the other hand, be a kind of milestone for a man who just a
few years earlier thought he'd be trading bonds the rest of his
life.

I suppose my house, that morning at breakfast, had
looked like your standard suburban domestic scene. Five years
earlier, like most of the men on my block, I wouldn't have
been in it. By the time my family stirred, I had long since
headed for the Commodities Exchange pit—the 'Nam of Wall
Street, my colleagues and I called it—for fourteen hours of
screaming, bluffing, sweating, relentless pressure, horrifyingly
high stakes, and frazzled nerves. More often than not, I came
home with glazed eyes, exhausted, hoarse, barely able to
speak. I pretended to notice how my kids were, went through
the motions of talking with my wife—she was rarely fooled—
and tried desperately and unsuccessfully to make amends on
the weekends.

I had thought it a pretty good deal at the time. We had
the black Lab, the Volvo wagon, the swim club. The kids had
plenty of friends and were doing well at school. The Suburban Lifestyle Checklist: Do you have a comfortable house?
Are the kids healthy, attractive, and reasonably well-man-
nered (meaning, do they eat with their fingers only at home,
not in public)? Do they have any values beyond how much
TV they watch or how cool they are? Do you have a few
friends with whom you could feel comfortable? If the answer is yes to most or all of the above, then you have a good
life.

But that was before the boom waned, taking my career

with it. In fact, I consider my life unfortunately emblematic of the much-remarked turn from the greedy eighties into the poorer and more reflective nineties. My firm was suddenly enmeshed in one of those nasty insider trading scandals.

Don't let anyone ever tell you the government doesn't have enough clout when it comes to combating white-collar crime. When the feds come down on you, it's like a hurricane, a tidal wave, and a typhoon hitting the same spot at the same time. There were multiple indictments and everything that wasn't indicted was impounded or subpoenaed. Everyone's guilt was presumed, in some cases correctly, and all of us were threatened if we didn't talk. After the FBI raid, I never again spoke to a boss, colleague, or subordinate. Our firm evaporated, as if by magic. My career, financial security, lifestyle— all the predicates on which I'd built my life—vanished with it.

I wouldn't testify against my bosses or my coworkers, for which the U.S. Attorney's office has never forgiven me and for which, they've made it abundantly clear, they'll happily punish me if they ever get the chance. But my lawyer was smart enough to cut this deal: no indictments or charges against me, no testimony by me, all I had to do was agree never to work in the financial industry again. I did and I won't. In desperation mostly, I went back to the only thing I had known before trading—the army, which had paid for my college, and where I'd worked for three years as a CID investigator. I had been pretty good at it; I'd sent a few officers playing the black market to jail, worked AWOLs and fraud cases, and investigated a half dozen homicides.

It had taken four months to get my New Jersey private investigator's license, using our dwindling savings to acquire the fax, the gun, the unkillable plant, and the two-room "suite" on the second floor of the Amway Mall, five miles beyond Rochambeau's carefully zoned residential streets.

Now there's only one item on our Suburban Lifestyle Checklist each month: Can we meet the mortgage?

My parking lot reverie wasn't as mindlessly relaxing as usual. Something alien and uncomfortable was intruding on the normal imagery, and I realized after a second or two what it was: a vision of two dead bodies up on that frigid, dark hill.

5

Ida Flowers never drove past 8 P.M. It was the arbitrary but absolutely rigid line of demarcation she had drawn in her head between safety and danger.

Have another cup of coffee, her friend Rita would say every Tuesday at seven forty-five, as their weekly dinner together drew to a close. Ida would thank her but demur. At her age, she would insist, she couldn't afford to be reckless. Eight P.M. was stretching it as it was.

The exchange had become something of a ritual between the two women, widows and friends for nearly a quarter of a century. Rita suspected her friend's stubbornness had as much to do with getting home for some television program as it did with safety, but it didn't really matter what she said because, at seven-fifty, Ida was in her old Mercury heading down Chambers Street.

Just one mile separated Rita's apartment from Ida's own one-story cottage. She always left the light on along the driveway in front of the house so she could see to get in, and she always called Rita, letting the phone ring twice before hanging up, to signal that she had arrived safely. Sunday, after they'd attended church together, the same procedure was followed even at midday, although neither had ever heard of a robbery committed against an old woman in Rochambeau. It wasn't like New York or Boston or Washington where their old friends were trapped inside their apartments at night, where even broad daylight no longer offered much protection. This was Rochambeau.

Burglary was what they feared, especially surprising burglars inside their homes. So when Ida pulled into her driveway, she would honk the horn and rattle her keys good and loud and bang the car door shut, just so anybody inside the house would have plenty of time to get out without feeling cornered. She was feeling even more cautious since that awful news about the Brown estate up the hill. The abandoned old house and grounds were enough to give one the spooks as it was, with teenagers and God knows what else crawling around up there. Even though the chief said it was a simple murder-suicide and there was no suggestion of a madman running loose, Ida knew too well what living alone could do to your nerves and imagination.

It was time to start thinking—Rita was coming around to this—about selling both their houses and moving into the Presbyterian Church complex down the parkway. She and Rita knew what it really was, a place to die. Suburbs used to be where you went to start a life, but now there were places where you went to end one. Total care, they called it. You gave them everything you had, and you got a roof over your head and someone to help take care of you until you passed.

But as depressing as it was to think about life in a place like that, there was too much to be afraid of these days, even in a town like Rochambeau. Ida pulled up to the red light at Baker Avenue, the only stop she had to make before her house, which she could already see ahead through the bare trees. As early as it was, the streets and sidewalks around this neighborhood were already deserted in the winter dark.

·   ·   ·

Rita called Ida's house at 8:07 P.M. Like other elderly people, she was not casual about safety checks. When there was no answer, she called the police immediately and without hesitation. The worst that could happen was that some patrolman would waste a drive. Ida might have had difficulty with the car, in which case she would, as they had discussed so many times, lock the doors and wait for the help Rita would summon. Rita attributed the chill she felt, as she called Ida's house again and the phone rang unanswered, to the cold.

Officer Jim Calcagno had swung his big Ford onto Baker Street at eight-fifteen, on his way back to the station to file a report on a fender bender. The call was a 748—"possible distress"—usually meaning somebody was worried because a friend or relative was supposed to be home but wasn't or because an alarm had sounded. The dispatcher asked Calcagno to watch for a blue '81 Mercury between Hope Street and the address he had been given.

He saw the car right away, just around the corner.

Calcagno was an eleven-year veteran of the Rochambeau PD. Like others on the force, he had fled a bigger city, in his case Newark. But his internal radar still functioned well, as is often the case with experienced cops, and all of his warning bells were clanging as he pulled up behind the Mercury. He radioed for a backup car, then unstrapped his holster as he noticed some movement in the brush off to his right.

A darkly clad figure moving awkwardly in the shadows disappeared into the bushes and up the base of the hill, out of sight. Calcagno shined his flashlight up into the brush, but whatever it was, was gone. And whatever it was gave him the creeps.

He turned towards the car. A little blood spattered the

side of the driver's door and bits of glass were strewn along the road side. The driver's window had been smashed in. Calcagno saw the white hair moving in the cold wind. He used his shoulder transmitter to radio for an ambulance and for the captain, then ran around to the trunk of his patrol car and pulled out his first aid kit.

There seemed to be a single wound on the left side of the neck, just below the ear, but it didn't seem to have hit an artery, judging by the relatively small amount of blood. Calcagno pressed a gauze compress to the wound, snapped his capsule of smelling salts, and murmured reassuringly as the old lady moaned and opened her eyes. She looked bewildered but calm as Calcagno gently probed her head to feel for other wounds. "It's . . . Good Lord, I can't believe this . . . it's just the neck," she whispered. "Not as bad as it looks." Game old lady, he thought. No tears, no hysterics.

"I . . . all I did was to stop at the light," she said before he could ask, her voice growing a bit stronger, her eyes fixed on his. "It was so strange, I think perhaps I was . . . There was someone at the window, someone all dressed in black. In a cape and a strange tall hat. The window just seemed to break into a thousand pieces, then I felt this pain in my neck. He said 'Caroline.' I think that was what he said."

Calcagno radioed for the captain to call in the State Police and their dogs. He started to give out a description of a man in a tall hat and black cape but hesitated, knowing that once it went over the radio, the town would go nuts. He decided to wait for the captain and the chief.

The sirens were coming from two sides, two Rochambeau cruisers from the north, the ambulance from the east. The chief's unmarked blue Plymouth pulled up behind him. Calcagno stepped back to let the paramedics at the woman.

"Hit-and-run?" Chief Leeming asked hopefully.

Calcagno shook his head. "Stabbing. Some guy came up to her at the light, smashed the window, stabbed her in the neck. I think I saw him run up there." Calcagno and two other officers plunged into the brush, but there was little chance of finding anyone. The woods ran all the way up to the Brown estate, acres of dense, unlighted growth.

A fourth officer leaned over the side of the car and picked up something. A thick piece of rope. Leeming took it from him, his usually inexpressive face registering disbelief.

"What is it, Chief?" asked the officer, while Leeming turned the rope over, looking at the freshly cut edges.

"This rope," he said finally. "It's old. They don't weave it this way anymore; they haven't for years."

The officer looked down at it. "So?"

"So it's the same kind of rope the kid used the other night to strangle his girlfriend and hang himself in his fucking car."

"Shit," said the other officer. The men looked simultaneously up the mountain.

6

Sitting in my office the next morning at the American Way, waiting for Plumbing Inspector Daupeen to tremble before the irrefutable weight of my investigation, I had a couple of minutes to file and review the mixed results of the previous day's efforts.

I had spent a half hour successfully importuning Em's principal to switch her to an English teacher who didn't run the class like a Special Forces unit.

My visit to Trenton, on the other hand, had yielded little. I couldn't connect the fraud suspects I was investigating to one another, except for the fact that six of them lived within five miles of the river where I knew cars were being dumped. That investigation would have to wait while I raced back to Rochambeau in time to drive Ben and Emily to soccer practice and art class, respectively. Time has a way of melting through your fingers when you take care of kids. The Volvo was rarely in the garage.

Because Jane had been at the clinic late, I hadn't seen her for much more than five minutes after she got home and staggered into bed. We turned on the little black-and-white TV in the bedroom to get the weather report and heard about Ida Flowers instead.

"You feel comfortable taking this case, Kit?" Jane had asked. "It isn't exactly up your alley. And now, this poor woman—it's creepy." Her tone suggested *she* sure wasn't comfortable. But it would not have been in her nature for her to have fussed about it. Jane granted as much independence as she demanded, and more than any other thing, I think that was why I loved her so much and why our marriage was so strong. I frankly didn't see how I could possibly expect to be a private detective and not take the case, but I had told her I didn't know yet.

The morning's encounter with Mr. Daupeen, who had resumed his stiff gait in honor of the occasion, went smoothly. The former plumbing inspector enthusiastically accepted a cup of coffee, nodded when I showed him the photos, shrugged, and signed the forms releasing my client, the insurance company, from all claims in exchange for a promise not to prosecute him. He said that he might just stop by at the Channel hardware adjoining the mall on his way home for some tools he needed for his home workshop.

"I knew I shouldn'ta bowled, but to tell you the truth, this is a relief. I missed work. I guess I gotta go back," he said. "No hard feelings?" I assured him I didn't have any, though he might not have an easy time getting disability insurance. But considering he could have been charged with fraud, he hadn't come out that badly.

But the Ida Flowers attack had lit up Rochambeau again. We'd heard a few details on the radio that morning and had another brief and unsatisfying discussion with the kids before they went off to school. If Ben was worried, he didn't let on of course, but Emily was showing all of the indirect manifestations of anxiety. She wanted to know where we would be all day, if we would be there when she got home from school, if we would keep a careful eye on her stuffed animals while she was away. "Why would someone hurt an old woman?" she asked.

I didn't have an answer, and I realized that nothing in Em's short life could possibly have prepared her for this. I often read or saw TV interviews with city dwellers whose children heard gunfire all night long and thought of it as the inevitable backdrop against which they lived. But we lived in the other America. Random violence here was rowdiness on the school bus. My kids had nothing to measure this against, no experience to draw on.

But instinctively, I knew I had to clear the decks. I called Sam Mellman's father and left a message on his answering machine. Then I spent an hour trying to track down two more errant ex-husbands.

Will Mellman returned my call toward noon. He apologized for the delay, explaining that he had been called out of town suddenly on business and had just returned.

Sam was as good as his word, as I sort of guessed he would be. His father was proud of his son's loyalty and trusted his instincts. There were parents, I'd noticed, who listened to their kids, and parents who thought kids couldn't possibly know what was good for them. The first kind turned out better kids, as far as I could see. "Sam is a clear-headed kid," his father told me. "I trust him, and even if he's wrong I want him to know that I trusted him.

"He's combined money from his jobs with his allowance and his friends' and has got more than a thousand dollars. I'll kick in at least that much. Call me if the bill tops twenty-five hundred, and we'll take it from there. I know what you did for Lou Keiser's boy and that's good enough for me. I hope you take this case, Mr. Deleeuw. Ken Dale practically lived in this house, and I can no more see that boy killing anyone than I can picture myself voting Democratic. Do what you have to do. I'll be happy to sign anything you send over.

"And Mr. Deleeuw—I heard about your troubles. I work on the Street. I think you were done dirty. I don't need to say any more." He hung up. Nice dad. Wish I'd had him.

I think I was a bit disappointed, though. I was counting on a conventional Rochambeau dad to tell me how cute but fuzzy-headed his kid was, or to bellow that of course he wouldn't allow his son to waste his hard-earned money on a wild-goose chase for a dead buddy, especially when said money was being turned over to a disgraced bad guy. But that hadn't happened; it was my case now. Whatever happened, I could say that I didn't spend the rest of my life chasing sleaze-bag husbands and insurance cheats.

I called the clipping service I use from time to time when I'm doing background checks and ordered all the articles on the Brown estate deaths from the *Bergen Record*, the *Newark Star-Ledger*, the New York papers, and the *Rochambeau Times*. I also called my *only* real police contact—a lieutenant who worked in the state narcotics strike force—a nice, if gruff, guy I'd met while working on the Keiser case.

I'd tipped Bill Tagg to the biggest bust of his career, and according to the tribal ethics that dominated our work, he owed me. I hated to wipe the slate clean on so long a shot, but I had few options. Tagg made it clear that he would cooperate this time, but that next time I called he would tell me to fuck off. He reinforced my suspicion that I would be calling Sam shortly to tell him that the cops were right.

"You never know," said Tagg, "but this one is pretty buttoned-up. You got opportunity—the girl knew him and would go up there with him. You got motive—jealousy. And the press don't have this yet, Deleeuw, but you got a suicide note the boy left behind in his computer that they say amounts to a confession. Don't touch this case if you figure you're gonna bust it open. You want my advice, it's tight. And—don't take this wrong—you're not exactly Spenser for Hire. You still got that old Volvo wagon that sounds like a moose farting?"

"Yup. I don't see your exploits on 'America's Most Wanted,' either, Tagg. Thanks for the encouragement," I said. "Any loose ends?" I might not know much about homicides, but I could do macho banter with cops.

There was one thing, said Tagg. "Just a nasty contusion on the boy's forehead. Probably came from banging his head on the dashboard when the car stopped. He might have reflexively hit the brake—who knows? It's a rough bruise that bothers the lab boys a bit, since it ain't clear exactly where it came from. But not enough to shake their faith in homicide-suicide. I'll fax you the report. Anything else you'll have to earn. Is someone actually paying you, Deleeuw, to take on this mess?"

"What about the old lady?"

"Hmmm. The local cops think it's a copycat nut. Even got the same kind of old rope to leave at the scene. Could be anything. Can't help you there. Gotta go, buddy. Lunchtime."

Within minutes, my fax was purring. Along with a surprisingly thick batch of newspaper clips, I also got the preliminary Rochambeau Police Department report. Since the town PD rarely, if ever, got to work on murders, the state detectives were automatically sent in on a homicide. The report, Tagg had said, was a snap to pilfer.

I had to start with the local police, of course.

The bitter cold snap had broken overnight; it was just another drab winter day as I headed downtown for the Rochambeau Police Department. Chief Leeming, I knew, would be about as happy to see me as he would have been to see Ted Bundy rise from the grave and buy a two-bedroom condo in town.

Leeming had spent twenty years with the NYPD, and the deaths on the mountain and the stabbing below, splattered all over the media, were the sort of craziness he must have thought he had left behind. I could guess at the quantity of flak he was catching. Deaths and stabbings didn't exactly lure newcomers to a town.

It had required no special sensitivity, in our previous glancing encounters, to see that the chief was suspicious of me, partly because of the local FBI's assurance that I was a crook and partly because I was additional aggravation, perhaps the final annoyance he couldn't bear. In the city, private detectives could get lost in the general mayhem, but in Rochambeau my very existence was an affront to suburbia's smug notions of itself.

People with those notions don't understand what Woody Guthrie wrote—lots more people got robbed with fountain pens than with guns. There are plenty of unfaithful (sometimes vanishing) spouses, kids in trouble with drugs or hiding out in the East Village, nannies with arrest records, unemployed marketing veeps whose fancy cars are being repossessed, and résumé frauds.

A couple of employment checks and missing-kid cases had taken me into one of Leeming's old precinct houses in Manhattan a couple of times, where his pals remembered him fondly and respectfully. "Leeming? Good man. Good cop. But he's seen too much, too much." That was all they would mumble; this was one inner circle I would never crack.

The Rochambeau PD is stuffed into a red brick building two blocks off Main Street, a onetime elementary school

abandoned in favor of a more modern facility. The cluttered
headquarters reflects the ambivalence of the upper middle
class towards cops, as if putting major money into policing
constitutes a tacit recognition that crime exists even here. In
the suburbs, police departments are either in old buildings
ready to be abandoned, or sleek new public safety facilities
that look like elementary schools. Neither style suggests what
is inside, and the parking lots are *always* in the back. The cars
that line the Rochambeau PD lot are painfully discreet, the
town seal discreetly stickered onto understated gray doors.
Inside, the department looks frozen in the early sixties, when
it moved from City Hall. Peeling gray cabinets line every
hallway, and stacks of yellowing manila folders collect on
vacant surfaces, topped by a layer of dust.

Except when they bust the stray baddie driving through
town with a trunkful of cocaine or catch a burglar red-handed
with somebody's Trinitron, you don't hear much about the
local cops, which is sort of the point. Drunk driving and
youthful pranks are handled quietly and efficiently. The town
has hardly any racial tensions to speak of.

Every couple of years, kids from other towns go on a
burglary spree, busting into houses on school Open House
evenings and carting off VCRs or jewelry. After some to-do in
the paper, things always quiet down in a week or two. One
neighborhood tried to organize itself and put those crime
watch stickers on front doors, but local realtors quickly
squelched the program, arguing that it is not the sort of signal
you want prospective home-buyers to pick up on their first
trip into town.

No wonder the police dispatcher looked unusually tense
that morning, befitting a department that suddenly had a murder-suicide and a nasty assault on its hands and didn't quite

know how to act. He was on the phone, so I walked down the hall past overflowing cardboard cartons and the table with the Mister Coffee and the jar of powdered creamer, universal symbols of impoverished bureaucracy. I don't think I ever encountered Cremora in all the years I worked on Wall Street; now I keep the jumbo size in my office.

Leeming, standing outside his office and holding a coffee mug that said CHIEF, spotted me instantly. "Deleeuw. Haven't seen you for a while. You still making a living as a dick?" He was beefy and compact, his muscles straining the crisp white uniform shirt, a slight smirk on his broad face. Leeming offered a tough hide to the world, but I thought his old cronies in Manhattan were right: The face was weary, not mean.

"I wouldn't say I'm making much of a living, but I'm still at it," I volleyed back, failing to sound hard-boiled and worldly. Leeming chuckled. "You must feel like you're back on the Lower East Side, eh?"

The chief shook his head. If the crimes rattled him, he clearly wasn't going to share it with me. "You branching out into homicides, Deleeuw? You'll get pretty hungry out here." His grip tightened on his coffee mug; he did not seem pleased by my appearance at his suddenly busy headquarters. "Who're you working for?"

Most private detectives never reveal their clients, even under intense police interrogations, but I've never understood why. I had nothing to hide, and if my clients did, I wouldn't take them on. Sam had made no secret of his crusade to clear his buddy. "Some high school kids asked me to check into the murders on behalf of Ken Dale. They don't see him as being able to kill anyone."

Leeming waved me brusquely into his office and kicked

the door shut. "You're working for a bunch of kids? On a murder? Hope you touch base with their parents, pal. That's the sort of thing that would send me up the wall, my daughter telling me she'd given her last two years' allowance to some private dick." He looked up at the fifties-style clock over his desk, one of those big round black-and-white numbers that school kids gaze at so impatiently.

"I've got the state boys coming in here in two minutes, Deleeuw, so I'll be direct. You know, of course, that I don't like your being on this case. Even *you* probably know that you have no business working a homicide. The movies are right about the way cops feel about private eyes: There's no reason to like them. They're either competing with you, making you look bad, or screwing up your cases. Once in a blue moon, one of them gives you a helpful tip, but in no way worth the grief they cause the rest of the time. Especially true of an amateur like you, who I'm just as apt to have to rescue as not.

"You got a bad rep with some people. You've never done anything sour out here that I know of, but I have no reason to trust you, either.

"And this is a murder case, not some car repo," he went on, enumerating the many reasons I should butt out, ultimately resorting to the universal male communications channel—sports analogies. "Fact is, Deleeuw, you're triple A and this case is All Star. You work alone, have no resources; all you have is your army training, which is not bad but was twenty years ago. You do background checks and I know you helped a kid out of a drug jam, which should qualify you for a spot on the school board, but not this case. You could easily find yourself face-to-face with some psycho in a park all alone. Or he could come after you—or your kids. This case is *way* over your head."

Leeming gulped the rest of his coffee down and banged the mug down on his desktop.

"Now, I got two girls in college and four years till my pension, which is a polite but candid way of telling you to piss off."

I wanted to crack wise, but when no snappy retort came to mind, I decided to try a different tack. "Chief, I can't make you talk with me," I said calmly, "but I can't drop the case either. I know the FBI probably whispered in your ear about my troubled past. But you've seen a lot. You can look me in the eye and make your own judgments, can't you?" This sounded lame, even to me. A veteran New York cop would know better than anyone that you could tell nothing by looking somebody in the eye. I'd met some doe-eyed soldiers who'd done things I couldn't bear to remember, let alone describe.

But before he could give me a tongue-lashing on my moral state, one way or the other, Leeming's intercom buzzed. The state police had arrived. "Well, forget it, Deleeuw. I'm prepared to give you the benefit of the doubt in terms of your general character, but don't expect squat from me on this case. It's just not kosher, and whatever you might think about suburban cops, I do try." His voice quieted, and he dropped some of the tough-guy persona.

"I sincerely hope that when you think about it, you'll see you have no business taking money to work a case like this. But if you stay on it, and you find anything—*anything*—that conceivably would help our investigation, you better haul your butt in here with it. You get in our way, I'll have your license pulled in ten seconds. That's one thing we *can* still do."

I took him at his word—that is, I thought he meant what he said—but he shook hands without any rancor, considering that he had just threatened to destroy my livelihood once more.

As I turned to leave, though, he frowned and motioned me back. "Deleeuw, I feel bad for his buddies. But did you ever hear a teenage kid accept bad news about a pal? Ken Dale strangled that girl. Then he strangled himself. And believe me, that's not just intuition."

"You mean the computer note," I said. Leeming's eyes widened, then his mouth opened, and he sputtered a bit. He didn't insult my intelligence by asking me where I'd heard it. "Shit. I won't confirm that, we weren't letting that out—"

"It's still not out," I said, by way of letting him know the depth to which the Deleeuw tentacles could reach. "I think you're a good cop and a decent man. And I see how you think I'm overstepping myself. But don't underestimate me either, okay?"

He glanced at the clock again, gave me a long appraising stare, and seemed to make a quick decision.

"Keep that note quiet, Deleeuw, and I'll tell you what it said, okay?"

I nodded. He opened a folder on his desk. "Dale left a message on the computer in his bedroom. It said, 'I'm sorry, I couldn't bear her loving someone else. I couldn't bear not knowing who it was. I just couldn't leave things the way they were. I'm sorry.'

"And Deleeuw," Leeming added in a quiet voice, "it takes a password to get into this computer program. Even his parents didn't have it. It was logged on at 7:45 P.M. when his whole family was in the house. Dale left right afterward, and his father reminded him the car was low on gas. This kid had a motive: He was wacko over his girlfriend."

He paused, pondering whether to set me straight. To his

credit, I guess, he did. "And look, let me tell you something about the suburbs you may or may not know, Deleeuw. Every parent, every friend, every relative thinks just about every kid here is perfect, thoughtful, and sweet. Parents come in here to pick up their kids who are so stoned they can't stand up and they'll tell us their boy never drinks. Even when you can smell it twenty feet away.

"Nobody out here is ever going to say, 'Yeah, well, I can see my best friend putting a rope around a beautiful young girl's neck and choking her until her face turns purple.' 'Cause it gives the lie to their whole lives."

Maybe the chief had just been going through the obligatory motions when he'd threatened me. We'd traveled pretty quickly from yanking my license to giving me advice. "Meaning I have to believe that Dale did it?" I said.

"Meaning it's true and you know it. Now, will you go away?"

"Okay, Chief. I'm appropriately stunned. But it doesn't explain everything. Why'd he leave the engine running, for instance? He could've rolled down the incline." I thought of mentioning the bruise on the forehead, but I'd tipped my hand enough for one conversation.

Leeming shrugged. "I don't have all the answers. People think we can wrap up every detail, but we can't, especially when the people who were there are dead. My hunch is, he and the girl were talking before he killed her. It was cold as hell up there, and he probably had the heat on so he kept the car running. And if you believe it was a murder-suicide—and I do—he would've wanted the car in motion so that he could strangle himself quickly. The radio was on, too. Maybe he just wanted company at the end."

"And the old lady? The knife attack?"

"Nothing to do with the two kids," said Leeming firmly. "Totally unrelated. Some cuckoo who heard the local news and wanted to be on it. Ask any detective in New York: Somebody kills somebody and half the city comes out and confesses. Here you got some of the most exciting action in town history, lots of people want a piece of it. It's not your business anyway. Go away."

"Dammit, Chief, I wish you'd knock off this patronizing shit," I snapped back, surprising the both of us. "The FBI is up my ass because I wouldn't turn in my buddies at work, not because I stole anything. If they had anything on me, I wouldn't be tiptoeing around your delicate sensibilities; I'd be folding laundry in Danbury. For that matter, if I'd stolen money, I wouldn't be sitting on a sofa with the stuffing hanging out, driving a car that sounds like a tugboat. I'm a detective now; I'm gonna stay one. Nobody is ever going to screw me out of my livelihood again. I've got kids, too, and they're going to go to college just like yours, and I'm earning a living just like you are. If you don't want to help me, that's your business, but I don't have to sit here and let you dump all this bullshit on me."

Leeming blinked. The room seemed unusually quiet for a police chief's office. As for me, I was already regretting my outburst, considering whether he would slug me or just toss me out of his office. But Leeming seemed to be at least considering what I had said.

"You're pals with Benchley Carrolton from the Historical Society, aren't you, Deleeuw?" he asked matter-of-factly, as if I hadn't exploded.

I nodded. He obviously knew it.

"Well, he'll probably tell you this anyway, since someone in the society will surely spot it. It's probably unrelated. But we think we know why the word 'Caroline' was used in the knife attack. There was another murder-suicide up on the Brown estate, about a hundred years ago. Girl killed by her boyfriend, a farmboy who went nuts and killed a half-dozen people before they got him and strung him up. On the Brown estate. Your pal Benchley has some old newspapers he's going to show me."

We looked at one another. I said nothing at first, waiting to see if he would volunteer more. He didn't.

"Let me guess," I said softly. "They hung him from a tree in the hollow."

The chief nodded. "More or less. Same place he strangled his girlfriend. Caroline. I know, I know, it sounds weird as hell. But Deleeuw, I'm telling you this for a reason: so you won't go off on some stupid wild-goose chase. I'll lay it out for you. First, the Dale boy strangles his girlfriend. I saw it a hundred times in the city, although they used guns, not station wagons. Teenagers surprise you. Then he kills himself. Then some deranged young man—the kind it always is— reads the story and remembers something he learned or heard about this old murder. He gets himself some old rope and an old hat and it's terror time in suburbia. He gets his rocks off watching all the moms in their minivans race back and forth across town in a panic. So that's the story. Let your kiddie clients keep their money. Bye."

He opened the door. Three fit men in suits came in, looked me over professionally, and dismissed me as unimportant. Perhaps they were thinking I looked like a bond trader trying to play a private detective.

I sat in the Volvo, my yellow legal pad on my knees, and tried to get organized. The suicide note was a pretty damning repudiation of Sam's notions. It didn't seem likely that someone else could break into the Dale house unnoticed and figure out

Ken's computer password. The "Caroline" reference *did* suggest a copycat, someone who knew about the old killings and was acting out a sick joke or impulse. But none of this kept the shiver from going up my spine. None of this explained why a popular, easygoing kid like Ken Dale could turn killer. We were into strange stuff here, not what people plunked down $200,000-plus for in a town with quiet shady streets and fine schools.

Was there anything in Ken's past, I wondered, any record of psychiatric care or history of instability, that would even partially explain what happened? What connection could there possibly be between Ida Flowers and the kids who died on the mountain that freezing night?

The chief's unsubtle threat had succeeded in shaking me up a bit. If he pulled my license, I'd end up living in the Volvo, not driving it. In the years since I'd left the Street I hadn't exactly been plied with job offers or acquired many useful skills and contacts. I could probably work summers for Benchley in the nursery, but I'd have to give my kids and dog away.

Fortunately, in tense moments like this, private investigators, like reporters and criminal lawyers, can turn to a whole range of books, movies, and TV dramas to shore themselves up and remind them how they're supposed to behave. Soldier on, I thought. You've got an orthodontist and a vet to pay, soccer uniforms and Mario Brothers to finance, not to mention six trips a year to Gap Kids, the running account at Domino's, craft bills at Creative Expressions, and summer camp. There's no greater driving force than two growing children to motivate you to face hardship and danger.

Besides, another notion had been haunting me ever since I had looked into Sam Mellman's earnest eyes and heard his inarticulate but moving defense of his friend. I sure didn't want to believe Ken Dale had killed his girl or himself. Most of all, I didn't relish being the one to tell my client that he had.

One of those Eyewitness News vans with a satellite dish perched on top like an ill-fitting hat pulled into the police parking lot as I was heading home. Local television, which had always seemed filled with rampaging pillagers from across the Hudson, was now portraying the town as a combination of Amityville and Jonestown, a vision of semirural horror. Not exactly the slice of the American Dream for which all those rich young professionals in Manhattan were saving their bonuses until the biological clock began to chime. The only thing saving us, at least temporarily, was one of those spectacular mob trials in Brooklyn, with all kinds of quotes from hidden mikes and courtroom shenanigans, that was pulling some of the cameras away from Rochambeau.

No community could be expected to accept that so peaceful and livable a place can possibly be seen as something out of Stephen King. But the media love contradictions, none more fervently than those that belie the apparent placidity of suburban life. "Suburban Nightmare" was the logo that led one station's report. HELL MOUNTAIN HORROR headlined one of the tabs.

In three days, the town had been subjected to more violent crime than in the previous five years. Anxious residents saw the deaths and assault, the kind of violence the outside world is subjected to daily, as pieces of shrapnel that had overshot their targets and landed astray. When Chief Leeming reassured them by reporting that some out-of-town copycat must be getting his kicks by aping a local tragedy the town had forgotten decades ago, but that there was no real danger, they believed him, mostly because the alternatives were unthinkable. There was a near riot at the Township

Council meeting, where hundreds of fearful parents and the ubiquitous outraged taxpayers—who seem to think the act of paying taxes gives them the right to scream at everybody who receives them—demanded better and more police protection pronto and vied with one another to sound the most enraged. This was a quintessential political solution, viewing violence as a matter of municipal competence, a problem for which solutions could be demanded and found.

In nearby Paterson, where Jane's clinic battled against the tide, kids died with some regularity, picked off by stray bullets, killed in gang fights, beaten by parents driven past the point of endurance. There was much pain, but not much shock.

Rochambeau was different and anxious to prove it. A team of psychologists had swarmed over the high school immediately after the deaths, dispatched to counsel grief-stricken friends. In this morning's paper, the school board announced a series of meetings at which professionals would advise parents about danger signs in adolescent behavior. The elementary schools had sent home hastily photocopied pamphlets advising how to discuss the tragedies with younger siblings. Jane and I were planning to attend the memorial service for Ken Dale and Carol Lombardi tomorrow afternoon.

I drove home. I tried to be there when the kids got back from school at three-thirty, even if I had to go out again later. I somehow had decided that this routine was vital, though it produced little in the way of tangible communication. I figured that I was planting in their distracted, inscrutable brains the notion that I was there, that I cared and could be talked to.

7

Next day, I dropped Jane off and drove nearly three blocks before I could find a spot to park the Volvo. I guess everybody had the same idea.

The high school is new, its auditorium one of the school system's prides. It features some of the best acoustics and lighting in the state and more than fifteen hundred upholstered seats, every one of them filled this afternoon, with another hundred people lining the back wall. I had never seen so many kids together in so muted a way. There was some murmuring and whispering, but mostly there was silence.

"This is going to leave a lot of echoes," Jane said, squeezing my arm. Jane was like Benchley in that way: Nobody's pain was too far away for her to feel. These deaths hit her in several places—as a neighbor, as a mother, as a therapist who worked to prevent tragedies like this one.

It hit me, too. From the descriptions I'd read and heard, Ken Dale didn't sound all that different from Ben. Was it likely, or even possible, that Ken's wholesome, well-adjusted manner had been just a veneer finally worn thin?

The lights were turned low and, across the edge of the stage, scores of candles flickered in small glass holders. The stage was draped with black. John Lennon's song "Imagine" was playing over the PA system, and the sobbing was infectious.

Across the room, Benchley offered a sad little wave. I'd never seen him look so down. I don't think he knew either Ken or Carol, but Ida Flowers was one of his oldest customers, one of those indomitable ladies who garden to the bitter end and would no doubt be back at it in a week or so. Benchley had kept the Garden Center closed since the kids' deaths. When I'd called earlier to tell him about Sam Mellman's offer, he'd told me how he'd been wandering through his greenhouses, misting the rows of perennials. I told him I'd stop by tomorrow. I wanted to keep an eye on him. I also wanted to hear about "Caroline."

Mr. Goleman, the principal, spoke briefly. I recognized Richard Handley, whom I'd met at the Historical Society dinner, as he walked to the podium—his informal clothes, his salt-and-pepper beard, his white, haggard face. As Ken Dale's and Carol Lombardi's teacher, he'd been chosen to memorialize them.

Handley cleared his throat, and the auditorium grew still. He reached for a glass of water. I couldn't see any visible signs of emotion, but I had the sense nonetheless that he was fighting to control himself.

The sobbing in the room quieted, although I could see some of the seniors dabbing their eyes. Sam Mellman, off to the left, was sitting erect in his chair, a tear running down his right cheek. He made no effort to hide it or wipe it away. I liked that kid.

"When two people as smart, as loyal, as decent as Ken Dale and Carol Lombardi die, everyone near them has a dual responsibility," Handley began soberly. "First, to mourn them, to honor them and their best qualities, and to say a proper good-bye. Then, to begin the process of asking some painful questions. I can't tell you what your questions ought to be, but I can tell you mine. Was there something in their behavior I should have seen? Warnings I should have noticed? Pleas for help I should have heeded? I don't have the answers yet, but I will be thinking about them for the rest of my life.

"Carol and Ken were both the sort of kids that teachers want to teach, that parents hope to raise, that friends want to know. They were blessed with brains, good values, kind hearts. I don't know what happened on the mountain that night, but I know that our world is a darker place without these two people, that our lives are diminished. Godspeed to both of them. And for us, for all of us in this room, for teachers, parents, and students, let's begin the process of working as hard as we can to see that we never gather again in so pointless and unspeakably tragic a way."

He reached into his pocket and unfolded what looked like a much-handled piece of paper. "Ken Dale wrote this poem in English class," Handley said. "It was part of his application to Kenyon College and, as his advisor, he shared it with me. I want to share it with you:

"We will grow and cool, our lives that are now on fire
Will harden and calm, all of us
Nostalgic for the passions that tormented us,
Forgetting their anguish,
Filled with lessons for those that come behind,
Remembering the hurt, but not that there is no
    soothing of it."

It wasn't great poetry, but not bad for a seventeen-year-old, I supposed. There wasn't a sound in the auditorium, not even a cough.

Handley cleared his throat and smoothed the crumpled paper. "I was surprised by that poem. I bet a lot of you are too," he went on. "Perhaps we all should have let him know in clearer ways that he didn't have to hide the part of himself that thought such thoughts. Ken was always proud to wear his soccer captain's jacket, but not to show his poetry. Carol had no ability to hide anything. She was as open as she was giving and warm. I don't honestly know . . ." Handley stopped and seemed to struggle for a few seconds. But good teachers, like good actors, never really lose control of their audiences. "I didn't want to give a lecture. There's enough for all of us to think about. Good-bye, Ken, Carol. God rest."

He returned to the row of chairs at the right side of the stage and sat down, crossing his legs. His eyes were clearly moist now. I reached for Jane's hand and squeezed it. If kids' lives could be snuffed out so brutally and irrevocably, where did that leave all of us and the kids' world we had worked so carefully to construct? Afterwards, on the steps outside, one of the blue letter jackets veered off and headed my way. Sam Mellman, controlled again but somber, his right hand outstretched. He politely acknowledged Jane, then turned to me. "Hey, I talked to my dad. He says you're taking the case."

"Whoa," I said, hoping that Ben would turn out to be as gracious and poised. "I'm still sniffing around. I saw the police chief today and he says there's precious little doubt about Ken's having killed Carol and himself. He says I'd be wasting my time and your money if I took this case. But I'm going to take a good look," I said, partly in response to his suddenly crestfallen face. "Where would you start if you were me, Sam?"

"There," he said, pointing to the back of a young woman retreating down the street. "Judy Cole. Carol's best friend. If anyone knows anything about Carol's life, she does." Judy Cole was already out of sight in the throng.

"Was Jamie Harte here?" I asked. Sam pointed down the street toward the school gym. There were lots of kids around, but I picked him out right away. He was all alone. He had a decidedly nonsuburban strut. Even the jocks at Rochambeau didn't look tough. Jamie Harte did. Judy Cole first, but Jamie Harte would definitely be worth a visit.

"Damn, I hope you take this on, for Ken's sake," Sam said, sadly. "Does that poem sound like it was written by somebody who could choke his girlfriend until she died?" Now that he mentioned it, it hadn't. I said good-bye, patting him on the back and promising to get back to him quickly.

As emotional as the memorial had been, there was a sense of closure afterwards, a kind of farewell the town seemed to want badly. The crowd began to drift off into the pale winter light. I dropped Jane off at her car—she was heading back to work—and out of an impulse to be near one of my kids, drove to Lucretia Mott School to pick up Emmy.

"Dad," said Em as she piled into the car with one of her buddies who was coming to dinner. "Don't forget—tomorrow you promised to bring you-know-what into my science class. Put one of those Post-its on the car. You promised!"

"Yes," I lied. "I hadn't forgotten." I scribbled "ERNIE" on a Post-it and put it on the rearview mirror. I dropped Em off and headed for the mall. I had to spend the rest of the afternoon and much of the next day trying to nail down some employment background checks and a couple of still-missing Daddy Cheats. These were cases that couldn't wait, in fairness to my clients. The next day I'd hit the school with Em's secret project, try and track down Judy Cole, and, of course, attend Camp Night. Tragedy or no, summer decisions had to be made.

8

I'm quick to see other people as being child-obsessed. Me? I'm a conscientious, attentive parent. I laugh, trade stories, and cluck about the degree to which other parents in Rochambeau are entwined with their offspring, but I know the truth. There are those lots worse than me, but there are those who aren't as bad, either. This is all by way of explaining why I was rushing from Vincenzo's Seafood to the Lucretia Mott Elementary School with an enraged two-pound lobster in the seat beside me before I stopped at Judy Cole's house and went to see Benchley. It was a sacred commitment, made well before I'd heard of the Dale-Lombardi case, and one which I could break only at the risk of shattering my daughter's trust in my word. I had promised, and I would never in life, I swore to my Ben and Em, break a promise.

Vincenzo had shrugged philosophically. "It's cold out. He could live twenty-four hours, but I've had 'em drop like that." He'd snapped his fingers. This obviously wasn't the first time some loony-toon parent had come in looking for a lobster. In the way of nine-year-old girls, all living things, even those unseen, were cute and had names. His was Ernie.

Em's class was studying invertebrates, and everyone had to bring in reports and exhibits. Tiffany, Em's snobby, clothes-obsessed rival—Em called such creatures "status girls" —had confided to her best friend in the girls' room that she was bringing in a lobster carcass her family had presciently obtained in Maine the preceding summer. Tiffany's sister, who had had Miss Archibald ("Miss Pumpkin Head" to her students) two years earlier, had tipped her to this annual assignment and to the fact that Miss Pumpkin Head went wild with joy (and good grades) when the real thing, or a facsimile, was brought in. Tiffany was ready, she giggled to her friend. But Em had overheard.

Em had come to me in desperation, suggesting that someone—why, who?—bring in a live lobster. Of course I would. We couldn't have a status girl ace out my kid, could we?

Ms. Welty, keeper of the visitors' log, took one look at the squirming plastic bag I was holding at some distance and encouraged me to go right up to the classroom without signing in. Like New York City cops, she had that I've-seen-it-all look.

"Science?" she asked wearily.

I nodded.

"It's alive," she noted. "It's not a snake, is it? 'Cause if it's a snake, I'm telling you right now, I'm just hitting the fire alarm like I did last year when that joker brought in a boa."

"No," I said reassuringly. "It's a lobster. Its claws are pegged." I decided not to introduce him as Ernie.

When I slipped into the classroom, I saw Emily nudge her friend Georgia. As luck would have it, this had the effect of distracting Tiffany, who was already midreport.

I didn't like her. I wouldn't like the adult version I could picture either. She read from her three-page computer-typed (clearly by a parent) report in its clear plastic folder, with three illustrations and a brochure from the Maine Department of Fisheries. At the end of her report, she triumphantly

reached into a paper bag and pulled out a remnant of a lobster.

"Oh," cooed Miss Archibald. "You brought in a carapace.
Excellent. Please pass it around."

Meanwhile, Ernie's struggles with the plastic bag were
growing faint. The countertop I'd set him on, I suddenly noticed, was a radiator cover. This couldn't be a healthy environment for a lobster, could it?

Em went next. Her report was concise, factual, and au-
thoritative. Every eye in the place was on my plastic bag.

"And," said Em, with a flourish, "my dad has been kind
enough to bring in a *live* lobster. Dad, if you please." I reached
into the bag and pulled out Ernie. We were a smash. No
Broadway show ever made an audience happier. Despite Miss
Archibald's scolding, the boys were out of their chairs in a
flash, jostling one another for a good view and a chance to
touch Ernie. Everyone in the class but Tiffany and a couple of
her henchpersons were in a circle around me, poking Ernie,
peppering me and Em with questions.

"Gross," said one girl. "He's spitting."

"Awww," said two others, in all sincerity, "he's so cute!"

A giant bubble had formed at Ernie's mouth. As it grew,
Ernie waved his claws one last time, and expired. With appropriate thoughts of appreciation and farewell, I disposed of his
body in a trash can on the parking lot.

My plan was to try and see Carol Lombardi's family before heading over to Judy Cole's house. But Carol's aunt dis-
abused me as soon as she picked up the phone.

"I don't mean to be rude," she said, "but my sister needs
complete rest. If you call or come by here I will file a lawsuit
that will have you in court for the rest of your life. Please
excuse me for being threatening, but Carol was an only child,

and I can't imagine how Harriet will ever get over it. She's in no position to talk to you, I swear it. And by the way, she doesn't know anything, anyway."

There was nothing I could—or should—say to that. I headed for Judy Cole's house.

The phone book had listed a Lee Cole on Ramona Place, but the mailbox said Lee & Sara Cole. It, like the grounds and front porch, was unadorned and a bit faded. The house was small by Rochambeau standards, and indifferently kept, which could mean various things. Sometimes it meant old-timers, people for whom a house was a shelter, not a statement. Sometimes it meant hard times, that severance pay was being stretched for food and mortgage payments and that gutters and paint would have to wait. There were people in town who would be embarrassed to walk outside if every flower in every windowbox wasn't perfect, and people who would no sooner put ribboned wreaths on their doors than run naked across their front yards. There were people who peered through their curtains, angrily watching for dogs shitting on their lawns so that they could politely rush out and ask through gritted teeth if the dog walkers couldn't be "more considerate." There were also people who laughed off dog poop as an inevitable consequence of having an overpopulation of retrievers.

"Yup," said Lee Cole, who had a newspaper in one hand. He held the door open a few inches with the other and looked anxious to tell me to get lost as soon as I started my sales pitch. His look was familiar to me from the financial district: angular body, slicked-back hair, icy blue eyes, an air of command. I was sure that the door had been slammed hard in many a salesperson's face.

"Sorry to bother you," I said, smiling my best aw-shucks neighborly smile. "I'm not selling anything, and I'm not running for office."

"That leaves charity," he said with a thin smile. "I'm busy. Please get to it."

I held up my plastic laminated state ID card. "My name is Kit Deleeuw. I'm a private investigator—"

He seemed startled, then he focused on me. "Now," he said. "That's what you are now. That's not what you used to be."

"We've met?"

He shook his head. "No. I've heard from Judy that you were hired by some boys at the high school to look into what happened to the two kids. She sort of expected you'd be contacting her. Besides, I had already heard of you." He said this without any particular emphasis or intonation, just matter-of-factly. But not with admiration. I couldn't tell whether he was cold by nature or if the frostiness was aimed at me. My guess was both.

"Well, I appreciate that you and Mrs. Cole—"

His mouth tightened further. "Mrs. Cole died of cancer almost eight years ago. It's just Judy and me. And it was Carol, too."

"I knew she and Judy were close."

"They were like sisters. You know how girls are, when they make those friendships. There were very few weekends over the past ten years when Carol wasn't sleeping over here."

An awkward silence followed. I wanted to talk to Judy, but he showed no sign of moving aside to let me in.

But Cole broke the impasse directly enough. "What do you want?"

"I'd like to talk to Judy," I said. "I—"

"Look, Deleeuw, I'll be open with you. I don't like what I've heard about you. The whole Street was talking about your firm. Everybody said the SEC wanted you in jail, that a slick lawyer got you out.

"I don't like your coming around here. Judy has dealt with the death of her mother, and now with the murder of her best friend. I'm sure that for enough money you or some good lawyer can find twenty bits of mitigating evidence that will raise just enough questions about Ken Dale to make him a martyr and turn this into some sort of civil rights issue, but I don't have to help you. Especially you, somebody who could as easily be in jail as standing on my porch."

The words stung. I guess I'd known that there were people who thought that of me, but outside of the federal agents I wouldn't cooperate with, nobody had actually come right out and said it.

"Because you've heard rumors doesn't mean they're true," I began, trying to hold my voice steady. But he broke in, the veins in his temples growing more prominent.

"Deleeuw, I'm not making myself clear. I don't want you bothering Judy, upsetting her, scrounging up dirt to clear that crazy kid's name. I don't want somebody with your reputation hanging around here." That threw me. *My* reputation? He seemed upset about my inquiries on his own account, not just on Judy's, as if any effort to clear Ken were offensive. But why?

It's unnerving to confront someone who thinks you're a thief. But losing my temper wouldn't help my clients. Remembering that my first duty was to the case, I decided not to tell him to go piss up a tree.

"Friend, I see you don't like me, or what you think you know about me, but if you continue to be pompous and strident, and I walk away, you'll end up wondering what I came for. Why don't you get off your high horse and hear me out?"

I should have left politely or sent a letter, perhaps had some mutual acquaintance call him up and explain that I wasn't Bugsy Siegel. It was crucial that I talk to Judy. Alienating her father only meant that I'd have to skulk around and catch her on the sly—tricky stuff when you're dealing with a high school student.

Lee Cole was now brandishing his *Wall Street Journal* like a weapon, he so clearly wanted me to go away. But there I was, standing like a mule with one hand planted on the door jamb, plowing heedlessly on. "And I'd prefer to talk inside, if you don't mind. I'm freezing, and the heat is pouring out of your house."

He mulled this for a second, then opened the door wider.

"Taking kids' money in a hopeless cause like that," he muttered as I walked past him into a colonial living room with a mantel full of knickknacks and ruffled curtains that wanted cleaning. "You got a lot of heart, Deleeuw." Wall Street was full of good-looking midlevel executives with tight assholes and contempt for the rest of the world, and he was one of them. Poor Judy, losing her mother and being left with this stiff, then losing her dearest friend.

"You knew Ken?" I had to concentrate on the fact that I was making progress. If I kept talking, I'd become more of a human and less of a slime with a reputation.

"Not as well as Carol," he said grudgingly. "She practically lived here. And sometimes she came over to the club to play tennis with me—doubles," he added quickly, as if that was safer. "I'm sure you knew that. It was almost like having another kid, I suppose." I hadn't known that, but everybody assumes private detectives know more than they actually do.

"Judy wouldn't come to the club after last summer. Some damned history teacher of hers told her it was a racist institution." He spit the words out as if the teacher—Handley?—had told her it was peopled with Martians. Though if he was talking about the Rochambeau Country Club, she and Handley were dead right. When you apply, board members visit your house and check your genealogy to see just how WASPy you are.

"You seem angry that I would take this case?" I pressed.

The question was an invitation to bring sharply into focus all Cole's resentment: at people who steal money and give Wall Street a bad name, people who snoop into others' private lives for a living, people who defend accused criminals, people who decide certain country clubs are racist, etc. He responded with The Voice, the one executives use to deny raises or fire somebody. The it's-a-dirty-world-but-somebody's-got-to-do-the-tough-stuff voice.

"I'm *uncomfortable* that you're not in jail with all the other people who wrecked Wall Street. My firm went under two years ago and I've been fortunate in putting together a little consulting business in the city, but some of my colleagues weren't so lucky. I'm *extremely* uncomfortable that you're defending a murderer. I'm *irritated* that you're coming to my home." He had hit his stride now, the tone he had used to chew out many an employee, I was sure. "If you think you're going to get to my daughter, think again. The only reason I let you one foot in the door was to tell you that. Now please leave."

I headed home, wishing I'd slaughtered him with some piercing wisecrack or maybe even humbled him with a jab to

the jaw. It was an unwelcome look at what people had probably been saying about me all along, perhaps at why my son
seemed barely able to talk to me. It was the kind of feeling
that sometimes sent me to the Lightning Burger for long talks
with Luis. But not today, I told myself, swallowing and squar-
ing my shoulders. There was too much to do.

9

The new guard on the Brown estate was a twenty-eight-year-old Salvadoran who usually kept well away from the police, since he had smuggled himself across the border in the back of a truck full of tomatoes. Like many of his friends, he had worked at first as cannon fodder in small stores in Newark, Paterson, or Queens. Since he had no papers, that was about as good as work could get, and better than he might have expected. His job in America, a cousin had explained, was to get hired by Americans to get shot or stabbed in their place. The odds were still better here than back at home, where two members of his family had been killed for union organizing and a similar fate probably awaited him if he ever got sent back. And if he survived, he would make more money in three months than his father could in a year at home.

So he'd jumped at this new job, which his cousin—personnel officer for a Newark-based security firm—had spotted. He had never spent much time in an American suburb before, and though he couldn't stray far from this abandoned old palace up on a hill, he had found the town below to be almost exactly what he and others back home had pictured when they thought of America. The spot where the dead teenagers had been found was disturbing—he crossed himself when he had to pass by—but he was unlikely to get shot at up here. Life had gotten easier.

He was making his afternoon rounds on foot—a simple stroll around the big old house, alert for evidence of vandalism or mischievous trespassing kids—when he saw the crows circling a bush off the main driveway.

He assumed that a dead squirrel or raccoon was attracting the birds, and was almost upon the bush when he practically stepped on the body—a bluish young face, eyes open, scarf tightly knotted around the neck. He froze, fought back the nausea, waited until the instinct to run abated. Risking deportation was preferable to risking time in an American prison for murder. And wouldn't they blame *him* if he ran away?

He did not, could not, touch the body, but ran to the guardhouse telephone, afraid to look back over his shoulder, his body chilling with sweat. The job had seemed too easy, too good to be true, and he now saw that it was. If he wasn't arrested, he would quit at the end of the day and slip back into the secret life of the illegal people. Three ghosts were too many to abide; better to face the crackheads in New York City.

Officer O'Brien came up the twisting roadway at forty miles an hour, tires screeching at every curve, dust and gravel forming a cloud behind him, siren at full blast. If anything had been coming down the hill, pieces of him and his cruiser would have rained all over the town below. O'Brien was excited: This was real police work, though it was a hell of a lot more than he'd bargained for when he left his welder's job. At least the call had come in daylight this time. He hoped the body wasn't too gruesome, that it was recently dead and intact, and he hoped someone else was close behind him. The state cops were always looking for signs that bonehead locals had screwed up evidence or fucked up in some other way.

The dispatcher had told O'Brien that he was the closest, thus would be the first. Don't touch anything if she's dead, he was warned. Don't let the guard who called it in leave or talk too much—save that for the state guys. The radio was emitting continuous and urgent reports: The chief was on the way, the state police had been notified, the Rochambeau Volunteer Ambulance Squad and most of the department were en route.

My, my, O'Brien thought. What the hell was happening to this town? Last week, he had been staking out the mayor's block, where there had been a spate of stereo and VCR snatchings. This week he was Dirty Harry.

The car lurched over the last rise and shot up the main drive. He saw the security guard waving his arms. He flicked off his siren, clicked on his mike to tell the dispatcher he'd arrived, and grabbed the first aid box from the trunk. Rushing across the small patch of lawn that separated him from the ashen-faced guard—a kid, and a terrified one—he could already see from the bluish hue of her skin that she was dead. He slowed his pace and watched where he was stepping, in case he was mucking up footprints.

The frightened-looking guard eyed him warily. "I have touched nothing," he said nervously.

"See anybody? Any car? Anyone at all?" asked O'Brien. "Hear any sound? A car? Motorbike? Noise of any sort?"

The small young man shook his head, looking helpless and cold in his outsized brown shirt. Illegal, O'Brien thought, but nobody would give a shit about that today. Let the INS worry about it. Last week this would have made a nice arrest, he might have reacted differently, but today he had graduated from speed traps to homicide. "I speak only a little English," said the guard. "Habla español?"

"Kid, I barely learned English," said O'Brien. "The chief speaks Spanish. Just wait," he said, holding up his hands in a gesture of patience. O'Brien scanned the body. Jersey girl, probably from some other town. Gold jewelry on the neck and wrists, long frosted hair with a perm, heels—this was a working-class kid. All that gold still on her, he thought suddenly, spotting the leather purse sticking out from beneath the body. So this wasn't robbery. It was weirdo stuff or a drug OD.

He leaned over her. No sign that the clothing had been removed; no blood. The tongue protruding from the corner of the mouth suggested strangulation, he thought, his mind racing as it always did when he was nervous. No signs of a struggle that he could see. Any chance she had done it herself? He'd responded to a couple of suicides, although none of them had afterwards been reported truthfully in the *Rochambeau Times*. They were always described as deaths occurring "suddenly" or after a "sudden illness," fooling no one but allowing the families to save some face. More than anything else, those families had made O'Brien glad he couldn't afford to live in Rochambeau. Within a year of the deaths, all of them had left town.

But there was nothing overhead that this young woman could have hung herself from, and she sure hadn't choked herself to death lying on the ground. Someone had twisted the yellow scarf around her neck.

Was there a serial killer working in Rochambeau? The chief would go berserk. So would the town. Not what people paid all those high taxes for.

He shook his head sadly at the sight of the girl, but he was scared about his job, too. Probably everyone on the department would get fired before this was done. When they met for coffee at the Dunkin Donuts on Route 23, cops from other departments liked to trade stories about how quickly

towns went nuclear when something terrible happened. Suburban police departments were never prepared for such
things. Residents refused to accept such crime, and local cops
always got the blame. Some video cam got ripped off and
people expected Kojak to suddenly appear.

He pulled the small mirror out of his first aid kit and
pressed it against the girl's nose and mouth. No signs of
breath. The skin was ice cold. He felt under her neck—no
sign of a pulse. He pointed his flashlight into her eyes and
clicked it on and off. No pupil movement. The state cops
thought they were all huckleberries, but he was a professional,
he knew what to do with a corpse.

He stood up and reached for his shoulder transmitter.
He could hear the wail starting up the hill.

"Dispatch, this is O'Brien. Over."

"Read you, go ahead."

"We have a ten-ten. No vital signs. I'm securing the area."

"O'Brien—any descriptions, any one-elevens?"

He looked at the trembling kid again. No scratches, dirt
on the knees or elbows, signs of dishevelment, nothing that
would suggest a struggle. If he'd killed the girl, he was unlikely to hang around and call the police. He'd be in the back
of some truck heading south through Virginia by now.

"You sure you didn't see anything? Anybody?" The guard
shook his head.

Fuck, thought O'Brien, this town is going to go nuts.

10

When Danielle Husick charged towards me across the school playground I assumed she'd heard of my new case—it seemed everyone had—and wanted to talk about developments on the crime front. Foolish of me, really, since two dead people paled into insignificance next to her daughter Heather's social needs.

Heather wanted to play with a friend today—not most days, just today—so her mother Danielle, cruelly nicknamed "Heatherwants" by the other mothers, was patrolling the schoolyard trying to scare up a playmate. There was another mother, related only sociologically, that everybody called "Rachel-isn't-ready" as in "Rachel isn't ready for overnights/ PG-13 movies/cable/9 P.M. bedtimes/books that aren't about cats or Native American myths."

"Don't you dare," Em hissed to me as Danielle waved warmly and steamed toward us, sullen Heather in tow. I no longer, in fact, arranged play dates on Em's behalf. It had taken me a couple of years, but I had eventually learned that arranged friendships die the painful deaths they deserve. Real ones come from the kids and their own curious, invisible signals, impulses, needs, and rituals. So I left it to Em and her pals. Usually.

"Kit! Em!" trilled Danielle. "You both look great." Neither Heather nor her mother had much to do with either of us when Heather didn't want to play. But today, her mother announced, sliding one arm around Emily's shoulders, she did. "Is Emmy available?"

"You really should ask her, not me," I said, trying to unclench my jaw. "But today is Em's piano lesson, so it wouldn't be a good day. Why doesn't Heather call Em later and schedule another date if she wants to?" Heather looked impatient. She never communicated directly with me or any other adult if she could help it.

Fine, said Danielle, looking around for another target. Heather was not into delayed gratification. I knew Heather wouldn't call Em, tonight or any other night. Why should she? She had a Yale-trained social secretary to handle such chores.

"Danielle," I cautioned as she was heading off, "there's still a lot we don't know about what's happening. You know you need to be careful."

She looked startled, casting a panicky don't-mention-this-in-front-of-Heather look at me. "Oh," she said. "Yes. Talk to you later." Nothing much was going to be discussed in her family until Heather was playing with a friend, which she felt like doing that day.

I felt more than a little sadness, mixed with annoyance, about Danielle. She'd been a union lawyer a few years back, before her daughter was born. Now she was an upper-middle-class yo-yo, her life dictated by Heather's constantly shifting needs and desires. Heather wanted to take violin lessons this year. Or didn't. Or wanted time by herself that day. Or wanted to see a movie. Or didn't want her parents to see one. I stifled the urge, every time I saw Danielle, to pull her aside and say, "Look, you had a life once. Take it back and let Heather have hers." But I didn't have the guts. Investigating deaths seemed easier and more likely to succeed. And was I much better? It was easy to cluck at everybody else, to feel superior to such neurotic notions, but was I ever easy when Ben and Em weren't? It's strange about life out here. You want other children to succeed, yet you don't want any parent to be better than you are.

"Thanks, Dad," whispered Em, who didn't actually have a piano lesson. Play dates with Heather were notorious. She insisted on playing only games she liked and refused to help clean up. When her mother came to fetch her—always five or ten minutes early—she stalled, refused to leave, threw tantrums. To this performance Danielle, the former fearsome negotiator, could only whimper, "Oh, Heather, honey, I know you aren't ready to leave, but it's time, sweetie. Daddy will be home soon, and we have to be there to help with dinner." Sometimes, after this drama had gone on for a half-hour, I would lose it, pick Heather honey up, and carry her to the car, for which her mother seemed grateful.

It was beginning to snow; the radio had predicted an inch or so. The mothers—there are still very few dads around schoolyards in Rochambeau—were rounding up their chicks for after-school cocoa.

I had my usual sense of mass interrogation under way. Did Jason have a good day? How was Jennifer's music class? Gym—was it hard? Lunch—was it satisfactory? Whom had they played with? Were they happy? Were they all right? Weren't they supposed to deal with any problems by themselves?

"You okay, sweetie?" I asked as Em maneuvered awkwardly into the Volvo with her lunchbox, backpack, and rolled-up artwork.

"Yup," she said. "Why do you ask?"

"Oh, I don't know, I get the sense you're a little down lately."

"I'm not down at all," she countered. "Well, maybe a little."

Whatever might be wrong would have to wait until our nightly before-bedtime chat.

"You working on that murder case on the hill?" she asked.

"Yeah. Just a little."

"So. What's the poop?"

"You mean scoop."

"Whatever. What happened?"

"It's private, and anyway, I just got started so I don't have any conclusions yet." Em got a kick out of my most unsavory cases, but I wasn't comfortable chatting about murder with my daughter.

I pulled into the back driveway and watched Em bound through the drifting snowflakes toward the back door. She had never noticed, but I often sat for a minute or two watching her disappear into the house. One day she *would* notice, and I'd have to stop. Actually seeing them grow up was a stunningly different experience from merely tucking them in every night; I shudder when I think how close I came to missing most of it.

How they turned out was the real sweepstakes, wasn't it? The point of the game, the ultimate roll of the dice. Wasn't that why we all got so crazy about it? For the simple truth of it, reinforced brutally by the deaths on the mountain, was that life could be unimaginably short and breathtakingly fragile.

My backyard reverie was interrupted by a sound I was used to in spring but wasn't prepared for in midwinter.

A roar went off in my left ear, setting Percentage baying furiously by the back door. My neighbor Charlie Pinski's garage door shot up and, like a rodeo contestant bursting out of the gate, Pinski roared out riding his snowblower.

He waved, shouting something I couldn't hear.

He turned into Gene Autry on those machines, his bellow of "Yo, Kit!" audible when the wind turned in my direction and he was downshifting.

I yelled pointlessly to Percentage to shut up. (Why do people tell dogs to be quiet? They never comply.) Pinski, somewhere in his early sixties, had been laid off from Wall Street himself a few years ago, but much later in life and under circumstances vastly superior to mine. He'd gotten a fat enough severance to slide him into early retirement. Much of the money, I think, had gone into purchasing the best suburban home maintenance machinery available.

Pinski owned some loud, polluting, wasteful machine for every twist and turn of nature, gear for every season. There was a leaf sucker and chopper, this new snowblower that rode into three-foot drifts and sent plumes of white through the air like a fireboat, trimmers, mowers, chippers, wheelbarrows and spreaders, rakes, trowels, and bulb-hole diggers.

He turned the engine to low, bringing the roar to a grumble. "Could be a big storm," he shouted, as he always did when the first flake fell. "Getting a jump on it. Don't worry about hiring anybody—I'll get yours, too." I waved and yelled thanks. At first I had declined his offers, not wanting to take advantage, but Jane pointed out what should have been obvious: He was in heaven. With his giant blower, it took a scant four minutes to polish off his walk, not nearly long enough. He would have been happy to clear the whole block. Or the entire town, for that matter. Have a gas, Pinski, I thought as I got back into the car. We're both having so much more fun since we lost our jobs.

. . .

The Volvo glided into the back of the Garden Center. If you kept going, the road forked two hundred yards beyond the center, one branch leading out of town, the other climbing up the hill to the Brown place. Two state police cruisers were coming down off the mountain, mopping up after the deaths of the two kids, I assumed.

It was a pleasure to have so much space to park. It wouldn't last. The Garden Center lot, deserted in midwinter, would become a riotous scene from April through October, requiring tanned young men and women with walkie-talkies to direct the traffic that backed up down the road.

People can never get enough of dirt and trowels and grass seed. In the suburbs, you can be a leftie or a rock-ribbed Republican, a white-maned WASP matron, a Jewish labor organizer from Brooklyn, or an orthodontist. One thing shared by all of the above is fussiness about their yards (or grounds). Benchley frequently, and not unhappily, points out that men's lawns are their signatures in suburbia, as well as the only form of therapy most of them find acceptable. Jane allows that he has a point, a rare psychological concession from her, but cautions against generalities.

Benchley's house, a Colonial, is sprawled against the base of the hill. It's a beautiful old place which has seen a lot of history. Generations with differing tastes and needs have resulted in its branching out in all sorts of unpredictable white clapboard additions.

Benchley came out of the kitchen door in response to the delighted squeals and greetings of Melody, his yellow Lab. She loves me, but then she loves everybody. Perhaps the supply of liver biscuits I keep in the back of the Volvo adds to the wiggling and squirming my arrival always sets off.

Benchley still looked weary, a frightening state for someone who so rarely appears anything but indomitable and enthusiastic.

He even dispensed with greetings.

"Kit, do you know about the trouble up on the hill? One of my sales clerks says they've found another body up there today. A young girl. I can't really understand it. I've lived my whole life in this house, and now it seems—well, come in out of the cold. You don't need to stand out here and listen to an old man whine."

But the fact was I was too stunned to respond. I looked foolishly up the hill, as if there might be something to see. A girl. Dead. What could it mean? How would Leeming fit that into his murder-suicide-copycat theory? My first response was that Sam's instincts about his dead friend had just been given a bloody but dramatic boost. Maybe it was a suicide? Or an accident? Even as I thought it, I knew better. Benchley and I stared mutely at one another for several moments. I was supposed to be coming up with answers, but the questions were outdistancing me as Rochambeau was turning into a bloody and nightmarish battlefield.

Collecting himself, Benchley told me that he'd discovered something important. "You'll need to see it quickly, if you're going to be working on this case," he said over his shoulder, leading the way, actually a bit excited.

"This isn't about 'Caroline,' is it?" I volunteered.

Benchley whirled around. "You know," he said, shocked.

"I know you think I'm just a lost soul who couldn't survive a week without your guidance, Benchley," I said, a bit smugly. "But I have a few tricks left in me." And I'll sure need them, I thought, wondering about the girl up on the hill.

"But how could you . . . ?"

"Chief Leeming mentioned it to me yesterday. He didn't seem to think it was all that significant, and he said you would probably be onto it pretty quickly. But he didn't tell me much, so I'd be grateful for any details."

Benchley managed to smile. "You *couldn't* survive a week without my accumulated wisdom," he said. "But I'm glad you've taken this on, Kit, because maybe you'll help stop this—" He gestured helplessly out the window.

Usually Benchley, Melody, and I passed our winter visits in one of his heated greenhouses. It felt like being magically transported to Florida. But today he was steering me into the library where he kept his Rochambeau Historical Society files and whole crates of old newspapers. One of them was spread open on the oak library table, its yellowed pages held open by heavy binders. Benchley went to fetch some mulled cider, and set the tray on a side table well away from the old papers. "I called Chief Leeming to tell him about the files, and, of course, I offered to show them to him. He's coming by later. But I think you should see this as well. And you'll have time to look it over; the chief's up there on the mountain."

The *Rochambeau Times* was dated September 11, 1872. The story Benchley pointed to was one column wide, just like all the others on the page, but the headline stood out visibly enough: NATHANIEL GOWDY HANGED AT NOON WEDNESDAY. PRAYERS SAID FOR SIX VICTIMS.

I pulled up one of Benchley's huge oak chairs and took a gulp of cider. He had vanished, leaving me alone to absorb what I was reading. It was strange even to look at the newspaper; the last thing I associate with the suburbs is history. People come and go so often that we don't see ourselves as having much common heritage, yet I was looking at some pretty powerful local lore.

Sheriff James McDowell reports the death of Nathaniel Gowdy, a Rochambeau farmer, nineteen years of age, hanged by order of the Superior Court at noon Wednesday last from the giant elm on the hilltop where the first murder was committed. Gowdy was sentenced to death for the murder of his betrothed, Miss Caroline Clark, who was also nineteen years of age. Sheriff McDowell said deputies had evidence that Mr. Gowdy also killed five other women in Rochambeau over the past three months. All were strangled by rope of a type that Sheriff McDowell said was purchased recently by Gowdy.

According to the testimony at the trial, Mr. Gowdy was believed to be unbalanced by reports that Miss Clark was considering breaking their engagement. He lured the young woman to the estate on some pretext, then strangled her not ten feet from where he was hanged. He fled, leaving the body behind, and hid in the woods. According to the sheriff, he kidnapped and killed five other women in precisely the same manner at different locations throughout Rochambeau. The crimes constitute the greatest tragedy to occur in Rochambeau since the deaths recorded in the War Between the States.

It took me a second—maybe a few—to take this in. Leeming had told me about this case partly because he knew Benchley would, and partly because it suggested to him that some nut was getting his kicks attacking an old lady while dressed like a man of the last century, like Nathaniel Gowdy.

But it had a more chilling ring to it for me, and I suspected the rest of Rochambeau would react that way as well.

Benchley came in with a plate of biscuits.

"Finished?" he asked, sitting in the next chair. Melody sighed and plumped down next to him.

"My God, Benchley. Our lives have gone from the mundane to the horrific in less than a week. What do you make of this? Had you known about these murders on the hill, this Gowdy stuff?"

He nodded. "I had," he said. "We even devoted a meeting of the Historical Society to it some years ago. There was a manuscript on the case written by a local reporter years ago, although, curiously, I can't find it now. I'm sure it's here, because Evelyn de la Cretaz, who works at the library, and who does our filing, is quite meticulous. A couple of old-timers in town still talk about the Gowdy murders, but like you, most people in Rochambeau have arrived more recently and could hardly care, it was so long ago. Six murders is a mild weekend in New York these days. . . . You have two choices, really, don't you?" he said, coming abruptly to the point. "You can either believe in ghosts, which I sometimes do, or you have to conclude there's a disturbed man out there who knows about Nathaniel Gowdy and, for one reason or another, is yelling the name of his fiancée and stalking the town."

Benchley had something on his mind beyond the obvious. I could see he wasn't disturbed only by the violence, but by other memories as well. He looked down at the yellowed newsprint for a moment, then said:

"The Gowdy case was quite extraordinary, Kit. My family was peripherally involved, you know. After Gowdy was hung, his family sold this land—this Garden Center was the site of the Gowdys' farm—to my ancestors. It's been in my family ever since. The newspaper report doesn't say so—some things never change—but Caroline Clark was disreputable, at least by the standards of the time. She was seeing another man, and was quite open about it. Gowdy was passionately in love with her, and when he found out, he simply went mad. He asked her up to the mountain, then killed her, or so the authorities said at the time.

"Gowdy seems a puzzle, especially tragic," Benchley said, lapsing into the sort of reverie that questions of good and evil tended to induce in him. "He was, by all accounts, a decent, hardworking young man. He made a point of driving injured war veterans around town in his wagon. The people who knew him simply couldn't imagine him killing anyone under any circumstances—just like young Ken Dale. And he vehemently protested his innocence. But people do step out of character, don't they? And, of course, there was quite a bit of evidence. I believe Gowdy was captured running from one of the murder scenes. When he was caught, the police found the kind of rope used to kill his fiancée and all of the other women right there in his barn."

Benchley frowned, looking around the library in exasperation. "That investigation by the journalist raised some disturbing questions. I *know* it was in here somewhere, but I can't put my hands on it. Getting too old to know what room I'm in, I guess."

I'd seen no evidence of that, but the library *was* so cluttered with boxes and files that it was probably easy to misplace things. "I'd love to see that manuscript, Benchley, when you unearth it. It does make me understand the chief's attitude —lots of people in town probably know of the Gowdy case. Some disturbed kid could have taken it on himself to stir up old ghosts."

Benchley sighed. "It stirs up ghosts for me too, Kit. There's history here—my family's history. My great-grandfather grabbed this land from the Gowdys when they were in no position to bargain. He bought the property for a song and left the family nearly penniless. It's a blot; it troubles me that this wonderful place was acquired in that way."

"Are there any Gowdy descendants left?"

"You do have an instinct for this, Kit." He smiled. "There is a relative of old Nathaniel's. He won't speak to me. I've tried a hundred times to make recompense for this land, to pay a fair price, restitution if you will. I think he's obsessed with what's happened, what happened to Nathaniel that is, and what it did to the Gowdy family. There've been any number of small incidents of vandalism here over the years I am quite sure he was responsible for, although they ceased years ago. But he's a pig-headed old bastard. He won't let me help him."

He pulled a slip of paper out of his pocket. "He's a great-great-nephew. His name is Blackhead Abraham Gowdy, the grandson of Nathaniel Gowdy's brother Julius. He's eighty-six and lives in a nursing home downtown, you know, one of those old Victorian mansions. Not likely he could hurt anyone or would have waited so long to do so." I took the paper. Even if what had happened to Ida Flowers had no connection with the deaths on the mountain, improbable tips are worth a brief trip; otherwise, there is the nagging sense you have overlooked some tiny piece that could make the puzzle work.

Benchley was looking out at the falling snow, which was getting heavier, obscuring his view of the mountain. "Kit, this isn't normally the sort of thing I would reveal, but if you look into all this you'll probably come across it anyway. You see, I tried in personal visits and through lawyers, every way I could think of, to pay Blackhead back. He'd have nothing to do with me. But when he was no longer able to pay the taxes on his home, I arranged a subterfuge with my lawyer. We had some money bequeathed to Blackhead, anonymously, through a different law firm, and said in a letter that it had been discovered in an old family trust. Blackhead was weak and ill and unable to live by himself. The money pays for his nursing home. I was afraid you would stumble across this arrangement and somehow reveal it to Blackhead. You mustn't."

I wanted to take Benchley in my arms, he looked so bleak and conscience-ridden. I had the sense he had still other things to tell me, but he seemed hesitant, and in any case, there wasn't time. I heard a car pull up in front of the Garden Center.

"Whoops," I said. "That must be the chief coming down from the hill. I'd better scram. He's unhappy with me as it is. Thanks, Benchley." I let my hand rest on his shoulder for a moment. Whatever my problems with Leeming, I thought, Rochambeau was probably lucky to have him around. I hadn't met anyone else in town who had had any practical experience with violence at all.

The wind had picked up and the temperature had dropped again. Glancing out the library window, I saw the medical examiner's van, two state cruisers, and three Rochambeau PD cars sliding down the hill. I didn't wait to be thrown out. I had a slight jump on the rest of the town, time best spent taking advantage of being one of the few people who knew much about Nathaniel Gowdy. But then I thought, hurrying towards the kitchen door and feeling my neck tingle, it looked as if at least one of them *had* known enough to get a knife and whisper a name.

"Benchley," I said. "Doesn't this make it seem that Ken

Dale might have been the murdered, rather than the murderer?"

"Why, Kit? Because of the body they found today?"

"Maybe, though we don't know anything about that. But the police seem quick to assume that some crackpot who knew about the Gowdy case decided to run around and scare the town half to death by attacking Ida Flowers. But those women Gowdy killed were all strangled. Why wouldn't it be as reasonable to assume the killing of Dale and Lombardi were in a similar vein—someone obsessed with the case, perhaps, calling attention to it again?"

"I suppose it's possible." Benchley shook his head. "It makes me sad—and dizzy. This is far beyond me. I'm more tired than I can remember feeling. I'll sleep on it. We can talk tomorrow."

I headed off, planning to spend some time on the phone calling nursing homes until I found one Blackhead Gowdy. With a sick eighty-six-year-old, it was probably imprudent to wait. Except, of course, for Camp Night.

The choosing of summer camp is one of Rochambeau's most nerve-wracking and complex rituals, primarily because the culture accepts that it is healthy for kids to go away but contrives day and night to postpone the inevitable parting and to agonize over the destination beyond all reason.

By ten or eleven, most kids went. Some were deemed not ready. Some parents decided that even if the kids were ready, *they* weren't. Some kids wanted to go with friends, some by themselves. Some got too homesick and only went once or didn't go at all.

Like cars (van people versus station wagon people) and dogs (pedigreed versus mutt), camps made statements. Some had special ethics and values—the environment, athleticism, brotherhood. Some emphasized special skills—computers, music, riding. Religious camps. Sports camps. Sailing camps. Lose-weight camps. Rich-kid camps with cabins you'd be happy to live in year round. Travel camps bound for Europe. Camp Whispering Pines. Camp Diversity. Camp Empowerment. Camp Runamok.

For years, camp representatives had dashed from one living room to another with their slides and happy testimonial letters before somebody got the bright idea of holding Camp Night at the junior high, when all the reps could set up booths in the auditorium, pass out brochures, and answer questions. There are lots of questions. There is much murmuring about counselor/camper ratios, junk food policies, and sunscreen and Lyme disease vigilance. By now, the reps are slick as car salesmen about what will hook kids. There are not inconsiderable financial stakes involved. Most good camps require at least a month's enrollment. That could set a family back two thousand dollars or so per kid.

Camp Night protocol required that the kids stay at home. Camp was too important and expensive a matter to be left to children, and they were too easily swayed by pictures of snorkeling.

Jane and I always split up. "Look for a camp with some values," she instructed gravely. "Something besides just having a good time, although that's important. I want the kids to hear about the environment. I want Em to be in a place where they transcend gender roles. I want Ben to do more than throw baseballs for four weeks." Good luck, I told her.

We agreed on several ground rules. No camps with Indian names. No camps with Jell-O wrestling. No camps with glossy brochures and colored pictures of sailboats. No air-conditioned cabins, no chefs as opposed to cooks. That narrowed the field considerably.

She could barely make it through the evenings anymore. She didn't like crowds or salespeople, and was losing her patience with the intense parental input that characterized so many suburban activities. She strode up and down her assigned aisles in a businesslike way, deflecting the eager reps and collecting literature. I dawdled more, eager to pick the thread of this year's questions.

Outside, the town was beginning a collective nervous breakdown about the deaths and the attack on Ida Flowers. Inside the gym, there was no mention of that trouble. Instead, in an atmosphere of serious business, a throng of eager, concerned parents encountered a force of earnest, reassuring counselors, reps, and owners spread out in nearly a hundred stands around the gym. It looked like a high-class crafts fair, except the commodity was your kid.

To wait past mid-February was to risk getting shut out of the good camps, and that meant some dumb camp in the Poconos called Fuck-A-Duck or something, cabins with holes in the roofs, no large bodies of water, campers of lazy or lackadaisical temperaments, and your kids deprived of a major-league meaningful experience. But to commit too early raised unnerving social problems. Would your kid still be speaking to January's best friend in June? What if he developed a sudden aversion to computers? Jane and I had taken a blood oath to seek out a sane, pretty place with a diverse group of people and sign up, regardless of social complications and transparent child-enticements. When I wavered, tempted by field trips to Montreal, Jane kept me steady. The kids had to go sometime, she said. We wouldn't like it any better than anybody else, but camp was one of the places where they—and we—could best learn how to start the process of living apart. We couldn't blow it. We owed it to them. We owed it to us.

Around me, the questions swirled: "Are boys allowed in the girls' camp? In the cabins? Is the exercise too strenuous? Are bedtimes enforced? Are kids allowed to bring pets/candy/Gameboys/Walkmen? How many visiting days? Are there any wild animals? Have there ever been any wild animals? Have wild animals ever bitten any of the campers?

The spectacle was jarring, but it was reassuring, too. Rochambeau, I decided, was becoming a town you might want to send your kid away from for a while.

11

The town was possessed and hysterical, its very reason for being turned upside down. Everywhere I looked, over the next few days, I saw things I had never seen here before. No one in Rochambeau ever had. In front of City Hall, three men and a woman set up a booth and offered to exorcise the demons that had taken over the town. An evangelist volunteered to help the lost souls who lived here come to Jesus.

Meanwhile, television crews in their buglike vans cruised back and forth along Main Street, past the high school, and up to the Brown estate's driveway, where they were turned back. Dejected, the crews often stopped at the Garden Center at the foot of the hill, trying to interview Benchley, frantic for fresh visuals. Reporters from the New York tabloids and from the supermarket horror sheets paraded into the police station and hung out at the local coffee shop. Several homeless men and women suddenly appeared, on the apparent theory that there might be large and generous crowds in the vicinity. Bad guess. One trio tried to set up a makeshift tent in a park before the cops swooped by and, according to local rumor, drove them in unmarked cars into Newark.

The county sheriff, facing reelection, sent in gaudily marked giant cruisers full of fat desk jockeys to patrol the streets between coffee breaks. State police cruisers were a gift from the governor. Adjoining towns sent their cops over the line as well, their burglaries and underage drinking investigations finally interrupted by something truly dramatic. Police detectives gave lectures to school assemblies on dealing with strangers, and went door-to-door asking townspeople if they knew anything suspicious, had heard anything unusual, or had seen anything—anything at all—out of the ordinary.

The rituals of suburban life collapsed in the face of so stunning an invasion. Maids were picked up in Paterson and Jersey City, spared the sudden terror of public transportation. Baby-sitters moved into guest rooms. Basketball league practices were moved to midafternoon so people wouldn't have to drive home in the dark. Psychologists and counselors roamed the public schools, declaring their availability. PTA meetings, swimming classes, school science fairs, and Weight Watchers' sessions were all canceled or rescheduled for weekends during daylight.

Security company vans raced from one home to another, installing new locks and iron grilles over ground-floor windows. My eeriest memory of those days is the sudden sensation of sensor spotlights switching on and off all over town. Plumbers and electricians gave previously agreed-to passwords at front doors before being admitted. Door-to-door salespeople, already hurting because of the number of women away at work, suspended operations completely. Editions of the *Rochambeau Times*, which speculated fruitlessly about the connections between the deaths of the three young people, sold out within hours. The 5 P.M. train from New York— usually half empty—became thronged with Wall Streeters rushing home early to guard their nervous broods. At night, the trendy Emporium de Edibles—a market whose seafood and deli sections were bigger than most small stores—was eerily empty.

At our house, Em began sleeping with the lights on, her

stuffed animals arrayed in combat positions around the bed, her usually placid sleep interrupted by nightmares. Even the normally taciturn Ben got chatty and seemed interested in my work. Meals became therapy sessions and discussion groups, over which Jane expertly presided.

"First thing," she would say when we all sat down, "let's exchange all of the rumors we heard today." They were always wild.

"I heard there are ape men pulling children out of their bedrooms and eating them," Emily offered one night.

"It's a cult," Ben offered. "They suck the blood out of the corpses."

Jane emphasized again and again that while the news was terrible, she wanted the children to know that they would be safe, that they would be taken care of. We asked them to not wander off to friends' houses without telling us. We asked Ben to make certain he knew where his sister was at all times and insisted that even when he went to the video store two blocks away to rent a Nintendo game he take Percentage—a security measure that brought howls of derision from everyone.

Our phone, which had not rung much in a long time, suddenly grew busy. Parents called Jane for counseling tips, neighbors and acquaintances called to press me for any fresh details as word spread that I was working on the case. I didn't have anything to pass along yet, but I took a stand as coach of Ben's soccer team, urging that indoor practice sessions take place as scheduled at 7 P.M. in the high school gym, a gesture in opposition to the panic. I lost. Every one of the players' families pulled its player out.

I was pleased, in a way, to have my work as a detective ratified as important by people who usually acted as if I were cleaning stables at the track. I wanted, like everyone else, to be worth something.

"Kit," Jane announced one of those tense mornings, "I'm thinking of going to half-days for a while. I want to be around more for a couple of weeks. The kids are spooked and so is everybody else we know. Maybe I can even help you." The kids were in the playroom, Emmy cheering Ben on through the sixth level of Super Mario whatever; we were having our weekend postbreakfast cleanup, when the kitchen chaos of the preceding days was supposedly set to rights.

"That would be great, but I don't want us to overreact," I said. "I want us to lead a normal life—"

"Overreact? Everyone in this town is freaking out. Your being involved doesn't make it easier on the kids, either, I don't think. It all comes right into the house. You may have to be coming and going at all hours. If you're going to stay in this line of work, then you have to be able to throw yourself into it. But, Kit." She put a cautioning hand on my shoulder. "After what we've been through, you know, after we've come this far . . ."

I laughed. "And just how far have we come? We're broke. We couldn't send either kid to college for one year. I have no health insurance, no pension. At Camp Night, I walked past half the interesting camps because I knew we couldn't afford them—"

Jane is invariably supportive, but she is prickly about whining. I loved whining, started many of my days with it. "You're whining," she said. "This is no time for a significant depression. Instead of worrying about camp, how about getting off your butt and nailing this nut so our kids can ride their bikes again?"

"Tough love," I said. "I'm off."

12

We had suspended Jane from attending athletic events a year earlier, when she had gone to one of Ben's soccer games and watched a dentist who lived across town scream for nearly an hour. He screamed at the coach for leaving bad players in or good ones out, he screamed at the refs for bad calls, he screamed "Go," or "Yo, Bobcats" at everyone. His boy was often visibly close to tears.

Such behavior was a little extreme, by the prevailing standards of Rochambeau soccer games, but I wouldn't go so far as to say it was unprecedented. Parents often stormed up and down the sidelines, cursing, bellowing, and generally making their kids feel conspicuous, ashamed, or uncomfortable. You know, instilling the will to win.

Jane's defense was twofold: first, that she had endured several years of this boorishness in silence, and second, that in her work, she frequently saw the damage overinvested parents could cause. "It's an upper-middle-class form of child abuse," she contended. "Poor people hit their kids. The middle class invades them emotionally. No responsible person can sit by silently and watch it."

She didn't. When the dentist starting screeching "Replace him, replace him!" as the third goal slipped past the Bobcats' abashed goalie, his own son, Jane lost it. She marched halfway downfield and jabbed Dr. Rendell in the chest.

"Look, you macho bozo," she announced, as the other parents froze in shock. "I've been listening to you berate kids on soccer fields for several years. You're humiliating and degrading your son, you're making everybody in the stands miserable, and you're making a total asshole of yourself." It was a great speech as far as I was concerned, a suburban classic, one I never would have had the guts to make in a million years.

Rendell's reaction was as good. He turned purple, gasped, and sputtered like a tire with a slow leak. Then he went to his picnic basket and pulled out a thermos of something, of which he drank deeply. I could swear his kid grinned at her, but maybe I was fantasizing. I, who loved Jane devotedly, swore even more eternal fealty after that, simultaneously noting my good fortune that I didn't have one of those jobs that required a doting, deferential corporate wife. Ben didn't speak to her for a week. The ultimate suburban parental crime, in my experience, was causing a scene in front of your kid's friends. Jane had staged a whopper.

Ben and I both thought it best that she take a protracted time-out from Rochambeau sports, to which she happily acceded. She decided to forswear crowded and expensive malls at about the same time, and insists she misses neither. After all, grumped Ben, if you yelled at every parent in Rochambeau who acted like an asshole around his kids, the town would look like the aftermath of one of those nuclear war movies.

In this context, I was conscious of how much Jane would have disliked Coach's Gym, which looked just like a seedy, run-down gym in a dying mill town ought to look. I parked the Volvo a block away, in a less than inviting alley. If the

Volvo hadn't looked like such a veteran, I wouldn't have left it there, but it was past being stolen. I could hear the shouts, banter, and grunts half a block away. If Jane couldn't bear the macho posturing on a soccer field, she'd go nuts in a place like this. And the guy I was looking for was no sensitive soul either.

By reputation, Jamie Harte was as close to the prototypical thug as you could get in a town like Rochambeau. Even Ben had had a couple of run-ins with Harte, he told me reluctantly when I pressed him. It was Harte's practice to slam younger kids into lockers, vandalize their books and backpacks, or come up behind them suddenly and hold their faces in water coolers until they choked. Minor stuff, I suppose, in an age where high school kids gun one another down, but still frightening and ugly if it happens to you. And the thing that made Harte especially menacing was that he was violent and explosive around those his own size as well. Ben said he'd heard stories "over the years" (interesting notion for a twelve-year-old) about Harte chasing kids off the playground and "suggesting" they give him a dollar a week if they wanted to get home safely.

At the Y, where Jamie could often be found slamming the Nautilus equipment around even in his junior high days, Ben had learned to give him a wide berth. It was interesting that Ben had never told me about these encounters when they happened during his swimming lessons, only under pressure and after repeated promises to keep them to myself. Public school kids and hardened prison inmates everywhere share these rules: Never snitch, never like cafeteria food, escape whenever possible, and remember that despite the rare exception, teachers/guards/principals/wardens are the enemy.

Jamie was right where his gentle-sounding mom (who

seemed to take in stride visitors looking for her son) had told me he would be. Coach's Gym, two towns over in Ridgefield, would never have lasted a week in downtown Rochambeau; it would have been supplanted by a mirrored exercise studio called Circulation, offering the latest advances in aerobics, with an adjacent activewear boutique. Rochambeau isn't your basic thick-neck town, but Ridgefield is.

The gym was a big old converted retail store, the furniture sign still stenciled on the outdoor window, with cracked vinyl-seated arm, leg, thigh, and chest exercise machines. As you'd expect from a room with fifty or so men and boys grunting and pumping in it fifteen hours a day, it smelled pungently of machine oil, liniment, and sweat. As near as I could tell, the only real ventilation was a fan that blew the rich odors all around the gym.

Every guy there seemed to have a neck the size of Percentage's head, and none of them looked anything like me. But I assumed I was safe enough, since every other T-shirt carried a local, county, or state police logo of one kind or another. The coach, who was over in one corner and looked more or less like a giant cinder block, was easily identifiable; this was the only T-shirt that said "COACH."

I recognized Jamie easily enough from the memorial service for Ken and Carol. He was wearing a Rochambeau High sweatshirt, though he didn't seem the school-spirited type, and a nearly handsome, Elvis kind of sneer. He was six feet or so, understandably muscular, wavy black hair cut above the ears, not quite a greaser but definitely not a preppie. He was pressing 150 pounds with the help of an even beefier partner in an Essex County Sheriff's Department T-shirt.

No one had ever seen Jamie Harte's parents at school events; he was listed in no extracurricular activities. I remembered that Sam had said his father was a drunk who'd taken off.

There were only a handful of blue-collar families left in town; most had inherited rather than bought their small brick rowhouses or wood-frame twins. In a way, I thought, being working-class in Rochambeau was tougher than being Hispanic or black or Asian. You were just as much a minority, but it wasn't unfashionable to discriminate against you or ostracize you. And blue-collar kids could never keep up. Their parents couldn't afford Sid Green's high-quality materials for school projects, or supply them with Murray Grobstein's hot sneaker of the month or the latest in keyboards, CDs, and torn jeans. They didn't have new cars or big houses to throw parties in. It had to be rough.

But none of that could fully explain why Jamie Harte was such a hard case. I didn't like him. I didn't like what I'd heard about him. I didn't like the way he looked, his face frozen in a perpetual sneer. I'd seen plenty of mean-eyed bullies in the army and I would have put a good chunk of money down that that's where Jamie would end up, if he was lucky enough.

But I cautioned myself to be a little more open-minded; it would be hard to take to anybody so many people had warned you about.

"Yup," he grunted, when I came up beside him. His partner looked right through me.

"Jamie, I'd like to talk to you for a few minutes."

"What . . . about?" He was bench pressing, lying flat on his back, breathing hard. Sweat poured off his face and onto the mat. It already seemed to me a poor call to seek him out in this most macho of lairs. He would hardly confide in me in the middle of a gym.

"Give him slack," growled his weight partner, a blond

with a crew cut. "If he loses his concentration, he could drop that thing right on your foot."

I nodded politely, tried to look cool, stepped back. "Jamie, I'm a private detective. I'm investigating the death of Carol Lombardi. I need your help, just for a few minutes."

The crew cut looked at me and grinned. "You?" I could almost hear him thinking. "Pretending to be a detective? Who you kidding?"

"Forty-eight . . . forty-nine . . . fifty . . ."

Jamie slammed the weights down on the forked stand above his head, blondie guiding his arm. I jumped back. Jamie sat up, gasping, and looked directly into my face for about thirty seconds. He had cold, hard eyes, the kind it wasn't fun to stare into for any length of time.

"Suck my dick, faggot," he wheezed.

Blondie laughed loudly. "Hey, guys. The faggot here is going to suck Jamie's dick." Jamie wasn't smiling. His eyes were blazing, his body tense, ready to spring, and eager for an excuse. He wouldn't get one from me.

"Well, Jamie," I said, "it's nice to meet somebody who so precisely lives up to his reputation. I'd like to hear from you." I dropped my card on the floor next to the bench, then backed away.

Just some more male bonding, I thought.

There were a few grunts and guffaws. Coach paused in his screaming, looked over at me, and jerked his thumb towards the door. We both knew he wouldn't have to tell me twice.

I headed for the Volvo, hoping it was still there. Downtown Ridgefield was a boarded-up, litter-strewn wreck. That it wasn't a place I cared to hang around was the last thought I remembered having before the left side of my head seemed to cave in. I thought I heard somebody say, "And stay away, dickhead," but I couldn't swear to it.

I woke up a few minutes later, as I later reconstructed it, since my watch and the few bills in my wallet were gone. I tasted a bit of the blood where whatever had slammed into my head had pushed my teeth into my lower lip. I assumed the message came from Jamie, but I couldn't be sure, and I wasn't about to go back to the gym and ask. I thought of calling the police, but I had no appetite for answering their questions or taking their ridicule. Nobody in the gym was going to testify for me. And the Ridgefield PD would surely call Chief Leeming. All I'd end up with was another lecture about what a boob I was, and my head hurt enough. I opted for an ice pack at home.

Jane went a little berserk when she first saw my puffy cheek—I was touched to see that she even cried—but then her excellent training and instinct for action kicked in.

"Who did it?" she demanded.

"I dunno," I mumbled, refusing for the fourth time to go to the emergency room. "Maybe somebody just mugged me for my watch. This is what they mean by being blindsided. Look at the bright side; there wasn't any rope found by my body, right?"

"This, my love," said Jane, as she pressed an ice pack against the growing lump on the side of my foolish head, and kissed me gently on the forehead, "is called total lack of common sense. I'm not giving you any lectures tonight, but we're going to sit down tomorrow and talk out some procedures."

"Procedures for what?" I mumbled thickly.

"For being careful," she said. "Why did someone slug you?"

This was a good question. I assumed Jamie had done it. The only thing that made me pause was that he didn't look like the kind who would have waited—he would have happily slugged me right in the gym. And why? I hadn't done anything. Or better put, it certainly wasn't because of all the important information I'd gathered.

13

Over the weekend, Lisa Caltari's name had been released. The second dead girl found on the mountain became another element in the media drama Rochambeau had become. I had fed her name to my state police source and my credit mole as well as to my clipping service—the combined resources of Deleeuw Investigations—but come up blank. Tagg said the state boys working on the case were flummoxed.

"Pardon my French, Deleeuw, but she was a tramp. She could have gotten aced anywhere. So the big question is, why there, up there on that mountain, where only a nutcase would go? Although, there are a lot of nutcases out there. It might signify, as the British say, or it might not." For now, I thought, the best course was to put the Caltari killing on hold and stick with Ken and Carol. I had to get to Judy Cole, the best and most promising link I had to the case. I dialed her number.

My old buddy Lee Cole answered.

"This is Kit Deleeuw," I said.

He started to bluster. I'm sure secretaries in New York trembled at the sound all day. "Deleeuw, the minute you left I called the FBI in New York and told them their old buddy was out here nosing around. They seemed quite interested. They urged me to keep them informed. Special Agent White said my instincts about you were sound, as far as the FBI is concerned. And I *will* keep them informed, I promise you. In fact,

I intend to call the local cops as soon as this call is over. And this had better be the last call." But he didn't hang up. He paused.

"Cole," I said softly, "I'm not going to get in an argument with you about my reputation. You seem to have made up your mind about that, and you're entitled. But I need to talk to your daughter."

"My daughter," he exploded, "is off-limits to lowlifes. I warn you—"

"You warn me all you want, you arrogant windbag," I shot back. "I'm getting sick of your pontificating. You don't know a thing about me, or what I did or didn't do. According to the class yearbook, your daughter turned eighteen a week and a half ago. She's an adult. If she doesn't want to talk to me, she can call the police herself. But if she's there, please put her on. I want to ask her about her friend Carol, and I want to ask her about—"

This time, he did hang up. I flushed, furious. Our relationship was not progressing. It was none of his business what I wanted to talk to Judy about, anyway. Cole got to me because he actually seemed more substantial than a mere windbag, more menacing. He was smart and angry. I couldn't imagine it was easy to be the daughter of somebody like that when your mother had died, or the friend of the daughter either.

The mall was teeming. It was afternoon, time for the late-rising high school kids to start pouring in by bus, van, and Mom's wagon for their weekend cruising. Out here, the wagons are Chevies or Fords, not Volvos. The American Way is a more working-class hangout. True, Murray Grobstein's latest nuclear-powered sneakers are likely to cost a hundred bucks, and every kid seems to scrounge up the money for a pair. Murray had been in the doorway signing for his latest shipment when I'd pulled in; he'd waved, too busy to come out and chat.

The kids tend to swarm mostly around the west entrance, where there are an ice cream place, Murray's Shoe World, a discount tape and CD store, and lots of benches. Their mating rites are beyond my or any outsiders' understanding. Everything—every shirt and pair of pants, angle of hat, earrings style, and body gesture—has some encoded meaning.

You can see the most amazing demographic changes on those benches if you pop in and out all day, as I do. In the morning, they're empty. Weekdays, 11 A.M. on the button, the Silver Warriors, as the mall people call them, begin appearing, elderly widows looking for company, couples who come to the mall to exercise (some with pedometers attached to their belts to ensure they walk the prescribed mile a day), or for the $2.30 breakfasts offered at Lightning Burger.

At lunch, they are joined by waves of weary blue-collar housewives, stopping in at Foodway or hitting J.C. Penney's specials. They sit on the benches only to rest for a minute or two, change their babies, or chat, briefly and always distractedly, with a friend; they are harried and rarely linger for long. They always seem to have less energy than they need, not to mention less money, and one or two more kids than they can patiently or comfortably handle.

Jane says a lot of them—or their kids—end up in clinics like hers. Too much time to fill, she says, too much repetitious drudgery to fill it with. You almost never see them in Rochambeau, where failure and discouragement are more submerged. There, working women are commonplace, and many of those who stay home by choice have time for tennis and facials and lunches with friends. In Rochambeau, says Jane, there is too much space between the houses for people to know the kind of unhappiness often experienced inside.

Anyway, by two-thirty weekday afternoons, almost by prearranged signal, the old folks vanish, piling into their big old Buicks and sedans and lumbering tentatively towards the highway. They are undoubtedly well aware that the after-school wave is about to wash over them.

So is the rest of the mall, which seems to palpably tense in the afternoon. Stores that don't sell sneakers or tapes hate the kids, seeing them as intrusive, noisy, and without commercial reward. Proprietors are always fussing to mall security to keep the kids moving, to quiet them down, to remove the benches. But the protests are pro forma, and, I think, mostly unfair. Kids buy a lot of tapes, sneakers, jewelry, T-shirts, stone-washed denims, burgers, pizzas, and shakes, and they have a perfect legal right to be there.

I kind of like having them around, actually. They're colorful, high-spirited, and, except for an occasional jostling match, generally law-abiding. I wondered if Ben and Emily would ever hang out in a mall. Would I care? Was it harmful? I suspected that, if they did, they'd choose Mountain Lakes, where the more affluent Rochambeau kids tended to congregate.

Adult males are almost never in evidence in the daytime. They appear around 7 P.M., after dinner, tired from work, sullenly pushing strollers and glowering at wives who want to buy things and kids who won't be still. I greatly prefer the teenagers.

I popped into Lightning Burger to say hello to Luis, who is the smartest investigative strategist I know. He must be in his sixties now, but he's where I head when I feel confused or overwhelmed or just want to bounce things off somebody smart. He has a good trial lawyer's ability to slice through the lard and get to what matters. It's a delicious irony of my current life that the two people I rely on the most heavily are the owner of a garden center and a fast-food manager.

Luis was having a cup of coffee in the westernmost window of Lightning Burger, the one that caught the afternoon sun, and going over the lunch hour receipts. I'd rather avoid bright sunshine, especially the kind that gets superheated by pouring through plate glass like a magnifying lens, but Luis can never get enough of it, especially in the winters. This is his verandah.

Though he lives in Union City, a Cuban enclave near the Lincoln Tunnel, he's always at Lightning Burger from 5 A.M., when he turns on the grill, until at least eleven when he closes. I know he has three sons, but he never refers to them or brings them to the restaurant. He has declined several invitations to come to dinner at my house, and I sense—though he has never quite said—that he feels uncomfortable about it. It seems to me that this gracious, educated, polished man has dealt with the loss of his membership in the upper middle class by avoiding replications of it.

Luis is a fatalist. I'm no world traveler, but that seems to me not an American trait, to accept what is. Americans seem continuously astonished by the world's ups and downs. In suburbia, perhaps more than anywhere else, the good life is dangled in front of you like a big sweet bunch of grapes on a hot summer's day. To accept the premise that it's beyond you for good is almost inconceivable. Luis suggests, in his conversation, in his gallant demeanor, in his wise, resigned face, that he understands the cards life can deal, the kind he's been dealt.

"Kit, this is a wonderful surprise. I haven't seen you in

weeks—much too long. But it's a blessing that you stopped by today, so I mustn't reproach you." He motioned to one of the pouty teenagers behind the counter, and a cup of coffee, two packets of sugar, and two plastic creamers quickly appeared at my elbow, along with a wooden stirrer. Lightning Burger might be a dump, but Luis always acts as if it's the Plaza.

He scanned my face curiously, too polite to ask outright what I was doing there. When I stop in, it's usually for lunch —we eat together once a week or so—or for coffee in the morning. My coming by in the afternoon usually means a problem.

Luis pulled a Camel out of the pack on the table. He always asks me if I mind. I always say no. He tilted his head back. Luis was making the transition from handsome to distinguished, his full head of black hair graying around the fringes, his body still lean and unstooped. Even in his manager's polyester jacket, I could always picture him in front of a courtroom, captivating a jury, dominating the room. That he never would again seemed inexpressibly sad.

He smoked in the old-fashioned way, drawing the smoke deeply into his lungs, and exhaling deliberately. "Trouble?" he asked quietly. He took in the bruise developing below my ear, too polite to ask where it came from.

"No, not yet," I said, "unless you count the fact that I'm suddenly getting drawn into a serial-killer case and feel like I'm so far over my head I can't even see the surface." I explained the sequence of events, which he had obviously been following in the news, and my own increasingly problematic involvement. "Luis, this is deep. A lot deeper than alimony deadbeats."

He chuckled. "I'll never get used to how blunt you Americans are. It's one reason you get so much work done; you don't beat around the bush. In Havana, we would have had three lunches and two long walks before you would have told me what was bothering you, and even then you would have referred to it indirectly."

He sat up, stubbed his cigarette out, lit another, and was suddenly all business. "Kit," he said. "This is horrible, horrible. The violence in this country is unspeakable. I have no love for Fidel, as you well know, but to kill children like this? To attack an old woman with a knife? This would never happen in Cuba." His look was briefly one of longing. I suspected that he often missed Havana, though that wasn't something he would acknowledge.

"But Kit, this is a major breakthrough for you, this case. I take no pleasure in its happening, but it's important. I remember my first big criminal case—a banker arrested for murdering his wife and her lover. He was acquitted. It made my career. In our work—" he smiled, suddenly self-conscious, "in yours, other people's tragedies are your opportunity. You mustn't be frightened. You are smart, resourceful, and you have nothing to lose. Tell me everything."

I did. His eyes glistened. He nodded once or twice, then asked for details, most of which I didn't have.

"I've tried Carol Lombardi's girlfriend," I said. "But the father—an unpleasant Wall Street type—made me unwelcome, to say the least. He thinks I'm a thief. He's a forceful man. Angry, scary in a way. I've got to approach her directly. And I've already encountered an angry young high school student and jilted lover of Carol's—as you can see," I said, gesturing towards my bruise. "For all this running around and getting worked over, the only person who has actually had the decency to talk to me is the chief of police."

Luis nodded, smiling sympathetically.

"We must know whether the second dead girl was connected in any way with the young man who killed himself and
his girlfriend. That is crucial, don't you agree?" I had gotten
that far by myself, but it was reassuring to talk it through with
Luis.

"Yeah, that is crucial," I said. "But I think I'll try old Blackhead Gowdy first. At least I don't have to worry about his
father."

Luis and I chatted about a couple of cases he remembered, both of them murders, and as usually happened, I felt
easier.

"Come and visit whenever you need to, will you?" he
said. "Like most amateurs, you tend to overrate the police.
Trust yourself. See where your instincts take you. You're always telling me this is what you want to do with your life, so
do it." He put his hand on my arm. "Kit, this is an opportunity
that may never come again. This isn't a case where a drug
addict shot someone down in the street; this is a thinking
man's case. There is an intelligence at work here, however
twisted, and it will take an intelligence to solve it."

"However twisted." I laughed.

Luis nodded. "However twisted."

Inspired, it took me only five minutes of phoning nursing
homes to locate Blackhead Gowdy, for twelve years a resident
of the Rochambeau Homes Nursing Center. The attendant
there seemed shocked that anybody would be calling Gowdy
and said he couldn't care less if I came to visit or not. "He's of
drinking age," he chuckled. "He can see who he wants."

I drove over, stopping by to pick up Emily and drive her
to her best friend Molly's house. Normally, she could have
ridden her bike the three blocks, but we were succumbing to
the hysteria a bit ourselves. For the next few weeks, the rule

was, she couldn't be anywhere or go anywhere except under adult supervision.

Without anyone having to communicate it, Rochambeau had adopted new rules. Before the killings, kids came and went and adults entered the equation only if somebody wanted to stay for dinner or beyond to watch "The Simpsons." Now, there was a new etiquette. I waited until Cindy— Molly's mom—came to the front door and waved before I pulled away. "Dad, jeez," was Em's disgusted observation when she climbed out of the Volvo. Giving up hard-won independence was bitter stuff.

Rochambeau Homes was a mile from my house. Despite the town's obsessive zoning, its old Victorian mansions off Main Street, built by the merchants who'd ruled the town for generations, had all been occupied by law firms, doctors' offices, and nursing homes. These all had misleadingly elegant names—Rochambeau Plaza, Rochambeau Woods, the Inn at Rochambeau—on discreet wooden signs out front. I never saw anybody, old or otherwise, on their porches or front lawns. They sat quietly like huge docked ships, disconnected from the life and commerce of the town.

The outside of the Rochambeau Homes was carefully maintained, the yellow clapboard fresh and clean looking, the gingerbread trim perfect. The remaining sprinkles of snow contributed to the Currier & Ives feel.

There was no bell, just a tiny sign on the black wooden door that said "Please Knock and Come In." I got the creeps two feet inside. The inside hallway was an abrupt change, dimly lit with exposed fluorescent bulbs, the floor lined with cracked tiles. A row of motel-style chairs had stains all over their fabric. There was no one in sight, but I could hear some faraway-sounding noises: a groan, a chair or walker being scraped across the floor, some faint conversation. The smell, rich and unpleasant, was hard to identify—part disinfectant, part musty overheated air, medicine, aging flesh.

I had switched to my more formal investigative attire— losing the baggy sweater and flannel shirt in favor of a blue oxford cloth shirt, actually adding a jacket and tie. I keep one of each in my office. I had put my suits away for three years, then taken them out and donated them to a homeless shelter. I never wanted to be in a position again where I might be tempted to wear them.

A tired-looking woman stuffed a little too tightly into a white uniform, midforties, I guessed, had apparently heard my knock and entered the hallway, looking both surprised and curious. She stubbed out a cigarette in the ashtray stand by the door, nodded coldly, and waited. "I'm Jeanette Evans. What are you selling?"

"I called," I said, handing her my card. "I'm here to see Blackhead Gowdy."

"About?"

"Private," I said, surprised that she had even asked. "He's allowed to have conversations with people, I presume."

"Well, you're not family." She didn't look at my card. "He doesn't have any family living. His fees here were paid in advance—" She stopped and glanced at the card. "I don't guess there's any harm. But you know Mr. Gowdy's well into his eighties. He's a little touchy at times, if you know what I mean. I wouldn't expect much in the way of conversation. He hasn't had many visitors in the nine years I've been working here—just a few, no family. And we'll have to bring him down. People upstairs get upset at strangers."

"Or," I said, "do visitors get upset at what they see upstairs?" The Rochambeau Homes, a place I didn't even know existed despite having driven past it a thousand times, was making me edgy.

I expected her to get huffy, but she softened. "Mr. Deleeuw—am I pronouncing it right? I sort of wonder whether I ought to call the owner. I mean, a private investigator and all. Look, I'm sure you're thinking this place is a dump, but we try to do our best, I mean, if you're from his estate or something. We're all legal, inspected twice a year. We do more than we're required to, which isn't that common, I can tell you, because I've worked in a lot of homes. So we're not afraid of visitors. Maybe embarrassed sometimes, but not afraid. I just don't want to cause the old guy any harm. He's feisty, that one. And he's been extremely agitated lately, and none of us can figure out why. Joey DiNardo, that's the young man who takes care of him, is worried about him. Joey is very protective of Mr. Gowdy. I just want to make sure you're not trying to sell him anything."

I regretted my tough-guy outburst. What did I expect a nursing home to be like, anyway? I didn't exactly spend my weekends volunteering to keep the people inside them company. I explained that I just wanted to know about a dead relative of Mr. Gowdy's, that I would be gone in fifteen minutes, that I wasn't the least bit interested in Rochambeau Homes, and that I hoped we didn't make this a long drawn-out confrontation as I was busy and she was busy and weren't we both anxious to get back to our work.

"Honest, Ms. Evans, there's no hidden agenda. Please bring Mr. Gowdy down and I'll get out of here." She insisted on making her telephone call (so much for my persuasive powers), but the owner apparently didn't care any more than the man I'd talked with on the phone had. Fifteen minutes later, I heard an elevator open down the hall and in came

Blackhead Gowdy, slouched in an aluminum wheelchair pushed by an orderly. I noticed a few cut white hairs on his shoulder. Perhaps he'd been touched up for our visit.

The young orderly pushing him had his name—"Joey"— sewn onto his white jacket. He hovered, giving me a pretty solid once-over before he seemed ready to leave. "Not too long, okay? He can walk, but he's tired now, so I put him in the chair. And Mr. Gowdy, I'll be right in the next room. You got a problem, I'm right there."

Gowdy nodded, I thought almost affectionately. Joey's concern seemed genuine. Maybe I was too hard on the place.

Gowdy was dressed in a frayed black cardigan sweater, a blue shirt, and wrinkled brown slacks. His frame was emaciated, but he still had a forelock of thin white hair drooping across his forehead. He had several fresh scratches across his hands and one alongside his chin—probably from his overgrown fingernails, I thought. His legs were splayed, as if he couldn't hold his knees together. My first thought was that he was only a few years older than Benchley, but in comparison to my friend he looked ancient and frail.

His eyes, though, were quite alert—piercing, in fact. He was taking me in. "Mr. Gowdy," I said, leaning forward. "My name is Kit. I'm a private detective."

His eyes held mine. I thought he understood. "Did Carrolton send you?"

"What—you mean Benchley? No. He didn't send me. Why would he?"

"*Benchley's* sent people before," he jeered. "To try and get me to take things from him. So he won't feel so guilty for living on land I might be living on, so he won't feel bad because his family destroyed mine. If you came from him, you can just get out." His voice was rising, and I saw Joey pop his head into the room, then withdraw it.

"Mr. Gowdy, I do know Benchley, but I promise you he didn't send me. Do you read the paper? Do you know what's going on in town these days?"

He opened then closed his mouth, looking almost frightened.

"I wanted to know about Nathaniel, if anybody in town has been asking about him, or if people know what he was accused of—"

I froze at the shout that came out of his mouth. It was an animal cry, part fury and part pain. "I've tried to get people to pay attention to Nathaniel and what happened to him—to us —my whole life and nobody gave a damn. Nobody gives a damn! Nathaniel was innocent. There was proof and nobody wanted to hear it, not when he was on trial, not later, not ever. Now you're all coming around."

"Who's coming around?"

"It's none of your damned business!" he shouted. "Who comes here is none of your damned business. You don't want to help Nathaniel. Why would you? You're working for Benchley, aren't you? I don't want to talk to you anymore!"

He raged for me to get out. His voice became a howl, a shocking anomaly in a matchstick body. It brought Joey and Ms. Evans on the run. Nobody had to nudge me out the door; I was happy to go. Joey stayed behind to quiet Blackhead.

"Well, I tried to warn you." Back in the hallway, Ms. Evans smiled and shook her head. "He's been awfully touchy this last day or so."

"Ms. Evans, Mr. Gowdy mentioned someone else coming to see him. Has he had another visitor?"

She frowned. Behind us, Blackhead was still yowling in fury. "Not on my shift. No one mentioned it to me. I told you he doesn't get many. And I don't think I'd be able to give you that information anyway. Miss Whitmore, the manager, she keeps the log book of visitors locked up. She's not here now, but you could call her later. I'm sorry."

I asked if I could question Joey, but she shook her head firmly and guided me out the door. Two more orderlies appeared behind her, watching me suspiciously.

I gave everybody in sight my card as I backed out into the bitter cold, then fled. Some private eye. Since I'd been on the case, the police chief had told me to butt out, a martinet father had slammed a door in my face, a punk kid had knocked me out, and I had been run off by a crotchety old man. Not a glorious start.

The street seemed bleak and depressing. Rochambeau had always seemed such a bright place to me, especially when I commuted to the city. Whenever I stepped off the train, I had relished the station wagons pulling up to pick up the frazzled daddies, mothers behind the wheel, the kids squealing, sometimes jumping into their fathers' arms. On sunny days, the sidewalks filled with children in strollers, on roller skates, on bikes or skateboards. That felt like some other place this afternoon.

I steered the Volvo toward Judy Cole's neighborhood. She, not to mention her father, would undoubtedly be as welcoming as Blackhead Gowdy had been. His enraged face and howl would stick with me awhile. Whatever he was, he was no frail old man. His body might be failing, but his anger and hate burned brightly.

14

The details of Lisa Caltari's life and death dribbled out slowly. She was an eighteen-year-old who had dropped out of high school in Elizabeth and had last been seen at midnight at the end of her shift at a diner on Route 3. Her father was dead, her mother a nurse's aide in Bergen County. She had no known boyfriend, and if she had any friends, reporters hadn't located them. The only comments were the charitable platitudes about her quiet harmlessness offered by neighbors.

She wasn't beloved by her former classmates, adored by her teachers, admired by her colleagues. There wasn't much on which to keep hanging stories about her, other than the way in which she died.

She was a working-class North Jersey kid, bound for secretarial school if lucky, Hardee's if not. There was absolutely nothing to tie her to Rochambeau. In fact even some of the town's more well-meaning citizenry would see her as uninteresting, different from them or their children. Since Elizabeth was more than twenty miles away, police theorized that someone had taken Lisa Caltari to the Brown estate after work for the express purpose of strangling her.

I didn't buy it. I doubted that Leeming really did either. It was possible that your random psychopath got excited reading the paper or watching TV and decided to grab a young girl, bring her to Rochambeau, and kill her, and that the same or a different psychopath tried to stab Ida Flowers. But I thought the odds slender.

Her death made me even more certain that Ken Dale had been murdered. I knew I wasn't really being objective. I had lots of good reasons to be a skeptic: If the cops were smart, what future did I have? And if there were a massive conspiracy, then my client was right and I had a case to break open.

But couldn't the same person or persons who killed Lisa Caltari have killed Carol Lombardi and Ken Dale? Wasn't it as reasonable to assume that as it was to assume random wackos being turned on by the first killings and flocking to Rochambeau to stab and murder its inhabitants? Not to the chief.

"As horrible as this is," the chief had announced at a local press conference, "I do not believe Rochambeau or its residents are targets of a serial killer. We believe the murder-suicide to be an isolated incident. We feel the attack on Ida Flowers was brought about by the publicity that resulted from the first incident, that some twisted individual wanted to see his or her crime on television. We feel that whatever happened to Lisa Caltari was initiated in Elizabeth, not in Rochambeau, and that the perpetrator was drawn to the Brown estate by the media attention. We urge restraint on the part of the media. The more coverage there is, the more likely this is to happen again. There are unfortunately a lot of disturbed people out there. But Rochambeau is not under siege; we will not tolerate this kind of violence, whatever the source or the cause."

The *Rochambeau Times* carried an equally telling interview with the head of the town Board of Realtors, who declared that most firms had pulled their listings off the market. Real estate transactions, he said, were at a "standstill," and some purchasers had already reneged on signed or verbal agreements. Prospective buyers were postponing their moves to Rochambeau or looking elsewhere; residents who wanted to move were hunkering down. Chief Leeming had good reason to hope there wasn't some determined psychotic stalking the town.

In addition to various and sundry corporate and financial bigwigs, Rochambeau had one U.S. senator, a congresswoman, and two members of the governor's cabinet living within its atmospheric boundaries. So Leeming announced that the FBI had joined the case, since the Caltari girl might have been kidnapped. He also took advantage of the increased police presence to slip into his statement the fact that the town's previously rising burglary rate had plunged by sixty percent. The *Times* had devoted almost as much space to the plummeting burglary rate as it had to Lisa Caltari's murder. I figured that burglars, like the rest of us, were scared to drive around.

Local principals who had initially scheduled school assemblies on dealing with fear and loss had begun issuing warnings about how students should deal with the media. The schools were suggesting the same thing we had instructed Emily and Ben: no interviews.

But town teenagers were having a blast, spinning cock-and-bull stories to reporters about fear and paranoia in the burbs. One high school senior told a story that had aired the evening before about a dozen children who gathered nightly in a church basement to pray for their lives. The mayor went berserk, first trying to find out where the church was, then unsuccessfully demanding a retraction from the TV reporter, who insisted he would stand behind his "sources." This touched off a spirited competition among the town's kids to see who could mislead the media in the most imaginative way. By week's end, the winner was a high school senior who got a New York tabloid to go for a Satanic cult among the town's wealthy kids that met weekly to sacrifice a family pet.

I had stopped by the public library to check the high school yearbook again to see if there was any other information on the Cole kid that I ought to know before I tried again to talk with her. Judy had edited the high school literary magazine, it turned out, was a runner who had finished second in the Rochambeau ten-mile Cerebral Palsy run, and had been voted most mature. I would be happy if Em's yearbook read the same way in nine or ten years.

I paused for quite a while over a photograph of Cole sitting next to Carol Lombardi, fellow members of the school's debating team. She and Carol were both beautiful kids. The death of a kid seems to me to be Nature's most unnatural act.

I pulled the car over in front of the house, wondering what I ought to say if I ran into Daddy Cole again. He would call the cops at the sight of me, I was sure. Maybe he and Jamie Harte had become pals and would work me over together. I knew I needed to talk with Judy Cole privately—no high school kid was going to spill secrets in front of her father, especially not secrets about her best friend. Then again, how would I feel if I came home from work one day to learn Emmy had had a tête-à-tête with a private detective without my permission? But Judy was a high school senior, I reminded myself, and an adult.

When I looked at the rearview mirror—crucial habit in suburbia, where kids on mountain bikes have a habit of slamming into car doors as they open—I was surprised to see her coming up behind me. She was running, even in the cold, in navy sweats with a red bandana. The yearbook picture had not quite done her justice. She was very pretty—youthful, vigorous, expressive. Impulsively, I stepped out of the Volvo and held up my investigator's shield. It was the only really coplike gesture in my pathetic repertoire of private-eye techniques. I had learned in the army, though, that people want to see some ID. They don't read it, or particularly care what's on it, but they expect it. Judy stopped and glanced at my license and picture, clouds of breath puffing rhythmically from her mouth.

She looked puzzled, but not frightened. I was expecting a kid, but she certainly didn't look like one, more like a graduate student I might have tried to pick up when I was in college. Maybe I had misconceptions about eighteen-year-olds.

"Judy? Kit Deleeuw. I'm a private investigator, as you can see from my ID. Sam Mellman and some of his friends have hired me to look—"

"I know," she said, regaining some of her breath. "They want you to prove Ken didn't kill Carol." She gave no indication of how she felt about this, though I'd half expected fury at the suggestion that her best friend's killer might be innocent. "I'll be happy to talk with you. Do you want to go inside?"

I hesitated. That didn't seem a good idea, being in a young girl's house alone. And if her father was there or came home, I'd have to fight my way out.

She seemed to read my mind. "My father's working this afternoon. You probably also know my mother is dead. I'm sorry about Father," she added. "He's very quick to make judgments and slow to listen to anything that would change them. It's been tough for him since Mom died. It's just not the life he pictured, I don't think, being alone with a child so much."

And what, I wondered, would it have been like for her, being alone with an angry, detached man who had sole responsibility for a child?

"Dad doesn't want me talking with you. But I trust Sam. He told me he hired you and that you were okay, and that's good enough for me. I loved Carol, she was my closest friend. She practically lived over here. She was one of the few people Father could stand to have in the house. He even taught her tennis at the club. That's one of the reasons, I think, that he can't abide the thought of you. He thinks you'll try to clear Ken's name, get him off the hook. But I'm guessing here, because he doesn't talk about those things."

She spoke about him matter-of-factly, simply describing him. There was no judgment or complaint in her voice.

"But if there's any evidence that Ken was innocent, well, I don't want to stand in the way of proving it," she added, meeting my eyes. "Is there?"

"I don't know yet. But I very much appreciate your trust. As I'm sure you know, in some circles I'm considered a criminal who narrowly escaped his just punishment."

"Won't you come in?" she asked. "Father won't be home for hours."

"I think we'll both be more comfortable if we talk out here. I mean, your father hasn't invited me into your house. He would love to call the U.S. Attorney and tell him I trespassed in his home with his teenage daughter. Let's sit in the car. I'll pop on the heater. It's old, and smells of dogs and kids, but it's a fitting portable office."

Judy sat in the front seat fingering Em's favorite Cabbage Patch Kid, Gandalf, named after the wizard in *The Hobbit*. "I had a dozen of these," she said, almost sadly. "I guess I still do, upstairs somewhere. How old's your daughter?"

"Emily's nine. Quite a piece of work. She's at her pal's now."

"Her best friend?"

"Yup. Molly. They're inseparable, joined at the hip. Her soulmate."

She nodded. "Yeah, I know. Carol was that for me, my soulmate, since fifth grade. I have this feeling I'll never have another one like her. I mean, we went on vacations together, whispered about boys together. I won't be staying in the same place that long again, I don't think, to make those kinds of connections. In the fall, I'm going to Vassar. Leaving without Carol . . . she was going to school in upstate New York too. I don't know."

She shook her head and changed the subject. "Excuse me, Mr. Deleeuw. I don't mean to be inquisitive, but you don't seem much like Tom Selleck. You don't strike me as a private detective, not the kind I've read about or seen in the movies. I realize those are probably foolish stereotypes."

"I don't know many private detectives, myself," I said. "My career fell apart, and the only other thing I'd ever done was criminal work for the army, so I've been doing this for a few years."

"Do you like the work?" She cradled Gandalf, smiling down at the battered doll.

"Yeah. Usually. I get to take care of my kids, who I never saw before. I get to be my own boss. I love the life this work lets me have. Investigating dead kids isn't fun, though. It's frightening as a parent, I guess. And as a detective who hasn't done much of this kind of work, it's just depressing."

I blinked. Why was I pouring my heart out to an eighteen-year-old kid I'd come to pump for girlish secrets about Carol Lombardi? This girl ought to be shattered, and here she was gracefully laying me open. I guess I'd expected more of a kid and less of a woman. I heard myself saying:

"It must have been rough, your living here with your father. I'm sure he's handled a lot. I don't mean to be—"

"Oh, it's all right. It has been difficult. It's been lonely— for both of us. He tries very hard, he truly does, but it's really been more like two people with separate lives sharing the same house than it has been like a family. I think we're both relieved I'll be going off to school. Having Carol around made it so much easier for both of us, so much more—" She choked. I waited. "It was tough on Dad as well. He really extended himself to make her comfortable. In some ways, he was closer to Carol than to me." She shook her head. "He growls like a bear, but he's warmer than he lets on."

I couldn't swear I would have been a whole lot better in the same circumstances, if I'd had to watch Jane die and then raise the kids by myself. I told her as much. She said nothing, merely smoothed Gandalf's hair with her fingertip.

"Excuse my blather," I said. "I'm straying off the mark. I was hoping to ask you some questions about Carol. I need to know about her relationships, about this mysterious other man. Forgive me—I think I'll need to ask you some blunt questions. Could the other guy possibly have been Jamie Harte?"

Judy threw her head back and laughed, although more bitterly than humorously. "No. Jamie is a bully, cruel and offensive, not the sort of person Carol could have loved. She didn't take him as seriously as everybody else did. When he got crazy, she'd just say, 'C'mon, Jamie, chill,' and he would. Nobody else could say that to him, but she could. But after the fight he had with Ken—she had to keep away from him, for Ken's sake if for nothing else. Jamie has the capacity to really hurt someone." We both took in the implications of that. "But not to kill. Jamie's a bully, not a murderer, and Carol is the last person he would ever have hurt."

"Well," I said, "I know he can hurt people." I fingered the purpling bruise below my ear.

"Did Jamie do that to you?"

I shrugged. "Don't know for sure. Somebody slugged me while I was leaving a gym where Jamie was working out."

She shook her head. "For whatever it's worth," she said, "I don't think Jamie would have had any hesitation about punching you out face-to-face. He usually doesn't need to sneak up on people." The thought gave me the creeps. It's a lot more comfortable to know who whacked you than to wonder.

"Do *you* hate Jamie?"

"No," she said. "He never bothered me. But I sure hate what I see him doing to people. Groping girls. Beating up boys. Stealing. Cheating. He's in a perpetual rage that he's stuck in a culture he can't keep up with, understand, or be a part of. It's a tough spot for him. But he can be incredibly hateful."

"Then why are you so sure he couldn't kill somebody?"

"Well, I'm not a shrink, Mr. Deleeuw. But Jamie plays the role expected of him, it seems to me. I know from his sister that he's really devoted to her and his little brother. His anger is right up front; he doesn't hide anything. Could he damage or even kill somebody like Ken Dale—somebody who had everything he wanted, including Carol—in a fight? Maybe. Could he strangle Carol and Ken in the middle of the night up on a mountain? I don't know. I just don't see it."

But then, I thought, what experience would you have with murder?

"Any truth to the rumors Carol and Jamie dated?"

That one seemed to throw her a bit. She shook her head. "I . . . I think they may have gone out one time. Carol sort of alluded to a crazy night with Jamie one time when she and Ken had split up for a couple of weeks. I'd forgotten about that. I don't think it was any big deal." There was little point now in protecting Carol, I thought. She'd have to be protecting Jamie. She would have known that knowledge might have made him a suspect if the police decided the deaths were a double homicide.

Judy looked at her watch. "I've got to go, Mr. Deleeuw. I've got to get to my job. I'm working part-time at Sally's Boutique down on Walnut. And I've got to look just so, or Sally has a fit."

She smiled indulgently and tossed her head back, flipping the dark brown hair off her pretty face. Her teeth were perfect—white and straight. Her dark blue eyes were wise, I guess that's the best way to describe them, penetrating and thoughtful. I felt a stirring I didn't recognize at first as sexual, then a sharp stab of embarrassment, as if I'd been caught looking through a bedroom window.

"Tonight," she said, "my father will be in the city quite late. Let's meet at Gennaro's, on Route Forty-six—you know where it is?" I said yes, and offered to drive.

"Why, Mr. Deleeuw, I have a car and a license to drive it. I even lock the front door all by myself. See you at eight."

She hopped out, closed the door, and continued on her run, waving with one hand as she rounded the corner. Her self-possession and confidence were as startling as those knockout good looks. Watch it, I thought. Fantasizing about a teenager is inappropriate for a man driving a decaying Volvo with 100,000 miles on the odometer and a Cabbage Patch doll in the front seat. But I have to confess, I was looking forward to seeing her again.

15

Sherry Peterson called her mother back into her bedroom twice to make sure the closet door was tightly shut so that the witch who lived inside couldn't get out.

"Don't worry, honey," her mother cooed reassuringly and patiently, as she had every night for nearly a week. "Seven-year-olds often go through periods where their rooms seem scary. I've turned the night-light on. I'll be right downstairs. Daddy is nearby in his study, and Midnight is guarding you in the hall."

At the mention of his name, the German shepherd in the hall thumped his tail against the floor.

Sometimes Sherry feared the space beneath the bed and the floor, sometimes the narrow black area between the headboard and the wall. Her father laughed whenever she yelled for help, pretending to look all around the room. But she knew he didn't really believe there was anything there.

It was the closet that caused her the most trouble. There always seemed to be something inside it. Her mother made a big deal out of being sure that her window, which looked out over the backyard, was closed, but Sherry was never frightened about the window. Her room was on the second floor and nothing could get up there.

It was the witch in the closet, the one who slept all day but strained to get out at night, that's what kept her up. One night, she might forget to remind her parents to snap the door closed and the witch, who was furious at being locked up, would come storming out while she was asleep, chop her up with an ax, and kill her big brother Bobby and her parents. The witch had the power to turn Midnight, who frightened people when he wanted to, into anything she wanted. That was why Sherry couldn't quite relax, no matter what Mommy or Daddy said. They made it all seem like a joke—her mother was smiling as she turned off the light and went downstairs—and one day Sherry would forget, and that would be the end of her.

Still, she was surprised at the noise outside her window. She looked right away at the closet, but she could see that the door was closed. Maybe the witch was pounding to get out. Sherry froze, terrified that if she made a sound the witch would know she was there. She couldn't speak or call for help. If they didn't hear her right away—the TV was on downstairs—it would be too late.

When Sherry saw the dark shape outside the window she was confused. She couldn't make it out. She did not understand why she couldn't move or scream when the glass shattered not five feet from her head.

Frank Upsall had lived on Pine Lane for twenty-three years and had never, in all that time, heard a single disturbing sound from the Petersons or from their predecessors in the big old Georgian house. The back of the Petersons' house was more than a hundred yards from the Upsalls'; it would have taken a pretty loud noise to carry that distance.

So Upsall had a hard time crediting the piercing scream that cut through the bare maples. Two weeks earlier, he might have waited to see if it were a teenage prank or some other kind of mischief. He might even have gone outside in his robe with a flashlight to check for himself. Rochambeau, at least until lately, was the kind of town where you felt foolish calling the police.

He'd done it only twice in all these years—once when a young guy had cracked up his sports car and wrapped himself around a tree out front, and a second time when the Upsalls' corgi was missing and he called to inquire whether it might have been stolen. The sergeant who answered had laughed. "Sir, we haven't had any reports of stolen dogs lately. Just leave some cooked meat out back. He'll show up." The sergeant's snotty attitude had nettled Upsall, but damned if he hadn't put the meat out and damned if Charles hadn't returned.

But that might as well have been in another life, Upsall thought, throwing open the window with one hand and reaching for the phone with the other. The screams had resumed, even more intensely. Upsall thought he heard something rustle in the trees and peered out, but it was too dark to see. He felt a distinctly unfamiliar flutter in his chest. He had never been frightened in his home.

But sadly, Rochambeau was just another dark corner of the world now. He and Marge had been about to put their house on the market in preparation for the long-planned move to Boca, but he'd called the realtor just that morning and told her to wait. Rochambeau was a tougher housing market than the South Bronx at the moment.

"Marge, wake up! You hear that? It sounds like a child. Like a girl! I'm calling the police. You can bet they won't laugh at me this time!"

Pine Lane is right near Benchley's house, and I saw the stream of flashing blue lights pouring into Pine Lane and pulled in behind them. When I jumped out of the Volvo, I could hear what sounded like a child screaming. The scream stopped abruptly, or perhaps it was drowned out by the helicopter that swooped suddenly over one house, a piercing beam of white light cutting across the roof and back. A second helicopter appeared almost immediately behind it, the two shafts of light playing over the street, the yards, and the narrow park half a block away. I began walking towards the house.

The street instantly filled with sirens that bounced eerily off bedroom windows and empty porches. Brakes squealed; car doors slammed; radios squawked; gun belts were unsnapped; flashlights slashed back and forth across the sidewalks and backyards. Dogs yelped all up and down the street as poodles, retrievers, and yippy lap dogs found police shepherds and bloodhounds sniffing around their territory. Neighbors were peeking from their windows, and a few threw on parkas and boots and ventured out, to be waved back by rifle-toting police pouring into the neighborhood. One of the neighbors, a man, swore in wonder that the first squad cars were in the street less than thirty seconds after he called. Could this be the same town that got excited less than a week ago at the sound of a fire engine?

Chief Leeming was standing in front of the house I learned was the Petersons'. I went over and stood nearby— visible enough for him to throw me out if he wished, but far enough away not to tempt him. I didn't know the lady's name at the moment, but I watched a woman bully her way with a tray of cookies past three state troopers and two county sheriff's deputies and up to Chief Leeming, who stood with a walkie-talkie to one ear. Stan Peterson stood quietly next to him.

"Chief, it's Marge Upsall; I live just across the way. I'm here to see if I can be of any help and I certainly won't let these big men and their rifles stop me." Troopers carrying automatic rifles in Rochambeau; I'm sure Mrs. Upsall never thought she would see it. "Stan, what the dickens is going on? Is everyone all right?"

Peterson looked at Leeming, who shrugged and nodded.

"Thank you, Marge. It's good of you to come over. Sherry could probably use a cookie about now. Dear God, Marge, somebody tried to break into her room. They took our ladder from the garage—Chief says they wrapped rags around the ends to muffle the noise—smashed the window and stuck a knife through it, Sherry says. She's all right, but we couldn't stop her screaming. God, when we heard that screaming, we were sure she was . . . Whatever it was scared her half to death, as you could imagine. Then, it seemed as if the whole U.S. Army came storming in, choppers, men with dogs and rifles. Some of them came right through the windows . . ."

Marge's cookies were sliding off the tray and onto the ground.

"Why, I can't believe it. Did he hurt her?"

"No, he broke the window, and then she said he stuck a knife in. She was too frightened to scream at first. Then, I don't know whether she screamed and the dog came running, or whether the dog got there first. But by the time we got to her room, there was nobody at the window, the dog was barking like crazy, and Sherry was hysterical. I can't believe somebody would do this. Could it have been a burglar?" Stan sounded almost hopeful. Three television vans careened down Pine Lane, screeching to a halt in front of the house. The police ushered Peterson inside, shooed Marge away. She looked glad to head for home.

I kept expecting the chief to give me the boot, but I would have sworn he was glad to see me. I moved closer.

"Shit, shit, shit," he was saying, staring numbly at the

teams of police officers fanning through the neighborhood backyards. "Deleeuw, I've survived twenty-three years of New York City's worst precincts—the South Bronx, Williamsburg, the East Village, I've seen everything. Bodies bombed, stabbed, crippled, machine-gunned, dismembered; newborns left in trash cans to die; corpses rotting in apartments for weeks while neighbors slept on the other side of the wall; homeless people set ablaze; fourteen-year-old boys with dead eyes who kill a cop as naturally as they take a leak. The rule is you take it for as long as you can, get your pension, and then leave for a quiet town where the good guys are still in charge."

"You catching a lot of stuff?" I asked quietly.

People thought he was running scared, he said, and they were right, though not in the way they thought. Hell, he could retire in a second. Rose was ready; they even had the condo in South Carolina all picked out. But he wouldn't end thirty years of police work a quitter, walking away from a town with this . . . this evil at large.

The same instinct that had kept him in the thankless toilet bowls of New York trying to hold the lid on for twenty-three years would keep him here—if the town didn't toss him first, which seemed increasingly likely. I peered around the corner at one of Leeming's officers, who was carrying a plastic bag containing something that looked like a foot-long piece of hemp. Leeming saw it and stepped in front of me to block my view. I didn't push it. It was miraculous he hadn't ousted me already.

The chief put his hand-held radio to his mouth and asked the helicopter to sweep the side of the hill with its spotlight. "Anything, anything that moves, I wanna know. Even if it looks like a deer." The pilot acknowledged the order.

"You expect to see people get killed *there*, Deleeuw. But this is the other side of the line, this is what they were all putting their lives on the line to protect. What kind of fucker could walk into the armed camp that Rochambeau has become, pull a ladder up to a kid's window, and poke in a knife? What kind of crazy motherfucker could do that, then slip away as if he lived in a mole tunnel?" He radioed dispatch to contact the Corps of Engineers and have them check for tunnels first thing in the morning, all around the Brown estate and in this backyard.

Then he seemed to snap back to reality, back to business and back to the pariah he was talking to.

"You still on this? You're a strange duck, Deleeuw. You can't possibly know what you're doing on a murder case, and the FBI swears you smell bad from Wall Street. But I have to be honest: The FBI don't know the difference between a serial killer and a mongoose. You obviously weren't frightened off by my speech the other day. But then, I didn't think you would be. Get lost."

"I'll only stay a second. I was driving by, on my way to meet somebody for dinner. I figured it might be connected."

Leeming gave me a long, hard look. "This turns it, Deleeuw. This sends it into a whole new stratosphere. The murder-suicide was bad. The old woman, bad. The kid from Elizabeth. But barging into a seven-year-old kid's bedroom — that's a blade right into the heart of a town like this. This place will detonate tomorrow."

The chief lit up a Marlboro and inhaled deeply, his weary face taking in the scene. "Look at me, I'm smoking again. Now, go away. You're okay by me, but you still have no business on this case. I have to direct my troops in the field and I'm still not going to tell you shit. Have a good dinner."

16

I had pulled away from the madhouse on Pine Lane, headed for Gennaro's, when I remembered with a sudden jolt that I'd nearly forgotten Emily. I'd told Jane that I'd bring her home from Molly's before I met Judy Cole for dinner, so that Jane wouldn't have to leave Ben alone in the house. We didn't like either of them to be unattended anymore.

I'd been responsible for most of the numbing amount of chauffeuring that goes into the lives of suburban children. Generally, I liked it. Every man carries a snapshot in his head of what a successful life should be, and despite all the change I'd been through, mine had always involved driving kids around in a station wagon.

Now and then you screw up, necessitating frantic phone calls. Another kid's parent usually steps into the breach to drive yours home or keep them until you connect, a narrowly defined fellowship that extends more readily to kids in distress than to adults. Still, the notion of your child standing on some soccer field watching all the other players leave is a breath-stopper. Despite the police armada circling Rochambeau, I headed to Molly's house going well above the speed limit.

Usually I swung into Molly's driveway and beeped, and Emmy would come bounding out. Tonight, I left the car's headlights on, turned off the engine, looked around before I opened the door, then locked it and went up to the front door.

"Yes?" came Cindy's voice anxiously through the thick wood.

"I'm here to pick Emmy up, Cindy," I said, slowly, so that she'd have time to recognize my voice. I saw the curtain on the living room window lift, and a few seconds later the bolts were pulled back and the door opened.

She was holding a horn alarm, a portable telephone, and a can of Mace. Normally I would have laughed out loud at such an arsenal, and it *would* have been laughable. Now it wasn't funny or even particularly inappropriate.

The fatigue and fear were visible in Cindy's face. Jane and I had evolved our own classification for people we meet in Rochambeau, especially the women, who tend to be more complicated.

There are the Untamed Women (I put Jane in this category), essentially undomesticated, whether they stay at home or not. They are good mothers and loving wives, but they have no innate interest in or aptitude for the chores that used to be such staples of women's lives. You never see potted mums by their front doors, and they seem incapable of contributing to bake sales properly or evaluating wallpaper patterns. There are things lying around their houses, their children have odd clothing combinations, they frequent the deli counters of the supermarket where instant meals can be bought, and they would no sooner give a dinner party than plunge into the Hudson for a dip. They recognize one another, exchanging deprecating but good-humored jokes about the quality of food and the lack of tidiness in their homes.

Then there are the Supermoms, who race their Volvos like stallions all day, securing the right dessert topping or birthday gift or end table. Their homes are always perfection, no matter who drops by or when. Their children tend to be equally well produced, every decision from piano teacher to school clothes advanced as carefully as any presidential campaign.

The saddest category, to my mind, are the Lost Women, who started out on fast career tracks, stepped off to have kids, and then somehow lost their ability to climb back on. They grow so enmeshed with their children and with their children's schools and social lives and problems that they can't seem to untangle themselves. Men in suburbia are berserk in many ways, but they don't seem to fall as often into this particular tarpit. The Lost Women seem just that; they can't find real satisfaction in the details of domestic life, but they can't get back to work, either.

They are so anxious about their parenting that they can't even get much pleasure out of their kids. They seem to live in near terror of what might happen if their offspring ever got out of sight. Jason isn't allowed to cross a street by himself, even at age eight, because there's too much traffic. Rebecca can't go to the candy store because you never know who's going to be hanging out there. Mark isn't allowed to see movies with any conflict in them, because they might be violent or he might pick up foul language. You don't need to be as well trained as Jane is to see what this fear is usually about: not about the kids' safety, but about letting them go, about not being needed or necessary. Jane puts it this way: In many ways, she says, the Lost Women are married to one or more of their kids, not to their husbands. I think that's right.

Cindy was one of these, obsessed over every detail of Molly and her four-year-old sister's existence. I could usually laugh about the endless discussions we'd all had about fourth-grade politics in Mott Elementary School, where Cindy had once hid in the coat closet for two hours, peering out to observe Molly's social skills. Jane has a tougher time with Rochambeau's neurotic side than I do because of her work. She can spot family dysfunction, rifts between couples, and parental overinvestment a mile away. She thought Cindy a tragic waste.

Now, the trauma enveloping the town had snapped Cindy out of her customary fussing with the minutiae of childhood and given her a license to obsess. I was relieved to rush away with a curious but relatively unafraid Em in tired tow.

"Em," I told her, "there's been an episode you will hear about."

"I know," she said, buckling her seat belt. "We heard Molly's mom on the phone. Somebody busted into some kid's window and waved a knife around. I'm going to sleep with the bedroom light on tonight. Will you be home?"

"I'm meeting someone for dinner, but Mommy will be there. I know it's frightening, but Mommy and I will keep you safe." Jane's standing instructions: If the kids became alarmed, reassure them that we were concerned about their safety and that they would be well cared for.

"I know." Em yawned. "It's the only good thing about having a detective for a father. Nobody will mess with a detective's kid. You got any leads yet?" She'd been reading a lot of Nancy Drew lately.

"I'm working on it," I said. She would feel a lot less safe if she knew the extent of my progress so far.

Judy Cole was waiting for me at a rear table in Gennaro's facing the door. In her white cotton blouse and navy pleated skirt, she looked like a young college student meeting Dad for dinner in the best restaurant near campus.

Gennaro's was in an old brick farmhouse tucked behind a discount computer warehouse about fifty yards back from the highway. For one reason or another, it had escaped the highway widening and mall bulldozers. Every now and then, you could spot these lonely and atmospheric reminders that real life had once existed before all this concrete.

"I have to get home pretty early," she said, smiling and picking up the menu. "I have a paper to write for my philosophy class that's due the day after tomorrow. Things are a bit crazed."

"How did you find this place?" I asked, mostly to make conversation. It looked like every little café in Greenwich Village thirty years ago—brick walls, checked tablecloths, even a candlestick in a Chianti bottle. Most of those were gone now as well.

"Carol and I started having dinner here once in a while, after we got our licenses and took to acting like grown-ups. Once we came here with Ken and a friend of mine. It seemed such a sophisticated thing to do, going out to dinner with your friends at a cozy Italian restaurant." She looked dreamy, distant, clouded over.

"Must have been nice," I said.

"I miss her. With a friend you can totally trust, you're not at the mercy of every bitchy, cruel girl. You don't have to always worry about who you're going to sit with at lunch or who you're going to hang out with. It helps you ride out difficult or lonely times because you know you have a constant, an anchor. She helped me through so much." Judy shook her head. "Do men have friends like that?"

What a question. Right between the eyes.

"I don't. I have some old friends, but I'm not in touch with them anymore."

"Since your Wall Street troubles?"

I opened my mouth in surprise. Nothing came out.

"I asked my dad about you. He gave me quite an earful. My dad believes that people don't get in trouble with the law unless they've done something wrong. He thinks you were involved in dirty stuff but that you got off because they didn't have enough evidence to convict you. Some FBI agent he talked to says you should've gone to jail and he still hopes to put you there."

"I had no idea I'd become so notorious. So why don't you believe that I'm a crook?"

"What makes you think I don't?"

"You're here."

She met my gaze for a long four or five seconds, then chuckled. This was not the giggling, awkward, petulant teen-aged girl other parents had been warning me to expect when Emmy got older. "I don't pretend to know what happened on Wall Street. People love to underestimate kids, but I know better than to take people's versions of things at face value. Things are always more complicated than they seem. But I really have no idea whether you're a crook or not. Sam Mellman says you're straight, and if there's any possible grounds for clearing Ken and proving that he didn't kill Carol, no one would be happier than I would."

"But you must be furious at him . . ." I offered.

"Look, Mr. Deleeuw, I don't know what happened up on that mountain, any more than I know what happened to you. I'll never think of Ken as a killer, even though I realize people can be driven to almost anything. I'd like to know for sure about Carol's death, one way or the other."

We ordered pasta and salads, and then she asked, "So is that why you don't have any friends left? Because of the Wall Street thing?"

No one had ever asked me about the Wall Street "thing," shockingly enough. People either didn't inquire about my previous work, or they steered clear of me altogether. Which generally was fine by me: I tried to avoid situations where I would run into people who knew me from the Other Side, as Jane called it. I can rationalize this any way I want, but the fact is, my instinctive response is embarrassment and shame, the first because I got into trouble, the latter because I'd put a lot of pressure on my wife because of the trouble. In the suburbs, without densely populated neighborhoods or big anonymous apartment houses to melt away into, failure feels so visible. Someone like me might as well walk around Rochambeau with a flashing neon sign that reads *I Screwed Up*.

"Mostly," I said, "friendship comes hard for men, even when things are normal. When your career blows up or you get into trouble, other men run for their lives. It's too scary for them, I guess. They look at me, especially in a town like this, and they see how fragile it all is. One day you're making six figures, which you need to live here, the next you're driving around checking insurance fraud in a car you should have traded in fifty thousand miles ago."

"The Volvo you were driving today? I love that car."

"Thank you," I said. "I'm attached to it myself."

"You haven't mentioned your wife—"

I felt a twinge of discomfort at talking about Jane. On some level, I realized, I didn't want to acknowledge her in front of Judy. Maybe I wanted the fantasy to last just a bit longer, my *intime* dinner with this lovely, bright young woman.

"Her name is Jane Leon. She's a psychiatric social worker, working as a counselor in Paterson. She went back to work when my career went up in flames and my phone got very quiet. Before all that, she was bored out of her skull, taking graduate courses and mucking around in the kids' business. Now she's busy and happy and we have more of a partnership than we ever did. The change is we're always broke now, always borrowing and scrambling. It's still a decent trade-off."

She took a sip from the glass of white wine she had ordered, so smoothly that the waiter hadn't given a thought to carding her. I swear I almost told her to drink milk or something healthier.

"I feel like I'm losing control of this conversation," I said. "I'm the detective, remember? Things have gotten even more bizarre since we talked this afternoon, as you've surely heard." She nodded. "And you've already told me you're on a tight schedule. So if you don't mind, I ought to get this information first, and if we have time after that you can continue pumping me about painful episodes from my past."

"I intend to," she said, unflustered. "I'm interested in hearing about it."

Judy was right—we do underestimate kids. I rarely think of teenagers as being empathetic, self-possessed, or perceptive. Why would I? In movies and on television, they're invariably portrayed as brainless twits. Astonishingly, this person was only nine years older than Emily.

"Tell me about Carol," I said in a businesslike tone, switching approaches the way the army had taught me. "Broad brush. Just a few words to describe her."

Judy stopped, as if she needed to step back and consider her friend from some distance. "Carol. She was a fantasy friend—cheerful, loyal, warm, generous. She wasn't brilliant in an academic sense, but she was quite smart about getting around the world. More adventurous than I am, always up for the scary ride, the horror movie, flirting back with strange boys. But it was illusory, you know, it was more in the nature of pretending than actually being irresponsible. She was conservative sexually. If she had a weakness, maybe she was too quick to romanticize men, especially mature men. I think she liked being around older guys. She even enjoyed hanging around the house or the club when my father was there; he probably was the closest thing to a father she had, though. My father gave her advice on college, taught her tennis, wrote job references for her. *Her* father—her parents are divorced—moved away, and they had no contact whatsoever. He was abusive when he was there, so maybe that made her likely to fall for somebody warm and supportive. Which Ken sure was."

I leaned forward. "Carol sounds almost too good to be true—cheerful, generous, popular, close to your dad, who isn't all that easy to warm up to. Was that hard for you?"

She looked at me with her straight-on gaze and nodded. "Sometimes. All the things that came hardest to me came easiest to her. I had one friend, she had lots. She was open, I found it difficult to relate to kids. She was girlish, I never knew how to be. I was off-putting to boys, she always had the best ones—like Ken—doting on her. She had a mother. I didn't. I don't even play tennis, and I told my dad I wouldn't go to the club unless they started admitting Jews and blacks."

"Did you ever have a crush on Ken?"

She smiled. "Well, you're pretty good, after all. Sam chose well. Sure, I was in love with Ken for a while. So were about a half-dozen other girls. When Mr. Handley got up at school the other day and said we should have known the literary side of Ken better, I wanted to cry. I did know it. He showed those poems to me." Her eyes had misted. "So, you've established that I was jealous of Carol and had a crush on her boyfriend. Am I a suspect?"

"No. You know you're not. What you are is honest, and it's nice to know that. Let's get back to Carol and the other man. Were there any earlier episodes, affairs with older men or people outside school?"

"Never that I knew of, and with best friends you can't really keep things secret for long. We knew every detail of one another's lives. Except for these past few months, I never felt Carol did a single significant thing I didn't know about, from age nine on."

"But you didn't know whom Carol was seeing. And according to the police, she was definitely seeing someone."

Judy nodded, looking down at the table, seeming to sag for the first time as if forced to acknowledge a painful failure. "A few months ago Carol admitted to me—after we nearly had a fistfight—that she was involved with someone else, but she never said a word about who he was. That's what was so strange. There was no giggling, no excitement. Girls always get goofy when they're involved with someone new, especially when they're talking with their friends. But not this time. She simply closed up. There was something about the relationship she was frightened or ashamed of. I think Ken could have handled the situation if he'd known what was going on. But it was almost as if she had changed personalities overnight. One day she was deliriously in love with Ken, the next she wouldn't see him at all and she was tense and distant. It was just like that—" she said, snapping her fingers. "And I never could break through and get her to tell me. It was like this Berlin Wall had gone up between us. She just wouldn't let me help her."

I thought she was going to cry. I would have, had I been telling the same story. But she just cleared her throat and sat up straighter. I wondered how she came to be so composed.

"Judy, forgive me, but I find it astonishing that you have no idea—whether she told you explicitly or not—whom Carol was spending her time with."

"And I'm sure there are people who find it difficult to believe you weren't involved in any wrongdoing on Wall Street," she said politely. "That's their problem. The truth is, I don't know. And I've been up most nights tearing myself apart trying to figure it out, because whoever it was was really messing her up.

"Carol started behaving real strangely about six months ago. She'd burst into tears for no reason, withdraw for days, get all moody and depressed. It was totally out of character. She even told me she wasn't sure she was going to go to college. She said she hadn't made up her mind but I could tell that she had—she wasn't going to go. She stopped talking about it, or mentioning it at all. She would only tell me there was something going on that she had to handle herself."

"Did she say why?"

"No. And she was the most trusting person, usually. But she became furtive, hunted. I thought she was getting paranoid. She seemed jumpy all the time, short-tempered, ill at ease. It drove Ken crazy. He couldn't understand it, either. They'd been going together for two years, and up until that point she'd never even hinted anything was wrong. They couldn't keep their hands off each other, which made me crazy sometimes. In the car, y'know . . ." She flushed a bit, which I was pleased to see—a crack in the impenetrable cool.

"Drugs?"

"Never. Carol was a church girl. She never even smoked a cigarette. A glass of wine would put her to sleep. It's always possible, I know; they always taught us in Family Life Ed that drugs can account for sudden mood changes. But she said no, and I took her at her word. She was involved with someone else, romantically or in some other way, someone who scared her. Someone she couldn't talk about, even to me."

The food came and we both ate quietly for a couple of minutes. I was off balance, surprised by the whole conversation. The girl knew little about me, and most of what she did know was unflattering. And we were, after all, talking about murder. But she remained quite poised, handling a situation in which considerably older people would be babbling like fools. Meanwhile, I had to fight to keep the conversation from drifting towards me. Why did I allow myself to veer off on personal tangents in the presence of this kid?

"Carol was doing something wrong," Judy offered suddenly. "Guilt was all over her. It wasn't an emotion she could hide, being a good Catholic girl. She was in trouble. She even had to drop the project she and Ken were going to work on in school, and that was strange, because the whole town's talking about that project now."

"What project?" I asked.

"It was about that guy who was jilted and started killing women—the one who was hung on the Brown estate near where Carol and Ken were found. The thing is, Carol and Ken were assigned to do a research project on that case."

"They did a history project together? On the Gowdy case?"

"Yes. In the senior year, any two people pair up and take on a research project that lasts half the year. Mine was about how Clarence Darrow would be an impossibility today. He wouldn't pass the bar, and none of his tactics would be admissible in court. Mr. Handley loved it—told me I was heading for an A-plus." Her pride was one of the few adolescent gestures she permitted herself.

"But about Carol and Ken's project . . ."

"Well, they never finished it, obviously. At one point I know Ken was quite excited about it. Carol never discussed it much—I guess she didn't get very far before they broke up. They asked Mr. Handley to assign them other projects with different people. But I remember her telling me about this young farmboy who killed a bunch of people and they caught him and hung him. It's hard to imagine now, but there was quite a rampage. Some people were strangled. One of them was stabbed, or chopped up in pieces. Ken was fascinated by it."

"Jesus. The Gowdy case." Rochambeau was getting a tragic lesson in its history.

"Well, that's the name people are using now. But I didn't know his name before. Carol never mentioned it. The paper wasn't due till May, so I don't know how far they got, but the police know about it. The chief, Chief Leeming, asked me about it. He obviously thinks that's what gave Ken the idea to —well, to kill Carol. Apparently whatever this Gowdy did was prompted by jealousy. Ken told me once there was considerable doubt even at the time about whether he was guilty, but it was suppressed by the people who were after his land. It's incredible, how it ties together . . ." She stopped, her emotions breaking through.

"Well, his name was Nathaniel Gowdy, and the chief is

correct about that tragedy hanging over this one," I said. "He was a young farmer who strangled his girlfriend. She was apparently unfaithful."

We picked at our food halfheartedly. The conversation didn't leave either of us with much of an appetite.

"Do me a favor," I asked. "While this is fresh, while we're sitting here. Considering what you know of the Gowdy case, and of Ken and Carol, what does your gut tell you happened up there? You knew them both, and you know about Gowdy —what's your instinct? Don't think too much, just tell me."

She didn't hesitate. "I think the police are right, Mr. Deleeuw. I think Ken got deeply into this Gowdy case. You know boys Ken's age will do that, they'll obsess on Dungeons and Dragons or some video game and it almost takes them over. I didn't see it happening, but in retrospect, it seems logical to me that he got upset over Carol's breaking up with him, crazed with jealousy at some man whose identity he didn't even know, and decided to do what the Gowdy kid did. I don't find that hard to believe—just indescribably painful."

It was painful for me, as well. Here was a levelheaded, obviously intelligent kid who knew Ken Dale well and *could* picture him killing Carol Lombardi, then himself, under certain circumstances. I had talked myself into near-certainty that he was innocent. I still thought so, but now it was not as close as near-certainty. It's fashionable, especially in my line of work, to dump on the police. But cops like Leeming usually do know what they're doing. This case had already become a roller coaster for me, and I had just taken a plunge.

But I had to do right by my client.

"Isn't that a contradiction, Judy? You tell me you trust Sam Mellman enough to talk to me without reservation. But you don't seem to trust him enough to accept his belief that Ken Dale—*his* best friend—was utterly incapable of killing Carol or himself. That's why he came to me, you know."

This time she paused to sip from her water glass. She seemed to be selecting her words carefully. "Well, I do trust Sam, and I like him. But boys like Sam, well, they have these tribal loyalties. He's a good buddy, and a good buddy is honor-bound to try to clear his pal's name. I respect him for that, but that doesn't mean it's true. Carol was obviously into something I wouldn't have pictured her doing, either. I just think in the absence of other information, you look at what's logical. I feel the same instinctive loyalty to Carol that Sam feels to Ken—but at some point you have to be able to grow beyond that, to look for the truth." Whew, I thought, how mature would she be when she *graduated* from college?

"What about the attack on the woman in her car, then? And the death of Lisa Caltari? Or the guy who scared the little Peterson girl half to death? Ken couldn't have been involved in those."

She shook her head. "They're all terrible, but there's something especially horrible about frightening a child in that way. I can't believe anybody would do that. And she's as sweet as girls that age get."

"You know her?"

"Yes. Carol did too. Not well, but the Petersons belong to Dad's club. Carol baby-sat for Sherry more than I did, sometimes at the club, sometimes at her house. We haven't done any baby-sitting for a few years. You do that sort of thing before you really have a social life or interests of your own. But that was horrible."

I felt another Post-it coming on after dinner. Perhaps I needed to know a bit more about Peterson—I couldn't remember his first name.

Judy wiped a napkin delicately across her mouth. "I don't have answers for you, Mr. Deleeuw. Or even theories. But once Ken and Carol were found, then every other screwed-up kid in North Jersey probably started hearing about the Gowdy case. I've seen these obsessions start to take hold. There was a period after those four kids in Bergen County killed themselves when I thought we were going to lose half the junior class. Something about the Gowdy case is like that; it can get into kids' brains. But I don't know. The thing that gnaws at me is this other relationship Carol was into. There was something creepy about it and it's hard to leave it at that. I'd like to know who she was seeing and what he was dragging her into. Although I'm not optimistic we'll ever find out."

"Why? Why won't we? This is a small town."

"That's my point. All her friends knew she was seeing somebody, but nobody had a clue who, including her best friend. Unless this person comes forward, and I would hardly expect him to now, how will we ever know? Only two people knew, and one of them is dead."

She had grown agitated, confused about what she was hearing and what it meant. I realized for the first time what a toll her rationality and reasonableness exacted. "Don't you agree? Don't you see it that way?" she asked me, almost pleadingly.

"Well, you have a good point," I said, trying to sound calm. "In my line of work, you sometimes get lucky. You learn that somebody saw them, or they had a picture taken—usually people leave some traces. If this man was awfully clever and left no tracks, then you could be right. But I don't totally buy this notion of a lot of disturbed people flushed out of the woodwork because of the deaths and the old Gowdy case. It might have given Ken—or somebody—some ideas about method, but I doubt it gave him homicidal tendencies in the first place. The attack on Ida Flowers, well, that doesn't fit. The attacker didn't kill her; he almost seemed to be announcing his presence. Whoever crashed into the Peterson girl's room also seemed to be sending a message more than he wanted to harm the child. The one that really jars, that seems so far away from all the others, is the Caltari murder. That doesn't fit in at all except that her body was found on the Brown estate. I just don't know enough yet to have many conclusions."

I leaned back, stretched my legs out, and rubbed my hands against my temples. "What you're saying mostly suggests, Judy, that the person Carol was seeing might not have been a kid. That would explain why nobody in the class knew who he was. What if it was a person nobody knew, someone outside the school environment? Then it would make sense, wouldn't it, that no one knew?"

She mulled that, seemed to accept the logic of it. She nodded, slowly, although without much enthusiasm.

"Mr. Handley knew of the Gowdy case from the beginning, right?" I said. "That has to be where the police first learned of the connection." I was thinking out loud. Handley was clearly somebody I needed to see quickly. I was impressed by him when we met at the Historical Society the night of the killings, even more so when he spoke at the memorial service. He seemed perceptive and insightful. If he shared Judy's belief that the Gowdy case had obsessed Ken, that would come close to tying it all up. I wasn't being paid to investigate the Caltari case or the attack on Ida Flowers, just to reach some conclusions about Ken. If his teacher and his girlfriend's best friend were in agreement, that was something I had to listen to.

"I believe some of us had heard of the Gowdy murders

before this," said Judy. "Somebody had read something about it or heard something about it. I know I had—I just didn't know any of the details. I don't think we first learned of it from Mr. Handley."

"Well, I'm sure the police told him not to say a word," I added, as an afterthought. "But it would be valuable to know exactly what other students knew about that old case."

"I'll have to think about it," she said. "We hadn't made our reports to the whole class yet. I really only knew a few details about their project because Carol told me, and that wasn't much—just that some kid went crazy. She didn't mention the Brown estate—I didn't hear that until a few days ago. Mr. Handley must have told the police or else Chief Leeming wouldn't have asked me about it. Who else could have told him?"

We both passed up dessert. For all her authority and command of herself, Judy had clearly found the conversation distressing. In a way, I was relieved; it was human.

"You can't picture Jamie Harte as a killer, can you?" I asked. I could; I had interviewed several killers in the army, and most of them were just like Jamie Harte. The side of my head still ached.

"No, but I'm not reliable that way," she said. "I can't understand the logic of murder. I can't picture anybody killing anybody." She took a sip from her wine. She wasn't a drinker.

"So in *your* gut, following *your* instinct," she said suddenly, looking closely at my face, "you don't believe Ken strangled Carol. You think he was innocent. That someone else killed them both."

What did I really believe? I'd never been in a situation as a private detective where my instinct mattered terribly much. Insurance cheats were easy enough to spot; delinquent husbands were uncovered much more by computers and perseverance than by guile. Until now, I don't honestly think I knew what I thought of the client I'd never met, a healthy kid whose life ended so gruesomely. It was time to decide.

As much as the army had taught me, it was as opposite an environment as there was in the world from Rochambeau, with its overpowering face of normalcy; nothing aberrant was on the surface. Surely someone capable of choking Lisa Caltari could have killed Ken and Carol both. But Ken didn't write his farewell note for nothing. Judy was watching me closely. The babble of polite conversation all around and the clinking of silverware on plates seemed surreal.

"No," I said. "No. Ken didn't kill Carol Lombardi." I said this quietly, in a near-whisper, but the authority behind the statement surprised us both.

A shadow of fear crossed Judy's face. "How can you be so sure?"

"I don't think I was sure until you asked. But I learned in the army that even though people can certainly shock and surprise themselves and their friends, they rarely reinvent themselves. It's too easy to say kids are so emotional that they're capable of anything. It's unfair. Ken Dale wasn't a turbulent kid. There weren't a lot of currents swirling around below the surface. No one ever knew him to be violent, even when provoked. He was honest and good-natured. I don't think people step out of themselves so completely as he would have had to do to put his hands around Carol's neck and choke her to death. That would have taken a very sick puppy."

Judy shook her head, slowly, as if she were struggling to

accept what I was saying, but reluctant for some reason to do so.

At that point, the case abruptly stopped being something I'd undertaken out of curiosity and deference to a nice bunch of kids. I'd said it aloud: I didn't believe Ken Dale was a murderer. Now I had a mission.

17

I parked my car next to Jane's in the driveway, a hundred or so feet from the back door. Was I being cavalier about her safety? This was just the sort of dark, secluded spot someone would pick for an attack. I reminded myself that all of the victims so far had been female, with the exception of Ken Dale who, the police kept insisting, was the victim only of his own crazed despair.

Maybe we ought to install a new spotlight over the back door. Jane didn't share the notion that I was responsible for her safety, claiming that this was a caveman legacy men would do well to shed.

She was sitting up in bed with her reading glasses on her nose, surrounded by several stacks of files. She had cut back her hours at the clinic, so she could be at home more until this crisis was over, but she wasn't comfortable taking off completely. The families she counseled would have had no relief from their troubles while she was gone, especially on short notice. She felt responsible to them.

Occasionally, she let me read through some of the records, always careful to fold back the name on the folder. I was always aghast at the flow of misery through the clinic and her life. And these were people strong and smart enough to get themselves to a therapist: victims of sexual abuse, stabbings, and shootings; alcoholics and schizophrenics; child beaters and addicts. I didn't know how Jane listened to their stories all day and then chatted with our kids over dinner about their spelling tests. But she did. Sometimes, alone in our bedroom, she would break down over a case.

Two of her clients had tried to kill themselves, a third had pulled it off, a fourth was stabbed by her husband who was furious that she had gone to the clinic. It was a chilling and powerful counterpoint to the sheltered lives we lead in Rochambeau. Or used to lead.

"Hey," she greeted me, smoothing her hair back off her face. "The kids are asleep, finally. Everyone seems to have heard about what happened on Pine Lane. We could hear sirens and helicopters all over town. I gather the child's okay?"

"I was there—it was crazy," I said. "It was like the scene in *E.T.* where every cop in the world converges on the house. But nobody got hurt. The weird thing was the cops were there in seconds, hundreds of them. I just don't see how anybody could've gotten away from there."

She was looking at me so curiously that I wondered if I was so transparent to her by now that I was looking guilty. Even more interestingly, I was *feeling* a bit guilty. I had mentioned the Peterson house, but not dinner. It was an odd sensation; in fifteen years of marriage, I'd never done much of anything to feel guilty about. I had one of those marriages where you didn't really need to talk after a while: Opinions were presumed and grunts sufficed for conventional dialogue.

For all my problems, it wasn't my nature to join in the macho banter of Wall Street or take advantage of the lonely single women who hung around the office late at night rather than go home. I was determined, on pain of death, to avoid the clichéd manifestations of middle-aged male stupidity so often demonstrated by former male colleagues and friends.

"You okay?" Jane has a mind that is part X ray, part computer, soaking up everything at a glance for subsequent sorting and classifying. People in Paterson are lucky to have her, especially considering she could have made twice as much with a private practice.

If I were feeling guilty, was it just because I'd had dinner with an attractive, unexpectedly impressive young woman? Or because I was getting so pulled into this case that I was forgetting to talk to my wife? Come on, Deleeuw . . . how about the former?

"I just had dinner with Judy Cole, Carol Lombardi's best chum. Interesting stuff." I filled her in on the day and the dinner, most of it, then waited for her to process the raw data. She took a swig from the bottle of seltzer on the night table. Jane had kept her reedy body through both pregnancies and beyond, but the price was that anything much more caloric than lettuce or whole wheat toast was generally off-limits.

"I'm actually thinking about that Peterson incident—that little girl. It was more revealing, you know."

I was relieved she didn't want to talk more about Judy, although I was still mulling over my peculiar discomfort. Glancing infatuations with young women were okay, weren't they? I was human. Or was this a bit more than that? Jane and I trusted one another completely, and for good reason: We'd been through a lot together and had never let one another down. She, in particular, could have walked away from my troubles as easily as some of the other wives in the firm had. Instead, she had saved my ass. I owed her, and I loved her. Oh, God, I thought, spare me the humiliating notion that I was flirting with an eighteen-year-old girl. Please, please, never let me be one of these men I chase around all day.

"You see, the police are undoubtedly working 'round the clock in search of a psychotic. But maybe that's too pat." She rolled onto her back and took another swig from the seltzer bottle. Percentage, always thrilled by the sounds or prospects of sex, came snuffling over. I pushed his nose away with my foot.

"Looking for a psycho isn't that unreasonable," I said, "when you consider this guy's crawling through a young girl's window with a knife." I had checked Em's and Ben's rooms on my way to bed, making sure the windows were locked.

"There's something studied about this, something that has the air of acting out a script," she said tentatively, trying out an idea. "Ken Dale and Carol Lombardi were both killed along the lines of that Gowdy case a century ago, same place, same technique more or less, except a Volvo used for the hanging instead of a tree. And Mrs. Flowers wasn't killed, or even critically injured. Psychos get off on hurting, on raping and killing. Don't confuse what he did with a real psychotic. He—or she—didn't harm the Peterson kid either. He broke the window, scared the hell out of her—I sure don't minimize that—then took off. But she wasn't harmed, not by the standards of the real world. It was almost a taunt, a dare, to the rest of us.

"Don't you see that he's striking not just at these people but at our life, at what Rochambeau is and wants to be? At our notions of security and, of course, at our children. That attack tonight is designed to freak out every parent in town. It's exactly what I would suggest to someone who came to me and asked, 'What single act could I commit that would shake this community to its roots, ring everybody's loudest, most sensitive bells?' I would say, 'Go into a quiet area in town, put a ladder up to a young girl's bedroom window, smash it, and lunge towards her with a knife.' It's every suburban parent's nightmare except—"

"Except he didn't hurt her."

"That's right. We don't dread our children being frightened as much as we dread them being harmed. That's the precise fear that makes so many parents here drive themselves and their kids crazy. They want to keep them safe everywhere, at all times. And of course, that can't be. It's not attainable. Life intrudes eventually, even here. So this man brought us to the edge of our worst nightmares, then stopped. If he wanted to kill her, he could have shot her while she was out playing, fired right through the window. It's easy enough to get a gun these days. He clearly wanted to sound an alarm. Somehow, this guy is at war with us. With you and me, Kit, and with all the people around here like us."

"I see what you're saying, but don't you think you're getting a little dramatic, a bit metaphorical for a nutcase?" I mulled the theory. Jane was levelheaded, and her ideas were always worth listening to, but there remained some big holes in this one. Why would someone be "sounding an alarm" by threatening a child when he'd already brutally strangled Lisa Caltari? That was no shot across the bow; that was real. Tonight's scare could have been a strike at the heart of suburbia, as Leeming suggested. But it could also have been a diversion.

"It is metaphorical, Kit, but what greater metaphor is there for Rochambeau, than that a child be frightened in her own bedroom, with both of her parents in the house? We have parents who fight to get their kids the best spot in ballet class!" She had a point there.

She leaned on her elbows, more excited now. What a good straight man I was. "But that's almost the clincher for me, Kit. Sherry Peterson was a red herring. Either one that was really unrelated, or a grotesque effort to make us take all this seriously, once and for all. Suburban teenage suicides are horrible, but sadly not that rare. To get the kind of attention this person wants, you have to kill an attractive young woman —or attack a child. Caltari could have been the credibility-builder, the corpse that convinced us he wasn't to be dismissed, that he was to be feared. Another button to push. Although tonight's incident could surely stand on its own.

"I don't know how the two kids fit into it. Teenagers can be incredibly fragile. Maybe it was just a busted affair, or maybe he killed them but was disappointed at the way it was interpreted. I'm not sure I'd start tracking outsiders or a psycho, Kit. Look among us. He knows what we fear and react to. He's one of us, if he's even a he."

"You're losing me, Jane." I stood and started to pace the room. "You think the two kids on the mountain were murdered and the killer is disappointed that they were interpreted as a murder and suicide? That doesn't make sense to me. If so, why did the killer make Ken's death *look* like a suicide?"

"I'm just talking out loud, Kit. I do think they were killed. I think the killer made it look like a suicide. I don't know why. There was some sort of message he wanted to send, one that he gets and we don't, or that he thought we would get but haven't. I don't have any proof, just an instinct: Those deaths were a ritual, symbolic act. The clue to what happened lies in understanding that. The thing about the Peterson girl that keeps eating away at me is that it was the act of a person disturbed enough to send us a message but too decent to actually harm the child. That makes it different from the deaths of Ken Dale and Carol Lombardi, or even from the attack on old Mrs. Flowers."

"And Lisa Caltari?"

"I don't know, I really don't. She seems to me a body dumped on the road. I don't know."

I took a swig from her bottle. I tried to remember if I'd

even heard of seltzer in the army. I felt a shiver up my back. The hooded man outside Mrs. Flowers's car. The Gowdy case. The spooky, haunted spot where Ken and Carol had been killed all suggested Jane was right—there was some symbolism the town had completely overlooked in rushing to declare the deaths another tragic, troubled passage in adolescent life. I was getting overwhelmed. I needed to talk about something else.

"Well, enough about my mundane life," I said. "What about yours? How are your patients weathering your cutback in hours?"

"Well, I was there for the tricky ones. My multiple personality—the obnoxious one—came out with me today. I like the quieter, more reflective one that comes out on Mondays. And I saw this teenaged girl who has been coming to the clinic for a year and never spoke before. She babbled all afternoon about how she saw her mother's boyfriend stab her stepfather to death five years ago. A drug dealer with HIV and a six-year-old boy whose mother pressed his hand against a hot plate for fifteen minutes because he woke her up. And that was a half-day." Small wonder Jane seemed to be losing patience with Rochambeau's more fluttery parents. After days like she had, how else would she react to parents like the ones in Ben's class last spring who got hysterical because the new bookcases hadn't arrived at the school yet?

Any given day at Jane's clinic contained more bloodshed and mayhem than Rochambeau has experienced in its most hellish week, yet every reporter in the Northeast was pouring into our town while she and her coworkers labored in complete obscurity, budget cut after budget cut, tragedy after tragedy. I gave her a long hug. I didn't know what to say anymore. As I snapped the light off and got into bed she snuggled onto my shoulder, and cried for a few minutes at her own helplessness. I talked about mine.

"Jesus, Jane, can I sort through all this? I feel like I'm a thousand feet below the surface looking up way over my head. Am I taking this kid's money in good faith?"

Jane sighed. "I don't have a theory for that, hon. What you're asking me is, can you work as a detective or not? I'm afraid that's between you and the great Private Eye in the sky. For what it's worth, I think you can do it. I think you'll bust this one."

Smart as she was, she hadn't always been right. But Leeming, I recalled, almost seemed to be saying the same thing at the Peterson house as she had; that something was taking us all on. A chilling thought.

I finally went to sleep thinking about another woman, if you wanted to call her that.

18

Sam said he had just about three minutes before class. Behind us, students were pouring into the building, passing below a doorframe that listed—on separate bronze plaques—the graduates who had lost their lives in the World Wars and Korea, plus a small plaque from my own era. I wondered if any of the laughing, jostling kids had even noticed them or had any notion of what they represented.

How could I ever reconcile Ben's leaving his life in some place like Vietnam or Kuwait at nineteen or twenty years of age? Such monuments seemed outdated to me, inappropriate and expensive. Maybe it was just wishful thinking, but I found it hard to imagine such a fate for Sam.

Even amidst the horde of healthy, lively kids, his tall frame stood out as he ambled down the hall to meet me. I had called before school and offered to give him a brief status report—and a chance to back out of our deal. He had sounded surprised to hear from me, as if it were not really conceivable that I was working for him, let alone reporting to him. His young face was trustingly expectant, which made the news I had for him all the more difficult to deliver.

Around us, the population of Rochambeau High swirled in transcultural waves, a riot of colors, styles, sneakers, jangly earrings and torn jeans, cornrows and flattops, leather and denim, a raffish funky celebration that discomfited certain straitlaced citizens but delighted me.

"Sam, this is the stage in any investigation where I give the client the option to back out before any real money is spent or wasted."

He looked back at me without expression, shuffling his Reebok pumps like some young stallion pawing the stable floor. "I don't understand, Mr. Deleeuw." Some of his friends, probably privy to our general business, shot us a curious glance or two, but most of the babbling crowd rushed past, parting as if we were a huge rock against an incoming surf.

"Well, here's the long and short of it. I agree with you: I don't buy Ken's being a murderer either. But I haven't a shred of evidence to back that up. I have no assurances to give you at this point that I can do better than the police at unraveling all this, or even that I'll end up with a different conclusion than they have when I'm done. And continuing to work at the unraveling could be expensive. There's my hourly fee, mileage, taking people to dinner, going through records, making copies and all. I know your dad's supportive of the Dale family and of what you're doing, but you are a high school student and I have qualms about taking too much of your money when there's so little to go on. We know Carol was seeing someone else and we know Ken was upset about it. He even seems to have left a suicide note on his home computer."

He looked stricken.

"I'm not here to bring you down, Sam, I'm really here to talk to Dick Handley. But we have to—"

"Mr. Handley?"

"Yeah, I want to ask him some questions. We know Ken was studying old town murders—stranglings—in the months before this happened. Did you know about his history project?"

Sam frowned and searched his memory. "Just generally. We weren't supposed to tell each other very much about them, so that we would be detached. Mr. Handley wanted us to be curious when everyone else's work was presented—you know, to be able to critique their projects. Ken just mentioned something about this guy who was hung a hundred years back or so. He and Carol were working on the project together, at least until they broke up. But that was a while ago."

"And had you heard of that old crime before?"

"Never before Ken was assigned it," he said, "not a word. And I was really shocked, man, because Susan and I go up there all the time, when we—" He flushed. "Between us."

"Not a word," I said solemnly.

The crowd had begun to thin out and I guided Sam towards a more private alcove near the water fountain. "Well, what would you say if I told you the guy was a teenager named Nathaniel Gowdy who was accused of strangling his girlfriend in a jealous rage up on the Brown estate, then killing five or six more townspeople during a rampage that ended when a posse caught him and hung him? How would you react to that?"

I was deliberately being a bit sharp, but I was thinking of the mounting bills. I wanted to make sure that Sam wasn't going on blind loyalty, that this represented a clear, conscious decision on his part and on his father's.

Maybe I would even feel relieved to get off this case that seemed to grow bigger and uglier each day while my grasp of it remained tenuous at best. If my clients declined to pursue things further, I could leave it a winner, a detective who moved on to other things before he had a chance to fall on his ass in front of the whole town.

"I have no trouble responding to that, Mr. Deleeuw," Sam said firmly. "I would still know Ken couldn't kill anybody." He was too polite to get nasty but too determined to let me off the hook. "That's what I—we—all felt, and that's what we'll always feel until you can look me in the eye and tell me you know, as far as it's possible to know, that Ken killed Carol. Is that what you're telling me? Because I'm kind of confused. You're saying you don't think Ken killed Carol either, but you can't prove it."

I put a hand on his shoulder. "I'm saying I don't think Ken killed Carol and I don't know whether I can prove it or not. I just want to be up front with you. This entails some risk on your part. I haven't worked a murder case in years, and there's no guarantee at all that I can crack this one. I'm willing to give it my best, though, and I will if you want me to."

"The whole school is obsessed," said Sam, not responding directly. I think he was too confused. "The other kids all say Ken did it. But if he did, then who stabbed the old lady? Or murdered that girl? What about that little kid up on Pine Lane? Do you or the police have any answers to that?"

"Nope."

He looked sad but resolute, and reached out to shake my hand again as the bell clanged. "I haven't changed my mind," he said. "I would like you to try to prove that Ken didn't kill Carol." That, I guessed, was that.

As for Sam, this constituted more introspection and agonizing in a few minutes than most boys his age faced in a month. "Jeez, this is like talking to my dad. 'Bye," he said. "You'll like Mr. Handley. He's in three-oh-six."

The teeming halls emptied in a moment. Sam, shouldering an enormous book bag as he loped down the hall, waved and turned the corner. I was learning things about kids this week. Had I possessed equal degrees of conviction and loyalty when I was Sam's age? Wouldn't it have been easier for him to follow the conventional wisdom, keep his money, and forget about the whole sorrowful and confounding affair?

I could see Richard Handley through the glass insert in the door of room 306, a classroom that seemed to have only four or five kids in it. When I tapped on the glass, he looked up, puzzled.

He came out and offered his hand. "Kit Deleeuw," I said. "I'm a friend of Benchley Carrolton's. We met at the Historical Society a week ago, and I very much admired your talk at the memorial service."

He nodded, my face and identity seeming to click. "You're the private investigator some of Ken's friends hired to try to clear his name?"

"That's me."

"I sort of expected you'd be getting in touch. You actually picked a good time to talk. Most of my class is off on a field trip to the U.N. The tardy few who are behind on their projects are about to head for the library. Let's go into the Teachers' Lounge. It should be empty now."

It was, except for one grumpy-looking elderly woman heading out. We sat on two overstuffed and sagging chairs, undoubtedly havens for the bottoms of generations of weary mind-stretchers commiserating with one another about their restless charges. The lounge had a refrigerator in one corner and the obligatory coffee maker that looked even more discolored than the one in Chief Leeming's office. But it was the beginning of another long and probably frustrating day and I needed a jump start.

Handley filled a cup. "I can't say offering you this coffee is exactly a hospitable act. But here it is, anyway."

He had about twenty minutes, Handley said when we had settled in, but I was welcome to meet him at the end of the day if we needed more time.

"I appreciate your making yourself available," I said. "I'm not crazy about taking money from high school kids, so I imagine everybody will be especially wary." I took a sip of coffee. He was right. It was awful.

"Not at all. I have a lot of regard for Sam and his instincts, and I would do this and a hell of a lot more for Ken Dale. He was one of the best, one of the five or six kids a year that make dealing with the rest of it worthwhile. I don't know what happened up there, but I had a great deal of faith in Ken. If I could help in any way to clear him, it would be a joy. It is almost impossible for me to believe that Ken could put a rope around anyone's neck, let alone Carol's."

I looked at my notes. "I know you were close to Ken. That much was clear at the memorial service. And I gather that Carol was a student of yours also. Were you close to her as well?"

He shook his head. "I liked her, but our relationship wasn't as strong. Ken had writing talent, and he shared it with me. Carol had great fun in school. She liked all her teachers, she had loads of friends, she was a member of everything. She had a good time. It was nice to watch. I guess I tend to get closer to the broodier, more complicated ones. Although it's dangerous to oversimplify. Carol wasn't without complexity or problems. I remember that she shocked me five or six months ago, when she turned down an offer of a scholarship through the Rochambeau Country Club."

I must have looked puzzled.

"Well, you know," he said. "A lot of the service clubs and organizations in town give them as a community service. They go to kids who aren't necessarily the best in academic terms, but who need the money and are involved in community work or athletics. Usually it's four or five thousand dollars. Carol was going to a school in upstate New York, I think. She asked me for a letter of recommendation, and I could tell she was proud. But I never got the chance to write it. One day after school she came to see me—she was very emotional, very upset—and said she didn't need the letter, and that she wasn't going to take the scholarship. I asked her why several times, but she flatly refused to talk about it. I could see she had been crying, although she didn't in front of me. But her eyes were red, and her makeup was smeared."

"You never wrote the letter? Hmm. That's curious. Why would she reject a gift like that? Do you remember how much time elapsed between her asking you for the letter and then telling you she didn't need it?"

Handley frowned. "It was just a few days. I always write them very quickly, because I write a lot of recommendation letters and if you don't do it right away, you tend to forget. Or at least I do."

"How long was she upset?"

"Oh, not for long. At least not that it showed. I can tell you she was quite troubled. But you know, you could ask Judy's father, Lee Cole, about it. He was on the club's scholarship committee. I was supposed to have written the letter to him. You should really talk to Judy Cole about Carol, too. You know she and Judy were great friends."

Yes, I said, I had already talked to Judy and had been particularly impressed with her.

"Judy is one of those students who should skip over adolescence." Handley smiled. "She never has any time for the silliness that goes on around here over clothes, boys, any of that. She always seems ready for the adult world. To me, she always struggled with childhood, but thrives when she is allowed to be as grown-up as she is. Do you know what I mean?" I did. It was my precise impression of Judy.

"How do you account for her friendship with Carol? They weren't much alike."

"Well, that's common. You see that all the time in high school, opposites do attract. Kids often find friends who complement them. But I think it was tough for Judy. Carol was everything she wasn't—bouncy, popular, always having fun. But they were close. I gather Carol spent a lot of time at the Cole household. About the only kid who did, I suspect."

"You mean her dad? I've already encountered his charm. I'm surprised anybody would voluntarily spend time there. Although, to be fair, it sounds like he had good reason to be glum."

Handley nodded. "It was an especially painful process, I'm told. I was teaching in the middle school then, when Judy was in fifth grade. She was only in one of my classes, but we all followed it. Judy's mother had cancer of the liver, one operation after another, before it finally spread past the point where they could do anything about it. The poor woman was in dreadful agony. But Judy never missed class, always did straight-A work, and, of course, never refers to it. Judging from the conferences I've shared with Lee Cole, I can't imagine it's been easy for her. He seems angry and remote. He obviously cares for Judy, but I doubt he shows it much. But there, I'm off the track. You've got me gossiping about parents —something I do not ever do, Mr. Deleeuw."

"Well, you know us detectives," I said. "Always working

our wiles." I was grateful to talk to someone who didn't think I was a thief or a birdbrain and wasn't armed with a barbell.

Handley looked haggard, though, the smile lines etched sharply around his eyes and mouth. I had no doubt that he'd done what he predicted at the service—agonized about the deaths ever since they'd occurred.

Then: "Shoot," he demanded almost abruptly, as if he couldn't take much more small talk.

"Tell me about the Nathaniel Gowdy project."

"So it's around," he said, sighing. "Chief Leeming was trying to keep the lid on it for a while. He told me not to say anything, but if you know the name, you know the story."

His eyes reddened slightly. "You see, it was my idea," he went on in little more than a whisper. "The project was my idea. I thought it would be fascinating. It's one of the richest and most poignant stories I've ever heard, the most moving bit of history I've ever encountered about Rochambeau. I spend nights and weekends going over old newspapers and journals to find topics for Historical Society lectures. I'm a nut about town history.

"I found this one in old newspaper files. Also, a retired reporter decided to do a book about it back in 1903 or '04, while some of the principals were still alive. The manuscript was never published, but I can understand his fascination: This thing makes *Gone With the Wind* seem like a third-rate soap. Aside from the drama in the story itself, it speaks so powerfully to the suburbs."

Handley shook his head as if to shake off the grief and, perhaps, the guilt. "Gowdy was a prototype of the fortunate, likable Rochambeau kid, at least in the first years of his life. Adored by his mother, respected in the town. By all accounts, he was crazy about his fiancée, Caroline Clark. They'd been engaged for a year.

"In those days, though, things had a way of turning quickly—sudden illness, accident, tragedy. Gowdy's father joined the army when things got financially rough on the family farm. He died in one of the Indian wars out West.

"Nathaniel helped raise his younger brothers and took care of his mother. He worked the farm, which adjoined what's now the Brown estate and is now the Garden Center. Everyone held him to be honest, responsible, and reliable, so the town was totally stunned—just as it is now—when Caroline Clark's body was found on the property in Gowdy's buggy. There was no trace of him."

Handley's fatigue seemed to lift as he told the story. The historian in him, or perhaps the storyteller, seemed to take over, as the mourning teacher receded.

"Then, over the next three weeks, five other young women were killed—all of them strangled in the same way, except one man, some landowner, who was hacked to pieces with an ax. Nothing like that had ever happened in this town before—then or now. Several witnesses say they saw a young man with a stovepipe hat—the kind Gowdy wore—around two of the murder scenes. And one of his friends told the sheriff that Nathaniel had learned that Caroline Clark was about to break off the engagement in favor of someone else. Of course, the fact that he'd vanished was a powerful condemnation. As the bodies piled up, the town was, of course, no longer rational. At first, people couldn't believe him capable of murder; eventually, no one believed him innocent."

A bell jangled suddenly in the hallway, and the roar of hundreds of students hurriedly on the move caused Handley to stop, instinctively. But he made no move to leave and no one came into the lounge.

"A posse roamed the town in a fury—the entire county was in a terrible rage. They found Gowdy hiding in the back of the estate, down at the base of a small valley behind the house. It's still there, you know."

Gowdy seemed stunned and disoriented, Handley said, but denied his guilt, telling the jury that it was true that Caroline was about to end their engagement and that he was upset. But on the night of the murder, he claimed, he had been set on by three or four men whose faces were shrouded in sacks, and then blindfolded in an unfamiliar cabin in the woods for days before being roughly hauled out one night and released—just minutes before a posse came charging through the brush with hunting dogs. He had run toward the posse, grateful to be rescued, filthy and disoriented and having eaten little for days but porridge and sour apples.

The prosecutor had thoroughly ridiculed Gowdy's story: There was no sign of any gang of men, no motive for kidnap, no ransom or other demand. The tale was widely perceived as desperate and incredible.

The youth, said Handley, was shattered. Handley appeared transfixed, almost spellbound as he told me the story.

"The trial was pretty pro forma," he concluded. "The evidence against Gowdy was circumstantial but it seemed overwhelming. The defense argued that there was nothing in Gowdy's past to suggest violence, that it made no sense for him to have been hanging around the estate if he were trying to hide, that the whole thing was some trumped-up plot to grab the Gowdy farm. Developers were salivating over the suburbs even then, because Rochambeau was becoming a summer residence for rich New York merchants. There was also enormous pressure to wrap up the case, which was attracting sensational publicity. And, in fact, the killings ceased as of Gowdy's arrest. The jury convicted him in minutes. And he was hung on one of the elm trees on the estate, perhaps the very stump Ken Dale used to strangle himself. Or, I should say, is accused of using. I'm spinning over this, as you can see.

"It's the parallels that transfix me," he said. "A young man everybody likes. A town anxious to preserve its property values and make the bad news go away. A young girl suddenly struck down amid suggestions of another man—a rumor that was never substantiated in the Gowdy trial, by the way. It's a powerful story, perhaps even powerful enough to take over a young man. . . ." He left the thought unfinished.

"True," I said, "but the differences are pretty compelling as well. Ken Dale never got a trial. I guess, in a way, Sam wants me to give him one." Handley nodded, drained.

"Is there a part of you that thinks he killed Carol? Given the parallels that you yourself find striking." It was a blunt, even tasteless question and it surely broke the spell of the Gowdy saga.

But Handley didn't recoil.

He ran both hands through his hair, took off his glasses and rubbed his eyes, and leaned back in his chair. The school suddenly seemed eerily quiet to me. He considered for at least a minute before sipping his coffee, replacing his glasses and looking me in the eye.

"I have plenty of character flaws, but I don't lie well," he said, "so I've learned not to try. It's surely possible, given what I know about teenage boys and about the Gowdy case, that Ken got distraught and was drawn to replay a tragic version of it. A lot points to it. But I taught Ken Dale for three years. I saw his mind at work, almost watched him grow up, tutored him. If he were capable of murder, then I misread and misjudged everything I saw in this young man. And that raises terrifying implications about my perceptions as a teacher, doesn't it? A part of me says strongly, 'No, Ken didn't do it. I'll never believe he did,' yet I am aware we only know the part of these kids they wish to show us. I can't predict how my students will turn out. And the evidence, well, it's hardly circumstantial."

"No, no," I objected. "You can't blame your teaching. You're not a psychic. There are too many variables, almost none of which you created or control. An unexpected shock can transform anyone, even someone like Ken, and take him out of character. My wife is a psychiatric social worker and she tells me that all the time."

Handley didn't seem convinced, and why should he be? Teenage psychosis wasn't exactly my specialty. He seemed uncomfortable now, in a good bit of pain, and I was glad I only had another question or two.

"What happened to the manuscript you mentioned?" I asked. "The one the reporter was working on."

"Well, that's murky," he said. "The reporter claimed to have found disturbing evidence, according to some newspaper accounts, including one farmhand who confirmed that a group of thugs *had* been hired from Newark to kidnap Gowdy, then release him in front of the noisy, drunken posse that was stumbling back and forth across town. There was reportedly some pressure to suppress publication of this book, or so the rumors went at the time, and they've been passed along to the town's few surviving original families. I'm not really clear about the reasons, but the manuscript never got much further than the Historical Society files. I suppose the story loomed larger in Rochambeau than in the rest of the world, and then, of course, it was largely forgotten during the waves of immigration into town over the past half century. But it should be revived. It would make a wonderful book."

The bell sounded again. Handley seemed to return to normal.

"That's just the bare bones," he said, looking up at the clock. "I'd give anything to read that manuscript. Anyway, God forgive me, I suggested that Ken and Carol research the Gowdy story together, having no inkling, of course, that she was about to break off the relationship."

"Would she have told you when you made the assignment, do you think?"

"I'm sure she would have, now that you mention it. I'm sure she wasn't expecting any problem when the assignment was made. You see, this is the reason that Chief Leeming naturally is convinced that Ken killed Carol—because it matches in so many ways the story he was researching. I feel more dreadful than I can say. I'm not a religious person like Benchley, but if there is a God, I hope that he or she is merciful and will forgive my role in this."

"Isn't that harsh? Surely Ken would have found some other way, if that was the course he was set on."

"I'm trying to reach the point where I can accept that and believe that if Ken killed himself and Carol, then there was nothing I could have spotted, nothing I could have done. I'm not there yet." He paused; I could see he was still quite a distance away. He looked hesitant, unsure.

Was there something else? I asked softly. Something about Ken?

There was a long silence, broken by school sounds; the echoes of a few voices in the hallway, the slamming of a locker, a thump, perhaps of a basketball on a gym floor.

"Only this," he said at last. "I haven't told anybody about it, because I don't want to fuel the police in their certainty that Ken did this. But a few weeks ago, he stayed after class to show me one of his poems. It was so bleak—chillingly so, really—that I asked him if he was depressed about something. He just shrugged. We couldn't talk any more that day, and we never spoke privately again. I haven't told the police that. It would just make them blind to any other possibility."

"So you think he was depressed, then? Just before the deaths?"

"The poem—he took it with him—would surely suggest that. But that doesn't mean he could commit murder."

I empathized with Handley's confusion about Ken Dale. In a way, I was in the same pickle. I wanted—in fact was being hired to find—evidence of the boy's innocence. But all I was running across were suggestions of his guilt.

"Dick, let me ask you a delicate question. In confidence, as is everything we're discussing. Jamie Harte. I think he brained me the other day when I went to interview him. Everyone says he's violent, a bully, and that he loved Carol Lombardi. This all suggests to me that he's someone who deserves a thorough look. Yet no one is giving him one. Am I missing something?"

Handley looked even more stricken. Maybe helpless is a better term, as if I'd reminded him of another situation he was unable to deal with. "Kit, I don't know. He's a student of mine. It's a very awkward situation for me. I can't speculate."

"Dick, I'm not asking for speculation. If I don't come up with something in the next few days, the police will close the books on this one and Ken Dale will be a murderer for all time. His friends aren't easy with that. Neither, I can tell, are you. If you know something about Jamie Harte, I'm asking you to tell me."

Handley shook his head, sadly but firmly.

"Do you think I'd be wasting my time investigating him?" I prodded.

He pressed his hands together, troubled. "I'll say this, and I'll only say it for Ken's sake. I have no evidence whatever of Jamie's guilt. None. If I had any, I would have given it to the police."

I nodded.

"But in all the years I've been teaching, I think I've never encountered an angrier, more vengeful young man. We've called in the Child Study team a half-dozen times for Jamie, and they've recommended special ed, counseling, you name it. But his mother won't follow through on any of it, and we can't make her. The system ought to help kids like that. But it doesn't, and we can't. You can't make someone get assistance. I wish to God you could." He seemed drained. Still, his answer wasn't exactly subtle, and it seemed as if I would be risking another crack or two to the head.

I got up to leave. "I appreciate your candor. I would be even more grateful if you could find me that manuscript, the reporter's aborted book on the Gowdy murders. It might be helpful to read it over."

He frowned. "It's odd. The Historical Society files are all catalogued and itemized, and it's supposed to be among them. But it's lost or misplaced. It was supposed to be in the Society library at Benchley's place. In fact, he called me the other day wanting to know if I knew where it was. The truth is, I saw it, but I never got to read it."

I was startled. "But you were so fascinated by the story. Why not?"

"Stupidity. And distraction—I was grading finals at the time I learned of it. Anyway, the old clips in the paper suggested it was just a crackpot theory. It wasn't until I came across an article in one of the Newark papers, a bit more balanced and disinterested, that I realized the writer had serious credentials and had done some solid research. I decided to get to it as soon as I could—but now, it seems to have gotten mislaid."

"What condition was it in?"

"It had held up pretty well—high-quality white parchment, good thick paper. I'm sure it's among those piles of Benchley's somewhere. I'd welcome your help in finding it."

I left the high school, feeling especially middle-aged and bland. Chinos and blue oxford cloth shirts seemed conspicuously unimaginative among the riot of colors and styles around me. I think I'm beginning to understand why so many elderly men favor madras pants.

I headed for the pay phone outside the school to call my answering machine. It obligingly delivered a message about something else that had been misplaced that morning—and it wasn't even 10 A.M. yet.

The Rochambeau Homes supervisor had called. Blackhead Gowdy had vanished from his room overnight. Someone must have helped him, she said, since he couldn't have walked far by himself. She was notifying the police, she said in a scared voice, stammering a bit, but she was also calling me because my office number had been found scrawled in barely legible handwriting on the wall next to his bed. Would I please call immediately if I knew where Mr. Gowdy might be? Directly after that message came a brisk, formal-sounding Rochambeau Police Lieutenant Richard Adams asking me to call him immediately regarding one Mr. Blackhead Gowdy and his possible whereabouts.

I decided to call Adams first.

"Detective Bureau," came the brisk answer. I suppressed a mild guffaw. My notion of Rochambeau's plainclothes division wasn't exactly Scotland Yard.

Adams explained, in a bored but professional way, that Gowdy went for walks once in a while, but had never vanished for so long.

"He sometimes goes away for a few hours—once, he was gone overnight—but he always turns up or someone calls the Home. He's got a card sewn in the back of his jacket with the Rochambeau Homes number. They get nervous because he's a diabetic, and needs his medicine." Adams cleared his throat. "Excuse me, Deleeuw—you're a private dick, right? Can I ask you what your business might be with Mr. Gowdy, just for our files?" I wasn't exactly a household word in Rochambeau; if Adams knew who I was, it could only be because Chief Leeming had told him, which meant the interest in old Gowdy wasn't as casual as Adams was making it sound.

"Sorry, Detective Adams. I appreciate your interest, but I don't think so. Clients and all, you understand."

"Perfectly." A steely edge had replaced the tone of diffident collegiality. He hung up. I put the obvious thought out of my head: Blackhead Gowdy couldn't have strangled a plucked chicken. But like Detective Adams, I wouldn't mind knowing where he was.

19

There was a time, embarrassingly recent, when I would have been delighted to spend an afternoon at the Rochambeau Country Club, tucked at the foot of the Watchung Mountains on the northwestern corner of town. But that was past. As I drove into the oak-lined parking area, the nearby greens velvety even in midwinter, I knew I could look forward to being hassled, put off, and held in contempt.

The main building is a sprawling Georgian mansion with a number of modern additions. I can picture the gents in their tuxedos and the ladies in their gowns attending one another's coming-out and anniversary parties here. The front driveway is the sort of place where car companies shoot commercials for those boring, big-ticket passenger sedans that are supposed to connote class. The Rochambeau Country Club scarcely misses a beat in cold weather. The old duffers golf in every weather short of a snowstorm, and the indoor health club, tennis and racquetball courts, meeting rooms, and restaurants keep the parking lot full all year. I took a deep breath, and prepared for a bracing rejection. What snooty, racist country club in history ever wanted to see any private investigator, let alone one run out of Wall Street by scandal?

I was surprised Lee Cole would belong to a place like this. He had the arrogance, but as an ousted veep who'd turned to consulting, he might not be able to keep pace with the members.

But as I waited in the lobby, I figured it out. Hanging on one paneled wall was a photograph of him with Archibald Henry Cole, clearly his father. Archibald looked like someone who would have had no trouble getting into the Rochambeau Country Club; he probably had helped found it. At clubs like this, Dad was an automatic passport in, I supposed. You probably didn't have to do anything yourself except hate Jews and blacks and everything that had happened to America since 1958.

I couldn't picture Judy hanging around here, though. She wasn't snooty, and her politics seemed pretty advanced. I guess part of the tension between her and her dad was that she couldn't picture hanging out there either. But hadn't she mentioned that Carol Lombardi had played tennis here with him? That made the place worth checking out.

It took the management a full two minutes to inform me that I wasn't welcome, that no inquiries of any sort would be permitted or responded to, and that I was not to return for any reason whatever. Would I please leave now?

But I knew that more was expected of me. Detectives don't just trot away when some white-haired shithead with a pole up his ass tells them to. I walked around to the car, drove out of the lot, parked it along the road out of sight of the main building, and then walked back along the rear wall until I found the very sort of caddies' room that I had worked in during high school. There were no caddies in it, just a gorgeous tennis pro, crisp and glowing in whites and sneakers, hurriedly (and undoubtedly unlawfully) swigging down a small bottle of Jim Beam. He froze when he saw me.

"Shit," he said. "You work in the office? You checking on me?"

I was immensely flattered. Here was one of the first people I had encountered in my new career who actually took me on sight for a detective!

"Put that down," I barked, happily emboldened. This was going to be the easiest work I had done so far; the guy was twice as jumpy as a cat and half as smart. "You're—"

"Claffey. I'm the only pro working this week. Look, I just took a quickie. It won't happen again."

He was in his late twenties, I guessed, tanned and fit and dirty blond and handsome and—maybe this was stereotyping, but what the hell—as intellectual and introspective as a bridge piling. I bet he cleaned up on tips, though, with the Wall Street wives who hung around here all afternoon. He probably had been bounced somewhere else for drinking; from the panicked look in his eyes, he definitely needed the job.

"I'm not going to make trouble for you. But we've had a complaint—an inquiry, actually—about one of our members. I need some fast answers. It's connected to all this trouble in town. You following it?"

"Yeah, sure. Well, I mean I've heard it on the radio." Claffey looked like he kept up with current events via the Sports Channel. "What's this got to do with me?" He eyed his little airline bottle wistfully.

"Finish your drink," I said, softening my voice (and him) up. "I don't give a shit about your drinking habits." Then I pulled out my notebook. "Lee Cole. Know him?"

"Sure. Mr. Cole. Plays here twice every week. Wednesday nights, Saturdays. Strong serve. Weak backhand. Kind of stiff guy, you know what I mean."

I knew what he meant.

"Who does he play with?"

"He plays doubles usually, with three other guys in his range. But they've only been a foursome for the last month or so. Before that, he played doubles with a coupla guys and this knockout young girl."

"Who was she?"

"Dunno. Carol something."

"Were they . . . ?" I gave him my best male leer. Anybody with two brain cells would have burst out laughing at the sight, but it struck Claffey as perfectly natural.

"I don't know how a guy could not have wanted to get into those shorts," he laughed, taking another swig. No wonder he bought my leer. "But to tell you the truth, I thought she was too nicey-nice. She called him 'Mr. Cole.' He was her teacher more than her partner. Funny thing about that is he's a crummy player. Usually people like her come to me for lessons. God, I wish she'd come to me. I asked her out once, but she told me she was involved with somebody. Too bad. I don't get many turndowns around here, but then, few of the women look like that kid."

"So it looked like a teacher-student relationship?"

"Yeah, like he was in charge. They always came on Wednesday nights. Except one night—the last time—they had this big intense discussion. He seemed kind of upset. They finished their set, and I think she won, but then they left kind of quickly. Usually, they'd hang around a bit, recap their game, have a soda. I never saw her again, and a couple of weeks later, he showed up with his new foursome. He's still not very good."

"Did you ask him what happened to her?"

"You don't do that sort of thing around here. It's not

my business. I just teach who comes here. You don't get nosy. I never saw him touch her, though. He called her Carol, never honey or sweetie or some of the yukky things you hear around here. He seemed kind of like an uncle giving his niece lessons—except if she was his niece, she wouldn't have called him Mr. Cole, right?" Nothing slips by this guy, I thought.

Claffey had finished off his little bottle and looked at me longingly. I nodded, and he pulled out another. By now, he'd probably figured out I wasn't from the front office, but he probably didn't care one way or the other.

"Did he look upset, wistful, any change of mood?"

Claffey shrugged. "No, I wouldn't say that. He was always a cool one, kind of formal and distant. He doesn't have buddies, like some of the guys do, just partners. He wants to win real bad, though, and I've seen him throw a racquet around when he doesn't."

"Claffey, you've probably seen a lot of May/September things. Was this one of those, in your professional opinion?" I almost gagged on the term. I wouldn't take this guy's professional opinion on a jockstrap.

He shook his head. He probably was savvier than he looked. He had to be, to get his shoes tied.

"Well, I'd be lying to you if I said I was sure. I've known guys at clubs like this who never talk to women, and you find out later they've been screwing somebody's socks off. Lucky guy, Mr. Cole, if he was. She was hot."

Another wonderful guy, I thought. But this one I could rattle. "Does the name Carol Lombardi mean anything to you?"

His brow clouded, overloaded. "Well, that was her name, I think. That was Mr. Cole's little friend, wasn't it?"

"Yeah," I said, in my best wiseguy voice. "She was murdered up on the mountain."

For a second, I thought he was going to keel over, but he steadied himself. Maybe I'd been too hard on him, to drop it that way.

"She's the dead kid," he gasped, after a minute. "Oh, my God. I never actually connected her with that. I guess I never actually saw the girl's pictures in the paper and I don't watch TV news."

I threw him my card, asked him to call me if he actually thought of any details I should know, and left him sitting there.

20

Deleeuw Investigations has three unofficial and unpaid advisors on matters relating to the town of Rochambeau and to suburban life in general. Benchley is the primary consultant. Carroltons have been wise in the way of suburban New Jersey since George Washington was tramping across the southern edge of town, setting up one of his implausibly numerous overnight encampments. Benchley's lineage gives him historical perspective; his gentle, analytic mind gives him special insight; his Garden Center allows him to be wired into the town as closely as the CIA, a comparison that would horrify him, and probably the agency too.

Luis has the keenest understanding I've ever encountered of aberrant and criminal behavior—and with my years in the army and on Wall Street, I know plenty about both. Luis, in his grease-stained franchise, is as detached from this brave new suburban world as Benchley is enmeshed.

Perhaps because of his exile and his unspoken but obvious disenchantment with life in America, Luis is unflinching in his theories. He swats down most of my trial balloons quickly, steering me in more intelligent directions without ever being patronizing about it. Even when guiding me far from my own notions, he manages to make me feel as if I'm a genius, sharing theories instead of receiving them.

My third and, over the past few years, most important source of advice and direction is Jane, who in the wake of my nuked career is finally doing with her life what she so clearly should have been doing all along, and probably would have, had she not blundered into marrying me. Gifted at reading people, she has become the most valued therapist in her clinic. How many women, I wondered, puttered around their houses a few years too long—quite a few, sometimes—without the motive, encouragement, or opportunity to do what they were good at?

I know the answer, of course, since such women are as common as gas grills in Rochambeau. They populate the town's playgrounds, school bus stops, and gourmet delis. Sometimes I feel ashamed of the pressure that my drastically reduced income has put on Jane. But when I think about it, I feel even worse about the decade or so I spent rampaging through the financial district taking heroic risks with other people's money, oblivious to the fact that Jane was reading a novel a day and shopping too much, her hard-edged, inquisitive mind beginning to atrophy.

I realize now that Jane could never have made it as an upper-middle-class, child-centered hausfrau. I love her deeply, but I'm not sure she's all that likable. She's kept the same close friends she had in college and shows little interest in making more. She's bad at small talk, disdaining the school/kid/house chitchat carried on in Rochambeau supermarkets much of the day. Even before she had a full-time job, Jane was an A-B-C-D person, going from task to task in a straight line. It would never occur to her to stand at the corner with the kids to wait for the school bus, even as her fellow mothers marched out behind their offspring every morning, dogs in tow, to await the Yellow Rabbit or Green Swan or one of the other cutesy names bestowed on buses by the public-relations-savvy Rochambeau school system.

At PTA meetings, she watched in dismay as parents com-

plained about teachers, principals, facilities, budgets, schedules, lunch room routines, and discipline procedures. My
sense was that getting involved in the real world—especially
her real world—left her unable to deal with the bullshit. She
just lost her tolerance for it—for listening to it, participating
in it, taking it seriously. If she found this stance unusual, she
didn't say so. She seemed to find her balance the natural order
of things, and the more I lived in Rochambeau, the more I
thought it ought to be, even if it wasn't.

So when I found myself suddenly sitting at home like
some mobster under indictment, we both seemed to stumble
into our real selves. I loved coaching soccer games, and Percentage and I became fixtures at the bus stop. I loved bullshit-
ting about teachers and social problems, mostly, I guess, because I'd felt so cut off from it for most of my children's lives.
Of course, some people weren't and still aren't all that comfortable chatting with me, my being a principal in a full-
blown scandal and all, a veritable symbol of the corrupt and
valueless eighties.

As it happens, I did not commit any wrongdoing on Wall
Street, a declaration I would have made had anyone asked me.
I might as well have, however; the lines between what's illegal
and what's wrong are pretty fuzzy there. Had I agreed to sell
out my friends and bosses, I might still be there, part of the
Great Crapshoot, confident of having enough money to get
my kids through college and possibly enjoy my old age.

All the feds really wanted me to do was to wear a mike
under my armpit, take my bosses and colleagues out for
boozy lunches, and record some incriminating admissions.
They would have made a few, too. We'd all worked together
for years, long days, too many weekends to count. But it was
unthinkable. If they'd been dealing drugs or something, I

might have considered it. But all they were really doing were things everybody else had been doing for years; they'd just gotten caught.

If I had turned informer and helped send the faces I'd looked at all day to jail, I could never have lived with myself or my family. More than anything else, that's what these few years have been about for me: learning to be a partner and husband, to be a father, to be a halfway decent human. Detective work was in some ways a sideshow to the main event. I felt considerable guilt about Wall Street—at the soulless work I did there and the time I wasted doing it, at the unrecoverable costs to Jane and to my relationship with the children, in which I always felt I was coming from behind.

I feared still that I might never really draw even. I was on firm ground with Emmy, who was only a little past four when I abruptly stopped running off every morning. But Ben had been wounded in some way I couldn't quite get at, in a way he could not or would not share with me. Jane insisted that this wasn't true, that I was a great father and that the kids loved having me around. Ben, she said, was simply going through the painful adolescent rites of junior high.

My abrupt separation from my career was only one of the disorienting factors in my life. The other was my gender. People in suburbia aren't ground together like the urban stew; each subspecies has its place. If the poor and the elderly are nearly invisible, then middle-aged, middle-class men are visible only in certain ways—shouting on the baseball field, stuffed into tiny chairs at Back To School Night, hauling mulch and dehydrated manure back from the Garden Center, tossing red meat onto sizzling grills.

They are rarely seen tending small children, taking up space behind the wheels of the Volvos, Tauruses, and minivans that ply back and forth across the town. When they get together on weekends, at dinner parties or the sidelines of soccer fields, it's still to groan about the rising cost of things, the unpredictable nature of employers, the indulgent nature of teachers and wives, the coddled and unprepared-for-life nature of children. So much between men and women has changed out here, and so much has stayed the same. It always seems to be men who cluck that their kids need to take on more challenges and start learning the bitter lessons of life, and always women who hold their offspring close until the last possible minute. I occupy my own increasingly distinct ground, alienated from the Suits who pour off the trains and apart from the Supermoms in their station wagons. I'm not sure I know myself what I am anymore, only that there aren't many of me.

The morning papers gave shell-shocked Rochambeau another jolt, but a more welcome one. Shortly after midnight, the state police had arrested an unemployed twenty-three-year-old truck driver, a man who frequented the diner where Lisa Caltari had worked, and charged him with her murder. Pete Gosolsky had had lunch at the diner that day and was seen talking to Caltari, the cops said. He returned that night and they left together after her shift ended at midnight. Tire tracks found near the Brown estate murder scene matched those of his pickup. It looked pretty cut-and-dried and, at least at first blush, seemed to leave one less attack to worry about. It also seemed to substantially reinforce Leeming's constant public assertions that Rochambeau was not being stalked by some psycho, but had instead become a temporary magnet for disturbed outsiders. I called my state police detective contact, Lieutenant Tagg, at home.

"Can you tell me anything about the arrest in the Caltari case?" I asked him, knowing full well I was out of favors.

"Drugs," he said, and hung up.

This didn't seem to explain why a young man bent on murder would head for a place half an hour's drive from the diner where Lisa Caltari worked. Perhaps he had read about the Dale/Lombardi deaths and the scene provided some strange turn-on? I added the arrest to the already daunting list of things I needed to know more about.

After breakfast, I slipped a leash on Percentage and walked Ben and Em to the corner where their respective buses came less than ten minutes apart. I hadn't accompanied either of them to the bus in a while, and when I glanced towards the bus stop, I thought at first there'd been an accident. More than a dozen heavily bundled grown-ups—mostly mothers— were waiting with their kids. Two police cruisers swept by slowly, followed by a Channel 7 news van. Up and down the streets I saw city-bound dads—most usually long gone by this hour—huddled at corners, hugging their kids, hanging around to see everyone got off to school safely. All of the normal rhythms of the town had changed.

The crowd at our bus corner was a strange mix of suits, bathrobes, and expensive overcoats. The kids bounced among them, exhaling frosty puffs of breath, chattering nervously and excitedly. This was a pretty riveting break in their routine.

"All of us don't need to be here, you know," I heard one mother announce to the crowd as Ben, Em, Percentage, and I approached. "This is even scaring me. How 'bout if I stay here with the kids today, and tomorrow someone else can volunteer?" Frontier spirit at the Rochambeau school bus stop. True community, something I don't think we'd ever needed before.

"Who are you?" asked an uncertain male voice from the back.

"I'm Donna Bernstein. I live at two-oh-six. I'm in the book. I'll go home and get some ID if you want." It was startling how few faces in the crowd I could put names to. We had lived on the block for years and waved at our neighbors, but few were people we socialized with or knew well. I understood why the man was asking; the volunteer could be the lethal nutcase, for all we knew.

"Good enough for me," I said, glancing at my watch. Benchley was waiting breakfast for me at the Garden Center.

"No, Daddy, wait," said Em, hugging my waist. I hesitated. A couple of harried dads, glancing nervously at their watches and gauging the time it would take to dash the four blocks to the train station, were peeling off.

"Here comes the bus," some kid yelled. I looked at Ben, but he looked away; if he needed me, he sure wasn't going to show it.

Ten minutes later, I was back at Benchley's house. It had been only a few days since I had been here last, but it seemed longer. I didn't realize how glad I was to see him until he ushered me into his study—complete with logs blazing in the fireplace, mugs of hot cider, and a tray of sweet-smelling blueberry muffins (Benchley was the most intuitively hospitable person I knew) amid the stacks of yellowed newspaper and magazine clippings. It felt safe and comfortable here, a welcome haven from the craziness outside.

"Kit, we'll probably never catch up on what's gone on since we last saw one another," he said mournfully. "At the Meeting House, we're holding a special Meeting for Worship with a concern for safety." Benchley had invited me to one or two Quaker meetings. I couldn't quite get used to people worshipping in silence, and I didn't really have the patience for the kind of introspection that went on, but it was clearly a place where Rochambeau's wave of violence would resonate especially painfully. It took only a look at Benchley's craggy face to see how hard it had hit him.

I recounted my conversations with Judy, Chief Leeming, and Dick Handley, and my unsuccessful efforts to communicate with Jamie Harte and Blackhead Gowdy. "Any thoughts?" I asked him, cupping my hands around a mug.

He leaned back in his favorite overstuffed chair, folded his hands, and proceeded to voice quiet doubts about everything I was trying to prove.

"I don't know, Kit. I have to conclude that the chief's instincts are likely to be correct in the initial killings," he began. "I know that private investigators aren't supposed to like the police or think they're intelligent, but during his visit the other day, the chief struck me as quite professional. If Ken Dale had researched the Gowdy history at all—as I've been doing lately—then he would have had a perfect blueprint for murder. And wouldn't he have related to Nathaniel Gowdy and his girlfriend's betrayal? Every teenager in town has brought his girlfriend up to that mountain to neck. It's one of the town's few traditions that has endured from poor young Gowdy's time. And there is the computer message you told me about. I have no trouble accepting all that, Kit. I don't really see many holes in it."

"It's surely out of character for Ken Dale."

"For whom can murder be considered in character?" Benchley asked quietly. "We sit out here behind our tended lawns and pretty gardens and we define murder as something 'they' do. But you and I know that it isn't so neat behind the fences and the shrubs. We have our share of painful marriages, alcohol and drug and other abuse, plenty of broken lives. Since people in other parts of the world may be poorer, sicker, more pressed and hopeless, it does happen more 'there.' But when it happens here, the first thing everybody says is, 'I can't picture such a nice quiet man/woman/mother/ father doing such a thing.' That's how we make ourselves feel safe. It's not in keeping with the character Ken Dale chose to show us, but we know how troubled adolescence can be, how volatile. He was in love and suddenly he had lost her and he didn't know why. Quite a trigger at that age, when love is so passionate."

Benchley caught my raised eyebrow and shot back a mock glare. "Well, Kit, even I can remember what it was like," he harrumphed.

He got up, heaved another log onto the fire, and stopped on the way back to his chair to bring me another muffin. "The case against the man in the killing of poor Lisa Caltari seems quite strong," he noted, "and it isn't inconceivable that he read about the Dale and Lombardi deaths and thought this was a 'neat' place to commit murder. Such behavior is deeply disturbing, to be sure, but this young man might be highly disturbed."

Well, it wasn't what I wanted to hear, but it was certainly what I'd asked to hear. "So what do you make of the other incidents—the Ida Flowers stabbing, and the man who came through the window of the Peterson child?"

He had thought about that, too. "You'll learn, as Ben and Emily get older, that kids in a town like this have three things: the imagination to conjure up trouble, the money to fund it, and the time to carry it out."

"You love children," I protested.

"I do, and I resent the way people demonize them at times, but the mischief I've witnessed over the years . . ." He sighed. "I couldn't even recount a fraction of it. They've vandalized houses and cemeteries. Several times they've sprayed my seedlings with phosphorescent paint on Halloween and killed off hundreds of them. They steal tools, tie cans to my cats. If a gate is left unlocked, they come in and destroy as many pots and shrubs and flowers as they can, just for fun. The police have repeatedly urged me to get a guard dog or a burglar alarm. But I don't want my business to operate in an environment like that, behind barbed wire. I could never live with myself if a dog of mine bit a child." He shuddered at the thought.

I got up for more cider. The sound and warmth of the fire and the smell of the food were almost intoxicating, a comforting counterweight to the ugliness and hysteria outside. This was the way to start every morning, in vivid contrast to the spilled cereal, slobbering dog, misplaced textbooks, hurried reminders, panic, and mayhem that kicked off weekdays in my house. Maybe when the kids were gone, Jane and I could start our days with such civility.

"So you write off the stabbing as kid stuff?" An ingenuously phrased and loaded question, but it didn't fool Benchley.

"Too slight a term, Kit. But I have little trouble imagining some disturbed young man trying to terrify an old lady. Perhaps he never meant to stab her. Perhaps she moved too quickly or something startled him. It doesn't seem as if he meant to kill her, though, does it? If he wanted to, wouldn't he have? And clearly someone intent on seriously harming a little girl wouldn't crash through the window with a dog and both parents in the house and a small army of police cruising outside? A dangerous and frightening and foolish stunt, yes, but also something an adolescent might do, trying to impress his friends."

There was a long silence broken only by the crackling of the fire as we both pondered Benchley's assessment. It had taken me awhile to grow accustomed to the Quaker silences Benchley occasionally lapsed into. At other social occasions, quiet was considered a form of rudeness. Benchley's quietness was more companionable.

I wanted to listen to his convictions carefully. Benchley knew the town much better than I; he knew what kids were capable of. Still, it didn't sit easily with me. He seemed to be speaking out of character. These killings had changed him too. Benchley loved kids and was forever defending them against the patronizing and judgmental assumptions adults made about them. I had never heard him express anything like the notion that terrifying the elderly or frightening small children was typical kids' stuff. I had never known Benchley to assume anything but the best in people's behavior; here, he was taking the worst for granted. He was trying to talk himself into—or out of—something, I thought.

And he sure wasn't convincing me. There seemed an intelligence to all the bloodshed in Rochambeau, a calculation far beyond teenage malevolence; someone was stirring up old ghosts for a reason, and I would have thought Benchley would see that more clearly than I could.

"The part that bugs me is all this old Gowdy stuff, Benchley. It had an air of unfinished business even at the time, and the Gowdy thread is woven throughout these troubles. What if you took the position that every incident was related to the Gowdy case: the two kids' deaths because of where and how they happened, the Ida Flowers case because it resembled Nathaniel's attacks on other women in town, the Caltari case because it was also done on the estate, and—"

I was startled by the look on Benchley's face. It wasn't introspection, but pain.

"Benchley, are you all right?"

He was quiet for a moment. "My friend, the Gowdy murders aren't some abstract historic tragedy. My family was involved; you and I are sitting on Gowdy land. The Carroltons have always prospered from that point; the Gowdys fell into a long decline from which they have never emerged and, given that Blackhead Gowdy is the last of his line, I suppose it is tragically correct to say they never will emerge from it. I feel horrible about it."

Neither of us said a word for several minutes, the fire cracking, and smelling of cedar. Benchley came out of it by himself.

"The part of your theory *I* don't get, Kit, is the Peterson incident. Where would that fit?"

I paused, smiled, then proudly revealed my coup. "I was at that house within minutes of the intrusion. I am sure I saw one of the officers—McClure was the name on his uniform— carrying a piece of old hemp, the same kind used to strangle Carol Lombardi and hang Ken Dale, the *same kind* left next to Ida Flowers's car. I think the cops found it in the Petersons' backyard, below the little girl's window."

"You *think*, Kit?"

But I was still pleased with myself. "I called the Rochambeau PD yesterday and kept calling until Officer McClure came on with the night shift. I said I was from the county prosecutor's office and we were wondering where the length of hemp was that he found behind the Peterson house. Pissed him right off. 'Jesus Christ,' he said to me, 'you guys couldn't find your asshole with both hands. I gave it to the state guys. It went to the crime lab in Trenton. Where else would I take it?' "

Benchley looked grave, rattled. "Was any found on the Caltari girl?"

I shrugged. "I didn't quite know how to ask. I didn't read or hear of it. But Leeming is smart enough to try to keep some details quiet. He didn't tell reporters about the hemp found behind the Peterson house either."

"Good Lord, Kit. This may be so far beyond my comprehension that I'm not of much help to you. Your army experience is probably closer. I was right about one thing, though: You're better suited to this than you thought." I felt a surge of gratitude: it was Benchley who had suggested that I return to investigative work when we had our first talk in the greenhouse. He'd probably saved me from real estate school.

"But," he stammered, "the implications. That means—"

I cautioned myself to go slow. I had to remember that Benchley was at least eighty, even if he looked twenty years younger, and that bloodshed hit him harder than most people.

"It doesn't absolutely rule out a kid's stunt," I said. "But it tilts me more toward a madman. It fits that pattern—the obvious clues, the cleverness, the desire to be caught. They aren't really hallmarks of an adolescent. If you believe in ghosts, you could say that whoever's doing this is behaving just like Nathaniel Gowdy is supposed to have behaved, except for the merciful fact that he doesn't seem to want to kill everyone. My hunch is that only the Caltari case really is unrelated. At least, that's my hunch of the hour."

Benchley got up again to poke at the fire.

"Benchley, Dick Handley reminded me about that manuscript you mentioned, the one some reporter wrote years ago that supposedly raised some questions about the murders and about Gowdy's guilt. You mentioned it's been lost or misplaced?"

"Yes. The Perry manuscript. I asked Evelyn de la Cretaz, the society librarian, about it. She remembers filing it, but it's not there now. She looked and I did."

"Have you lost other documents, as well?"

Benchley frowned. "Not many. Evelyn doesn't take well to losing things. She's terribly competent. Occasionally, of course, something gets mislaid, but never anything very important. The maddening thing is that I read it, but can't remember the details. I try not to complain about aging, but it drives one mad, the things you aren't as good at anymore. And we've gotten so involved in current issues, like preserving the estate. Still, you know what a hive that is back there," he said, gesturing towards the library. "I'll call Evelyn and we can try one more time."

We had another silent moment or two.

"Benchley, how well do you know Dick Handley?"

"Why?" he asked, watching my face closely.

"I'm just trying to be thorough. He suggested the class assignment that Ken Dale and Carol Lombardi undertook. He knew them both, and obviously knew the Gowdy case as well."

Benchley was incredulous. "Kit, you can't be serious. Dick Handley is one of the finest teachers in the high school. He's a mainstay of the Historical Society. He's a good friend. I assure you that he could never harm another human and is utterly devoted to his students. Really, Kit—"

I held my hands up in apology. "Sorry, Benchley. I just

thought I had to ask. You know, he is a thread that runs through much of this, too."

"I hope he's not a thread you intend to mention to anyone else in Rochambeau. You can destroy someone's reputation with a lot less. One shred of suspicion and he could never work in a school again, however dedicated he is."

I reassured Benchley of my utter discretion.

"Besides, Kit, aren't you overlooking something rather obvious?"

I raised my eyebrows in inquiry.

"Don't you remember? Dick was with us at the Historical Society dinner at the time of the deaths," he said, with obvious relief. "The police said the time of death was between 9 and 10 P.M. Dick was at the dinner at least until eleven. He was at our table. He never disappeared long enough to go up to the mountain or anywhere else. And I can tell you something else, too—the night when Ida was hurt, a Rutgers history professor gave a talk at the Adult School about colonial life along the Watchung River. I was late and had to leave early, but Dick was there when I arrived and when I left; we waved to one another. When I got home, my phone was ringing with news of the assault. That's two alibis for two, and he probably has others if you checked on the other incidents."

I surrendered. "Okay, okay. It never happened, I never said a word. Good grief, I hope you're as protective of me." It was a good reminder of a lesson I already knew—don't shoot your mouth off about somebody without some hard evidence, especially in a murder case. There are no secrets in a town this size. I was embarrassed at the slightly reckless way I'd nearly slandered a person I didn't really suspect of anything anyway, a person I couldn't help liking. It was fine to scratch

Handley off of my list of suspects. The only problem was that there wasn't anybody else on it.

Benchley broke the quiet. "Mike Cardone called me this afternoon to ask if I could supply some trees for a development in Clifton he's representing as a realtor. He told me one bit of good news. He said the buyers that were circling the Brown estate have all dropped away, at least for now. The trustees have agreed that he shouldn't even show it. I hate to see a silver lining in anyone else's misfortune, but the development proposed up there would be hideous. Hundreds of town houses, a multiplex theater, fast-food restaurants—what a nightmare. Bad for the town, bad for the estate." He looked out the window and up the hill, with its inviolate swathe of hemlock, oak, and chestnut. "But I don't believe it will happen," he said, so quietly and with such assurance that I couldn't tell if it was faith speaking or some special knowledge.

"It must be strange to look up that hill," I said softly, "knowing that it once belonged to your family and that it could easily have been yours today."

Benchley stared out the window a moment longer and then turned toward me. "Am I being investigated as well, Kit?" He smiled, more in sadness than in pique.

"Not intentionally," I said. "I went by the town records office as a matter of routine—detective handbook stuff—to review the history of the Brown estate. It was startling to come across all those Carroltons a hundred years ago."

"I like to block it out, myself, the fact that my family owned that land. I probably should have mentioned it, but I didn't see any relevance to it, although I suppose that others might."

"I vaguely remember your mentioning it once, Benchley.

I'm not suggesting you were hiding it, but I guess I forgot about it. How long ago?"

"When they first came to Rochambeau—it was called Springbrook then, in the early 1700s. My great-grandfather was a sharp businessman, like a lot of Quakers. This land where the Garden Center is was considered worthless for decades; too rocky and hilly to farm or clear. But the railroad wanted it for a right-of-way, and it was clear even then that as Rochambeau grew, any major road into the town would have to run past it. The Gowdys owned it and wouldn't sell, until after Nathaniel was executed. They had no choice then but to sell it and leave the town. It was probably not my family's finest hour, taking advantage of the Gowdys' misfortune like that. It's nothing that I'm proud of, Kit. I still don't like to talk about it. We sold off the hill above to the Brown family. They were wealthy traders and merchants, even then. My family retreated wisely to the bottom of the hill, quite comfortable on the money earned from the sale. The railroad was never built.

"The house up there now dates from the 1880s. It was probably the oldest continuously inhabited property in Rochambeau. It's sad to think of the place sitting empty this past ten years while Eustace Brown's heirs hire lawyers to squabble with one another. But sadder yet would be another shopping center. Too much history there. Not enough anywhere else."

It was good to hear what Benchley thought. But what did *I* think? My meager years of detecting had convinced me it is important to stop often while working a case and sum up. You talk to so many people and gather so much information that you can be overwhelmed by it. You have to stop and sort through it.

I stood up to leave, reluctant to venture back into the

cold and the confusion. About all I'd clarified was that I still didn't feel as if I were earning young Sam's money.

"I hope Chief Leeming *is* right about all this," I told Benchley slowly. "I hope the murders are all solved. Because if he's not right, if there is some connection with the Gowdy case, then Rochambeau's troubles might just be starting."

21

I now knew as much about the Dale/Lombardi deaths as anyone except the police, and maybe the killer. It was time to
make some decisions. I was oriented, employed, and enmeshed, ready to push aside everything else and plunge in.
The case would have to wait, though, at least for an hour. I
had to take Em for an after-school visit to her new pediatrician.

This time—part of my new independence campaign for
her—I wouldn't go into the examining room. I was thinking
ahead to the day when there might be intimate questions to
be asked and answered and Em might need to negotiate doctors' visits herself. She was nine, but not for long.

The office was on the ground floor of another boxy old
Victorian, just down the street from the nursing home that
Blackhead Gowdy had apparently walked away from in the
middle of the night. Gowdy had no warm outdoor clothing
and no means of transportation, the nursing home administra-
tor had said, but the door leading to the second-floor fire
escape was unlocked and he either was carried off or toddled
away under his own steam. I told both her and the inquisitive
cops I wasn't sure whether Gowdy had even understood who I
was during my brief visit. The detective taking my statement
sounded irritated, as if he and Chief Leeming had had a good
heated exchange about what happens when amateurs muck

around in police work. But I was baffled. Had those old black eyes taken in more than I suspected? Or had someone decided to squirrel Gowdy away for a while?

Gowdy might be dead, as well, another one of Rochambeau's victims. That prospect made me numb. I felt uneasy that I hadn't mentioned his disappearance to Benchley and unsure why I hadn't. I guess I wanted to hear what he had to say about the old man before I told him, and then it had seemed too awkward to throw it in. I made a note to call him. He had never lied to me; I wanted to keep my record as clean. Yet I was learning how to be a detective, and one of the first things I'd learned was that information was the most powerful tool I ever had. I had learned to be careful about what I did with it.

"You coming in, Dad?" asked Emmy, her pigtails bobbing, when the receptionist called her name.

"Nope. Why don't you try it yourself this time? I might take a walk, so if I'm not here when you get out, just read for a few minutes." She nodded. She supported the independence campaign, considering it just and long overdue.

"Give her as many shots as possible," I advised the receptionist. Em threw me a murderous look.

The woman next to me held on her lap a four- or five-year-old boy with a prodigious stream of mucus pouring from his nose. "Excuse me," she piped up. "But do you let her go in there alone?"

I nodded.

"Do you think that's wise?" she asked, making it clear that she didn't.

"I think so. I don't really need to be there. She ought to be able to deal with doctors—it's an unenviable but necessary part of life."

"Well, you're more trusting than I am. I would really want to know what was going on." I heard a brief yowl from Emmy—a finger-prick blood test, I guessed. I nodded at my companion in the waiting room, stifling the impulse to suggest she call the state child abuse hotline, told the receptionist where I was going, and headed out.

The Rochambeau Homes Nursing Center was two blocks down, but I never got there. Walking past a big green '75 Chevy with its engine idling, I saw a man who looked familiar, but whom I couldn't immediately place, smoking in the driver's seat. He noticed my stare and rolled down the window.

"Hey, man," he hailed me. And when I continued to stare, "You don't recognize me, do you?"

"Not yet," I said, embarrassed. Weren't detectives supposed to remember this stuff?

"I work over there," he said, shrugging towards the nursing home. "I go on duty in fifteen minutes. Remember when you came to see Old Man Gowdy? I wheeled him to you. I take care of him." The last he said with what seemed to be a touch of pride. I remembered the affection he had seemed to feel for Blackhead. Joey.

He looked about twenty-five, his face locked in a permanent sneer, his hair slicked back with some kind of gel. I could see the top of an elaborate tattoo under his shirt. "You're a detective, right? Private?"

I nodded, leaning into his window. There could only be one reason for this encounter—he had some information about the case or about Gowdy and he wanted to sell it. "Mind if I join you? It's cold out here, and you can save me a trip."

"Man, it's my job if I do that. We're not supposed to give information to outsiders."

"Well, how about fifty dollars for three minutes?" I suggested. People who wheel elderly people around might not make that much in a day. Offering cash for information seemed too pat, but quite often worked; I had better start carrying more.

He consulted his rearview mirror, then motioned me in. Personally, I resisted this furtive glancing-in-the-mirror stuff. No tail worth anything would be caught dead sitting straight behind you. "I'm Joey. Joey DiNardo. Working in that tomb for four years. Talk about dead ends, man, any deader you got to go underground. I'll circle the block," he said, shifting into gear.

"Wait," I said, flushing. "Let me make sure I have fifty bucks on me." He looked at me incredulously. I had one check, which I needed to pay the pediatrician, who was sure to charge a hundred dollars for a full checkup. Plus I had stopped at Rochambeau Sporting Goods after leaving Benchley's to buy some heavy-duty sweat socks for Ben, now at the age when sweat socks had begun to matter. He had responded with his usual eloquence when I handed them over after school. "Yo," he said, stuffing them into his gym bag. "Later."

"I've got forty bucks," I said. "I'll stop by with the other ten later, I promise." I was aware as I said this that I sounded like a total yutz, as well as a highly unprofessional detective.

"Jesus, man, okay, anybody as weird as you has got to be honest. If you screw me for ten bucks, then piss on you." I liked Joey. We both were trying to sound tough, and neither of us was fooling the other for a second.

"I'll deliver," I said. "Look, I don't have much time. Could Gowdy understand what was going on?"

"You bet, man. His body is fallin' apart, but his mind is like a new blade. Those eyes, you notice them? They'd cut right through you. Nobody else there would give the old guy the time of day, but I talked to him all the time—"

"He ever talk back?"

"Sure. All the time, man. He doesn't take nothing from nobody, I'll tell you. I used to give him the papers, the *Star-Ledger* and the *Rochambeau Times*. He talked when he wanted to —asked me to read things over, certain stories, if they interested him. He talks when he feels like it."

We swung past the pediatrician's office. I wondered if they were sticking needles into Emmy while she shouted for me. In Rochambeau, what you actually pictured was the kid lying on an analyst's couch twenty years hence, recalling that time alone in the doctor's office, screaming for the father who wasn't there.

"He ever react?"

"Not much. But lately, man, he started reading about that shit up on the mountain, the Brown place. Jesus, man, I thought that old scarecrow was going to fly right through the window. He was blazin', man, squeezin' my hand, asking me to read the story maybe a dozen times. I said, 'Jesus, old guy, you sure like a good crime story, huh?' Every day after that when I came up there with the papers, man, he wanted to hear every word. He'd come alive, at least his brain had. His body couldn't follow as fast, you see what I mean?" He relaxed as we drew out of sight of the nursing home.

"The thing is, I worry about the old guy. You take care of people like that, if you got any heart at all, you start to care about them. And Gowdy, he had a lot of moxie. I hope they find him. Aside from the money you're paying me," he added, a bit self-consciously.

"Joe, this is important. Did he have any visitors lately? The manager, I forget her name—"

"Miss Whitmore. Miss Fucking Bitch Whitmore."

"That's it—Whitmore."

"She's a lyin' hag, man. Mean and cheap. The stuff she lets go on in there—"

He looked me over, probably wondering how far he should go.

"It must be rough, Joe," I sympathized. "You try to help those people. You try to amuse them when they're left by themselves, give them some human contact."

"That's right, man. I make two hundred and ten dollars a week. And the families—they don't give a shit. They stick old people in there because they don't want to hear nothing about 'em. And they don't. Nobody comes. I been there four years. Almost nobody's come to see Gowdy. Once in a while this old guy—white hair, looks like a judge or somethin', he'll come by and ask to see the old guy, but Gowdy would just shake his head back and forth and tell me to tell this guy—a nice old fella—to go away. Gowdy never would talk to him."

"Could you recognize him, this visitor? Did you get a good look?"

"Once or twice. Usually he came to the receptionist downstairs and they called up. I think I'd recognize him, though. Classy-looking guy. But other than him, nobody's been to see Old Man Gowdy, not—"

"Not until about two weeks ago, I bet?"

His eyes widened. It was a long shot but a reasonable one, someone showing up shortly before Ken Dale and Carol Lombardi's bodies were found.

"You been watching us, man? Hanging around the home?"

I said nothing, fingering the forty dollars I was so arrogantly flashing. Mr. Big Shot Detective, with his bribery fund eaten up by sweat socks.

"Wasn't that a different person, not the old white-haired

guy?" I asked helpfully, my tone suggesting that I knew so much it would be pointless to withhold anything.

"Yeah, this other guy came. I wasn't holding out, I just didn't think it was a big deal. I wasn't at work yet. Jorge, the day man then—we switch back and forth—he was on duty. I saw the log—some guy came about four-thirty. I asked Jorge about it, 'cause I was surprised the old guy had a visitor. Whoever it was gave Jorge a few bucks, too—and Jorge brought the visitor up. Hey, this guy's getting popular, you know."

"You have a description? Did you see the name?"

"Jorge said it was already starting to get dark and he didn't pay much attention. Said the guy was wearing an old sports jacket—patches on the elbows. Jorge thought he was oldish, but Jorge isn't so alert, especially when he comes right to work from the car wash. We figured Gowdy had to have a relative or two. It happens all the time, with these people. A cousin or nephew or grandkid will stop by, but they don't stay long and they don't leave any numbers, 'cause they don't want you calling them in the middle of the night. But they have to sign in. The log sheets are locked up in Whitmore's desk. Nobody sees the medical records, man, I hate to think what she's writing about these people." He stopped abruptly, then said, "You know, it's funny, now that I think about it, but this visitor, this last one, the morning after he came, Mr. Gowdy said he was missing stuff from his trunk. Real upset he couldn't find some old things he had kept there."

"Did he say what?"

"No. But he was unhappy."

"Joe, it's pretty important for me to know what was missing. Do you think you could go back through the room and try to remember?"

Joey shrugged, said sure, he'd try. I think he was enjoying this; probably a refreshing change from his daily routine. And I had more to ask of him.

"Joey. What time do you get off?"

"Midnight. And no fucking overtime either. Why?"

"I'm going to need your help later tonight. I'm coming by."

"Hey, forget it, man. I'm not helping anybody bust into Whitmore's desk, if that's what you're thinking. This may be an armpit of a job, but it's the only one I've got, and I'm not giving it up."

"Nobody's asking you to give it up, Joe. I'm asking you to not see me coming. You'll make two weeks' pay in the process."

"You're talking better than four hundred bucks."

"That's right. A long weekend at the Jersey shore this summer, maybe even a flight to Florida, you get the right fares. Besides, this could lead me to the old guy. The cops don't much care if he's alive or okay, but you do, despite all your tough-guy talk. These visitors could be the key to finding out where he is. Joey, I don't want to get melodramatic, but people are getting killed in this town, and there are links to the old man and to the place the bodies keep turning up. An ancestor of his—a kid a few years younger than you—was hung up there a century or so ago. Blackhead could be in trouble." Finally, I thought, I was sounding like a detective. I was on a roll.

Breaking and entering would be quite an escalation for an investigator who was running reference checks until last week and whose office was in a dingy mall above a sneaker store. Speaking of which, I needed to go there, pick up the mail, and check in with Luis.

Joe was quiet as we pulled around the block and back to the point where we'd started. "I'll agree to this much, man. I don't know what you're doing, and I don't want to know any more. I am worried about the old man, though. I want to help you find him. You show up at eleven forty-five—the night janitor is gone by then and I'm alone. Give me the money and I go upstairs. I don't want to know shit more than that. Fifteen minutes later, I come down, you're gone."

I got it. I hopped out of the car and walked back into the ped's waiting room. A surly-looking Emily was rubbing her arm with one hand and leafing through an Archie comic with the other.

"Shot?"

"Tetanus," she growled. "And just where were you? Off on some superinvestigative work, I suppose?" The disapproving mother, still sitting there with her runny-nosed kid, raised her eyebrow. Well, I didn't like to watch kids get needles. I couldn't stand needles myself.

Driving home, I debated whether to tell Jane what I was planning. Aside from the obvious fact that some strange and deadly person or persons were on the loose, the cops had the town as buttoned up as the White House. I had to be exceedingly careful, and the art of stealth was not one of my finely honed skills. A burglary rap would not enhance my reputation, my career, or my marriage. And breaking into Miss Bitch Whitmore's desk would be a damn sight easier than sneaking out of my house at midnight without Jane's noticing.

22

I drove back to the American Way, excited and anxious about my plans for burgling the dread Miss Whitmore's office. I would do it suburban-detective style, stopping in later at the mall hardware store for a screwdriver and hammer big enough to pry open the drawer of a standard metal office desk. The visitors' log could be crucial if Blackhead's disappearance was related to the rest of this, and it struck me that it almost had to be. I considered just asking Miss Bitch Whitmore to see the log, but I couldn't think of one reason why she should let me. And if I let her know I was interested, then I couldn't grab it later without leading the police straight to my decaying home.

I rarely joined the rush hour torrents pouring into the mall parking lot. Usually at that hour, I was rushing the kids home from a play date or soccer game. If the detective business went sour, my emergency fallback was to launch a suburban van business to ferry kids to and from friends' homes and playing fields and tap-dance studios. Couldn't miss, and you wouldn't have to crawl around strange offices at night, either.

I veered around to the side entrance of the mall, past Murray Grobstein's. Jane argued that I could just as easily work at home as keep an office out here and save some money. But I balked at the idea of not having a place of my own to go, and at having unsavory characters come to the house, should I ever be retained by any.

Besides, I had grown fond of the mall, of its tacky jewelry stands and T-shirt shops, even of the dreadful Muzak piped in over the fake waterfall and the plastic palm fronds that drooped out of their decorator pots. It was a cozy feeling to be ensconced in my spare little cell above the American Way's unswerving capitalist diversity.

I waved through the windows of Lightning Burger at Luis, who was circling watchfully past several new trainees—there are always trainees at fast-food restaurants. A third of his time was spent hiring or firing people, Luis complained. I wasn't surprised. Standing for hours, pretending to be courteous, awash in greasy smells and sounds—how much of that could anybody take? In a just world, Luis would have been thinking about a gracious Havana retirement, reaping the rewards of his distinguished career, planning deep-sea fishing excursions.

I never expect visitors in my office, one of the things about it I find relaxing, I suppose. If I feel lonely—it happened more frequently at the beginning than it does now—there are hundreds of people to watch one flight down. Few clients drop by an office on the second floor of a mall; they make appointments, or I go to see them.

But Judy Cole was standing outside my door, leaning against the wall, round glasses perched at the tip of her nose, reading the latest *Glamour*. She looked up as I rounded the corner.

The thing that had struck me from the first was how unteenaged she looked and sounded. She seemed to have skipped the awkward phase and become an attractive, poised adult, wise beyond her years. Was my understanding of late adolescence skewed in some way? I wondered. Were other kids like this?

"Hey," she said, as casually as if she waited for me every afternoon at this time. She was wearing jeans, boots, a navy pea jacket, and a long red woolen scarf that reached her knees. She smiled and rolled up the magazine, noticing my glance at it. "I admit to reading a beauty mag—that's the difference between me and everybody else. They don't admit it."

"You don't strike me as needing it," I observed, unlocking my office door and wondering if that were an appropriate remark to make to a high school kid.

"Typical male comment," she said, with a toss of her head. "Nobody's judging *you* on your wardrobe."

"Good thing, too," I said. "What are you doing here, not to be presumptuous?"

"I've got something to tell you. I should have told you the other night, but I wanted to think about whether you were trustworthy or not. I decided you are, and I hope to God I'm right. I liked the way you talked about your daughter. She sounds neat, and you were so proud of her, the way you lit up. So I decided my dad and the rest of Wall Street were wrong about you. At least I hope so."

"It's not just Wall Street," I reminded her. "Don't forget the FBI and the federal law enforcement apparatus, plus the local police, most of my neighbors, and the seven-fifteen Boonton-to-Hoboken train contingent."

I ushered her into my anteroom and around the pile of mail, mostly junk circulars, that had accumulated on the floor in the four days since I had been in. I flicked on the light and the baseboard heat; the room was freezing. It was dusk now, and the parking lot acquired a pleasingly eerie quality as the light from the storefronts spilled onto the asphalt.

From up here, I liked to picture vans and wagons full of

families going home happy, moms caressing plastic sacks of new clothes, kids waiting to cut open the cardboard toy packages, dads toting new buzz saws or tool kits, all that commerce, all that cash entering the money chain.

Of course, from the ground floor you got a different perspective. The kids were apt to be whining about something they wouldn't get, Mom was smarting over the dimensions of her hips and the unavailability of flattering pants, Dad couldn't afford much of anything, and the whole family was snapping in the threatening or irritated tones of tired people growing a bit sick of one another. I preferred the view from above, headlights slowly gliding by, the cars in the lot flitting in and out of parking rows like the little suburban fireflies they were.

Judy tossed her jacket onto the old leatherette couch below the window and unwound the scarf from her neck. She wore dangly silver earrings, one a circle, one a triangle. I felt a little uneasy, being alone with her in my office in the evening. Could I trust *her*?

"Is each earring supposed to be different?" I asked.

She nodded. Her teeth were so white I made a note not to induce a smile, her eyes a startling blue. So I was infatuated, no point in denying that. Was I imagining that she was too? I hoped I was. I wasn't even sure she wasn't a minor. Actually, I take that back; I knew damn well she was of age. But so what? I'd seen lots of middle-aged men risk their personal lives on such an impulse. That kind of vanity was scary in your over-forty male, especially one whose wife would respond to the hint of a fling by kicking me out to spend the night on the front porch with Percentage for a blanket. I had no excuse at all for such foolishness. I'd spent too many days of my work life chasing after or mopping up behind jerks who succumbed to vanity, intimations of mortality, lust, or just plain stupidity. Men had choices. They might all be tempted, but they could look back in satisfaction at the right choices they made, rather than be explaining or apologizing all the time.

As a man involved more deeply than ever before with his family, I had come to feel strongly about how men had to start behaving. There was no way I was going out into the woods to beat drums with other men. But I'd rot in Hell before I'd hurt my family in those traditional male ways.

"Kit," Judy said, taking my name in vain as if we were old buddies. She didn't act like a kid; why should I expect her to treat me as an elder? She looked tense and a little tired. Whatever she was about to say had been on her mind for some time.

"I got a telephone call from Carol two nights before she died. I haven't told anyone, not my father or the police—no one. That's one reason I didn't tell you when we met. I was— well, frankly, I was frightened. There are no courses on how to behave when your best friend confides a secret to you and then is murdered forty-eight hours later. She made me swear not to tell anyone, not to breathe a word. She was half demented with fear and guilt, I think, just out of her mind. I had the feeling if she didn't tell someone, she would have cracked. I wasn't shocked that something had been bothering her, that was plain to see. But I wasn't prepared for what it was."

Now that she had sat down, in the light from the overhead, I saw how drawn and fatigued Judy looked. Something had happened, or occurred to her, that had shaken her up.

She sat silently for a few minutes, as if she needed to crank herself up to continue. Blood-oath secrets between best friends probably weren't something you casually let slip. Or maybe she was struggling to confront something she just didn't know how to handle. The smells from Lightning Burger wafted lightly up through the floor.

"You're thinking about how carefully to treat an adolescent girl, aren't you?" she said suddenly.

I said nothing, wanting neither to irritate or patronize her. I wasn't sure how to avoid either. "I'm thinking that you look like hell," I said finally. "That you're either scared or shocked out of your wits."

"I sensed you were smart enough to read me," she said, "to get how difficult it is for someone like me to be around teenagers all the time, even though, technically, I am a teenager myself. It's hard, you know, to be an adult in a kid's body."

"I was struck by your maturity," I mumbled awkwardly. "By your presence. You're right, you are not like any kid I know or expected to meet. But I'm struck by how rattled you look now. Maybe you'd better tell me about it."

That was as far as I dared go. She looked as if she were ready to bolt. She'd come this far, she'd probably go farther, unless I said something dumb and spooked her. The murmur from the highway, soothing and continuous, filled in the silence, along with the Muzak from below.

"What you're seeing is fear, pure and simple, Kit. Carol told me something I don't know what to do with, something I didn't want to know. Something that may possibly have gotten her killed. Or maybe I'm just being foolish about it. I really don't know *how* to take it."

"Judy, just tell me. I can't promise I won't go to the police with your information—my license says I have to take them evidence of criminal wrongdoing. So if you're telling me you know who killed Carol, I may not be able to keep that kind of secret for you. But you're carrying a great weight around, and that isn't healthy. And to be frank—I'm not trying to alarm you—but if you know something that got someone killed, then isn't it possible you or somebody else could be in danger, too?" When I thought about it, her poise was almost scary, under the circumstances.

She pondered the question for a long minute, then nodded. She said softly, "Carol sobbed into the phone for fifteen minutes that night. She told me she was in some awful trouble, that she could be in trouble even for talking to me. She said . . ." Judy shook her head, clearly in pain for her friend; her voice wavered a bit. "She said she had gotten involved with a man, an older man. I guess you really rocked me when you suggested that at dinner the other night. I thought somehow you knew. She wouldn't say how, except that he had messed with her mind somehow, due to special 'circumstances.' She said he had 'arranged' to have some time alone with her, then gotten drunk with her, and they'd ended up making love. She said—Kit, you have to understand what a knockout punch this was, coming from Carol. She wouldn't even *litter*. She *never* looked at anybody but Ken. It was incomprehensible. She made me swear a hundred times that I would never tell a soul."

I pulled out my notebook and a pocket tape recorder, right in full view, then switched it on. Judy could stop if she wanted to, but it was insane not to get this recorded. She looked at the machine briefly, then continued.

"She said the man had secretly made videotapes of the whole thing with a camera hidden in the room. He said he was going to distribute it all over town—to Ken, to her parents, throughout the school—if she didn't have sex with him again. But she said she wasn't as frightened of that as she was of him. She said he was powerful and angry and she was just terrified to cross him. So she decided she had to continue the relationship and she did, more than once."

For a kid like Carol, that could make it a lot more frightening to come forward. I couldn't imagine Judy so terrified of what other people would think. And in that difference, I thought, might have hung a life.

I started to speak, but stopped at the sight of the tears streaming down Judy's face. I got her a glass of water and pulled my chair around the desk to sit next to her. When people start talking, it's best to let them talk. I handed her a tissue. Seeing her in such distress deepened the sense that she was an unusual person and that I had to protect her. As a grown-up protecting an injured kid? Or as a man drawn to helping a woman?

"She said she couldn't bear the thought of what it would do to Ken, or to her mother. You know, Carol was genuinely religious. I hate to think how this must have torn her up. I can't even imagine what the 'circumstances' were that would have led her to this. She said this man had apparently done this before, that he had other tapes he would show her to threaten her. He said he felt bad about putting this pressure on her; that he hated himself for doing it, but he had no choice. He would keep the tapes for insurance. Carol told me she couldn't handle it, but she was afraid to go to the police or to her priest. I suggested she tell Mr. Handley, that he would help her. I begged her to, but she said she didn't want to talk about it anymore and got off the phone."

She twisted the tissue in her hands, sobbing softly but still quite under control. "God, I will never know if I did the right thing or not." You sure didn't, my young friend, I thought. And it will be a black day for you when you figure out just how wrong it was. Adults aren't good for much, but there are still some things they handle better. But I said nothing. I put my hand on her shoulder and she slid a hand over mine. I felt a tingle travel up my back.

"I called Ken," she said, sobbing more openly. "I told him Carol was in some sort of trouble—I didn't tell him what—and that he needed to talk with her, that he was the only person she might listen to." She blew her nose.

"I begged her to tell me who it was—for her sake and protection, in case she was missing or hurt—or worse. But every time I asked her, she got hysterical. She said there was just no way she could tell me—of all people."

I asked her to repeat that. "Why 'you of all people'? Did she mean you because you were her best friend or you because of who the guy was?"

She shrugged, then blew her nose again. "God, I don't know. It could have been either. She just freaked every time I suggested she tell me, as if that were the scariest thing of all. As if she really didn't want me to know."

"But that's so odd. Why would she have told you at all, then? Why call you at that moment?"

"Because I think she just couldn't stand to keep it in anymore. I think the fear and shame were just driving her mad, and she couldn't handle it."

"Could she have been trying to warn you?" I asked, although I didn't have anything specific in mind.

"I don't know. I believe if Carol thought I was in any great danger she would have risked anything to tell me. I would have for her. So I can't imagine she wouldn't have told me outright if she thought there was a risk for me. I just had the impression she had to talk to somebody, and I was her best friend, but—"

"But the last person she was willing to disclose this guy's identity to," I said quietly.

Her shoulders slumped, then she buried her face in the tissue. She sat sobbing for several minutes. I didn't put my arm around her; I just sat quietly trying to take in what she'd said. Why could Carol tell Judy an older man was threatening her and forcing her to have sex with him but find it so impossible to tell her who? What was the point of going that far, but no farther?

"Judy, think carefully now, this is important. Are you sure she said an 'older' man? Do you think she meant older than a high school student or a really older man, as in . . . oh, I don't know . . . me?"

She managed a little laugh. "I may be forgetting some of what she said. I was so taken aback. I think she meant an older guy, and the way she used the term could be anything from college up. I don't think she meant somebody *really* old —like you." We both chuckled. "Mostly I think she meant somebody outside the group, outside our circle."

"But somebody like that would have to be resourceful enough to have a place to take her, a camera set up, and the force of personality to really frighten her. Somebody pretty powerful. Or pretty mean."

Judy seemed frozen, transported. She seemed to have forgotten I was in the room, as if some idea had just over-whelmed her.

"What is it, Judy? Did you think of something?" She shook her head, unconvincingly. She had thought of some-thing, and it was a doozy, whatever it was. "Don't hold out on me, Judy. This is way too important, and too dangerous."

"That's it," she said crisply. "That's my end of the story. I'm just tired, that's all. I haven't slept very well since, wonder-ing if I were responsible for their deaths, if Ken got Carol to confide in him, if he did something rash. I have no idea what happened, except that two days after I got the call from her and called him, they were both dead. I'll never stop wondering if I could have prevented it or not. Do you think they were both murdered? Or did Ken kill her?"

I didn't know what I thought. Mostly what I thought was that she was pale as a sheet and hiding something major. But she had clearly made up her mind not to share it. However, she was right about one thing. Even though it made me uncomfortable, I did feel close to her, and what I was seeing in her face at the moment was something between shock and panic.

"Did Carol say anything else about this man, anything at all which might suggest who he was, what he did, where he lived?"

She thought for a few seconds, then shook her head. The sobbing had abated. She seemed shocked, washed out, numb.

I debated putting my arm around her shoulders. Don't touch her, I cautioned myself. Don't start touching her. It seemed indecent; she was too vulnerable. Besides, I had to get to the hardware store to purchase burgling tools. I stood up and paced instead.

"Judy, I'm glad you told me this much. It was the smart thing to do. You have no way of knowing whether this was related to the deaths or not, so you're taking on a lot of guilt and responsibility for no reason. In fact, the evidence points quite strongly to Ken's being overcome with jealousy and deciding to end his pain. Maybe he wanted to end hers, too. You had no reason at all to think that keeping her secret— which she begged you to do—would be dangerous in any way."

"You're speaking to me like a grown-up speaks to a kid."

She finished the mop-up of her stricken face, stood up, and looked me in the eye. She was nearly my height. She stared at me for a moment, levelly and frankly, before kissing me hard on the lips. I stepped back, unnerved.

"Judy, look, that's inappropriate . . . I—"

"I know," she said immediately. "I'm sorry. I know you probably see me as a crazy high school kid and maybe that's all I am. I'm grateful to you for hearing me out, for believing me. Please do whatever you feel is right with the information. I'd like to see you again. Maybe dinner tomorrow night at Gennaro's?" Then she scooped up her jacket and rushed out. Anxious to get away? Or anxious to get somewhere?

I was still sputtering when she closed the door, conscious of being frightened, confused, manipulated, and aroused all at the same time. I had to go to the police; the information, however vague, was stunning. I didn't have much concrete to tell them, but Leeming had made it clear he would have my ass—and license—if I withheld information. But that could wait. I had an appointment with a young woman who wasn't as grown-up as she thought she was and who had touched me in a way that felt reckless but irresistible. Was this the onset of loony time for middle-aged men? Or just a grateful kiss from an unburdened kid? Maybe she would tell me the rest of it tomorrow.

I wrote the dinner date in my appointment book, which made it seem official and aboveboard.

Jane called just after Judy left. For a second, I thought she was going to beg me not to disgrace myself with a teenager or break into the nursing home that night, but then I remembered with a flash of guilt that she didn't know about either.

"Kit," she said. "Emergency. I've got an attempted suicide

by one of my patients. I've got to go. I called Sally Oliver to be with the kids, but we've got a 7 P.M. conference with Mr. DiGeorgio and Mrs. Steneman to talk about Ben's grades. Can you make it? It's a big one."

It *was* a big one. Ben had gotten two C+'s on his report card, the lowest grades of his life. In some circles, that would have been considered a bump. For a Rochambeau Junior High kid with Ben's record, it was an earthquake. Mr. DiGeorgio had written in the "comments" section, "Ben doesn't seem to care much about his schoolwork this term." We were furious, which is the standard parental reaction when kids get into trouble in school—be pissed at the school. No one had ever suggested that Ben was anything but a terrific student and a hard worker for his whole academic life. Neither of the teachers had talked to Ben about the problem or to us. It had taken several days to schedule this appointment. I could get there and still have time to fit in my shopping at the hardware store.

"Sure, I'll go," I said.

"Please let them know we're not happy," she instructed. "They might try talking with Ben about his problems, rather than sending notes like that home on report cards."

I parked in the curving driveway closed to traffic during the day, and walked into Ben's homeroom at three minutes past seven to confront the two grim-faced, weary-looking middle-aged people who had to face another incensed Rochambeau parent.

Naturally, nothing was ever the kid's fault. Every version of events parents heard from their children was true in every detail. There was nothing for the kid to take responsibility for, only the teacher, the principal, or the system.

"Mr. Deleeuw," began DiGeorgio, academic looking in his short beard, ratty cardigan sweater, scuffed Rockports, and chinos. "Thanks for coming. I'm sure you were concerned about Ben's report card."

"You bet I was concerned," I snapped back, adopting the aggressive posture so many other parents had recounted taking in their own teacher confrontations. I sure wasn't going to be outdone doing battle for my kid. The school system was good enough, went the talk around town, but you had to fight for your kid. You had to let them know you weren't going to let them shortchange or ignore your child. You had to keep making it clear.

"My wife, who's a psychiatric social worker, was disappointed too," I went on, a touch sarcastically. "We were shocked that no one had talked to Ben. We were disappointed that no one had talked with us about these so-called attitude problems, the first ones he's ever had. And frankly, we were both puzzled by the fact that nothing like this has ever happened before in Ben's academic experience. He's never had a grade lower than a B. It seems to us he isn't particularly stimulated. He seems bored, and when that happens, why, I don't know as I blame him for not paying attention."

Mrs. Steneman looked down at her desk, then up at the clock. It was a fifteen-minute conference and several minutes of it were already gone. Her tired, disappointed face reminded me of Benchley, of Handley, of everything that was pressing in on me.

I didn't like the sound of me. I thought I sounded like a convincing argument for tenure.

"I'm sorry," I said.

Her head shot up. His eyes widened.

"I'm sorry. I feel like an ass. Look, can we erase the last few minutes and start again? Sometimes we just do what's expected of us. Please forgive me, and tell me how I can help my kid."

Mr. DiGeorgio looked at Mrs. Steneman, and for a moment I thought they were considering calling security or bolting the room. There was an awkward pause.

"Well, Mr. Deleeuw," he said tentatively, as if I would change my mind and go berserk any second. "That's really what we'd like to do as well."

I said I knew. What was the problem?

"Well," said Mrs. Steneman, still looking suspicious, "it's not uncommon for eighth-grade boys to slump like this. There's a lot going on in their lives, as you may remember. They're worried about girls, their bodies are changing—sometimes there are problems at home?" The last was a question.

I said there were no problems at home, but that I had been going through a sustained career change that Ben was certainly conscious of. But I didn't really know if anything was troubling him; I hadn't really asked.

"Ben is quite bright. And extremely competent," DiGeorgio said. "That's why I wrote the note. If I thought this was his best effort, I'd give him a B and leave it alone. But something's troubling him. We had a conference during lunch on last Friday, Mr. Deleeuw. He seemed distracted, even angry, I would say. I'm worried about him. I think he's one of my most creative students."

"And usually one of the most diligent," added Mrs. Steneman. "But he's not turning in his homework regularly. Perhaps it would be helpful if you could talk with him."

I could see that DiGeorgio was hesitating about something. "I know I came in here like another nightmare parent; I won't do that again," I apologized. "But if something is bothering Ben, I wish you'd tell me. I sort of have the feeling you've got an idea, even if you're not sure."

DiGeorgio smiled, then cleared his throat, and closed

Ben's file. They still looked startled, which I took as a mild but powerful commentary on the parent/teacher relationship in Rochambeau; it was apparently shocking when a parent wanted to hear what the teacher really thought.

"I appreciate your attitude," he said. "I think Ben *is* having a problem. It's a bit unorthodox, but I see you want to know."

He hesitated again. God, was Ben taking drugs?

"Mr. Deleeuw, I don't know the specific details of your . . . work. I do know you are inquiring into the deaths of the two high school students." He shook his head sadly. "There's a perception among some of the other boys that you are working on behalf of the young man who the police say was responsible for the deaths. In their minds, you're working to clear a killer. Some of them have also apparently heard from their parents—I'll just be blunt with you here—that you used to work in the financial district, and that you had some difficulty with the authorities there." He blushed, looking to see how I was taking it.

I smiled and nodded. The Lee Coles of the world did, of course, have children.

My stomach was already sinking, and not from shame. From guilt.

"They call you names," DiGeorgio was saying. "You know kids, they can be pretty brutal. Ben's been in a lot of shoving matches."

The bruises Ben said he got playing basketball had just become more explicable.

"It's true," said Mrs. Steneman, now that it was clear I wasn't going to pull out a gun or something. "It's been going on in my class too. Whenever one of these Wall Street people is sentenced, the boys sing this song: 'Ben Deleeuw, it will happen to you, your daddy's going to Allenwood, too.' "

"He always defends you," DiGeorgio added. "He's very loyal."

I thanked them both and climbed back into the Volvo. Poor Ben. We rush them around to games, pick them up at friends', and can't even see what's going on a fraction of an inch below the surface. It was one thing to pay for your mistakes, another for your kid to pick up the freight. I had misjudged him as well as caused him grief. I had just assumed he was ashamed of me, and maybe he was, but he was also taking a lot of stuff defending me.

Still, I felt relieved by the conference, as if a weight had lifted. I knew better what was troubling my son, if not what to do about it. For starters, though, it would probably be helpful to avoid being arrested for breaking and entering tonight.

In Rochambeau, parent-teacher conferences like that aren't passed along casually to absent spouses. Jane debriefed me on that and other developments like I was a CIA agent back from a tour inside the KGB, when there was still a KGB. In one sense, we were both relieved.

"It's something specific," she said, when I had concluded. "We can deal with it, once this madness is past." I agreed, but I knew it wasn't going to stop eating at me until we got to tend to it, and that might be awhile.

Jane looked at me quizzically when, instead of climbing into bed with her, I began changing into dark clothes. I casually dropped the notion that I was going out for a while, but instead of obliging me by saying "Sure, honey" (do women say that anymore?), she bolted up in bed and demanded to know where I was headed.

In addition to the obvious, bedtime for us is also a chance to snuggle, to compare notes on the kids, and to catch up on news from work. The rest of the time we have an understanding that we're often rushing around too much to stop and talk. So she props her case notes up on her knees until I come into bed, trying to get set for the troubled parade she'll face in the morning.

We had a brief flare-up because I wouldn't tell her where I was going.

"What if you're not back? What if there's a problem and I don't know how to reach you?"

I tried to sound entirely calm as I pocketed the car keys and pulled on a jacket.

"Look, Jane, this is the part of my work we've never had to face but was inevitable. I'm not a Wall Street trader anymore. I work unpredictable hours sometimes. I've got to do something I don't want to talk about. It's better if you don't know all the details, and I surely don't want you trying to get in touch with me."

"Is it dangerous?"

"No."

"Then why won't you tell me where you're going?"

"I'm going to break into someone's desk, okay? I want you to be able to say you didn't know anything about it, that's all. I'm not trying to be Philip Marlowe—I just need some room here."

"Room to go to jail?"

I contemplated explaining the importance of a break in this case, the headway I didn't want to interrupt, the unwritten rule we'd always followed about giving your partner room when he needed it. Instead, I caved.

"I'm going to the nursing home, okay? If I'm not back by 3 A.M., call a lawyer. If I'm not back by 6 A.M. call the cops."

She accepted that, albeit uncomfortably. I guess the more she knew, the easier it was to handle.

"You know," I said, eyeing the thick purple quilt enviously, "this girl has knocked me for a loop, what she told me about Carol Lombardi. In the back of my mind, I was edging toward the notion that perhaps this could all be related to the disposition of the Brown estate. That's a huge parcel of land, one of the few remaining in the metropolitan area. Maybe somebody was trying to manipulate the price down, by spilling all this blood in and around the place."

Jane gave me her not-good-enough look, but avoided the look of total contempt she used when she thought I was coming from Mars. "Then why the Peterson child? She doesn't live anywhere near the Brown estate."

I shook my head. "I don't know," I said. "There are too many threads here."

Jane pulled the quilt up over her shoulders. She hates both heating and air-conditioning and the result, as far as I'm concerned, is that we're always either freezing or boiling. "Well, all of these incidents have one thread," she said, slowly and deliberately, as if she were thinking out loud.

"Yeah, what?"

"Well, don't they all have the effect of making Rochambeau seem less desirable, of making it a less inviting place? If you were setting out to frighten people away, you'd do any combination or all of these things—certainly you'd scare a child. That would frighten any resident or potential resident. Except that—no, this doesn't hold up, now that I run it through out loud."

"But why?" I said. "You were just beginning to make sense."

"Because of what Carol told your young friend." I looked

closely at her expression to see if it held any edge or double meaning, but I saw none. "She suggests some sexual motive for Carol's death. I suppose Ken could have seen a videotape or something and gone over the edge—that's possible. But that wouldn't explain the other incidents at all." She shook her head. "You know, honey, I'm sorry, I guess I don't see a thread, not yet."

Too bad, I thought. Now *I'd* have to find one.

A detective's life just wasn't as orderly as other suburbanites', I muttered to myself, trying to overlook how bizarre it was for a grown man who wasn't a thief to be heading out at midnight to break into somebody's desk. I put my claw hammer and screwdriver into a nylon duffel bag once used for racquetball equipment.

I went into Emmy's room to give her a kiss, then into Ben's to pat him on his forehead, not because I loved him any differently but because I knew he would find it gross and disgusting to be kissed by his father. I said a silent prayer that they wouldn't have to go to school in the morning explaining that their father wasn't a burglar, on top of everything else.

Jane held me for a long time before I left, but said nothing. Lots of character, that woman. My mind skipped ahead to tomorrow's dinner. I felt foolish about it, but had little doubt that I would go. What a goofy cliché, a forty-two-year-old man all atwitter because a beautiful young woman gave him a kiss. I should have said no to dinner. But Judy had put herself through a small corner of hell to talk to me; I couldn't walk away from her. And I guess I didn't want to.

I drove down Elm past the high school and toward downtown. A couple of police cruisers had pulled up alongside each other so that the officers could chat. I could see the Styrofoam coffee cups as I drove slowly around them, but none of the officers paid any attention to me. Ahead, I saw the lights of a helicopter, its belly lights flashing red.

I pulled the Volvo into the back of the Rochambeau Homes building, and stepped lightly out of the car. This late, Rochambeau seems a ghost town of darkened homes and denuded winter trees. Nothing in my town has any reason for stirring at this hour. I needed to move quickly.

23

Fannie Clark had always despised the midnight-to-eight shift, at least until all these troubles started. The most excitement a dispatcher got was a drunk driver smashing into a tree or a loud party once or twice a month. But since those dead kids up on the Brown place, it was always the Fourth of July in Rochambeau, a welcome transformation for a bored forty-three-year-old in need of some drama. Not that dispatcher Clark wished anybody any harm, but she had to be honest about it, she did relish the action. And she might need it to last a whale of a long time, since she couldn't afford to leave the Rochambeau PD and could barely afford to stay.

The county prosecutor and sheriff had been on the scene practically from the first. The state police had been here for days. Now a special advisory unit from the FBI had landed, with a fleet of well-maintained cars and truckloads of high-tech phone-tapping and computer equipment. She thought the headquarters might burst, that the side walls would blow right out if one more cop got stuffed inside. Thank God they'd moved all the reporters and camera crews to a special press center set up in the fire hall. They'd been worse than cockroaches, crawling all over the building.

The phone hardly ever stopped now. Every dog that barked at a passerby, every raccoon that knocked over a garbage can, every car that idled a tad too slowly, someone would hit 911. Enough cars were out there now to cover every call, too, and fast, that was the amazing thing. Ten days ago, there were two cruisers on the streets during the lobster shift, both frequently holed up at Kay's Diner on the edge of town. Now, there were eighteen units out there, and she and Harry, the late day dispatcher, were working double shifts. Harry was sitting alongside her now, handling Sectors 9 through 18, the south end of town. The state cop supervisors had put up an electronic map breaking the town into eighteen sectors, where before there were three. Calls coming in lit small red bulbs in the sector they were coming from. Yellow lights were radio beacons coming from the police cars themselves to show where all the units were. Another dozen marked and unmarked cruisers were in reserve out back and at each end of town.

Rochambeau had gone nuts, Fannie told Harry in wonderment. You hardly saw a child on the street anymore. Parents clogged the schools at closing time, picking the kids up themselves rather than entrusting them to the bus.

Harry nodded. People used to complain that they could never afford to live in Rochambeau, he pointed out. Now they wouldn't even drive through it, detouring all the way around Bergen County to avoid it. When they caught this fellow, whoever he was, they were going to roast his ass.

Fannie reached for her thermos and was about to pour a second cup of black coffee to get her through this cold but no longer lonely night when Sector 12 lit up, flashing red. Wasn't the high school there, on Elm Street, leading target of vandals and practical jokesters? Fannie felt a tingling. People tended to underestimate the importance of a good dispatcher. She'd saved at least a half-dozen lives by getting kids to stay on the line while she called the fire department, or putting parents through to the state poison center, or sending an ambulance to some man gasping from a heart attack. She flicked her earphone switch on the second ring.

"Rochambeau Police. How may I help you?"

"This is Jefferson Drake, down on Elm Street. I live across from the high school. I heard this godawful shout, scream is closer to it, so I opened the door—my wife wouldn't let me go out and look, she says at seventy-two I'm too old, wouldn't have it—"

Fannie interrupted. She spoke slowly and coolly, as she always did when talking with the old or the young. You could spook them easily if you jumped on their asses over the phone, demanding to know what you needed to know, namely What-the-hell-are-you-calling-for? "Mr. Drake, what is it? What crime are you reporting?"

"Well, it isn't clear what I saw, but I think I saw a body hanging up there from the flagpole. I know my eyesight isn't great, but since I couldn't get closer, and what with everything happening, I feel foolish. But I thought—"

"Mr. Drake, please stay on the line. I'm going to put you on hold but please don't hang up." Fannie hit the digital monitor which showed the number the call was coming from and recorded it in case they were disconnected or the old coot got embarrassed and hung up. Then she pushed the buzzer that alerted the sheriff and the state police, as well as the deputy chief, all of them smoking and swapping sports insights in the back of the station to give Chief Leeming a few hours' rest downstairs.

She pressed the on-air transmission button. "Attention Sector Twelve and nearby units. We have possible eight-eight-eight"—the previously agreed-upon code for undetermined trouble; mention a body over the air these days and the whole northern half of the state would light up—"in the vicinity of the flagpole at the high school." The room behind her suddenly quieted, and she became aware of a half-dozen or so men, guns protruding from their waists or armpits, gathering quietly behind her. She could feel their attentiveness baking the back of her neck like a sun lamp.

A dozen yellow lights began moving rapidly towards Elm and the high school. Several engines roared to life in the parking lot behind the station.

"Don? You on the mike?" she asked the squad car that arrived first.

"I'm here, Fannie."

"What you got?"

"Got a flag, Fannie. Looks like they forgot to take it down. Call everybody off—"

Chief Leeming's voice barked onto the frequency. "All units, this is Leeming. Return to your sectors immediately. Don't leave the rest of the town uncovered. Someone could be hoping for just that."

Well, thought Fannie, so much for her honed instincts. A flag. But these days, nothing seemed quite right in Rochambeau.

24

The back door of the nursing home was propped open. Above and beyond the call of duty, I thought gratefully. I had brought $430 for Joey, by far my biggest expense in the case to date, who might continue to be helpful, though there was no sign of him at the moment. I hoped to God it was Joey I could hear moving around upstairs. I liked him. He'd tried to affect a wise-ass demeanor, but I thought his concern for Blackhead Gowdy was real. I stood inside in the hallway for a minute or two until I got my bearings, then made my way to the front of the building where the office was, my duffel bag clanking too noisily.

The home's smell was distinctive—not death, but decaying life. I wondered if aged, uncomprehending eyes were watching me from the darkened rooms on either side of the hall as I switched a flashlight on and made my way through the double doors into the lobby. Blackhead Gowdy probably saw more than he let on; probably many of them did. I stuffed the wad of money, as arranged, into a pot that held a fading dracaena. Joey had no intention of even laying eyes on me.

A single lamp with a dim bulb lighted the way into the opened office. I walked through the outer room, which seemed to be used only for files and bookshelves, and back into Miss Whitmore's office. It was noticeably out of whack with the rest of the spartan building, which is to say it was tastefully and expensively furnished with a thick pile carpet, a plush velvet sofa, and three or four antique-looking chairs. Clearly, this was the room in which relatives agreed to consign their aging charges into Miss Whitmore's loving hands. I slid a pair of rubber gloves on, flicked on the desk lamp, and then froze—a wail of sirens passing through the town made me shiver. I heard at least four or five, growing closer. I switched off the desk lamp and my flashlight and crouched beneath the desk. But the sirens rushed past, racing up Elm. I wondered if our strange creature, with his stovepipe hat and ancient hemp, had struck again. I hoped not. Nor did I want some twitchy deputy to mistake me for him.

I decided to keep the desk lamp off and use the pencil-point flashlight I had purchased from Jim O'Brien at the hardware store. I told him I'd lost the key to an unused desk in my attic. He'd given me a hacksaw and instructed me to just slice through the thin band of steel most of them used for locks on the drawers. Those locks weren't worth a shit, he said, showing me how to pull the severed band out afterwards and leave no trace—nothing, he said, to mar the outward appearance of the desk, in case I wanted to sell it later. I thought Miss Whitmore would quickly figure out that the lock wasn't working, but maybe she'd think it was just broken. As long as I wasn't around, I really didn't care what she thought.

I pulled out my hacksaw and began sliding it back and forth. It took about ten minutes to slice through. Occasionally, I would hear someone groan or Joey—I assumed—slide something across the floor. I had to get moving; I didn't want to make my accomplice more nervous than necessary.

The drawer suddenly slid open. Using the pliers Jimmy had sold me—and with some pride—I popped off the band that locked the drawer. A spare set of keys, as Joey had promised, was inside. I opened the left-hand drawer, but found only tissues and paper clips. The visitors' log was in the big, bottom right-hand one. I felt my heart thump. Cold as the night was, I was soaked in sweat.

The log was covered in red leather, with the year embossed in fake gold leaf. I flipped it open and, keeping my gloves on, thumbed awkwardly until I got to January 8. The name I wanted to see was quite legible. And quite a shock.

I locked the drawer, blew away the dust from the hacksaw, pocketed the flashlight and headed towards the back door. I almost yelled when I heard Joey's voice shout impatiently: "Your time's up, man. Get outta here."

I did. I was outside in seconds, sprinting down the back steps and across the frozen lot. I had almost made it to the Volvo when a piercing white light blinded me and I heard that barked command I had never actually heard away from a television set or a movie theater: "Police! Freeze or I'll blow a hole in your stomach big enough for a cow to stroll through!" Blinded and paralyzed though I was, I recognized Leeming's city-honed accents and delivery. Keeping faith with the wisecracking tradition of my new profession, I gurgled, "Easy, Chief. I may be an amateur, and I might be a pain. But I am a taxpayer." My knees were shaking, honest to God.

I had a half-hour in a holding cell to ponder the loss of my investigator's license, my children's affection, and life in Rahway State Prison. It was certainly messy, and highly embarrassing; Jane almost had a stroke when I called her from police headquarters.

But it didn't turn out as badly as it might have. The chief had been driving away from the high school when he saw my Volvo, which struck him as familiar, and radioed in a license plate check. When he heard who the owner was, he came around the back of the nursing home just as I was dashing out.

True, he suspected me of breaking and entering, but he hadn't seen me break or enter. True, I was carrying freshly purchased tools of a suspicious nature, but nothing seemed to be missing from the nursing home and a thorough search revealed nothing out of place. Most of the desk drawers—including the one with the visitors' log—were locked. All the patients were fine. Joey DiNardo swore on his mother's grave, and on the Holy Mother as well, that he had been upstairs the entire time and never laid eyes on me. Which was also true.

"Walking across a parking lot isn't yet a crime, is it, Chief?" I needled, a touch surprised by my own cheek. It wasn't like I was risking valuable cooperation from the police —I'd barely gotten any—but I was plenty uneasy. Judy Cole's information would be of tremendous importance to Leeming and his investigation, yet I didn't want to pass it on. I was uneasy about where those questions might lead, I guess. If Leeming ever found out all the things I hadn't told him, I would be driving a New Jersey Transit bus, at best.

"Pal, walking across a parking lot at this hour in this town makes you a person who has a lot of explaining to do," he growled. My wisecrack had lit his fuse, and it only took him a few seconds to ignite and give me a nuclear dressing-down. I'll skip most of it. "And probably the worst of it, you fucking boob, is that if one of the county deputies had happened to stumble upon you, instead of me, they'd still be trying to stuff all the holes," he thundered. "If you're holding out on me, I'll put some holes in you yet."

He was not a foolish man, and he rightly assumed I had important business inside the nursing home. Miss Whitmore, telephoned at home, insisted that I must know where Blackhead Gowdy was and demanded that I be arrested. But despite numerous threats about hauling my ass off to the county jail, I was home by 3 A.M., smarting only from fearsome warnings and acute humiliation.

What stung was Leeming's parting shot, made more cruel than he had perhaps intended by the lateness of the hour and his frustration at the general situation. I had not been forthcoming, claiming only that I was looking for Blackhead Gowdy for the same reason he was—to see whether or not there was any connection between the spate of deaths on the Brown estate and the Gowdy tragedy a century ago. Why I was looking for the old man after midnight at a place I knew he had vanished from, I didn't say.

"Deleeuw," Leeming snarled, "you're sitting on information about this case, I can smell it, and I'm telling you loud and straight that you'd better pass it on. 'Cause not only are you going to feel like shit for the rest of your life, Mr. Wall Street, I'm going to see to it that you feel like *unemployed* shit."

I don't know whether it was New York City combat fatigue or whether, as I suspected, the chief sympathized with anyone the FBI didn't like, but it was clear he was looking for cooperation more than he was looking for trouble.

"Seriously, Deleeuw, I'm not trying to break your balls. But somebody's going to get hurt again. I want to stop that. I suspect you do, too. You have kids in this town, man, you have friends here. Help us. I want to know where that old man is, and I want to know what you're doing here at 1 A.M., and I want to know what the fuck you're looking for. Level with me."

He got to me more adroitly with the plea for help than with the bullying. I had to absorb what I had found out. I was numb, exhausted, and bewildered. And there was this: Leeming didn't strike me as a vengeful man, but he was tough as iron. If I couldn't end up giving a good account of myself, the chief would honor his threats. But I couldn't share what I knew. Not yet.

25

I brushed off my dramatic encounter with the local constabulary. I was just too busy. Besides, wasn't it inevitable that my middle-class existence would be jolted from time to time, if I was going to be successful in this line of work? I'd already been beaten, slugged, and screamed at more in a week than in the previous decade. Wasn't I a tough guy now? I knew Chief Leeming wasn't going to nominate me for any civic awards, but he was straight enough that I doubted my visit to police headquarters would make the paper. In terms of the family, that was all to the good. It would have been a great plug for the agency, though. At breakfast, I didn't mention my brief detention.

I had three stops to make this Wednesday. First was the files and old newspapers of the Historical Society, in Benchley's library. The second was to Carol Lombardi's home to try once more to get her mother to talk with me—she had refused several times on the phone, and would almost certainly do so again. Then there was dinner at Gennaro's with Judy Cole. This rendezvous with an eighteen-year-old was foolish and inappropriate, wasn't it? But maybe in that setting she would tell me what else was bothering her.

The schedule made me too fevered to partake of Benchley's usual hospitality. He was curious about the rush and my reason for poring over more Gowdy accounts, but too polite

to demand to know what I was up to. He also had to contend
with three flatbeds waiting to unload the first fragile ship-
ments of the pale spring forest that would soon be dispersed
across the lawns and gardens of the town. Benchley had confided to me during one of our midwinter chats in the greenhouse that for years he had painted a harmlessly small red V
on the bark of all the trees he sold, so he could spot them as
he walked and drove around town. Over the years, he said,
he'd come to feel like the Johnny Appleseed of Rochambeau.

I was, despite my hurry, worried about him. He looked
raw and haggard. When you've lived in a town for eighty
years and suddenly people start getting killed or attacked
there, it must come as a tough jolt. And he was evidently
enmeshed in the town's agony in ways he wasn't talking
about. I do not mean by that that I secretly suspected him of
killing or frightening people; I didn't. But there *was* some
connection, something he knew but hadn't told, something
he'd seen or feared. It formed a subtle barrier between us. We
were both conscious of it being there, but neither of us knew
how to address it. I could see it was bothering him, and I
knew it was getting to me.

"You know," he had told me after the Ida Flowers attack,
"I'm always reading in the newspaper that some quiet neighborhood of some city was stunned to experience the violence
—a rape or shooting or stabbing—that has long afflicted
other neighborhoods. I never thought that bell would toll for
us."

Frankly, it was difficult for me to relate to any of the
prevailing notions of Rochambeau, even Benchley's. He saw
the town as a rich and fortunate community with a unique
history. So did Dick Handley. In fact, when I'd first met Handley at the Historical Society dinner, he had spoken elo-

quently about the importance of preserving the character of
towns like Rochambeau. He was quite careful not to call it a
suburb. But it was a suburb to me, not a rooted place. The
overwhelming majority of its residents had moved there in
the last generation or two. Many of its working people were
attached to the city, not the town, for their jobs and for their
cultural life.

The fact that some of the houses went back 250 years
didn't alter the way it had boomed and changed, the way
developers still scrambled to plunk a tasteful Colonial or a
scattering of condos on every available lot. So many of the
old houses that gave Rochambeau its atmosphere of history
had become funeral homes, insurance agencies, doctors' offices, or residences for the elderly. People still came to the
suburbs to have and raise kids, and most still moved along
when they were done, to make way for others. It was curious
—and a little depressing, Jane and I found—that people
talked about where they would go when the kids were gone,
as if their only connection to the town was through their
children.

As horrible as the spate of violence was, I could clearly
see a time beyond it, even if developers and home buyers
couldn't. Having had my epaulets torn off on Wall Street had
done that much for me: I knew that ghastly things ended, that
things changed and that even humiliation faded.

But Benchley's aversion to violence was stronger and
more personal. His roots in Rochambeau were deep, and
some of its ghosts hovered right above him. Hard to distance
yourself when your living room window overlooked the foot
of a hill, the top of which had yielded three young, dead
bodies.

"I'm worried about you, Benchley. Is there something I

can help you with? I don't want to pry, but I hope you know you can talk to me, if you want to."

"Well, Kit, since you asked, I wouldn't mind knowing why you haven't told me about Blackhead Gowdy's disappearance from his nursing home?" He spoke softly, with a trace of sadness and hurt but no anger or resentment. I felt about the same way I did when I learned the kids at Ben's school were pushing him around because of me. I didn't seem to be bringing joy to those I loved.

"I don't know, Benchley. I guess I just didn't know what —if anything—to make of it. Sometimes, in my work, the only real weapon you have is what you know. I'm sorry. I intended to tell you today. How did you find out?"

He watched me closely, as if searching for any hidden meanings.

"Well, I believe I told you that I've tried to help Blackhead. Part of that is my attorney who checks regularly— Blackhead would be upset if I called—with the nursing home. He called me the day after. I assumed you knew, and that there must be some reason you hadn't told me." Typical Benchley, trying to be sensitive to what I wanted.

He seemed upset beyond my own secretiveness. This was something of a switch. Usually, he was worrying about me, about the long, black bouts of depression I would plunge into about my sudden unemployment, my choice of a second career, my finances. It was actually refreshing to be fussing over him for a change. I asked him if he had any thoughts about Gowdy, but he didn't seem to want to talk about the old man.

He shook his head, trying to shake off his gloom. He still wasn't going to say anything about his secret. He changed the subject, sort of.

"That poor Peterson girl. She'll carry the scars of that awhile, won't she, Kit? She was in here with her father yesterday, looking for African violets for her room."

I had pressed him and he chose not to respond. For now, that was as far as I could take it.

"I saw Peterson the night of the attack. What is he, a lawyer?"

"I think a banker. Perhaps in real estate here in Rochambeau, Kit; I'm not certain."

He pointed to the pot of coffee and biscuits he had left on the library table. Busy or not, you were never hungry at Benchley's. "I can't help noticing how energized you appear to be, how happy even, if that's the correct word to use under the circumstances," he observed. "You look like a hound who's beginning to catch the scent. Purposeful. I wish it could be in a happier cause, but I'm pleased to see it. Maybe this detective work was the right choice after all. The spirit takes hold of people in different ways, doesn't it?"

He smiled, then went outside to oversee the unloading. He was right; I felt as good as I had in years. In fact, although he would have been stunned to know it, I felt like something that had crawled out of the garbage. The damn thing was, he was right—after years of living in some foreign place, I had come home. I was pretty sure I wouldn't have made it this far without him. I was beyond defeated when we first met; I'd felt left for dead. When he invited me back into the greenhouse that morning a few years earlier, I was about as thoroughly vanquished as a middle-class man can be, broke, disgraced, unemployed, without my career or the prospects for another. Benchley couldn't have been thrilled about my becoming a detective; he thought everybody should get out there, house the homeless, and feed the hungry, so there wouldn't be any need for cops or detectives.

Whatever his reservations, he not only had encouraged me, he'd held me together long enough to get started, always urging me to follow my instincts, always helping push me forward. All it takes is one, you know. So many of the poor bastards I worked with who have lost their jobs never hear an encouraging voice from anybody. So it was especially hard to see him in distress. I was hurt that he couldn't or wouldn't confide in me, afraid I had hurt him.

But he was more than eight decades old, and had to make those decisions for himself. As for me, celebrations about my new life were way premature. So far all I had was a name from a desk drawer, and I didn't even truly understand what that meant.

I kept rummaging through the old papers and files. I hadn't told Benchley what I was looking for, mostly to protect him. I had to keep reminding myself that we were after somebody who had killed and who presumably would kill again, if necessary. "If you can't find what you need here, Kit," he advised, "go see Evelyn de la Cretaz down at the town library. She's our librarian, too. She's fearsome and intimidating but thoroughly dependable."

The smell in the room quickly turned musty. Apparently Benchley never threw away anything that even remotely related to Rochambeau history. Sifting through the cardboard cartons that lined one wall, I didn't find the mysterious missing manuscript. But in Box 9 (*Miscellaneous Newspaper Files Pre-1900*) I did find something else, perhaps the next best thing—a story dated July 11, 1901. The clipping contained an interview with Ezekiel Perry, former reporter for the *Rochambeau Daily Times & Gazette*, the writer who had claimed Nathaniel Gowdy might be innocent. The interview was about the book Perry was working on about the Gowdy murders, the book that was never published, and it was misfiled in the wrong century underneath a fat old folder containing letters from Rochambeau volunteers in the Civil War. Was this a misstep by the legendary filing whiz Evelyn de la Cretaz?

Why did I even look in that box? I owed that to Sergeant Mize at Fort Benning during my army CID training: "Son, when you're looking for something, here's how you do it. You see a rock, look under it. You see a drawer, look inside. You see a lock, open it. You see an envelope, read what's in it. You see a cushion, lift it. You see a carpet, look underneath." It was one of those lines that stuck somewhere inside the place things stick and I didn't really have any other advice to go by. The Barnes & Noble at the American Way didn't have any how-to books on being a private eye. I had looked.

On my way over, I had stopped at Creative Expressions and bought an oversized sketch pad, on which I planned to chart the Nathaniel Gowdy history, tying it to what I knew of what had happened in Rochambeau. If there was a connection, it might stand out more graphically. Of course, it was hard to believe the police wouldn't have done the same thing.

After reading just a few paragraphs of the interview, I felt a respectful pang for Perry. His proposed book, as he described it, was just the sort of true-crime story that could have been a best-seller in the 1990s but which probably seemed inappropriate and sensational a century ago, when people didn't find aberrant behavior so compelling (and, according to Benchley, when the newspaper was owned not by some chain headquartered in the Midwest but by the mayor's brother who was also president of the Rochambeau Merchants Association. I knew, again from Benchley and from discussions at the Historical Society, that while suburban prosperity is taken for granted now, it wasn't at the turn of the century. Towns fought savagely to woo residents and developers and bad publicity was even more damaging than it is now.)

The interview was fascinating, bringing to life Nathaniel Gowdy's remarkable life and death. I could well imagine why the whole saga had made such a strong impression on young Ken Dale. Perry was a clear, dispassionate journalist, talking in the more formal voice of his time, but relentless and obsessed with even the smallest details.

He was going to write, he told his interviewer, the real story of the crimes on what was now the Brown estate. The reporter from the paper was clearly skeptical, preceding and following the Perry interview with a raft of dismissals of Perry's theories and affirmations of Gowdy's guilt from the local prosecutor and the sheriff.

"Nathaniel Gowdy's life," Perry had said, "was as heartbreaking as it was puzzling." He described a model young man, loyal, industrious, and responsible. Except for friends' descriptions of him as headstrong, there was not even a hint of evidence that Gowdy was capable of enough violence to harm another human being. Perhaps the would-be author was whitewashing, or perhaps Gowdy's friends were, but Perry's conviction was so clear and reasoned that it was difficult to believe he would leave out incriminating information.

And he was more than skeptical of Nathaniel Gowdy's guilt. He was convinced of the boy's innocence. Perhaps that was another reason the book was never published.

"Nathaniel Gowdy was never placed at the scene of the murder of Caroline Clark," Perry had said. "There wasn't even conclusive evidence that he and his fiancée had broken off their engagement, outside of the testimony of Eugenia Hinds, a notorious town gossip. There was no physical evidence that linked the young man or his wagon to the murder or the murder scene, and nothing to suggest that criminal behavior was in any way in character. Being a poor farmer, Gowdy was forced to hire a local attorney who specialized in deeds, not homicides. His defense was accordingly haphazard and half-hearted."

The prosecutor, Nicholas Anderson, had told the jury that explicit evidence linking Gowdy to the killing of Caroline Clark wasn't necessary. There was more than enough to tie him to the deaths of five other townspeople, all of them women. Rope matching the thick-woven hemp found in the Gowdy barn was used to strangle all of the victims. Footprints matching those of his boots were found near the homes of three, and he'd been spotted near the scene of at least two of the victims. And Eugenia Hinds was not a town scold, Anderson told the jury, but a loyal friend of Caroline's. Mrs. Hinds claimed that the girl was terrified of young Gowdy's temper and convinced he would attempt to harm her if she broke off their engagement.

There were, Perry acknowledged, strong eyewitness accounts that had Gowdy running away from at least one of the bodies. But he said the lack of physical evidence concerning the death of Gowdy's fiancée was striking. Perry had also located one of Hinds's cousins, who claimed it was well known in the family that Eugenia was once smitten with Gowdy herself and had never forgiven him for choosing Caroline. Why, wondered Perry, wasn't this alleged "other man" Caroline Clark was involved with ever found or identified? Why, if he existed, didn't he come forth in his grief and anger? (Well, here we go again, I thought. There was no way I could accept *that* much coincidence.)

And why, asked Perry, didn't authorities more vigorously investigate the murder of a landowner—stabbed to death and buried on the grounds of his nearby Newark home the same week Nathaniel Gowdy was allegedly on his murderous rampage? If other killers were running loose, why couldn't *they* have killed the women in Rochambeau and perhaps even Caroline Clark? Any possible connection should at least have been investigated, he said, and it wasn't.

Gowdy, according to the account, was so devastated by his beloved fiancée's death and by the charges against him that he could barely participate in the trial. He wasted away and refused to see visitors. When he spoke, he unwaveringly protested his innocence, denying that his engagement had ever been broken off or that he had any motive for or inclination to kill anyone, let alone Caroline. He would never harm a woman, he swore; the very suggestion was a stain he could never erase. He claimed to have been kidnapped, blindfolded, drugged, and moved around town for days, then suddenly released in front of the posse that was hunting him. He ran towards them in hopes of a rescue, said Perry, only to encounter the horror of multiple murder charges and, ultimately, the hangman.

Perry added—this one also rang my bells—that one of the factors for the county's hurried prosecution of the young man was the impending sale of a huge tract of Rochambeau land to a consortium of New York City builders hoping to establish the community as a premier site for summer homes. The sale—thousands of acres and millions of nineteenth-century dollars—was being jeopardized by the spate of killings and the bad publicity that resulted. I was beginning to see that Rochambeau had a continuous history after all. Even then, the town knew how to push aside what it wasn't proud of.

Later that night, after Judy Cole had gone home to do her homework, I planned to take the clipping to Luis. The criminal-lawyer-turned-restaurant-manager and the Wall-Street-hustler-turned-private-eye would munch on a Light-

ning Burger or two (with fries) and see if we could connect
some of these disparate dots. Perry's doubts about Gowdy's
guilt left me spinning, wondering if anything about the case
was clear, then or now.

And where did great-nephew Blackhead fit into this historical suburban melodrama? Surely his disappearance had
something to do with all this? Could it have been accomplished alone? Could he have left the Rochambeau Nursing
Homes by himself? Maybe. But he had to be living somewhere. If he was on the street the divisions of deputies, state
cops, and double-shifted local gendarmes would have spotted
him, the way they spotted me within seconds of my first foray
into burgling. But who would put him up, and why? And as
long as I was remembering things, what about Emmy's swimming lesson this afternoon? And Ben's basketball game?
Would Inspector Maigret or Sherlock Holmes break off an
investigation to drop off kids at the Y?

I had met Evelyn de la Cretaz before, although we had never
chatted. Benchley did not misrepresent her. She was formida-
ble. Semiretired, she presided over the main library branch
two mornings a week in her rather formal dark suit and gray
topknot. Exuding order, competence, and logic—and perhaps
recognizing in me many opposite qualities—she was exactly
the sort of person you didn't want to be returning late books
to.

She was not one for preliminaries. Yes, she remembered
filing some documents relating to the Nathaniel Gowdy case
for Benchley. Others were in the public library. It was apparent the minute she started talking that she knew where every
document she had ever touched was—or ought to be. Evelyn
was not happy at the suggestion she had misplaced the Perry

manuscript, certainly not coming from me, upon whom she fixed a withering glare.

"Mr. Carrolton is a dear man," she said after I withered appropriately. "But not organized in his filings. It's a wonder we haven't lost more things. I am quite familiar with the Gowdy case, Mr. Deleeuw, and would be happy to collect material here relating to it. Tomorrow, of course, on my day off." She glowered two loud teenage boys into paralysis, and said her good-byes. Somehow, I felt comforted knowing she was going to be working for me. If there were pertinent files in the library that could help, I would soon have them.

This time, Handley's class was full. I stood in the hall and waited until he glanced towards the door and spotted me. He quickly scribbled an assignment on the blackboard, then came into the corridor.

"Kit, I'm afraid you got me at a bad time. I have a class in session. Can I call you, or is it something that can't wait?"

I almost asked Handley if I could sit in on his class and watch him teach. I'd heard so many good things about his teaching that I thought it might be fun. And Ben might be in that class in a year or two; it would be helpful to know what to expect. But even Handley, gracious as he was, seemed a bit put out at the interruption of his class. This, by the way, is something a private investigator learns to get used to. Nobody is happy to see you, with the possible exception of your clients, and if they were really happy they wouldn't need you at all.

"I think it's crucial. I need to know why you visited Blackhead Gowdy on January 8."

He looked irritated. The bell rang, spilling the students into the suddenly thronged hallway. "That's why you're here?"

I nodded. "Your name was on the visitors' log."

He gestured me inside, closing the door behind us. "Well, I should say so. I wrote it there. I mean, I wouldn't have signed the log if I were trying to hide something, would I?"

He had a point. "You know he's missing, don't you?"

Handley seemed astonished. "Missing! You can't be serious. He was in terrible health, it seemed to me. I assumed he could barely walk. His mind seemed clear, but he was in a wheelchair. You're saying he left by himself? Oh, my."

"Nobody knows how he left, he's just gone. His attendant told me he could get around pretty well with a cane, when he wanted to. But your visit is why I'm here. What is Gowdy to you?" I wonder if it occurred to Handley at that minute that he was the thread woven through almost every part of the last week and a half. He knew of the Gowdy case, had assigned Dale and Lombardi to work on it, and had visited old Blackhead. No one else in the case popped up in so many different ways.

Yet, I'll be goddamned if the man I was looking at seemed capable of deception or wrongdoing. He appeared deeply troubled by old Gowdy's disappearance, but he had none of the other symptoms of guilt or unease I'd learned to read. He looked me straight in the eye, he wasn't sweating or grasping for time to think, he didn't appear twitchy or uncomfortable. In my experience, what cops say is true: Except for genuine psychotics or veteran criminals, you can smell guilt on most people, especially amateurs, in a flash. They're not used to intense verbal pressure; they show stress in one form or another.

Handley was displaying none of it. He seemed completely at ease, concerned but at peace, thoughtful, soft-spoken, and candid. Yet everywhere I went in the case, he seemed to be there waiting for me.

"I'm thinking of doing a book on the Gowdy case," he explained. "I was planning to call Benchley today to ask if I could come over and make a more thorough search for that manuscript I mentioned to you. I want to do a book proposal —there's an editor in town who works at a substantial publishing house and who is very enthusiastic. I'd like to finish the job that reporter—Perry—started. I want to find out the truth about Nathaniel Gowdy and I want to tell it."

"Good luck. I've just come from Benchley's and there's no manuscript there that I can find."

"You've been over there looking for it?" He seemed surprised that I was looking, not distressed that I hadn't found it. I decided not to mention the Perry interview. I knew precious little that everybody else didn't, and I wanted to keep what extra knowledge I did have to myself for the moment.

"I don't see how I can do the book without the manuscript. But it's got to be in there, somewhere. It's a powerful story, and if that boy was wronged, I want to set it right. Maybe, in a way, that can serve as partial redemption for my role in steering poor Ken towards this tragedy. Perry believed that Gowdy may have been railroaded."

Maybe, I thought, we were wrong to be nostalgic for Rochambeau's past. "Someone wanted him convicted?"

Handley nodded. "That was Perry's premise. That, and the fact that this Newark landowner that was stabbed to death at the same time and chopped up might have been connected to the Gowdy case. Although there's no evidence of that."

"You think Perry found real evidence Gowdy was innocent?" I asked, still keeping mum about the tattered yellow clipping in my pocket.

"You see, that's part of the reason his book was never published. The legal climate was quite different then. Perry's publisher ran for the hills. The town, just really coming into being as a prosperous community, was terribly edgy about what Perry was poking around in. I wanted to go back over this ground; it's wonderful history and a great story." He shrugged. "So of course I started with the only living Gowdy. But I got nowhere. The man's eyes were fearsome, but he wouldn't tell me anything. He seemed so upset that the attendant asked me to leave. It's a shame—I'm sure old Gowdy'd be a wonderful resource—but you can't press somebody that age and in that condition, can you?"

I didn't know whether to be mortified or perplexed. Mostly, I was confused. "Dick, why didn't you mention this book to me the other day?"

"You don't mention 'possibilities' in publishing, Kit, not if you're a suburban high school teacher who's had scores of book proposals rejected over the years. Every aspiring novelist or fresh-faced teacher has a 'possible' book. Wouldn't it be foolhardy to tell somebody interested in this case about interest in a book before I even have a contract? Besides, it seems to me that, without the Perry manuscript, I won't get a contract."

"So why tell me now?"

"Well, you asked about my visit to Blackhead. And I'm not so foolish that I don't see that I need to give an accounting of my presence in this case, lest your thoughts inevitably move in more menacing directions."

I knew even less about publishing than I did about private investigation, but his argument made pretty good sense. Another of Sergeant Mize's investigative dictums: "If someone seems credible to you, odds are that he is." Did Sergeant Mize have any idea what he was talking about? I wondered.

"Dick, how did you find out all this stuff—about why Perry's book wasn't published, for example?"

Handley smiled. "Historians, like detectives and reporters, have their ways. There are newspaper files and library files. I can't give all my sources away. Don't ask me to unless there's a demonstrably compelling reason. Needless to say, if there's something about the Gowdy case you need to know, and I can find out for you, I will."

Handley's accounting of himself was credible and sincere, and enough of a relief that I dropped the next question on him without a pause.

"Dick, in an unrelated vein. Do you have any reason to think that Carol Lombardi was in trouble? Perhaps in over her head with an older man or something like that?"

This time, he looked shocked. "Carol? Involved? Where did you hear that? I can't imagine such a thing." He looked so stricken that I regretted having raised it so abruptly. It seemed to me he could hardly bear the thought that another of his protégés had been in trouble and that he hadn't known.

"Carol was one of the straightest students I ever had," he said, shaken, running his fingers through his sandy hair. "It's true she was distracted, troubled on some days, but I always assumed that was because she was involved with some other young man—"

"But, Dick," I interrupted, "if it were someone in the school, it would've come out by now, wouldn't it? This isn't a big town, and these kids are pretty close. Don't you find the fact that this mysterious romantic interest has never surfaced to be significant? Doesn't it suggest it was with someone beyond the school and her circle of friends here?"

Handley looked as if he had simply had too much thrown at him. The question had rocked him. His concern for his students was deep, and it seemed to me that he hated having this ground plowed over again and again. He exhaled deeply, then leaned against the wall. "Did someone tell you that? Dear God, on top of everything else, Carol was in distress? Jesus, what was I doing all year? What is a teacher supposed to notice, if not things like that?"

"You're not their parents," I said. "Nor their minister."

"No," he said softly, "and thank God for that. My wife— I'm a widower—used to tell me the same thing. But this is a shock. When something like this happens, it isn't just that you feel responsible, it's that you feel stone blind. An older man? Do you have specific information or—"

I shook my head quickly. "No, not at all. It's just a rumor. I don't credit it much myself, just thought I'd bounce it off you. But give it some thought. I'm sorry to have jolted you. Give me a call if anything comes to mind."

I gave him one of my cards. I loved papering the town with them—not only did it make me feel like a detective, but I had this notion that eventually everyone in town would have my private phone number and I'd have thousands of eyes and ears.

"Did you tell the police about the Perry manuscript, about your interest in Gowdy?"

He looked slightly abashed. "Why, no. I didn't really have anything to tell them. Gowdy didn't tell *me* anything."

"Dick, last question. I know you're very protective of your students. But I'm having trouble tracking down Jamie Harte. His mother says he's not at home, and she won't tell me where he is. He hasn't been at the gym in Ridgefield where he hangs out. Do you know if he'll be in class today?"

Handley shook his head. "Jamie hasn't been in class for two days. But that's not unusual. We're not piling up many successes around here this year, are we?"

I said my good-byes and walked away. On the way out of the building, I dialed Judy Cole's house. I intended to leave a message canceling our dinner; I was feeling ridiculous enough. But then something Handley had said clicked in my mind, and I decided to go. I hung up without leaving any word. It hadn't been tough to change that decision, had it?

26

The raucous din I could hear all the way out on the parking lot reminded me that the American Way was inaugurating its new northern New Jersey concert series, in conjunction with the Totowa Lions Club and the mall's very own Melody Organ Company. In honor of this occasion, the fountain in the mall lobby was spouting multicolored jets of water. The concert consisted of three retired organists playing old Lawrence Welk tunes on three of Melody's top-of-the-line keyboards. The audience was, not surprisingly, sparse and elderly. I hoped they planned to pep up the music selection for the kids.

Walking through the ground floor, I felt an enthusiastic and familiar thump on the back.

"Kit, come in here."

It was Murray Grobstein from Shoe World. He dragged me into the store, where two of his teenaged assistants were feverishly uncrating boxes. "Kit, you have a boy, right?"

I nodded. Murray was always offering me great deals on sneakers for Ben and I was always taking him up on them. But I was in a hurry this time. "Murray, I'm on a big case—my first, in fact. I don't have time—"

"You have time for this," Murray announced proudly. "You don't want to be telling your boy you could have had Skyrocketer Pumps before anybody else in his school and you passed them up, believe me."

He held up a pair of shoes as if they were one of the crown jewels. "The Skyrocketer Super Pump," he announced. "The mother of all pumps." They looked a foot long and at least as high, with a lightning bolt on the heel and a small needle attachment on one side. Murray plopped the sneakers on the countertop.

"Now watch this." He pulled out a small plastic box with an air hose attached, and inserted the hose into the shoe and an electrical cord into a wall socket. The shoes swelled until you could almost float in them.

"Murray, they could double as life jackets. Or air balloons. You could do some brilliant cross-marketing here."

He was aglow, beyond the reach of sarcasm. "Here," said Murray, "be a big shot at home. They go for a hundred and fifty dollars, but I'll give them to you at cost—seventy-five bucks. Pay me later. I gotta get to work."

I was still shaking my head when I got up to my office, but I had the giant shoes and their pump in a plastic sack. I scooped up the mail—lots of junk, a big brown envelope, and too many bills—and carried it into my anteroom, flicking on my coffee maker.

This was a quiet time in mall-land, when the kids went home for dinner, the night sales force came on, the security shift changed. The highway outside was thick with rush hour traffic but the mall itself caught its breath. Next week, the American Way's International Food Court was scheduled to open—good news for global junk-food aficionados like me. There would be tamales, an Irish potato bar, fish and chips, egg rolls, and knishes. The common denominator seemed that no matter what country it came from, the cuisine tilted heavily to fried.

Ben would, in fact, love the sneakers. I guessed they must give extra bounce, looking so much like trampolines. Ben, and our relationship or lack thereof, was bugging me. I knew gifts couldn't buy closeness, but they could go a long way towards letting him know how much I cared and easing the sting of what he had been going through at school. And despite my sympathy, we still had to have some tough talks about getting his homework done. C's were no good, father's reputation or not.

"Deleeuw and Leon residence," said Emmy, who was just learning to love answering the telephone.

"Hey, Em, it's Dad."

"Hey, Daddy."

"How was school?"

"Like always."

"You mean good?"

"I mean like school. The same as it was last week and last year." Emmy was always chatty about her day, but she was learning one of the immutable laws of childhood—never give them a break if you could help it.

"Is Ben home yet?"

"Nope."

"He's supposed to get home at three forty-five and it's four now."

"I don't know. He's not home yet."

"Ask Mrs. Oliver to get on."

Sally Oliver, our baby-sitter, was a retired nurse in her fifties, reliable, sharp-eyed, and tough. Homework got done, piano and guitars were practiced faithfully, wild play was brutally suppressed, TV was restricted to an hour, and snacks were kept to three or four a day. In short, a gem.

"Hi, Sally. Hope you're okay. I'm at the mall. Where's Ben?"

"Well, he's at basketball practice, Mr. Deleeuw. It's

Wednesday, and he called like he's supposed to. But he said he was going to be dropped off a quarter to four and it's just a bit past that. I was thinking about calling?"

Ben had said he would be dropped off by Mary Pugh, whose son Peter was on Ben's team, Sally Oliver said. The hair on the back of my neck was already rising when she suddenly said, "Oh, here he is, Mr. Deleeuw. He just walked in the door. I'll get them started on their homework." I made a mental note to call Mary Pugh and remind her that none of us were casual these days about kids being dropped off fifteen minutes later than expected.

The fat brown mailing package was the kind that oozes stuffing all over the floor when you try to open it. I squeezed it to make sure the contents were soft—maybe the general paranoia of the town was getting to me. It felt like clothing. I cut one end open with a scissors and pulled out a squashy shape that unfolded into a basketball shirt.

The hair on the back of my neck proved resilient and shot up again. I think it was probably the smell that tipped me to the fact that it was Ben's shirt. His number was on the back, under the lettering that said Rochambeau Junior High.

Ben answered on the first ring.

"Yo."

"Ben. You okay?"

"Sure."

"Ben, don't go out of the house. Not for any reason till I get home, you hear me?"

"Why?"

"Ben, promise. This is serious. No discussion. Just promise."

"Lighten up. I promise. Chill out, will ya?"

I asked to talk with Mrs. Oliver, and told her to pull all

the blinds in the house, make sure the doors were locked, and let no one in. My second call was to Chief Leeming, who said he would send a squad car to sit by the house and asked me to bring the envelope and shirt home with me.

I called Jane, who said she'd drive home at once. We agreed to stay calm and try to avoid scaring the hell out of everyone at home, including ourselves. If the message was intended to frighten me, it sure did. My Wall Street horror was a walk in the park compared to what I'd felt in the few seconds it took to hear Ben's voice. Was someone after Ben? I thought of the Peterson girl: If somebody wanted to hurt her or Ben, why didn't they? What was the shirt supposed to suggest? Was I supposed to quit? To not sleep anymore? To forgo sleep forever? To go back to Wall Street?

I didn't intend to do any of those things. I had no choice. I was way past the point of no return.

27

Once the initial panic and shock wore off, once Ben, Jane, Emmy, and I had settled down, after we'd had a forty-five-minute family talk about the whole thing and the kids had gone to bed and I had a few quiet moments to think, what occurred to me was that Jane was probably correct in her early diagnosis of whoever was running around Rochambeau in a stovepipe hat. It's a bit risky to tell someone like my wife that she's right about anything. She's already plenty assertive, not in need of further ego-strengthening. She already has a successful career, with lots of recognition from her patients, peers, and supervisors. I'm not sure how I feel about her being better than me at *my* career as well. In my new line of work, you don't get raises or glowing evaluations. You're lucky if you get clients. I mean, I'm supportive of Jane's psychological skills, but there's a line.

In an hour, I had a late-night rendezvous with Luis at the mall. It was a crucial point in the case for me, a point that comes even in a two-thousand-dollar insurance fraud—the moment when you have to make up your mind. I needed to sort some things out, to try them out loud. I needed Luis's experience and his distance. With a squad car out front and the kids asleep, I figured I could spare an hour of conversation. It was time to stop asking so many questions and start coming to some conclusions.

Whoever had sent me the package was not nuts, at least not completely.

Anyone had to know that this gesture was far more likely to get the kids a week with their grandmother in Florida than it was to drive me off the case. Or maybe this was mere bravado, a response to the clammy terror I'd felt in the few seconds it took me to determine that Ben was okay.

The person who put together that package didn't intend to harm Ben. It was a shot across the bow, a reminder that whoever was out there knew what I was doing, knew my vulnerabilities, and was letting me know he knew.

"You're right," I said a bit brusquely to Jane, who had half nodded off on the playroom couch. She'd been hoping, as always, to wait up for the weather report, a desire I never can quite fathom, since we don't exactly have a crop on the line. She rarely makes it that far into the newscast, invariably dozing off shortly after the headlines.

"Thanks," she mumbled, drifting back to sleep.

"This guy knows how to strike at people out here. He's calling attention to something. He may be crazy as well, I guess he couldn't be too well balanced, but there's definitely a message—" Jane's head lolled over to one side. Well, at least I'd acknowledged her triumph; it wasn't my fault she couldn't stay awake to hear it.

Our new wave of security procedures basically ensured that the children were never out of an adult's sight or care, but we tried to downplay the package to avoid frightening any of us to death. Not an easy balance. I thought the kids had been reasonably steady.

Ben had even seemed a bit excited. "I'm okay," he mumbled. Then, in a surprisingly polysyllabic burst, he went on, "I just think he wanted to scare you, Dad. And he accomplished that, didn't he?"

I nodded. But maybe, I thought, what he wanted most was to distract me. Maybe I was getting closer than I realized.

It was not lost on Ben, particularly after he'd called a few of his buddies, that he would be far and away the most talked-about kid in junior high the next day, a fringe benefit of my work he'd never anticipated. But he was right about the scare.

That was the point, wasn't it? The scarer's mission seemed to be to shatter the most central of our suburban beliefs—that we'd found a haven for our children.

To find him, I had to acknowledge Jane's point and look not for a psychopath but for an ideologue, somebody to whom the suburbs were somehow anathema. Someone who understood the place well enough to conceive and execute so blood-curdling and effective a challenge to what we had become. For the first time, a vague notion of who might fit that bill had begun to crystallize, and it was a stunning thought. But I hadn't a clue as to how to amass any proof of my suspicions.

Luis might be a help. It was always helpful to talk things out with somebody, and Luis brought some experience as well as perspective. I chased Jane off to bed, tucked her and the sleeping kids in with a kiss, took the cops idling in the cruiser outside a cup of coffee—I bet Leeming was tickled to be guarding me—firmly instructed Percentage on his responsibilities as a surburban dog, and headed for the American Way.

The corridor outside the Lightning Burger was deserted, except for the jangling of a guard's keys and the whine of a floor waxer. The American Way was in repose, its parking lot empty, the floodlit green fountain turned off, its shops shuttered and jewelry stands folded up. A dozing commercial beast catching its breath for the next day.

The Lightning Burger had been scoured within an inch

of its life. The grill was scraped and smooth, the computer-
ized register blinking zero, the pervasive stench of grease replaced by disinfectant. Lightning Burger didn't rest for long;
in two or three hours the early morning crew would come in
ahead of Luis to fire up the vats of boiling oil and defrost the
juice concentrate. This lull in between was about the only
time I found it soothing to be there. Luis, I suspect, felt the
same way.

I brought my Gowdy chart. I'd blocked out the major
developments in the old case on the off chance any parallels
popped up that hadn't already made themselves clear. Luis has
an intuitive talent for overview, the sort of aptitude good
criminal lawyers develop quickly, I assume. He isn't someone
you run to with every new morsel of detail. You wait until
you've acquired a major chunk of information, then lay it out
and watch him spot all the things you've missed. I taped the
chart up on the wall above our booth and filled Luis in on
everything I had learned so far. He had lined up two cups of
black coffee and three thawing Danish. The chart listed the
five women Gowdy had allegedly killed, along with Caroline
Clark.

The first one read:

> *August 8, 1872:* Caroline Clark found, strangled, next
> to giant elm. Girlfriend Eugenia Hinds tells police Clark
> broke off with Gowdy the night before and he was en-
> raged. Clark reportedly involved with another man.
> Strangled with a length of hemp police said was identical
> to kind Gowdy stored in his barn. Police, seeking to
> question Gowdy, discover he has fled the family
> farmhouse shared with mother, brother Julius, uncle Ed-
> ward.

The chart went on to list the other victims of Gowdy's alleged rampage from August 8 through 20: Henrietta Brown, fifty-seven, two days after Clark while riding in her carriage; Julia Pine, seventeen, on August 12, found in a local cornfield; Sara Delancy, age seven, attacked while sleeping in her bed (Gowdy had often been hired to do chores for the family and the dogs knew him, the prosecutors said, possibly explaining why barking didn't rouse the family); and finally two sisters, Peach and Gabriella Chauncy, forty-four and forty-nine, killed at the foot of what is now the Brown estate.

All the victims had been strangled with hemp that matched the coil in Gowdy's barn.

Then I read Luis a summary of the final events in the tragedy, the ones that sealed Nathaniel Gowdy's doom. I was summing up for myself as well, stepping back a few feet before any wild impulses were acted upon.

" 'On August 20, posse of militiamen with bloodhounds find Gowdy disoriented and in disarray, wandering in woods 250 yards from spot where Clark was killed. Can barely speak for hours after his capture, then claims he has been kidnapped, blindfolded, drugged, and held in a cabin in the woods, released moments before encountering posse. Asked about Clark's death, he appears stunned, then collapses. Semiconscious for several days. Comes to, maintains his innocence despite considerable body of evidence against him.' "

Luis inhaled deeply from his unfiltered cigarette, the smoke curling up into the spotlight near the door. A guard strolling past started at first, then waved when he recognized Luis. We must have been a strange sight.

"A sad, sad story. I would have loved to defend that boy. What a miserable job his lawyer must have done." His eyes fairly glistened. "To exhibit such murderous behavior, completely inconsistent with the rest of his life, that is extraordinarily rare. There is much to make one wonder about his guilt." He shrugged. Luis was well aware that injustice was possible. "So all were killed the same way?"

"Yup." Something bugged me about the chronology. I couldn't pinpoint what.

"And this Edward Gowdy you mention, the uncle he lived with. This is Blackhead Gowdy's direct ancestor, his blood?"

I nodded.

"And the killing stopped after Gowdy was hung?"

"I think so, although I'm not positive."

"Was it the original clipping that you read?"

"No, it was a smudgy photostat—I'd say thirty years old. The original newsprint would have crumbled by now, I should think. None of this was considered a big deal, mind you, since almost everyone in town had forgotten about the case and the book was never published anyway."

There was a hum from the rear of Lightning Burger, and some beeping. You might have thought you were in some dark, top-secret Pentagon chamber. But, said Luis, smiling, it was the deep fryer preparing for duty.

"Does Perry have any descendants here, any offspring?"

"That's a good question, Luis." I jotted Perry's name down on the yellow legal pad I kept nearby.

"And Benchley had no other thoughts about what might have happened to the manuscript?"

I shook my head. "Benchley is not given to devious rationale. He said the only thing he recalled when he talked it over with Evelyn de la Cretaz, the Historical Society secretary, was that Evelyn had done some additional research in the public library's archives, where she works. He said she'd once thought of writing something about the case for the society's newsletter. It seems a lot of people have."

Handley was the other person who'd inquired into the Gowdy materials, according to Benchley. "There is one footnote," I added. "There was another murder at the time—some guy in Newark. It was attributed, as many crimes were in those days, to starving bands of war veterans who roamed the countryside. Some of them were deranged and hid out to avoid being thrown into mental hospitals."

He opened his mouth, but I held up my hand, trying to get the sequence correct. "I stopped by the library to talk to Evelyn. Quite the grande dame. She wears one of those buns bees would be happy to live in. She's pretty much retired now, but she still comes in a couple of days a week. She remembers the Gowdy case quite well and she's digging out the file she'd put together on it."

Luis stirred his coffee. He seemed to be rolling something around in his mind. I paused to give him a chance to share it.

"Well, Kit, it's intriguing that the Gowdy boy allegedly attacked and murdered a child. That explains why the Peterson girl was frightened in that way, I suppose." He frowned. "But it's odd. I can't quite tell if someone is blindly following parts of the Gowdy story, or whether someone is waiting for the town to connect those long-ago crimes with these new ones."

I nodded enthusiastically. For once, someone smart was echoing one of my instincts. Or was it Jane's? "Exactly, that's my notion. It's as if someone's trying to send a different message than the one that's coming through, which is that crazy outsiders are running around hurting people and spooking them. But maybe I'm being too subtle, looking for nuance where there isn't any. I mean, there are plenty of sickos."

Luis leaned back. "I don't mean to be uncharitable, Kit, but in this country there's so much violence that it isn't easy to separate one kind from another. People can chop up other people and bury parts of their bodies for months. No one seems to want to know what the smells are, nobody seems to really miss the dead people. Shocking. Shocking. Subtle messages can easily get lost in such a place."

I told Luis I didn't follow.

"Well, the child frightened in Rochambeau wasn't killed or harmed. That seems to be an act designed to forge a connection of some sort between the Gowdy incident and ours. And while I know you were stricken"—he put an arm on mine —"the envelope containing Ben's shirt seemed designed to do the same. This person is smart enough to have harmed your son if he wished to. But an obvious connection to the Gowdy case was being made, almost as if someone out there is telling us, 'Look, you don't get what I'm saying.' "

I saw what he meant. I'd had the same reaction. But it got fuzzy from there. What could the message be, beyond "I can scare your children half to death, and you with them." What was the point of demonstrating that? So that we would move away? So that others wouldn't come? To call attention to our passionate involvement with our children's lives?

Maybe the intent wasn't to frighten me off the case but to continue to draw attention to the Gowdy tragedy. The *Rochambeau Times* had finally reported the similarities between this case and that one, but no one in town seemed to have made much of it.

"Kit," said Luis, obviously unsatisfied on one point or another, "I'm interested in this other murder, the one Handley mentioned to you. What do you know about it?"

"Well, it is curious. I came across it in the Perry interview. During the week of all the stranglings and Nathaniel's
alleged rampage, a wealthy businessman from Newark disappeared, and his dismembered body was found by some kids
playing in a field. A pocket handkerchief found on the scene
was identified by the wife's maid as being his."

I had this vague sense—too familiar of late—of having
heard about a crime like this one. Hadn't someone mentioned
it? I couldn't recall, but it had to be in the notes I was jotting
down every night. I needed to start talking into a tape recorder every day. Or get younger.

"Did the authorities connect this killing to Gowdy's supposed murders?" Luis wondered, lighting his umpteenth cigarette.

"No. No one at the time connected it to the Gowdy
case. Newark was a faraway place by the standards of the day,
remember. Perry believed there was some connection, but the
sheriff was quite anxious to close the Gowdy case and refused
to delve too deeply into it. I guess some things about suburban cops never change."

Luis stabbed out the cigarette he'd just lit. He had become almost catlike, his concentration intensifying. "And
Gowdy's land?"

"It's now Benchley's Garden Center."

"Any other loose ends, other things to be tied up?"

"Only every single important element about this case.
Like who Carol Lombardi was involved with. Next to the
Phantom of the Opera, that's the most mysterious relationship
in history. No one seems to have had a clue as to whom she
might have been seeing—assuming she was telling the truth
about that at all."

The only other significant thing my detecting had revealed, I told Luis, was that in the library, I'd sat down with

the phone book and the local business directory and ran through a bunch of names involved in this case, just to see if anything cropped up.

"Did it?"

"A footnote, maybe significant at some point, maybe not. Stan Peterson, the father of the girl whose window was smashed? Well, Benchley had mentioned he knew the man and that got me to thinking. Peterson's a real estate developer. He put together the deal to sell the Brown estate to the Toronto company that wants to build the mall and all those town houses."

"Didn't you tell me earlier that the murders had frightened off the developers?"

"Yes," I sighed, "but developers are like rabbits around a garden. They may stall until it's safe, but you count on them to always come back. I'm sure they're just waiting for the dust to settle."

"Was Peterson the prime developer?" asked Luis, surprised.

"No, a kind of middleman. When a prime parcel like the Brown property comes on the market, it's Peterson's job to spot it and get in touch with a company. He gets a cut of the sale. Of course, the company has reportedly backed out of the deal now. Money is tight enough without having to deal with serial killers. Peterson has probably lost the best deal of his life."

"Maybe," said Luis enigmatically, nibbling around a thawing Danish.

"What do you mean? How could it possibly help Peterson if this deal fell through?"

He shrugged. "A company is spooked. Why chance tens of millions of dollars on ground that might seem tainted and haunted, in a town that is getting terrible publicity? Companies don't have to take risks like that in a country as big as this; they can go elsewhere. They don't have to think strategically or long-term. That's why the Japanese are such effective managers. But Peterson may understand that these tragedies won't go on forever. One day soon, the guilty parties will be arrested, the crimes will stop. Time passes. Meanwhile, it might be very much in a developer's interest for the price to fall. I never knew a middleman who didn't wish to be a top dog."

He sipped the coffee from his cardboard cup. At such moments, I picture him sitting in downtown Havana, hands steepled together atop a wooden desk, a fan circling slowly overhead, desperate clients in linen suits and mustaches pleading for his time. I'll bet he was pretty pricey. Now, I get him for free. This is not entirely a pleasure.

"Luis, you're opening up a whole new track here," I objected, feeling tired. "It's got to be about the Gowdy case, especially since old Blackhead disappeared. I'm certain that's the key." And yet, why wouldn't someone kill to manipulate the price of land like that?

The lobster shift had come in the back door—represented by two elderly Cubans, probably friends of Luis from the old country—and begun filling the fryers that would turn out enough browned bricks to build a potato house. Luis was meticulous about changing the oil each day. As he put it with characteristic elegance, the Lightning Burger franchise reps had not been nearly so conscientious in their training program; two or three oil changes a week was considered quite sufficient.

I looked at my watch. One A.M., but Luis was just hitting his stride, spotting lapses in my investigation, suggesting new lines of inquiry. I had half a dozen matters to pursue, which left me both grateful and discouraged.

Luis approached a case in wide concentric circles, nibbling at one point, then another, but always coming around again to one or two aspects that stuck with him. He had little American directness: he avoided our worship of time. And the thing he was returning to most frequently was the Perry manuscript. He obviously didn't buy the notion of its accidental disappearance, and the more he noodled about it, the more it bothered me as well. But there were dark implications in pursuing it too far.

"In your work, Kit," he mused on, perhaps thinking of his own lost career, "the trick is to believe what people are telling you, and to not believe it at the same time. By this I mean, you can't doubt everything everybody says. But there are times when logic tells us that what people are saying doesn't ring true. When your dear friend Benchley—whom you know to be a worthy and honorable man—tells you the manuscript is not in his library, believe him. That is, believe that he means what he says. But that doesn't mean his understanding of what happened to it is correct."

I realized that Luis was approaching a delicate spot with extraordinary care. I had wondered about Richard Handley's numerous connections to the case, but I hadn't thought much about Benchley's. Luis was nudging me to do so.

"You're trying to tell me something, Luis," I said. He and I had spent too many hours to count in the Lightning Burger, often in the quiet hours before the mall opened or past midnight when the highway roar was reduced to an occasional buzz. "Out with it."

He smiled and nodded appreciatively. "I just want to say this," he said, no longer tentatively. The gracious upper-class Latin had vanished; the sharp-eyed lawyer had appeared. "In our work—I'm sorry, in *your* work—you must consider every possibility. Benchley is close to this case. He owns land next to the Brown property, thus he has a stake in what happens to it. In fact, much of his life has been devoted to keeping developers off the land, no? His family and the Gowdys have been connected to one another for a century, perhaps not pleasantly?"

He was just being thorough, I told myself; this wasn't really going to go anywhere. "So?" I asked, a bit more sharply than I had intended.

He raised his hands in a gesture of supplication. "So in a case you're investigating, no one is automatically off the list. No one. Is there any conceivable circumstance under which you could entertain the notion that your friend Benchley—whom I have never met—could feel too deeply about the Gowdy case, or the Brown estate, or possibly have a connection to either of the dead young people?"

I put the coffee down on the table and gave Luis as level a stare as I could manage. "No, sir," I said quietly. "The answer is no, no, and no."

Luis returned my gaze, but said nothing. The fact was, Benchley had lots of connections to the Gowdy case and to the Brown estate, and I had no idea whether he had any relationship to Carol Lombardi or Ken Dale or not. But the idea of investigating Benchley nearly made me gag.

It was time to get back home. What if Ben or Emmy woke up with nightmares? And both Luis and I had to work the next day. I had a full day of confrontations ahead. Luis would be overseeing coffee, hash browns, and eggs for the first wave of truckers and construction workers who would be descending on the mall shortly, one of the many stages of its life cycle that mere weekend shoppers had no notion of.

"This is complicated, Kit," said Luis, with what I thought

stunning understatement. "But some things do come to my mind. There are two choices. Either the person responsible for these horrible acts is an ideologue, a person committed to harming Rochambeau, to attacking its family life or structure in some way, and is using the Gowdy history as an inspiration or a blueprint. Or the person involved is using the Gowdy tragedy as a smokescreen to cover up another kind of crime. In either case, the Perry manuscript, which purports to offer new information about the case, is crucial. Crucial and missing. Your criminal here is smart, understands Rochambeau quite well, knows his town history. He—or she—is intelligent enough to use one series of events to either illuminate or obscure other, truer motives and problems."

I had two other people to ask Luis about—Jamie Harte and Lee Cole. But they would have to wait. Luis's last line was a trigger, popping what was bothering me to the surface like bread out of an old-fashioned toaster. I waved at the startled Luis, thanked him, and took off.

Upstairs in my office, I called and roused Sam Mellman, and told him to round up his friends from their beds and their living room sofas in front of MTV. I had an assignment for them, I said. Sam listened and accepted with enthusiasm. My ragtag little army, as savvy about the suburbs as any sociologist, would shortly fan out into its darkened streets. I called Benchley. No answer. At this hour, that didn't seem right. I headed for the parking lot.

I drove over.

It was only as I left the slumbering mall and cranked up my cold and balky Volvo that I remembered that I'd stood up a beautiful eighteen-year-old girl. Rattled by the package, I'd plain forgotten. I'd even forgotten to call. And she hadn't called me. What a relief.

Benchley didn't answer his door, even though the whole downstairs was lit up. Wishing I'd worn a warmer coat, I tried the back door. It was unlocked, customary in normal times, alarming in these. One of the doors to his large greenhouse stood partway open. Melody, tied up in the backyard, gave a perfunctory woof and then, having discharged her official duties, pranced at her post, wriggling and squealing in welcome.

Would Benchley be out so late on a night like this, leaving his precious plants and his beloved dog exposed to the cold?

On the kitchen table I saw a note that got those hairs on the back of my neck hopping again. I did what any good suburban detective would do in a similar situation—I called the cops.

28

The two of them stood facing one another across the big old stump. In daylight, the mansard roof of the Brown mansion would have been visible above the stand of hemlocks behind them. But now, they might as well have been meeting in some remote wilderness. They stood like two proud, grizzled old bears, sniffing the air, deciding whether or not to charge.

"Nearly two centuries between us," said one, a shock of white hair blowing across his forehead. "The whole history of the town is alive in us."

The other snorted in contempt. "There is no more town, and it has no more history. We are ghosts, and we've come to the right place for ghosts. I didn't think you would come here, not at this hour, not alone. I thought you'd bring those friends of yours, or maybe the police. I credit you with more courage than anyone else in your family had."

"My age and my faith are shields to me, my friend. I'm not afraid. And I don't need police."

The other man wheezed heavily, then spat. "Don't give me that pious crap, old man. Your ancestors didn't hesitate to commit violence, did they? And you don't hesitate to live off their gains, do you? They didn't kill with their own hands, of course, but they destroyed a family by stealing its land and casting it out in poverty. My grandfather cursed your grandfather then. I damn you now. This ground is drenched with injustice and greed and blood wrongly spilled. And this town has no honor and no reason for being, other than to rush pointlessly from place to place and go to stores like yours that keep dressing up the myth. Don't blabber to me of faith. The police are probably on their way up here now."

Benchley shook his head and pointed the beam from his flashlight down at the frozen ground. The night was clear and starry and intensely cold. "I know you've been living in my greenhouse for three days, Blackhead. Do you think I'm blind and deaf? I could hear you at night, rustling through the trash cans for food. I saw you before dawn, sleeping in back of the house plants. Where do you think the food in those cans came from? Did you believe I threw away fresh bread and unopened bottles of mineral water? Did you think the blankets you wrapped yourself in at night fell out of the sky onto the greenhouse floor? If I had wanted to call the police, you'd be back in the nursing home or worse.

"When I found your note, I decided it was time we met again. I'm eighty years old next month, Blackhead. God has blessed me with good health and enjoyable work and much to do, but I won't live forever. I'm prepared to settle these accounts with you. We have a kinship, you and I, however much you hate me or my family. We are two old, old men who share a terrible past. Maybe I can still some of your hatred and give us both some peace while we have time left to cherish it."

Gowdy tottered on his walking stick. It had taken him most of the night to make his laborious way up the mountain. He was certainly in better physical condition than he had revealed to Joey or to the other people in the nursing home. At night, in the darkness of his room, he had been exercising for years, doing knee and arm bends, walking in long circles as quickly as he could, sometimes even trying a few push-ups when he felt up to them. But that didn't mean he was well, or equal to the difficult climb he had just made. He felt light-headed, and his heart threatened to pound right out of his chest. His great moment, the confrontation he had planned for years, and here he was gasping for air, barely able to stand.

But he had to be here. Once he had heard of the killings on this mountain, he had redoubled his efforts to prepare for his escape and this climb. He had always known the time would come when he would have to leave. And he had, walking quietly out of the nursing home in the middle of the night, winding through backyards and parks in the clothes he had stolen from the attendants' locker and secreted under his mattress.

"It was you all those years, wasn't it, Blackhead? Of course it was. The dead rats left in the driveway, the broken windows, the poisoned dogs. How often I thanked God I have no children; I would have been so frightened for them. I must confess, I believed your health was deteriorating past the point where you could be a threat, to me or others. I would have had to act, if I'd realized that. Until these terrible crimes —then I knew you still harbored all that hate and anger. But I never believed you capable of killing. I still don't."

Gowdy swayed in the wind, which cut cruelly through his jacket to the translucent skin and thinning old bones below. His eyes teared, and the silver bristles on his chin glistened in the moonlight. A thin trickle of spittle ran down his chin, and strands of scraggly gray hair stood straight up in the wind. He was everything Benchley Carrolton wasn't—frail, dried-up, worn down by rage and disappointment.

"You haven't fooled me either, Benchley. I knew it was

you picking up the tab for that nursing home after I ran out of money. I knew years ago, when that lawyer you sent came and suggested I move into a better place, maybe my own apartment with a nurse. I knew that was you talking, and I hate you for every dollar that I took. I wouldn't move from Rochambeau Homes, dreadful hole that it is; I wouldn't give you or any member of your family that comfort. But I consoled myself with the thought that it was my rightful money, my due that you were sending me."

Benchley chuckled. He had rather looked forward to this encounter, an overdue reckoning, a chance finally to come to terms with the past. "So we both knew everything, all these years. I suppose that makes a certain amount of ironic sense. The lawyer told you that you could have had enough money to build your own house, Blackhead. Lord, I wished you'd taken it. You could have given yourself a few comfortable years, at least. I wasn't responsible for what my family did to yours, but it has weighed on me all these years. I wanted to set it right. We could have, if you'd let me."

Gowdy shook his head, as if the idea were beyond imagination. "That would have been rich, a Gowdy living in a house built by Benchley Carrolton. How long's it been, Benchley, since we've seen one another? Almost fifty years? Ever since I came to your old man and asked him for money —that would've been just after the war, when I got back from overseas. My mother had the cancer, my father was already dead. I asked your father to do the right thing by my family, to help my ma stay in her place, maybe get some treatment in New York. I remember you digging out in the backyard— always planting something, you were. Your father said no, said it wasn't his business."

Benchley shivered in the wind. He wondered how

Gowdy had ever managed to tackle this hill in the dark and cold. With the power of hate and anger, clearly. He remembered that day, too, his father angrily denouncing Gowdy, all the Gowdys, accusing Blackhead of vandalizing his house and killing his plants and poisoning his livestock. He and his father had argued about helping Gowdy's mother. "We owe it to them," Benchley had said; "Our family owes it to their family. We did take their land when they were defenseless and desperate. Our house is on the site of Nathaniel Gowdy's barn."

"You don't understand," his father had told him. "However just their case might be, Blackhead Gowdy is insane. He'll never be satisfied or sated; if the Carroltons give him money, he'll just come back for more and more. I'll send a check to the mother," his father had promised. "But I'll never give Gowdy a cent."

"Do you remember your collie, who was poisoned when you were a boy?" Gowdy hissed. "I did that." Benchley thought the emaciated old man was desperately trying to wound him, to get back at him, but there was little real pride in his voice. His statement was as much a confession as it was malicious.

"I could barely contain myself when I heard about the two dead kids up here." Gowdy was ranting now, over the trees' intensifying rustling. "Thought at last there was going to be some justice. We'd gone back to where it started, to the time my family was destroyed and sent on a long, bitter road of poverty and bad luck. Somebody who knew about the hanging had to have done it, some connection had to be there. I knew Nathaniel's case would get reopened and we'd get our land back, proper restitution. So you see, I must be crazy. People like me never get justice from people like you."

A swirl of clouds darkened the moon, so that Benchley

could see only a faint outline of the thin, wobbly figure before him. What a pair of relics we are, he thought, each more absurd than the other. Two monuments to the time when Rochambeau was something more than a place to rent videos, play soccer, and make money on real estate. In another age, another context, Blackhead Gowdy would be a local hero, the sort of person who was asked to ride in the Fourth of July parade, a living relic and historic prize.

As it is, he's shut away in a nursing home, the town's industrious new residents too preoccupied to know or care that he exists. Both of us, Benchley thought, our roots go deeper in this soil than those of the oldest trees shivering above us.

"You couldn't have killed the two teenagers or the young girl," Benchley said suddenly to Gowdy, startling him. "Do you know anything about that?" It seemed impossible that this withered, shaking old man could cross the street alone, let alone choke three strong young people to death.

Gowdy looked quickly over at the road beyond the old elm stump. Impossible to know whether he was imagining the hanging of Nathaniel or the deaths of Ken Dale and Carol Lombardi. And the Caltari girl's body had been found on the other side of the house, nearly a quarter mile away from this haunted little valley. Surely Gowdy was too weak and mad to have perpetrated such mayhem.

Gowdy pulled an old pea jacket, one that Benchley had ostensibly discarded, more tightly around his shrunken neck. Poor fellow, thought Benchley, even now he has to take my charity. He regretted telling him about the food and water he had left.

"I'm not a murderer, Benchley," Gowdy said softly. He was looking uncertain as to what he was doing here, exhausted by his effort. "I might be loco, and I might have done some dirty deeds, but I never could kill a person, not any more than Nathaniel could have. You know that, don't you, Benchley?" It was a plea, not a statement.

Benchley nodded tiredly. "I do know that, Blackhead. It's why I didn't call the police tonight. I had no fear of coming up here myself. And for what it's worth, I have no doubt that Nathaniel didn't kill anyone either."

Blackhead turned, his black eyes gleaming. "Truly, Benchley? You believe that? You swear? How strange," he said. "Because I have the proof now. I have proof. I mean—" But he had lost the thread. Benchley noticed he was carrying a plastic bag, that one corner of a thick stack of paper wrapped with string protruded from the end.

"You've got a copy of the manuscript, Blackhead. But how—"

"Yes, and there's proof now, proof that Nathaniel was set up. In here," he said, "there is a letter signed by the man hired to kidnap Nathaniel. He wrote it before he died, and that reporter got it. I knew him, you see. Perry came to me before he died, when he was sick. He told me about the letter, said they wouldn't let him publish the book, but he wanted me to have a carbon of the manuscript." Gowdy's eyes had begun to tear, and he seemed increasingly disoriented. It was almost as if, having staggered all the way up the mountain, he could barely remember why he'd made the effort. "I can't keep it all straight anymore, Benchley," he quavered. "I've been fighting too long. Take it. Do the right thing. I've hated you my whole life, but . . . I guess I trust you to do the right thing. I'm tired. I've kept my contract with my family. Help me. Please."

Benchley took the bag with the manuscript from the old man's shaking hand. He wondered at the determination and will that had brought him to the top of this hill on so bitter a night, at what it must have cost him.

"I'll see that it gets into the right hands, Blackhead, I promise. We are joined in a way, if you will. The last links in a disintegrating chain, between what Rochambeau was and what it is, aren't we? God help us both, we can testify about a place that was different then, that might as well have been built on a different planet."

"Not so different," said Gowdy. "Not so different. All they cared about was land and money, too. Just like these people."

Benchley started as some creature skittered a few feet away from them. Blackhead seemed not to notice. "But you stabbed Ida Flowers, didn't you, Blackhead? Right down at the bottom of this hill. You obviously knew how to get out of the nursing home when you needed to, didn't you?"

Gowdy sat down abruptly on the old stump, presumably the very spot where his young relative had swung and taken his last breath more than a century ago.

"I didn't mean to hurt her," he said, his voice growing more fatigued. "I thought she'd drive away when she saw me. But she didn't; she just sat there and screamed. So I poked her in the neck. I kind of panicked. I just managed to get up the hill to a ledge—it was one of the family children's old hiding places—"

"And the little girl," Benchley went on. "That was you, also, wasn't it?"

Gowdy looked up and met Benchley's gaze. "I felt bad about that. That was a mistake. Thought I would scare her dad off the development of this land. I had to keep attention on it, you see. If I didn't, why, they'd just hush it up and hurry back to their main business, which is fussing with their kids and jacking up the price of property. I couldn't let them build a mall up here, Benchley.

"Then there'd be no trace of the past. They'd be parking

cars right where we're sitting, right where Caroline Clark died and where Nathaniel was hung, where my family's fate was sealed for good. Lord, how I've hated living in this town. I might as well be a piece of cheesecloth, people just stare right through me. I have no place here, no place at all."

Gowdy looked up at Benchley, his defiance gone. He had shrunk back into a lonely old man, his eyes no longer blazing, just resigned. But it was clear what he was asking.

"I know, old friend. I know what you're saying. I couldn't let them build here, either." Benchley looked inexpressibly sad. What a bitter, troubled life this old man had endured. What a rich bounty he had drawn in comparison. And it was true, his own good fortune and Blackhead's miserable lot, both their fates had been sealed up here on the mountain, in Nathaniel Gowdy's life and death. Benchley looked down the hill at the lights illuminating the driveways and toy-strewn backyards of the town. What an irrelevant little drama they were playing out up here, he thought. The people below wouldn't care about the old tragedy anymore, once they could walk their dogs without fear and let their kids hop back on their expensive bikes. It had nothing to do with them or with their lives.

"But it must have taken an unimaginable effort for you to climb this hill. Why did you struggle up here to meet me, Blackhead?" he wondered, more curious than angry. "Why didn't you just walk into the Garden Center or my house and do what you wanted to do? To be honest, I was waiting."

Blackhead Gowdy seemed to sink further into himself, unable to summon enough energy to keep fighting this ancient, losing battle. For the first time, Benchley noticed the coil of hemp by the other man's feet.

"Nathaniel's hat and coat, this rope, these were the only

things left behind by time and by that thief, the only Gowdy heirlooms," Blackhead whispered, picking up one end of the coil. "No silver service for us, Benchley. Man came to see me in the home, and a day or two after that I noticed most of the rope was gone."

He was quiet a long time. "I wasn't going to do anything to you, Benchley. I was going to string myself up on that tree, the one right next to the stump where Nathaniel was hung, I swear I was. You would have found me up there, with the manuscript at my feet, if I weren't so worn out. That's a Gowdy ending for you. Too pooped to kill myself." His eyes welled with tears. "I wanted you to see it, damn you. To climb up that hill and walk across that grove and straight into my body hanging from that tree."

The rope slipped from Gowdy's fingers and dropped to the ground; his sobs blended with the rising wind. It was the final delusion, his plan to hang himself. He couldn't possibly have gathered the strength to accomplish it.

The first police car bounded over the bump at the entrance to the driveway just as it had a week and a half earlier when the watchman had found the station wagon. Its high-intensity light swept the ground until it stopped, as if the lamp itself were puzzled by the strange scene. Sitting on the elm stump was an old man, a too large jacket bundled over his thin shoulders. A more vigorous-looking man, also elderly, held him in his arms, rocking him back and forth.

"Freeze," boomed a voice over a police loudspeaker, somewhat ridiculously under the circumstances. Kit bounded out the back and started running towards the two men. When they turned to stare, the glare harshly illuminating their faces, he saw right away that both were weeping.

29

I couldn't find 86 Hope Street at first. I had left the Volvo a few doors down and almost tiptoed the rest of the way, straining to see the numbers posted on porches and front doors. They were hard to distinguish, but I was seeing signs of kids —bicycles, skateboards, swing sets—and I knew that the house I was seeking was kidless. Once you have one, you can smell the presence of suburban kids by the detritus they leave.

Compared to this attempt, the break-in at the Rochambeau Homes had been a picnic. The consequences of botching this one could be a hell of a lot worse than a chewing-out by Chief Leeming. It was infinitely creepier and I was dramatically more frightened, so much so that I even yearned for my old Wall Street job. Sort of. So much so that I'd woken Jane up to tell her exactly what I was up to and reminded her where our wills were. I think she was having second thoughts about my second career.

I was going to tell her where our other personal papers were, until I remembered that she knew and I didn't. I'd even considered stopping by the mall for my gun, but having it in my pocket would terrify me more than facing danger unarmed. My real armor, I thought as I crept towards the house, was the suburbanite's almost spiritual belief that he had made it to a safety zone, an island insulated from spontaneous tragedy. Rochambeau had already vividly demonstrated the delusional nature of this notion, but here I was anyway.

Hope Street was only two blocks long, and different from the more affluent neighborhood surrounding it. It was lined with small bungalows, "starter" homes occupied by either elderly couples, young families with small children, or single people who wanted the greenness of the suburbs but didn't need all that space.

It was below freezing, according to my car radio, but it might as well have been mid-July, the way I was sweating as I made my way along the pavement. It was clearly one of my many weaknesses as a detective, sweating when I was terrified. Ben's army knapsack—he would be outraged in the morning —hung over my right shoulder.

I spotted "86" on a Colonial light stand on a neat front lawn. Remembering my army training, I crouched on my hands and knees behind a trimmed yew, and listened for a full minute for dogs or the sounds of late walkers—I couldn't imagine there would be any at 3 A.M.—then scuttled along the side of the house, pausing every fifteen seconds or so.

I was trained in the army to listen so carefully I could hear a spider spin a web. But there were no noises, no barking. Suburban dogs had lost their edge from too many false alarms. Most were child-friendly slobberers as likely to crawl into a stranger's lap as to announce his stealthy presence. I was more alert for and concerned about the police armada that had invaded Rochambeau, and that was probably looking for me in considerable numbers, as Leeming had no doubt noticed my quiet exit from the dramatic scene up on the mountain.

I would be thinking about that encounter for months, maybe for the rest of my life, but not tonight. Tonight I was on fire, a hound on the scent. This, I supposed, was the pay-off, an overwhelming sense that I was closing in, an incomparable rush that blotted out almost everything else.

Maybe the armada had thinned. There had been signs in the last day or so that the cops felt they had everything comfortably accounted for and were withdrawing. (Leeming told me his detectives were leaning towards the notion that mailing Ben's shirt was a prank by some inventive kids in his class.) Though as much as I feared their spotting me, in a few minutes I might wish for platoons of cops.

Anger was balancing the fear, motivating me to creep forward. If I was right, the occupant of 86 Hope Street deserved far worse than I would ever deliver. Mine was a goofy plan, about the only reason I thought it might have the slightest chance of success. The clouds sailed over the moon, completely obscuring it. I looked at my watch again. About now Chief Leeming would be impatiently, even furiously, pulling up to the house, and Jane would be telling him what I'd told her. Poor unnerved Jane—in our marriage, she always seemed to get considerably more than she'd bargained for. And she always seemed to handle it, my abrupt rushings off in the night, that menacing package. But this was another dimension.

I had reached the back of the bungalow without incident. We had visited friends in a similar house on this block a few years ago, a single story of living space with a half-attic above. If I remembered correctly, and I certainly hoped I did, there would be a master bedroom here at the rear, with the living room, kitchen, second bedroom, and screened-in porch towards the front. A toolshed loomed indistinctly in the yard beyond, under a cluster of naked ornamental birches.

Staying below window level, I unzipped Ben's pack and

pulled out my props, courtesy of Nathaniel Gowdy's corner of Benchley's greenhouse. I put the hat on and wrapped the black cloak around my shoulders, my heart whirligigging. Don't think about it, I told myself, or you'll never be able to do it. Burglary charges would be the least of it, if this went wrong.

I took the butt end of the flashlight and smashed right through the closed window, reaching in to yank the curtain rod down. The crash of breaking glass was louder than I'd expected, the noise reverberating through the quiet backyards as the shards fell from the frame. A lot of fingertips would be reaching to punch 911, I figured, right at this very instant.

I had guessed right; this was clearly the bedroom. I could see the digital clock glowing across the room. I just prayed I had the right house and that nobody kept a gun near the nightstand with which to blow an intruder's brains out. If I read the occupant right, that would be uncharacteristic, but I had been wrong about a lot of things lately.

"Who's there?" someone shouted, startled and confused. I clicked on my flashlight, shining it onto my face and hat so that I would be grotesque and quite visible from inside, and howled as loud as I could. I'm not sure I had ever howled before. The sound prompted a scream, along with another shout.

"I've got the tapes, you bastard! You son of a bitch, I've got the tapes right here, and I'll damn you to hell." I tried to disguise my voice, shrieking and counting on surprise. I sounded slightly ridiculous to myself, and to about a dozen neighborhood dogs—even dumb suburban retrievers have some pride—who went off all around me like baying hounds on the hunt. Was there any danger, I belatedly wondered, of some neighbor with a hunting rifle taking a shot?

I held up two empty videocassette cartridges, waving them in front of my illuminated face. Then I clicked off the flashlight, ducked, and waited.

I didn't wait very long. In seconds, a large figure burst through the back door holding a baseball bat in one hand and an unidentifiable shape in the other, rushing toward the tool-shed in the yard about twenty feet away from me, tearing open the door.

"Get the fuck away from me," he was screaming. "I've got a gun, and I'll kill you if you don't get out of here."

I couldn't suppress a brief thrill, an elated jolt. Only somebody with something terrible to hide would run into the yard in boxers in the predawn cold because of my noisy appearance in a weird costume. Perhaps somebody who had good reason to know that I couldn't be a murderous supernatural apparition from the past. Personally, I'd be cowering under the bed with my wife and kids waiting for the cops, not racing through the night in my underwear.

Lights had blinked on up and down the street, with confused shouts bouncing back and forth between the nearby houses, when the figure emerged from the shed with some sort of bundle and dropped the bat. He extended the other object towards me. I guess this was the part I hadn't thought through. No jury in the state would convict him for shooting me under these circumstances. And speaking of misjudgments, it appeared I had been wrong about the gun. But how could that be? People didn't carry guns in the suburbs. That was why we had moved here, wasn't it? I saw someone else bound out of the house and run towards him shouting, "No, don't," and then it appeared the two collided. He cursed, and the gun erupted, first in a flash and then in a roar.

My side seemed to catch fire, and I fell to my knees.

Jesus Christ, I thought. I've been shot in Rochambeau. Incomprehensible. But I was alive. And I began feeling terror beyond anything I'd ever felt or read. Because the man began walking towards me, the gun outstretched. I braced for the next shot. There was no reason for him to keep me alive. Quite the contrary. But then a woman's voice screamed, "No, I won't let you"—and he paused.

Spotlights suddenly flooded the yard and the figure—I could see Richard Handley's stunned face quite clearly now. Judy Cole stood next to him, clinging to his arm, gasping for breath, wrapped in an oversized bathrobe. Even as Handley tried to yank his arm free from her, two burly figures crashed into him and knocked him to the ground.

Foolishly, I kept pointing to the duffel as if the troopers, town cops, sheriffs, detectives, and SWAT team members pouring into the yard couldn't see it. They came shouting from everywhere, the back and the side, with dogs, vans, bullhorns, lights, and guns. Judy tried to walk towards me, then sobbed and collapsed. Several officers were around her. The scream had been hers.

I rolled onto my back, still sweating, and looked up into the unforgiving face of Frank Leeming, who, far from being grateful for my assistance, was cursing me quite colorfully and demanding a stretcher almost in the same breath. Everything seemed supernaturally bright in the searchlight from the hovering helicopter. Dogs howled all over the block, as if the suburban canines finally comprehended that this was serious stuff, not garbagemen on their rounds.

I thought first of Jane, then Ben and Em, and then of my crummy little office in the American Way. I hoped I made it back to them and to it. What a way to pay the mortgage. Then I passed out.

30

"First off," Chief Leeming announced, "this discussion is off the record." He glowered menacingly at Evelyn de la Cretaz, who sat with perfect posture, attentive gaze, and poised steno pad. "The county prosecutor would have my neck if he knew I was out here yakking about the case. No tapes or notes, or I gotta leave." He harrumphed for emphasis.

I smiled at Leeming. We both knew perfectly well why he had come to this postmortem: to make sure there was no detail involving the case that he didn't know about. He wasn't risking his pension to honor me. But I nodded at Evelyn, who put down her pad and, with a frosty glance at the chief, picked up her needlepoint instead.

My answering machine at the mall had collected dozens of inquiries from people who wanted to hire someone the papers had dubbed "The Suburban Detective." I needed help in sorting through the requests, in itself a luxury. I needed help with lots of things.

A secretary was the only thing I truly missed from Wall Street. I hated typing my own reports and could never quite cope with billing. Evelyn had balked at my offer at first, wary at the idea of working for a private eye, and her eyebrows had nearly climbed up her forehead when she saw my office and its surroundings. Evelyn wasn't your garden-variety mall rat. But I had played on her bored semiretirement and the inherent challenge of bringing order to my life and talked her into a thirty-day trial employment. It was clear from the outset which of us was on trial.

I was sitting, somewhat melodramatically, in a wheel-chair in Benchley's coziest greenhouse. Though the bullet had only grazed my side, it was still painful to move quickly or to stand for too long. Jane had no choice but to coddle me, and was uncharacteristically treating me like an antique porcelain.

The ever-pliant Percentage lay snoozing by my wheels, as inert as he was at home. Benchley, attentive and gracious in his maddeningly effortless way, wandered through the small gathering with jugs of his legendary cider, refilling emptied mugs. He had regained his customary energy and good cheer, I was happy to see, as the dreadful pall that hung over his home and his town had lifted. Chief Leeming sat to my family's left, still grumpy but benign. He would almost surely make it to that pension now and see his two girls through college. The only unfortunate aspect was that I had helped get him there.

Sam Mellman and his troupe of suburban princes were sprawled vaingloriously around and on the chaise longues Benchley had dragged out, their caps and shirts and the positioning of their jean waistbands below their hipbones signifying something crucial but incomprehensible to the adult eye. Ben and Em sat behind me, momentarily ill at ease and intimidated by the presence of older boys.

Jane was chatting with Luis who, in his immaculate navy pin-striped suit, left the lot of us looking grubby. It was the first time I'd ever seen him outside the mall, and I suspected it might be one of the last, but he had politely agreed to drive to Rochambeau to honor my first truly celebrated case.

Only three principal figures were missing: Blackhead

Gowdy, still in intensive care at the Garden State Medical Center, engaged in probably the final struggle of his bitter life against the pneumonia that had overwhelmed him following his last stand on the mountain. Plus, of course, Richard Handley, being held without bail in the county detention facility. And Judy Cole, in seclusion, I was told, pending the police investigation and decision as to whether she would be accused of obstructing justice or witholding information, or even charged as an accessory to murder.

"You're going to have to testify to this," Leeming went on, "so there's no pressure to discuss it now. But I'm still curious to know more about how you settled on Handley, and why you stayed so mum about it." At this point, there was actually little, if anything, Chief Leeming didn't know, though that wasn't true of everybody else in the room.

"Chief, I had to get my client's permission to reveal his own heroic role. And he had to talk it over with his parents," I said, gesturing at Sam, who preened despite his naturally modest and good manners. "I didn't let the media in on all of this—his father didn't want the family in the papers—but it was Sam who was mostly responsible for cracking the case open. He and his pals got the evidence."

Sam stretched his long, muscled legs out even further and blushed. "C'mon," he said, "that's not true."

I ignored the disclaimer, which wasn't very vehement anyway.

"There were the obvious things pointing to Handley. He knew about the Gowdy case. He was close to Ken Dale. He could have planted the idea for murder, if you will, by assigning Ken the report. On the other hand, I was lacking evidence or anything resembling a possible motive. And even if I had one, Handley had a cast-iron alibi—he was with

Benchley and me and a lot of other people at the Historical Society dinner from seven till nine or so, when the deaths supposedly occurred. Besides, he was greatly beloved by legions of appreciative students. I liked him myself. I saw nothing in anything he said or did that suggested he could do something like that. It's quite a lesson.

"When Judy told me Carol was involved with an older man, he did come to mind, not because of anything about him, but because no one knew anything about this supposed romance. If she wasn't seeing another student, who else would she have come into contact with regularly?

"Now, Carol had a friendly relationship with Lee Cole, of course; they played tennis and she hung around Judy's house. She also had a relationship of sorts with Jamie Harte, who wasn't exactly an older man but who was outside their circle.

"But a couple of other things made me consider Handley," I said, leafing through my sheaf of notes. "He kept trying to steer me toward Jamie Harte by confiding how bad a seed the kid was—and to be honest, not many people were contradicting him. But he got carried away. He told me they'd called in the Child Study team a half-dozen times. I know that Rochambeau isn't shy about bouncing problem kids into special needs schools, so I checked with my sources in the psychiatric community"—I looked away from Jane; Leeming looked straight at her—"and found that the Child Study team had been called in only once, back when Jamie was fighting a lot in middle school and his dad was out of hand. Handley was clearly steering me in the wrong direction.

"Another way Handley was trying to derail me—he left trails all over the place, leading to everybody but him—was this story he told me about how despondent Ken Dale was, how he'd written this suicidal poem just before his death. I called Sam and he and his friends went through everything Ken owned and they didn't find it. Where was this crucial poem, which almost functioned as an ancillary suicide note?" Leeming was scribbling now. These were details that hadn't come out in my hospital grilling, mostly because I had been too doped-up to remember much.

"A big tip-off was provided by Judy. It was bugging me for days and I couldn't put my finger on it until I was talking it through with Luis. When she referred to the Gowdy case when we had dinner, she talked about how Gowdy cut up one of his victims. When I read the chronology of victims to Luis, I realized that this wasn't true. At the time, the papers reported that Gowdy strangled all of his victims. The only other person who mentioned anybody being cut up was Handley, who told me that a wealthy Newark landowner had been dismembered at the same time the Gowdy killings had occurred. Yet Handley said he hadn't read the Perry manuscript, the only reference to that other murder that anyone knew about. So how could he know unless he was lying about that, and how could Judy know unless he had told her? He was obviously confiding in her because the other killing wasn't reported anywhere else, and nobody else knew about it.

"Jane"—I reached out to pat my wife's hand—"insisted all along that I shouldn't be looking for your stereotypical murderous maniac; that the manner in which these crimes were committed—the hat, the cape, the rope—were all too staged. She pointed out that not all killers are crazy, as we have been led to believe. Some people kill for what seem to them perfectly logical reasons. Look for a stable person, she said, who knew the town's history but who had a contemporary motive for murder—"

Leeming interrupted. "I've worked a lot of murders, Deleeuw; I've seen teenagers do amazing things, including kill themselves. But you presumed from the first that the Dale-Lombardi deaths weren't what they appeared. Why were you so sure?"

Benchley circulated with another tray of cider.

"That's what I was getting paid to do, Chief, to take Ken's point of view. I had an easier job than yours. You had to suspect everybody; I didn't," I said, looking back at Sam and his transfixed friends. "I thought any kid that could inspire this kind of loyalty deserved at least the benefit of the doubt." The kids were nodding and high-fiving. The fact is, I thought what they had done for their friend *was* incredible.

"Besides, the deaths always seemed too pat. You might have thought I was a pain-in-the-ass rube"—on cue, Leeming nodded vigorously—"but I investigated a few murders in the army. I thought Jane was right: these were orchestrated to make them look like something else. I've learned something from this case. We always assume the worst of kids, and Handley was counting on that. But some of them can fool you."

More nods. I paused, sipping from my cider. "There was something else, too," I said. "I am especially sensitive these days to what it feels like to be accused of something you didn't do." I shot Chief Leeming a hard stare; he met it. But the more important look came from Ben. Finally, I thought, I got through, and all it took was my getting shot.

"So starting with the premise that somebody orchestrated these young people's deaths and made them look like murder, Handley eventually seemed the likeliest candidate, especially with what Sam and Company turned up. But with the media, with lawsuits, with people's touchiness about sexual issues, I didn't want to go to the police and risk destroying Handley and possibly Judy without clear evidence. She handed me the motive, of course. Coerced sex tapes—that was something people can get killed over."

Jane jumped in. "It struck me from the first that there might have been some sexual abuse Carol was hiding, once Kit told me she was seeing someone else and nobody knew who. Who could draw a sensible kid like Carol into so compromising a position? She wouldn't be apt to get involved with a stranger."

"My first thought was Jamie Harte, to be honest," I said. "Nobody had a good word to say about this kid. Shows you how clever Handley was. He let me believe he was reluctant to tell me how evil Harte was. He could barely bring himself to say it, and I bought it."

"Well, what *about* Harte?" Ben asked. "You thought it was him that night somebody mailed you my T-shirt, didn't you? Maybe Harte sent it. He *was* scary, man."

"Ben, I have to tell you, sitting here like a pasha patting myself on the back, the truth is that I don't know who sent your shirt. We may never know. It's possible Jamie got hold of one of your shirts from the Y or some other place and concocted a vicious prank; I guess I think he was capable of that. He's scary, and he's a bully. But there is really nothing to suggest he was a killer."

I took a breath. In any other context but victorious crowing, I would have needed a nap by now. But under the circumstances, someone would have had to shoot me again to get me to stop. Leeming looked as if he was thinking about it.

"At first, Lee Cole looked strong as a prospect for Carol's mysterious other man," I went on. "She had occasion to be in his house a lot. He played tennis with her once a week, which still strikes me as a little creepy, although that's probably unfair. When the lunkhead tennis pro told me they'd had a disagreement, and when Handley told me she'd turned down a scholarship that Cole arranged, then I got even more interested. Cole had put Carol Lombardi up for the country club's annual scholarship fund; he had introduced her to some of the other men on the scholarship committee. He just couldn't understand when she suddenly turned the scholarship down. My hunch is that Handley was terrified of Carol's going off to college. She would be out from under his control, in an environment where there would be other friends and support—"

"And where she might talk about what had happened to her," offered Leeming.

"Right. Away from constant contact with Handley, away from the force of his personality, she might very well have gone to a counselor, or a roommate. So he pressured her into turning down the scholarship, perhaps into not going away to school at all."

"And Judy didn't pick this up?" Jane frowned. "Or hear about it at the club?"

"No. Remember that she and her father had had a big fight about the club. Judy thought it was racist and wouldn't go there. And Carol had decided she couldn't fully confide in her, even though Judy did pick up on some disturbance and Carol told her she wasn't sure about college. But that happens. I bet Judy wouldn't—or couldn't—face up to the reality. When Lee Cole told me that what he and Carol were arguing about was her refusing the scholarship, I realized I had probably misjudged him. But Handley probably knew that his time was getting short. So he killed her."

"Her teacher, especially one she respected, seemed a strong possibility," Jane put in. "The man was feeding on the respect and admiration some of his female students held for him."

"I know Dick Handley," said Evelyn, shaking her silver head. "He cared quite deeply about his work. Do you think that this, this—perversion—was his only motive, his only real interest?"

"Oh, no," I said, "that's what threw me off. When he heard Carol was telling her best friend she was in trouble, he figured he had to act quickly. So presenting it as a jilted-teenage-lover case seemed a plausible way to kill her off, especially since he had so much influence with Ken, and since people see teenagers as inherently unstable anyway."

"Then why did he tie it so carefully to the Gowdy case?" asked Evelyn. "Why didn't he just leave it as a jealous lover killing his girlfriend? Unfortunately, people would have accepted that, wouldn't they?"

"Yes," I agreed. "But invoking the Gowdy connection would draw the police completely away from him. There must be other students he's abused. It was brilliant in that regard. And it worked. Only temporarily, of course."

Leeming shot me an irritated glance, mostly for show; he knew I was just needling him.

"This way there was not only a motive—jealousy—but an actual modus operandi, an old case Ken Dale was known to have studied. And maybe there was another reason. You know, we still cling to the notions of black and white and good versus evil. But it's possible for people to do horrible things and also have considerable good in them. I think Handley justified the murders to himself by insisting that they would help save Rochambeau from growth and greed. The more he argued that line of reasoning, the more he believed it. By the end, I suspect he wasn't killing people to protect his sexual obsessions, but to rescue the town. He would not, of course, have anticipated that the deaths of Ken Dale and

Carol Lombardi would spark Blackhead Gowdy to attack Ida Flowers and the Peterson girl, or inspire a trucker to kill Lisa Caltari on the Brown estate."

Jane nodded. "That's right. And those crimes further unsettled an already unstable personality. Because if people thought a psychotic serial killer was on the loose, then they wouldn't see the noble cause in which Handley had convinced himself he was acting. Although the other crimes did suit his purposes, in a way. They further muddied the waters" —Leeming nodded wryly at that—"and they made it even less likely that people would want to move to Rochambeau. So he must have felt quite ambivalent about them."

Chief Leeming was transfixed; so were Sam and his pals.

I continued: "Things spun out of his control. And the fact that it's a righteous cause only further blurred his ability to separate reality from his own tortured rationales. In his mind, he was committing these crimes to send a message."

Benchley rose and headed for the cider jug. "And a valid one, in many ways," he said sadly.

"But people in the town were taking it just the way they took Nathaniel Gowdy's alleged spree, as the incomprehensible acts of a lunatic. Which was correct, too, in a way," I said.

"That's right," said Jane, "and the less the media and the town understood the crimes, the more difficult it was for Handley to keep on deluding himself."

Leeming had sat grimly through the discussion so far, analytic crime recaps in public not being his habit, but he seemed to be relaxing. I had learned over the course of this case that Leeming was, in fact, a first-rate investigator himself who had been neck-and-neck with me every step of the way. Almost.

Suddenly we all jumped at a shout—"Yo!"—from the

doorway. Two men in aprons lumbered into the room carrying huge Lightning Burger sacks and began to pull out scores
of wrapped burgers, bags of fries, and trays of Cokes. Benchley watched, astonished.

"Please excuse my presumption," said Luis, bowing
slightly towards him. "I thought such an occasion should be
well catered." Benchley laughed, even as Sam and his wolf
pack bounded to the wooden pallet set up as a sort of buffet
and scarfed up significant numbers of burgers before the rest
of us could move. Ben and Emmy scooted over, looking ques-
tioningly at Jane, who normally forbade junk food of any sort.
But today was clearly an occasion that called for relaxation of
restrictions.

We waited until everyone settled down again. "So, sus-
pecting Handley," Luis asked me in his formal way, "how *did*
you gather the evidence that invalidated his alibi?" Was there
a trace of impatience in his voice?

"You got me started, Luis. You talked about learning how
to believe and disbelieve someone simultaneously, to accept
what everyone is saying but examine it all, to take nothing at
face value. The breakthrough came in busting open his alibi.
If Handley had killed those kids, then his alibi had to be false,
and since I was with him during the dinner that night, that
meant the timing of the murder had to be off. It just had to
be.

"I called the security guard, the old guy who had discovered the bodies in the first place and then took off for Florida.
He balked at first, but then admitted that he had skipped his
first round at 10 P.M., and had been skipping it for days because of the cold snap. He had nothing to lose by confessing
this; they couldn't fire him now.

"When I went back and read over the initial police statements about the case, the fuzzy part was the time of death. The county lab said that because it was so cold that night on the mountain—it was way below zero, counting the wind chill—the supposed time of death, 8 P.M., was partly based on the fact that the Volvo ran out of gas and the engine died just after the bodies were found. We know the tank was almost empty because Ken's father had noticed the warning light on the dash. He told Ken to fill the tank, but Ken said he was in a hurry and he had enough gas to get where he was going."

The sun was rapidly warming the greenhouse with a tantalizing taste of spring. It was hard now to imagine Benchley and Blackhead up on that dark mountain just a few nights ago; it was harder still to imagine the bitter night when Ken Dale and Carol Lombardi had died and life in Rochambeau had turned inside out.

"You see, that's what brought it into focus for me. Because the night watchman heard the Volvo engine running when he discovered the bodies; the first police officers on the scene heard the engine die. So I went down to the Volvo dealership and talked to the mechanics; even a gallon would keep it running at idle for a few hours, they said. It can vary, depending upon age and temperature and octane, but there isn't that much play. So a nearly empty tank and a car that died about 4 A.M. would be just about right if the time of death were 8 P.M. But what, I thought, if somebody had put a bit more gas into the tank? That could mean that the murders could have occurred much earlier—*before* the Historical Society dinner.

"Suppose that the killer had been watching the estate and knew that the watchman was skipping his early rounds but made his last rounds every morning regularly and punctually, because he'd watched him? All he'd have to do is go up on the mountain after the dinner and pour a bit more gas into the tank—"

"You mean with the bodies in the car?" Sam interrupted incredulously. "That would take iron balls . . . uh, excuse me. That would be unbelievable. Man, that creeps me out."

"It was unbelievable," I confirmed. "Nobody believed it. But it would explain Handley's alibi."

"Or mine," said Benchley, quietly. I had not been able to say aloud what I had begun to fear just a few days earlier, and what Luis had sensed at the Lightning Burger. Benchley, too, knew about the Gowdy killings. And he had a couple of motives, certainly more than were at first apparent for Handley. His Garden Center would be the least inviting spot in town if the hill under which it nestled were suddenly obliterated by mall parking and town houses. His feelings about the town's history were not abstract political notions but something about which his own blood and family history made him feel strongly. And Benchley would almost surely lose his land if the Brown estate were sold.

Next to the fact that it seemed I would be able to keep my house for a while, my greatest relief had been that my initial instincts about my friend had been correct. When I left Luis at the mall that night, I was determined to confront Benchley. How, I wonder, would he have taken my questioning? But I didn't get the chance that night and, after a few hours, it was no longer necessary.

"Yes, Benchley, it would have invalidated your alibi as well," I said evenly. "Let's just say my instincts—which my friend Luis urged me to follow—did not lead me in your direction. Not for more than a few minutes." He laughed, though the looks we traded weren't entirely comic ones.

"Anyway," I continued—odd how the suspense hadn't

killed anybody's appetite—"I called Sam and asked him and his pals to fan out among the local gas stations with their high school yearbooks and show the kids who work at night Handley's picture."

"And bang!" said Sam proudly. "In an hour, Danny scored. Billy Hamilton, who works at the Mobil on the town line, ID'ed Handley in a flash. Recognized him from Rochambeau High, even though he'd never had him. Said the guy had driven in on a freezing night with a five-gallon plastic jerry jug but only bought one gallon of gas, maybe less. Claimed he was getting gas for a generator or something. Billy thought it was strange, and probably wouldn't have remembered except it was such a bitch to go out and pump one gallon in the cold."

"We found the plastic can in Handley's garage," Leeming added. "Gotta hand it to you there, Deleeuw." As if everything else was a lucky fluke. "None of my smart guys thought of the gas angle. There was no reason to look too hard at the alibis when we got a murder-suicide note in the boy's computer. Although," he growled suddenly, "sending high school kids out like that without calling us was dumb. And borderline irresponsible. No, make that irresponsible, period."

I bowed slightly; he had a point about sending the kids out. But I hadn't wanted to call the police, because the same suspicions I harbored about Handley might have led them to Benchley.

"So Handley goes up to the mountain later that night, after the dinner." Leeming picked up the tale. "He puts another shot of gas into the tank—half a gallon was still in the can—pushes back our time of death by two or three hours, and locks up his alibi."

"Right," I said. "Handley's thing was to invite his favored

young women students to his house, to do his beloved-mentor thing, get them into bed, secretly tape their lovemaking, and then use the tapes as blackmail to keep them quiet. He picked his conquests carefully, choosing those who were the most vulnerable and were drawn to his warm, sensitive routine. And who would be horrified if their families and friends saw tapes like that. A kid like Carol worshipped him, and she was so concerned with being a good girl she couldn't bear the thought of Ken or her mother or anyone seeing those tapes."

"Kit," said Luis, who'd stuck to cider and muffins, eschewing the very fast-food bounty he'd unleashed, "why do you think Carol didn't ask Judy for help? She was her best friend."

I shrugged. "One reason is that Handley probably frightened her half to death. He was plenty sharp enough to have noticed if Judy started behaving angrily or suspiciously, and he would have blamed her." I harbored another notion as well, but I thought it was inappropriate to discuss it with anyone but Judy.

"One of the things that had led me toward Lee Cole, early on, was that that would explain why Carol couldn't tell Judy who the mysterious older man was. But that would also be true of the most respected teacher in the school. Besides, Carol might have known that Handley was a blackmailer, but she had no idea, I'm sure, that he might be a murderer."

Percentage shuffled over to a corner to water one of Benchley's plants, then dropped to the floor again to continue his doze.

"But I still don't understand," piped in Evelyn, over her canvas of woolen columbine and pansies, "why he didn't just shoot her or stab her to death?" A blood-chilling interjection from a bespectacled little needlewoman.

"He would have the problem," Leeming said, forgetting or not really caring about the county prosecutor's sensibilities, "of how that would look. We would focus our investigation on Carol's personal life, her sexual life, her friendships, and that might have led us to him. He had to find a way to steer everybody in some other direction."

"Almost everybody." Luis beamed proudly in my direction.

Leeming ignored the implicit barb. "He planned it magnificently. He was already close to Ken Dale but became even closer, acting as his mentor and poetry coach. He called Ken's father and suggested that Ken needed extra tutoring—said Ken was special, and what parent in Rochambeau could resist that idea?—and volunteered to tutor Ken himself at the Dales' home for free. He probably got Ken to open up about Carol's odd behavior after their breakup, under the guise of helping the kid feel better about it.

"He had already suggested the Gowdy assignment, so that everybody would conclude that murder was already on Ken's mind and that the Gowdy murders gave him a blueprint. We don't know every detail," Leeming acknowledged. "With Handley going for a plea bargain instead of a trial, maybe we never will.

"But before we talk any more, I want the kids here to take a ride with Sergeant Alvarez. I can't have this case blown out by some smart lawyer claiming we prejudiced the town or something. If Handley wasn't already cutting a deal, I wouldn't be here at all." Sam and his friends started to mutter, but the chief held up his hand. "The sergeant's brother is manager of the American Way video game room. You've got two hours' worth of tokens."

The muttering turned pro forma. Soon they were bundled into a Rochambeau police car, a kick in itself, and whisked away, Ben and Em thrilled to be tagging along with the high school gods.

We all relaxed a bit when they were gone, not only because of the potential legal complications, but because we weren't at all sure these were details it would be appropriate for the town's youth to hear. Chief Leeming continued his gory play-by-play.

"Handley is the only person both kids would trust enough to come to the Brown estate to meet, probably at different times. He'd probably told Ken he wanted to explore the findings in the Gowdy case. Maybe he told Carol he was going to give her the tapes back and help square things with Ken, or told Ken that Carol wanted to go back to him. He had that kind of leverage. He probably brought the girl with him, then strangled her with the rope he'd stolen from Black-head Gowdy when he visited him at the nursing home a few days earlier.

"I don't know whether he already knew the rope was there, or quickly put this scheme together when he discovered the rope gave him a great way to muddy the waters with the old Gowdy stuff. He must have killed the girl first. When Ken pulled up in his Volvo, Handley probably had him get out of the car and whacked him on the head—there was that contusion that bothered the medical boys, but was consistent with slamming his forehead on the steering wheel if the car lurched or stopped abruptly."

My side was beginning to ache, and I was breaking into a bit of a cold sweat, although I was grateful, as Leeming had suggested I should be, that Handley hadn't kept a larger-caliber pistol around. I hoped the chief didn't get windy. Jane was eyeing me warily, but I would have killed her if she interrupted.

"He carries Ken, who's unconscious, back into the driver's seat, and puts Carol's body next to him," I said, picking up the narrative. "He ties one end of the rope around Ken's neck and the other to the stump, and releases the car's brake. It rolls down the incline, stopping short—that's why the police figure the body has a bruise. Ken chokes to death, which is why the coroner was correct in establishing strangulation as the cause of death."

Jane frowned. "But surely so severe a blow to the head wouldn't be dismissed by the police. I mean—"

"It wasn't *dismissed*," the chief interjected. "But when you've got two dead bodies, and you've got a motive—jealousy, for which a lot of people die—and the means, and a suicide note from the boy, you tend to take things like a bruise and fit them into the context of the events. It's easy enough to second-guess later, but you play the odds," he said almost pleadingly to me, "just like in the stock market."

I thought he gave Jane a cautionary look before continuing, a touch defensively. "We looked at Handley at the time. But there was no motive in the world that we knew of and let's face it, the man had a solid alibi. Plus, Mr. Deleeuw here didn't see fit to tell us for forty-eight hours that the Lombardi girl was involved with some older guy who was blackmailing her." His glare this time was unmistakably fierce. "Which Mr. Deleeuw assures me will not happen again, since I could already have his license hanging on my wall like a certificate from Kiwanis."

He walked over to grab another soda, with a bow to Luis.

"Now," Leeming proceeded, satisfied he had made me

sweat, "the question is whether Handley knew, when he asked them to come up on the mountain that night, how he was going to accomplish all this. If he did, wouldn't he have bought that gas earlier and poured it in?"

"He was arrogant and meticulous, and I think he had every step planned," I replied. "But he couldn't have known how low on gas Ken's car was. He must have freaked when he saw the gauge, knowing it might help fix the time of the death. So he had to dash out to buy gas. It must not have seemed a great risk, because not many Rochambeau High kids work as gas jockeys. And he went to the edge of town. It was his only careless act."

Now I had a few questions of my own I wanted resolved.

"I don't know much about computers," I continued, as Benchley began collecting Lightning Burger wrappers, "but didn't you tell me, Chief, that Ken Dale's computer had a code? Even his parents didn't know it."

"Yeah," said Leeming, "but Handley knew it. Don't repeat this stuff, please, the prosecutor will have my butt, but Sam told us that Handley's home computer broke a while ago, or he claimed it did. And he asked if anybody in the class had IBM PCs. See, he would've known who had word processors from reading the kids' papers. Plus, Handley had been tutoring Ken. When Ken said he had one, Handley asked if he could come over and use it. Meanwhile, Handley gets closer to Ken and learns the habits of the house. He finds out that the parents don't get home until six-thirty and that the little brother stays with a friend's mother every afternoon. Handley was a smart sucker, I'll give him that."

And an especially tragic one, I thought. You couldn't fake the affection and respect he engendered in the classroom. What a waste.

"So sometime," Leeming resumed, "Handley would have

slipped through the back door of the Dale house, which was always left open, gone into Ken's room, turned the computer on, and left the suicide note."

Jane brought me some coffee and a couple of aspirin. My side was really aching now; I didn't think I could hold on too much longer.

"What got you onto Judy and her connection to Handley?" asked Benchley, turning the inquisition back toward me. "You told me how impressed you were with her."

"Impressed wasn't the word," said Jane, drolly. "I thought he was going to do one of those dumb middle-aged male things." Everybody in the room chuckled but me. I decided to be extremely open with Jane for the rest of my life, since any other course of action was obviously pointless.

"Judy's a complicated person," I said. "She's quite remarkable. Remember that Handley has probably been at this game for some time, as I'm sure the chief has already uncovered but won't talk about. He taught Judy in middle school, coming into her life right at the time she was the most vulnerable. Her mother was dying of cancer, her father loved her but was cold and remote. She had a tough life. She also had to watch Carol Lombardi have everything she didn't have—easygoing nature, family, friends. I'm sure Handley got his hooks into her then, emotionally. He was waiting like some bird of prey for her to mature. I'm sure he didn't tape her. She wouldn't have put up with it, and he didn't need to. He was everything she needed—a father, a mentor, and because of her maturity, a friend as well."

Leeming nodded but said nothing.

"But are you saying," asked Benchley, "that she knew when you talked to her that her lover, her teacher, had killed her best friend?"

"No, no, just the opposite," I said. "I think the idea surfaced the night we had dinner. When I said I thought the man Carol had been seeing had to be outside their circle, probably an older man, she seemed stunned. I think that's when she first started thinking about it, but the implications were just too much. Her surrogate father and lover murdering her best friend? I'm not sure she could have handled that. She didn't know for sure until Handley tried to shoot me outside his bedroom window. Then, she didn't hesitate to save my life. If she hadn't charged at him, I might not be here."

"What will happen to her, Chief?" Jane asked. "I hope they won't charge her with anything serious. She surely didn't participate in the murders."

The chief shrugged. "Not my turf," he said. "But given her intervention for Kit, and the fact she was an abused child, for chrissake, even the county prosecutor won't want to go to a jury with that one."

"She was—is—pretty impressive for an eighteen-year-old," I said lamely. Eyes were rolled here and there about the greenhouse. I changed the subject, clearing my throat.

"Handley stole the Perry manuscript from your library, Benchley, and the manuscript turned out to be key. It was his road map for engineering the whole affair, the trigger that gave him the idea and the method. Maybe, in some twisted way, the justification as well. So it was crucial that it not be left around for others to read, because while Handley wanted everyone to assume that Ken Dale was inspired by the Gowdy case, some of the details in the manuscript might have led us to Handley sooner. Of course, I didn't understand how it could have vanished so conveniently, particularly after I met Evelyn. Handley didn't know that just before he died Perry, the writer, had sent a copy to Blackhead Gowdy. Blackhead had buried it in a strongbox up here on the estate, because he knew it might someday clear Nathaniel's name.

And that was one reason he had to get back up on the mountain, even if it killed him.

"He meant to die with that manuscript at his feet." Benchley shook his head. "His final statement—his family would finally have the public's full attention."

Evelyn's head popped up from her canvas, her gray curls bobbing in anger and certainty. "I knew I filed that manuscript. And it would be there still, unless someone took it." She glared as if daring anybody to challenge her; no one did.

"We found the manuscript in Handley's toolshed," Leeming said. "Along with the videotapes he used to keep his victims in line. There were a half-dozen young women over the past five years. Probably there were also some, like Judy, he didn't tape."

"Judy had mentioned at dinner about a man being cut up, but it didn't click until after I'd read the Perry interview," I said, leaning forward excitedly but involuntarily wincing at the stab in my side. "You see, among the things Perry uncovered was the brutal stabbing murder of this landowner. That murder took place at the very same time that Nathanial Gowdy was supposed to be strangling all those women. But Gowdy wasn't charged with that crime, and none of the newspaper accounts at the time connected them."

Benchley stood up, trembling and flushed. "You're saying, Kit, that Nathaniel's being hung and this landowner's being stabbed—" He couldn't finish. Already tormented by the fact that his ancestors took advantage of the Gowdy family to buy their land at a bargain price, he now had to digest the fact that Nathaniel might have been innocent of the crimes as well. I wanted to go put my arms around him, but I couldn't get up.

In fact, my forehead had broken out in a cold sweat and I leaned back. Percentage came over and plopped his slobbery head in my lap. I liked to think he was concerned about my discomfort but knew, of course, that he wanted a scratch.

"It's true, Benchley," I acknowledged. "Perry clearly had stumbled on major new evidence in the case, findings that had they been raised at the time might have cleared Gowdy."

"What about the Caltari girl?" asked Luis. "No connection?"

Leeming shook his head. "The truck driver who picked up Lisa Caltari has confessed. They were doing drugs together, peddling a little on the side, and he brought her up there for sex. They both thought it would be a kick to do it where two people had just died, a sort of sick turn-on. Then he found a wad of bills in her purse and was convinced she was holding back the dope money. She freaked and he strangled her and threw her body onto the driveway. A random, freakish thing. He wouldn't have gone up there if he hadn't read about Dale and Lombardi."

"The Caltari death must have really shaken Handley," Jane put in. "He had become in his mind—this is where the delusion grew—Rochambeau's historic avenging angel. My God, when I think of him standing up there at the memorial service, the noble educator." She shook her head. "That was part of his grandiose fantasizing."

"By the time the Peterson child's room was broken into" —I took up the tale—"every cop in the state had come to town."

"And every reporter," Jane said. "So what he did was interpreted not as the selfless gesture his disturbed mind had declared it to be, but as one in a series of violent, psychotic acts. And he certainly could never have expected the real avenging angel in the case—Blackhead Gowdy—to rise almost from his grave."

"Blackhead had a genuine wrong to right," Benchley agreed grimly. "He told me up on the Brown estate that night that when he heard of the deaths, he knew it was his last chance. He was determined to keep the Gowdy case alive."

Leeming coughed, leaned forward. "But here's one thing I don't understand. Why didn't Handley kill Gowdy? He must have known that Gowdy could connect his nursing home visit to the missing rope."

"Blackhead didn't give him the opportunity," Benchley said. "He took off before Handley could get him. He hid in my greenhouse."

Leeming reached for the last of the burgers. I suspected he and Luis would be seeing more of one another. "But Jesus, Deleeuw, whatever possessed you to pull that stupid stunt at Handley's house—My God, we might have shot you ourselves if Handley hadn't."

I winced theatrically. "Well, I concede that was risky. And perhaps inspired just a touch by my need to prove something to myself. But Handley was clever. I knew a blackmailer never strays far from his evidence, and the Gowdy disguise was impulsive. I felt I had more leeway to provoke him than the police did. I found the hat and cape here at Benchley's when I came looking for him; Blackhead had hidden them in back of the greenhouse behind the dracaenas. I thought the sight of me shouting about tapes would have Handley scrambling for them, if he had them. Shooting me seemed out of character. I know it sounds stupid, to say that about somebody I suspected of committing murder."

It was past noon, after Sergeant Alvarez returned with Sam and the other kids, after everyone but Jane and Ben and Em had drifted away, that Benchley took me for a stroll outdoors, pushing me along in my wheelchair. I was wrecked. The emotional tumult and odd hours of the past weeks had taken some toll, not to mention the first and—I hoped—last bullet wound of my life.

"Do you have any questions for me?" asked Benchley quietly, as we circled the greenhouse that he had begun to fill with annuals. "Or suspicions, perhaps?"

The question was phrased with typical directness and warmth. It took some getting used to; most people didn't operate that way.

"No," I said, "but I have a confession of sorts. It *did* occur to me that you had a strong interest in what happened to the Brown estate. And that your family had a history with the Gowdys. My dread was that you had some connection with Ken Dale or Carol Lombardi that I didn't know about. Or some business dealing with Old Man Gowdy."

Benchley stopped the wheelchair and sat down on a stone bench. In a month or so this walkway would stream with eager gardeners gearing for massive assaults on their lawns and flower beds.

"I did have private talks with Eustace Brown," Benchley said, looking a bit sorrowfully up towards the mountain. "He was a son of a bitch, reclusive, tight-fisted, and difficult. But he loved his mountain. He loved this town, too, in a way few newcomers ever could. He had four sons, none of whom he felt especially close to. All greedy and spineless, he said. He saw what was happening to Rochambeau—this was the beginning of what we came to call the yuppie invasion. People who'd lived in the town for decades could no longer afford to live here. Gentrification was rampant. Everywhere we looked were construction sites.

"Developers were offering Eustace millions for his property, and his sons were badgering him to sell. He came to me before he died, troubled. I suggested that when we both were dead, our land be deeded to a private trust for a nature preserve that could never become a commercial property or be sold for any reason. Eustace knew his sons would challenge this agreement. Developers might, too, and so would the town, which would hardly appreciate prime acreage contributing nothing to the hard-pressed tax rolls. We had both lived here long enough to know how such contests invariably end. Nevertheless, we actually had our lawyers draw up an agreement.

"But I underestimated how relentless the developers would be," Benchley said sadly. "They badgered Eustace and his children day and night. He hesitated, then died before he could make up his mind. I know he wanted the land preserved. I also know his sons don't. I'm certain that this land's fate will end up in the courts. I'm sorry for that. In a way, the Brown estate is our last chunk of real history, not to mention open space and beauty. Suburbia never learns. That, I suppose, is its special fate. It was built on the ethic of growth; it doesn't really have any other. I probably should have told you that Eustace and I had talked. But I didn't, because nothing came of it. And Eustace had sworn me to secrecy."

"You never reached an agreement anyway," I said loyally.

"That's right," he said. "But I don't like to hold things back from my friends."

I had never really believed Benchley capable of littering, let alone some of the crimes that had haunted the town. But it was good to have the air clear between us, to have the air clear in general. Blackhead Gowdy, and perhaps even his distant relative Nathaniel, had been exonerated of murder.

I doubted that I would ever see Blackhead alive again,

but I was grateful to him for reminding me, all of us really, that we lived in a place that had a history, that was built at a cost, that needed some vigilance. When I looked up the hill, I tried to imagine teenaged Nathaniel, a distant antecedent of sorts to Sam Mellman and his friends. Would he be a prince of the suburbs today, bounding up and down the asphalt courts in his Skyrocketer Super Pumps, sauntering the wide streets with his army surplus backpack draped over one shoulder?

This morning, on the way to Benchley's brunch, Jane and I had driven Ben and Emmy up to the elm stump on the Brown estate and told them Nathaniel's story. I felt honor-bound to connect them with their history. When I was done, they both looked wide-eyed and impressed and said the same thing at the same time:

"Awesome."

31

Lee Cole opened the door. I instinctively braced for it to slam, but it didn't. Cole didn't exactly look wary, but he was visibly less hostile and malevolent. More like sad. He'd probably had to face a lot of things about his daughter and his own life in the past week or so. I figured he had enough to handle without any posturing from me.

"Hey," I said, "how you doing?"

He offered his hand, which I took. "I guess I owe you an apology of sorts," he said.

"No, not at all. You were protecting your kid from a person you didn't trust. I think that's the way it's supposed to work, isn't it?"

He nodded wearily. Perhaps the weight of the past few years—the sickness and death of his wife, the death of Carol, the loneliness and agony and danger of his daughter—had finally worn him down.

"Besides, Cole," I said, "I spent a few days convinced you might have killed Carol. That's a lot more damning than your thinking I was a crook."

He nodded again, then smiled. "If I'd thought about it all, I would have known that nobody who stole money on Wall Street would be doing what you're doing for a living."

I laughed. "I don't know—it has its perks. You pick your own hours and get to meet the most interesting people."

He hesitated, awkwardly. "I really have to thank you," he said finally. "When I think what might have happened to Judy, how much trouble she was in, how I didn't even see it, I'm very grateful. You see, Judy is exactly like her mother. Seeing her every day was like experiencing the loss of Julia every single day. I couldn't bear it; I just drew back. It was easier to be a father to Carol, who was nothing like either of them—she was so open and accessible. It was selfish. I hate myself every minute for not getting help."

Before I could respond, he collected himself, regained a more executive bearing. He was going to work, he said.

The family's lawyer had called that day to say the county prosecutor was satisfied Judy knew nothing of the killings, and would only require that she see a counselor, which both Coles were already doing. There would be no charges, no record, and Judy would cooperate with the police in any way she could. "She's just back from a few days at my sister's, away from the press," he said. "She wants to see you. I'll leave you alone." He gestured toward the living room, then walked upstairs. It seemed a long time ago that he had bellowed me off his property. Now he was leaving me to it. It seemed we had both misjudged one another.

Judy was sitting on the couch, an Anita Brookner novel in her lap. I doubted she was making much progress on the book. She was wearing jeans and a work shirt and thick sweat socks, and I saw her clearly as a wounded kid now, not a sophisticated woman. I felt around for the crush, but I was relieved to find it gone. I had wanted to believe in this vision of a grown-up, beautiful child, but I had misjudged that, too. There was plenty to keep me from getting smug.

She smiled, then waved. I sat down across from her.

"Thanks for coming," she said. "I really wanted to see you."

"Me, too," I said. "It's not often somebody saves my life. In fact, it's never happened before. I guess that binds me to you for life. I'm grateful. That was incredibly brave of you."

"Well, you saved mine," she said. "I would have stayed under his spell for a long time, until he got tired or I got smarter and healthier. He might even have killed me, just like he killed Carol.

"I guess on some level, I was beginning to put it all together, to see what was happening. But I couldn't come face-to-face with it, not yet. I loved him a great deal. There I was, telling my dad that I was sleeping over at Carol's one more time, knowing he was too detached to ever check or wonder why I was spending so much time there. But I was starting to see, and he was sensing it, I think. I think he knew that I was coming to learn what he was really about."

I started to say something, but she held up her hand. "Look, I'm in therapy now, four days a week. Dad's going too, sometimes. She's a great psychiatrist, she really listens. I'll get through. I just have so much to face.

"This all started way back in middle school, his literary discussions, his praise for my work. I remember him sitting down with me over a sandwich in his classroom—I've never been more flattered in my life—and he told me I was special, more intelligent, more mature, destined for great things. I was an intellectual athlete, he told me, and he wanted to be my coach. The sick thing was, I told my father about it, and we were both proud that I was being singled out. There were trips to New York for plays, visits to museums, he gave me books and tapes. You know how people always tell me I'm mature for my age, that I'm sophisticated? Well, one reason was Richard. I did love him; he did tutor me. I just never imagined how big the bill was going to be."

I nodded. "Was dinner the first time you suspected?"

"I thought sometimes that there were other girls. He would be busy on certain nights of the week. Sometimes I would smell perfume. But I never suspected Carol until we talked. It was a terrifying night, because you could have been talking about my father, too, as I'm sure you know. But I guess I never really believed Dad could do that. I knew he was able to be a father to Carol in ways he really couldn't be to me."

"When did it get sexual?" I hesitated to ask the question, but Judy was the part of the case I still had to close in my own mind. I knew she would tell me if she couldn't handle the questions.

"Well, only recently," she said. "Only in the last year. He was so popular, so powerful among his students. I felt I had been chosen by this remarkable man. You know, he had a very political side. He was always going to peace marches and working in soup kitchens. He knew literature and music. I was so lonely. It was as if he had been waiting just for me."

"The night of the shooting," I prodded.

"Well, I had actually told him that I thought we should be spending less time together. I was going off to college next fall, I was trying to deal with Carol's death. He was sympathetic, as usual, very understanding. Then you pulled your horrible stunt at the window," she said, smiling, "scaring me half to death."

"But not him?"

"He seemed to know exactly what was happening," she said. "I saw him grab a gun from the dresser drawer and run outside. I couldn't let him kill anybody else. When the police took him away, he looked at me and said, 'Judy, I love you. Whatever else you believe, continue to believe that.' I do, I guess, but the part that's unbearable, the part that I dread . . ."

She put her head in her hands. We both knew the part she was talking about; it was the part I had to know. Had she told Handley about Carol's desperate phone call to her? Was that why he had to kill Carol, and why he'd ended up killing Ken as well to cover it up?

"You told him about Carol's call, didn't you? That's how he knew Carol was cracking, becoming too dangerous. Not only might she go to her mother or to the police, or to Ken, but Handley would lose you, too."

She nodded. "All I can tell you is that crazy as he was— and I'm just beginning to comprehend that—I think he truly loved me. I think he loved me in a special way. It was so sick, but it was real."

"Is there any point in telling you this wasn't your fault? That you couldn't possibly have known he was a blackmailer or a killer?"

"Yeah," she said, wiping her eyes. "Say it as often as you like. One of these days I might even believe it."

"Kit," said Judy, putting the novel on the table, "why do you think Carol talked to me at all? Did she want me to help her? Was she expecting me to take more action than I did, to step in somehow?"

Warning bells went off when I heard the question. I was worried Judy was setting herself up for a lifetime guilt-trip. But I also thought she was too smart not to hear the truth.

"I think it's sadder than that," I said, "although I doubt we'll ever really know for sure. She probably sensed or picked up in some way that you were getting involved with some-body, and probably guessed as well that it was Handley. After all, he manipulated you both in similar ways. She might have sensed the same thing happening to you that happened to her. I think she was trying to warn you as best she could, hoping that you would put it all together. I think she was trying to save *you* more than trying to get help herself. Which was tragic."

Afterwards, I sat in the Volvo staring at the house. Mostly, I felt heartbroken that a young life like that could have been so pointlessly shattered. It would take her years to put it back together, if she ever could. We had agreed to have dinner at Gennaro's in a month or so, when she felt on firmer ground. I looked forward to that. It's a strange town, I thought. Nathaniel Gowdy, who was probably framed, was hung from a tree. There was no mob howling for Richard Handley's throat.

My reverie was interrupted by the honking of a horn. I looked over, surprised—not happily—to see Gwen Baker-Goldstein, dean of Rochambeau's Crazy Parents Brigade, sitting at the wheel of her Honda, gesturing that I should roll down my window. I was trapped.

"How's Em and Ben?" she chirped. "We have to get together. We have to start going after those people in the high school." In Gwen's world, adults serve no purpose except to communicate fears and concerns about their children's safety or the incompetence of the school system. I had just weathered the most amazing weeks of my life, but Gwen was probably not even aware of it. The kids called her "Eric Needs" (no relation to Heather Wants) because on most mornings, she could be found in the hallway outside one of her fifth-grade son's classrooms telling the teacher, "Eric needs more homework." Or less. Or wasn't being encouraged. He needed more math. Or social studies. Her son was the only kid I ever knew of who had been expelled from Rochambeau's outdoor soccer league because the mother almost drove the coach to a nervous breakdown.

It occurred to me, belatedly, that her Honda was idling in the middle of a street far from either home or school.

"Gwen, what are you doing here?" I asked. Her office was across town.

"Oh," she said. "Well, Eric takes the school bus on Tuesdays and Thursdays. Mondays, he has piano, Wednesdays he has Hebrew school, and Fridays he swims. I don't trust the bus; you know what happens with boys. But Eric likes it—he insists he wants to take it."

Of course. I *was* dense.

"So you follow it?" I said, looking down the street as the yellow school bus dropped three kids off at a distant corner.

"If he needs me," she said, "I'm there." She waved and took off after the bus. Things were returning to normal.

32
April

The murders on the Brown estate left me feeling more ambivalent than I would have expected on that morning two months ago when I sat lecturing like a wise old pasha in Benchley's greenhouse. My friends would be surprised to hear that I've felt anything but jubilation.

Things have finally settled into something of a routine, the most promising and pleasurable in years. Evelyn is working full-time to take my messy office and expanding workload forcefully in hand, bringing decades of experience as a librarian to the overdue organization of my schedule, my files, my life.

I am even considering hiring a junior partner to help handle my growing caseload. I still help kids with drug problems, find runaways, search for the secret assets of divorcing husbands, run reference and security checks, and follow up insurance claims. But I decline spouse-snooping now.

Now that spring's here, Benchley holds court at the Garden Center from nine to nine, fielding questions, prescribing for sick plants, recommending the right shade tree for a south-facing lawn or the appropriate deterrent for aphids.

Local realtors have plunged back into the business of moving property, and FOR SALE and SOLD signs have sprouted all over town like mutant saplings. At the American Way,

Murray Grobstein is working sixteen hours a day ordering, unwrapping, and selling soccer, baseball, and track shoes as well as the hundred-dollar sneaker-of-the-moment. Murray is thinking of buying a summer place at the Jersey shore, down the road from where Bruce Springsteen, whom he reveres, grew up.

The *Rochambeau Times*, to its palpable relief, is concentrating not on tragedy but on the impending state basketball championships, in which Rochambeau High is contending for the first time in twenty years.

As coach of Rochambeau's Kinderkickers soccer league, I had fared much worse than I did on the Brown estate case. My notion that each kid should play at least once in every game was not greeted with enthusiasm by many of the parents, who often stood along the sidelines and screamed at their six-year-olds to run faster or think defense. The team parents couldn't bear the notion that their kids might lose. I could never accept that they cared so deeply about winning. Jane knew better than to drop by.

"Why are you playing Jason?" a mother hissed at me one Saturday morning. "You know he's slow, goddamn it. We haven't won in three weeks."

"Because Jason came to play," I answered, "and on my team, everyone who comes to play gets to play." That philosophy collapsed in a few weeks, after a number of parents circulated a petition to have me removed as coach. I resigned. It wasn't much fun, anyway.

My encounter with Ben's teachers had served as a needed caution that I had no business feeling superior to other parents. Part of what spooked me about my own child-obsession that evening was a brief insight into what it can sometimes teach kids: They are responsible for nothing. My message to

Ben was simple: I love you; I'm here to help you. But if you don't do your homework and improve your grades, you won't be playing Nintendo, basketball, or soccer, listening to De la Soul tapes, or watching MTV until you do. Ben's back on the honor roll.

Still, the familiar language of Rochambeau has reemerged. No more talk about locks and police and passwords. We're back to "Joshua wants to go to Disney World" and "Jessica wants a Nintendo but we think it will cut into violin practice" and "Nancy isn't ready to be home by herself yet. Maybe next year, when she's twelve." The kids are back in charge. The police are nearly invisible again, their natural fate in suburbia, although I manage a monthly lunch with Chief Leeming.

It bugs me more than it used to, perhaps because the deaths of Ken Dale and Carol Lombardi—and let's not forget poor Lisa Caltari—made me think more about our unknowable kids and the dangers of providing children with all the trappings of a good life but little of the meaning. None of those kids died because of parents' failures; they were assaulted by sick people. But no one noticed Ken Dale falling under the spell of his manipulative mentor. No one even suspected, until it was too late, the trouble Carol Lombardi and Lisa Caltari were in. No one spotted the terrible trap into which Judy Cole so maturely strolled. Were we paying attention to the right things? If our kids don't have any problems, how can they learn how to solve them? And one thing we learned for certain—they will have problems.

Nathaniel Gowdy's poignant ghost has altered the landscape of Rochambeau permanently for me, as have the pathetic but half-admirable efforts of his great-nephew to restore his ancestor's honor. Nothing highlights the evolution of Rochambeau more than Blackhead Gowdy's hopeless battle.

In a way, I suppose that cursed land has claimed yet another life. Three days before the pneumonia finally broke his spirit and body, I visited him in the intensive care unit, where he'd been since the police and I found him with Benchley up on that freezing mountaintop.

Gowdy's gaze had lost its ferocity. He knew he was about to die, and he knew he would die having failed to accomplish the one thing that kept him alive: justice for his family, vengeance on their oppressors. He would live to see neither. He couldn't even hate Benchley anymore. His nemesis had come to visit him daily, filling the hospital floor with flowers and plants, seeing that Blackhead was well cared for, bringing him cider, and reading him the latest news. Benchley's a tough sucker to hate.

Gowdy only said a sentence or two to me. "If you come across any evidence that would help prove Nathaniel's innocence, you are honor-bound to pursue it. I'd be grateful if you'd bring it to the attention of the authorities," he managed to say, as if he'd prepared a speech. "I'm the last Gowdy, which is probably a blessing, since not a one of us has had an easy life. We haven't fit in Rochambeau for more than a hundred years."

"Mr. Gowdy," I said, "I can do you one better. Benchley has hired me to look into the new information that Perry had dug up—the information about the other killing. It looks promising. We've brought it to the county prosecutor's office and they say they'll reopen the case."

The old man smiled before he lapsed back into sleep. It was partly the truth. Benchley *had* hired me to sort through the new material, but the county prosecutor had laughed mirthlessly when I'd called to talk about it. "I've got a three-month backlog of cases," he'd barked incredulously, "and you want me to reopen one that was closed a century ago? Good luck." Then he'd hung up. But we would honor Blackhead's request. The Historical Society had taken up Nathaniel's cause as its special mission, and one of its members, a retired attorney, would look into the case.

Three days later Blackhead Gowdy was dead. Benchley, Jane, Joey, Miss Bitch Whitmore, Evelyn, and I were the only people at the funeral, which he and Benchley had planned. His ashes were scattered on the Brown estate. Maybe there was some justice in that, Benchley opening the urn and spreading its dusty contents around the stump's ancient roots. We observed a few moments of silence and then left. Three separate lawsuits—two from Brown descendants and one from a local developer—have been filed seeking to force the Brown estate onto the market. The revenue-hungry town of Rochambeau has filed as a friend of one of the plaintiffs. We have not learned much.

The psychologists have gone back into the high school, this time to work on repairing the student-teacher relationship that Richard Handley had so brutally and viciously abused. Handley has struck a deal with the county: guilty to two counts of second-degree murder, all other charges dropped. Chief Leeming tells me Handley will walk out of prison an old man, if he makes it that far. That's okay with me; I could never countenance the idea of capital punishment, and there will be no joy in that man's remaining days. I wonder if we will see one another when he gets out, to have a cup of coffee and talk about what he did to those young lives. What a dumb idea.

I did have my dinner with Judy at Gennaro's. She's still

planning to go off to Vassar, where she'll continue with her therapy. We keep in touch. I see her father around town now and again; we wave. In a few months, he's going to be alone. I think that will be tough on him.

I have mellowed a bit about Rochambeau, especially as the spring ripens. In many ways, towns like Rochambeau are comfortable beyond the imagining of the vast majority of people who walk the earth. In spring and summer, the sounds are especially rich—children splashing and laughing in the plastic pools, lawn sprinklers swishing, the cheers of Little League games in the parks, even those goddamn lawn mowers. We work so hard at such things out here, as if driven by the belief that if it all looks great, great lives will follow. It breaks your heart to learn it isn't always true. I don't think I'll ever quite put so much stock in the appearance of things again.

But at such times, Rochambeau's innate good heart and good will come to the surface. It wants so much and tries so hard to make the world perfect for its kids. Most of its excesses, after all, are in the best of causes, the health and happiness of children. And isn't it better, when all is said and done, to give too much rather than too little?

I suppose in the end there's been too much blood and sadness for me to feel much triumph, though I have felt some. I changed my life and left my sense of honor intact. I escaped Wall Street without causing anyone else harm. I've become a real parent, smack in the thick of things, driving everyone crazy and being driven. I'm no visiting dignitary. I've kept my contract with my family, which is to say I carry my load and keep their lives intact, if not as luxurious as they once were. I've met my responsibilities.

So, surely, has Jane. The fact that she went to work, that

she had work she was eager and able to go to, bought me the time I needed to recover from my own crushed career and begin again. Thank God for feminism. I point this out to my male neighbors and fellow fathers on those frequent occasions when they squawk about their wives' work aspirations or lack of domesticity.

I am now, in fact, the Suburban Detective. It's mostly interesting work and often a pleasant life. I still watch the seedlings sprout in Benchley's greenhouse. I gaze out the window at the mall parking lot whenever the phone stops ringing, and sup regularly and in style at the Lightning Burger with Luis. Murray's sneakers are now the size of small farm animals and look as if they could float to Europe. With Evelyn's help, I plan my schedule, still built around piano lessons, emergency rides to school, and playdates. My marriage has miraculously endured and even been enriched by these latest adventures. I have a few thousand dollars in the bank for the first time in several years. In fact, I've just enough to put a nice down payment on a new Volvo. Jane will drive it. I'll keep the old one.